THE FIX

ARJE SHAW

To Bina and Gabe
    For this gift of life
        The heart must break
            And mend...
                And break...
                    And mend...
                        And break...
                            And...

The Fix

THE FIX

Published by:
Library Tales Publishing, Inc.
244 5th Avenue, Suite Q222
New York, NY 10001
www.LibraryTalesPublishing.com

Copyright © 2011 by Arje Shaw, New York, New York
Published by Library Tales Publishing, Inc., New York, New York

No part of this publication may be reproduced, stored in a retrieval system, or transmitted in any form or by any means, electronic, mechanical, photocopying, recording, scanning, or otherwise, except as permitted under Sections 107 or 108 of the 1976 United States Copyright Act, without the prior written permission of the Publisher.

Requests to the Publisher for permission should be addressed to the Legal Department, Library Tales Publishing, Inc., 244 5th Avenue, Suite Q222,New York, NY, 10001, 1-800-754-5016, fax 917-463-0892.

Trademarks: Library Tales, the Library Tales Publishing logo, The Fix, The Fix logo, and related trade dress are trademarks or registered trademarks of Library Tales Publishing, Inc. and/or its affiliates in the United States and other countries, and may not be used without written permission. All other trademarks are the property of their respective owners.

For general information on our other products and services, please contact our Customer Care Department at 1-800-754-5016, or fax 917-463-0892.
For technical support, please visit www.librarytalespublishing.com

Library Tales Publishing also publishes its books in a variety of electronic formats. Every content that appears in print is available in electronic books.

ISBN-13: 978-0-578-07458-0
ISBN-10: 0578074583

Printed in the United States of America

The Fix

It shoulda never happened. A bookie's life is relatively safe. You can make a living, not great, but okay if you take the long view—that is, win in small increments over a long period of time. It takes discipline, detachment, and some honesty in a dishonest game, which Eddie's willing to play. It starts out like this: You take the bet, maybe put some of your own money in, but never *ever* use your bettor's bet for *your* bets. That's playing with fire, that's Moses sticking his hand in the burning bush, that's Eddie keeping his hand in. That's God saying:

"Take your hand out, *Shmuck!*"

The Fix

Chapter One

Eddie Parker whips off his grease-stained apron from behind the counter of Golishoff's Dairy Restaurant, stuffs a half-eaten buttered poppy seed roll in his mouth and takes off as Max Golishoff yells after him, "Run, *Meshugeneh*, run!" Eddie laughs, flips his collar, pops a cigarette, and slides recklessly along the icy sidewalk of Stanton and Orchard on the way to Houston, scissor-jumping the front door of his '65 fire-engine-red Caddy DeVille, landing squarely on the torn front seat of the beige leather interior, once white.

Like Eddie, nothing in the car works, save the engine. Brakes squeal, doors jam, wipers moan, tires shot, top dead at half-mast, headlights as ornaments, lighter missing, radio hisses. So, in one respect, the car's safe. He could only lose it on a horse, a card, a die, but never a thief. "Who would steal this piece of shit!?" But as Eddie says, "One man's shit is another man's collateral."

Eddie loves his car. Well, it's not entirely his. He's paid for it many times over, depending on his luck, something he doesn't believe in. Luck to Eddie is fate. Like an accident, you can't prepare for it, can't avoid it. Unlike Eddie's gambling cronies, who, when they win, it's skill, when they lose, it's luck. Not so with Eddie. To Eddie, winning's the flip side of losing, all one in the same, a mirror image depending on how you look at it. For winning's always an entitlement, and losing's a curse—losing being the challenge, for it requires an excuse and a lie. And, if you can lie to yourself, then you can lie to others so they can then believe you, a system of self-deceit Eddie's perfected.

Max Golishoff says Eddie was born under the "Ouf Tzeluches" star, the "you're-fucked-in-spite-of-yourself" star. On the contrary, Eddie thinks, "Just ride it out, ride it out, stay in the game; as long as you're in the game, you got a chance."

That's the gear his mind would shift to when caught in the heat of a hot losing streak. The power of positive thinking, that's the key. "Keep it up, keep it going and you stay invincible, stay untouched, can't get hurt. I can die, but I can't get hurt." In fact, from the time he was a kid, Eddie believed someone was watching over him, put on this earth not to win or lose, but to play, a toy for the universe, waiting to be played out. So, in Eddie's mind, it isn't so much that he has a gambling addiction as much as he's addicted to destiny. This allows him the convenience of forgiving himself for almost anything, the permission to push the envelope, see how far he can go, what he can get away with. Free will to Eddie is as free as you make it.

Eddie's free 'n' easy demeanor runs counter to his pigeon-toed walk, scurrying around the Lower East Side, a weasel looking for action, looking lost. But the minute he slips into his Caddy DeVille, Eddie rules. The wings, the slope, the chrome make him feel regal, and where Eddie lives, "Regal" rules.

He pictures himself the centerpiece of a ticker-tape parade down Delancey in his Caddy convertible, standing on a towel, flushed Florsheims wedged between cracked leather seats, waving to all the bookies, shysters, con men, hustlers, *yentas*, meddlers, peddlers, push-cart vendors, shoe-shine boys, *shmatta* store owners lining the boulevard, confetti-raining sky dropping flowers, knishes, cellophane-wrapped candy, and he, Eddie, his arm around his kid, The Kid, "The All-American Kid," the hoop phenom from Seward High who single-handedly carries a street gang of neighborhood jocks on his bony shoulders to a stunning triple-overtime, buzzer-beater upset over the number one seed in the City to win the City Championship! BAM!

The Kid pulls it out of his ass, drilling an impossible jump shot from downtown, hands in his face, knees in his groin, no foul! The Kid didn't need it! BAM! Downtown beats Uptown! Then the offers, the agents, the scouts, the steaks, wined and dined, Smith & Wollensky, suits from Barneys...

A cold wind snaps his head right back.

Get The Kid!

Eddie screeches to a stop at Junior High 65, leaps out, sprints up the back stairwell, tossing a pack of Luckies to some kids sneaking a smoke. "Hey, thanks, Mister Parker." He bursts through the emergency doors, running down the hallway, students and teachers stepping aside indifferently, the Red Sea splitting for Eddie Parker, The Golishoff Man, short-order cook by day, fuck-up at night.

Beating to the racing cylinders of his frazzled mind, Eddie's powerless. Always on the run, he's everywhere, he's nowhere, always making plans, always ahead of himself, one leg moving, the other stuck, one eye open, the other shut, and no sooner does one plan evaporate, than another takes its place. He doesn't know what he wants to do in life, but he knows how he wants to feel — happy, content, admired, respected. A respect he never got from Maddy.

The day she left, some ten years ago, she said, "You're a joke Eddie, a fucking joke! Where you been? Where you been for two days? Look at you, your eyes are dancing! You're an eel, Eddie, an electric eel, twitching and moving—do you ever stop? Has your heart, body, and mind ever been in one place at the same time? Do you know you have a home, a wife, a child?"

"Maddy, I—"

"Do you care?"

" I—"

"Does any of it mean anything to you?"

"I love you, Maddy."

"I love you too, Eddie, but I can't stand you."

She starts wiping the kitchen counter.

"You're toxic, Eddie, toxic. I'm beginning to stink just thinking about you."

What is it with women and counters? Every time they get pissed, they start cleaning.

"With you it always takes a two-by-four across the side of the head."

"I know."

"Why is that?"

"I don't know, guess I'm kinda thick like that."

Now she's scrubbing the floor.

"I can't keep up, Eddie, I can't. I love you, but I can't! I can't figure you out."

"Makes two of us, Maddy."

"For all the years, I don't know who you are."

"Yeah."

"And then I don't know who *I* am."

"I know."

If she got down on me half as much as the kitchen floor, we wouldn't be havin' this fight.

"You're work, Eddie. You're so much fucking work. Ten bundles of laundry a day don't hold a candle to you."

Eddie dips into his pocket and removes a Limoges figurine of a young boy.

"He's Dutch, Maddy. Looks a lil' like The Kid, don't he, Maddy? There was another with a striped hat, I'll get 'im that one next time. It's Limoges, from France. That's where they make 'em, honey. It's porcelain, thin shell, made of stone, flint… could be worth a lot *a* money some day… I promise, Maddy, first winnings on my bets go right to Limoges."

Maddy walks into the bedroom and comes out with her coat and valise. She walks over to Eddie, drops the valise, cups his slim, ratty face in her small hands and kisses him softly with a longing he would never forget. It was the saddest day of his life. Eddie felt an ache in his throat, wishing he could cry, but years of manufactured highs and lows grew him a skin of indifference.

The worse things got, the cooler he got. The less he said, the more he thought, the less he felt.

"You got a place?"

"Yeah."

"A guy?"

Maddy laughs. "No, Eddie. You're enough of a reason."

"What do I tell Bina?"

"Tell her I have cancer or something, something worse than leaving!"

"Nothing's worse than leavin'."

"Staying is."

Maddy threatened to leave many times, but each time he came back promising. But no sooner than it took him to convince her he'd changed, he'd go right back to his old ways. When threatened with loss or abandonment, he'd turn on the spigots full force using every faucet to win her back.

"Maddy, I promise—"

"Yeah, yeah, Eddie."
"No, really."
"Right."
"I'll be good."
"Sure, Eddie, sure."

What a high, to behave badly, incur the wrath, resentment, disgust, hurt the one you love, and reverse it with words, just words, talk, do nothing but talk, talk your way back, talk… talk, talk, talk… slow, fast, breathy, thoughtful, deep, almost sincere, inaudible whispery puffs of bullshit blown up the ass, pinched eyes, runny nose, snot retrieved by short inverted horse snorts obliterated by one smear of the sleeve.

At times like these who cares where the snot goes? For these are the times that try men's souls, the best of times, the worst of times, it's Eddie at his best. Win her over, fall or jump back into her graces, just talk, keep talking, talk. Oh, how women love men to talk… talk, talk, navigate, find a safe place to land, a virgin patch, a sinecure, a soft perch, a tender palpitating berth for Eddie to lay his smelly egg.

"I can change, Maddy."
"That's what Quasimodo said."
"If you give me a chance, if—"
"If I had balls, Eddie, I'd be King," and she smiles.
"Oh man, *that* smile, haven't seen that smile in a while."
"You haven't seen *me* in a while."
"It's not 'cause I haven't been thinkin' 'bout you."
"Yeah, I can feel your thoughts, Eddie."

He starts crying.

"So this is it, eh, Maddy?"
"Afraid so."
"End of a love affair."
"Not quite."
"What was the straw?"
"Straw?"
"That broke the camel's back?"
"It's a wheat field, Eddie."
"We go back a long time, Maddy."
"Oh Eddie, please."

"It hasn't all been great but—"
"Don't start."
"Start what?!"
"Apologizing."
"What else can I do?"
"Get the fuck out of my life!"
"I was on a hot streak, Maddy. Look!"

He pulls hundreds from his pockets, tossing them at her feet. She won't give him the satisfaction of looking down.

"You think I'm screwin' around out there? I'm workin'! Securin' a future for *you*, The Kid! Can I have a napkin?"

She hands him a tissue. He blows his nose. In a perverse kind of way, she's enjoying watching Eddie dance.

Fuckin' Maddy, makin' me work like this!

"You think it's easy for me, bein' away from home, from you, The Kid. You two mean everything to me!" Eddie would have made a great jazz artist. He took improvisational lying to new heights.

"Two days, Eddie. Two fucking days!"
"What did you want me to do, quit when I'm ahead?"
"I know. That would be a tragedy."
"It would. I'd get killed!"
"That's not a tragedy, Eddie. That's relief."
"C'mon, Maddy, have a heart."

And she did, with a mouth sharper than a knife. She knew Eddie's coda, "Have a heart, blah, blah, blah… "

"There are rules, Maddy, rules in my business."
"Marriage, too."
"That's right. You don't walk. You stay. You finish. Take it to the end."
"That's what I'm doing."
"Didn't the Rabbi say for better or for worse?"
"He's not married to you."
"You leave, you can't come back."
"Can I take a chit on that?"

Eddie drops to his knees, wrapping his arms around her legs. Now, this move made by most men can be seen as unbelievably moving, or pathetic, depending…

"Get up, Eddie."
"I love you."
"Get up."

He pulls her down on the floor. It's his favorite place; he finds one wherever he goes. Eddie's good on the floor. Just ask all the women he fucks on the fly.

He thought he had Maddy goin' pretty good, until she whispered, *"Oh, Vinny."*

He kisses her hard. Eddie knows Maddy's turn-on are his lips, beautiful contour, soft on bottom, firm on top.

She loves my lips.

Too bad they're attached to his face. But when he goes down on her, all is forgiven.

If I make her come, she'll stay.

Banging away with a ferociousness bordering on despair, Eddie's fucking for his life.

Down to my last shot.

Eddie never worked so hard for something he knew would end. He watches the come run down her nylon. She wipes herself. It was their last kiss goodbye.

"I love you, Maddy."
"Get up."
"Don't leave."
"Your *shmeckel*'s hanging out."

He won't let go, holding her tighter than a straight flush. She removes a speck off his shoulder, pulls one leg from his circle of love, then the other, then out the door. He goes after her, yelling down the stairs:

"COME BACK!"

Eddie hears The Kid crying. He runs upstairs yelling downstairs. She slams the front door so hard the building shakes. He grabs The Kid and lifts him to the window.

"HE'S OUR KID, MADDY! LOOK! OUR KID!"

He kicks in the window. Maddy's shaking. She knew he'd play his ace. If she takes The Kid, she's gotta take him. Two-for-the-price-of-one, the bargain comes with the package, it's all or nothing. For Maddy, it's nothing. An impossible choice, not "Sophie's," but close, a decision she agonized over from the time she brought the baby home and Eddie wasn't there. He was locked up for drugging a horse. Ollie Calamari, local mob boss, posted bail and Eddie got off.

This time he's not getting off. She's leaving. But she has to be careful. He'll need something and he'll be back. A persuasive barracuda, Eddie feeds on sentiment. If he smells a tear, a drop, a hint of hesitation, a crack in the fault, he lasers the empathy, milks it. Eddie can stitch St. Andreas together. If you help Eddie, it's as if you saved the world.

"If you do this for me... just this one time... "

She knows the drill. She's been watching him do it for years, the same con, over and over, practicing on her, and the tougher she got, the more she opposed him, the sharper he got.

A master of deceit, he honed his skills at home. It made her sick, but she allowed it, felt for him, loved him, knew him, knew his history, his family, where he came from, what he went through, how he got to be Eddie Parker... before he was Eddie Parker, when he was *Aryeh Pyatiegorskia*, eight years old, only a few short light years away from Tashkent, Krakow, Bergen-Belsen, starvation, cattle cars, refugee boats, landing in the hallowed halls of East 7th and Avenue C, a six-floor tenement walk-up, one room, bathtub in the kitchen, bathroom in the hallway, for four families.

To get to the bathroom, Eddie had to pass Maddy's apartment, where Captain Video, Flash Gordon, Milton Berle played. Another time, another place, when life was slow, mellow, and miserable. Eddie listened by the door, pushing it open with his foot, a thin crack left by Maddy for Eddie's next visit to the toilet.

For Eddie became a frequent urinator, transfixed by screen images, strange language, TV—"Tell-A-Vision," what a great name for a television.

The streets were different then. Busy, cluttered, open market merchants hawking second-hand items to those given second chances. The streets, the music, the air, the hustle, pedestrians, mostly white, mostly immigrants, all survivors from something or other. First Avenue, a mile wide to Eddie, used to the cracked narrow streets of Bergen-Belson, holds tight to Bina, her other arm carrying Maya, exquisitely Asian-looking little Maya, who at three could stop traffic with her beauty.

Bina held on to her children with all her might, having lost too many to war and starvation. But this is America! This is 1949 and "Irene, Good Night" tops the charts while Eddie downs Lime Rickeys, a deliciously sweet, ice-cold, red-green drink he gulps down quickly to get that stabbing pain in the upper right corner of his left eye... and then the relief that would follow... and then the diarrhea. Eddie was made for punishment, some inflicted, most of it elected, the sweet followed by the sorrow.

Eddie's salvation was games, street games. Only two weeks off the boat, wearing knee-high pants held up by suspenders, he went out looking for kids to play with. Not a good look for a tough block. A bloated blimp floats by, cornering Eddie with the question of the day.

"Yankee or Dodger?"

"*Vos?*"

"YANKEE OR DODGER?"

Eddie takes his first stab at English.

"Da-Dger."

The Mick punches the Hebe in the face. Strange, because they both like potatoes. Bloodied Eddie *shleps* up the six flights, passing Maddy and horrifying Bina who doesn't let him out of the apartment for weeks. Bored out of his mind, he begs Bina to go downstairs to play.

Deep into *Shabbes*, she pulls her hand out of the chicken's ass, wipes the sweat off her brow, washes her hands, walks Eddie downstairs, and sits on the stoop watching him bounce a ball off the wall for a monotonous hour. The repetition drives her nuts, and yet she sticks it out like she does everything else, working days, cooking nights, cleaning mornings.

Bina works at the Chunky Chocolate Factory until the Health Department Inspector shuts it down, mistaking a chocolate-covered cockroach for a fat raisin. Deep in the Health Inspector's bribe-sized mouth, the cockroach has made its last move. Not so with Bina, "The Greene K'zeenah."

She just moves to another job, another factory, sewing buttons, dressing jackets, stitching hats, lightning at the wheel, winged arms flapping, short legs spinning Singer sewing machines, pumping it out ten hours a day, a piecework prodigy waiting to be laid off any day when orders slowed, a seasonal business on the Grand, Lower East Side "Tour de la Sweat Shop."

But she's happy, grateful for work, food, a home. It beat Russia, ten in a room, no water, plumbing, food, electricity. Compared to that, this was *Gan-Eden*, Paradise. Feed your family for two dollars a day, eighteen dollars a month rent. Not exactly finding gold in the street, but more than they ever had. Still, you had to be careful, watch your money, watch how you spend.

Bina was a real *Yiddishe Momme*, Old World and New, naturally suspicious and trusting. She took one look at you and her mind was made up for the rest of her life, *and* yours. She knew no names, only disfigurements and flaws. Eddie's friends were *"Der Hoyche,"* the tall one, *"Der Grobe,"* the fat one, *"Der Kleinike mit der Hint,"* the shrimp with the dog, *"Der Tinkele,"* the dark one, *"Der Gestipelte,"* the pock-marked one.

As many times as he tried, "Mom, it's Henry, Donny, Danny, Ira, Herb, Marvin!" Bina called them as she saw them. And she saw them well, seeing and sensing things others didn't, possessing a clairvoyance enhanced by depression.

It started with sleeplessness and ended with electric shocks. Eddie saw it coming long before anyone else. Before Sol, Max, or even Bina herself.

"Zayst Epes, Kind? You see anything, my child?"

"Nein, Momme, bist gut. No, Mama, you're good."

But as he looked into her eyes, he knew it was coming, the tip-off being those dark watery eyes. Behind the eyes, a strangeness, a black abyss—the Dybbik's annual visit every December, anniversary of her father's death, conscripted at forty-one, shot dead in Stalingrad, 1941, the year Eddie was born.

Only a matter of time before the eyes give, then the screaming, the craziness, police, ambulance, straitjacket, shock treatments, two kids watching, Sol's head bowed as she's taken away. But Bina was strong. The Dybbik knew he was in for a fight, unlike Sol, who knew the Dybbik had 'em by the balls.

On visits to Kings County Psychiatric, Eddie finds Bina crouched in a corner. Roaming the ward are lost souls in white sheets shuffling aimlessly in thin slippers, mumbling and nodding, depressed and denied, deprived of lives, lives which did not rhyme, Bina among them. When she sees Eddie, she lights up, then withdraws, embarrassed for Eddie to see her like this. One poor old soul's banging his head against the wall, pulling the hair out of his head.

"OH GOD! PLEASE STOP! PLEASE STOP!"

Invaded by high frequency waves only *he* can hear, Paul's head is the zenith for all the world's *tzures*.

"STOP! OH STOP!"

Bina walks over. "Is this a good time to introduce *mein* son?"

"OH GOD! OH GOD! PLEASE STOP!"

"He came to visit me."

"MY HEAD! MY HEAD!"

"He's a *gute* boy."

"OH! OH! OH!

"Paul, stop *benging* your head, I *vant* you should meet *mein* son."

And miraculously, Paul, the high-voltage human antenna, stops banging his head, a trickle of blood drying on his ear.

"Good to meet you, son. Your mother's very nice."

Then Bina would tell him how Eddie almost starved to death in Russia during the war. How she kept him alive. How, after two days of waiting on a long hospital line, she broke through, demanding doctors see her baby, his eyes shut for three days, so that when his lids were popped open, green pus sprayed all over the anointed.

"'Will my child be blind?' I cried. 'Yes,' the doctors said, 'if you had not broken through.' 'Is *your* baby more important?' the line shouted. I screamed, 'YES!'… And did I tell you, Paul, how I lost my father in the war?"

Bina had a loving heart. She had compassion for those who suffered. She saw what could happen to people through no fault of their own—how you can wait patiently in line for death to come, or spray pus on everyone. Bina listened to everyone's story, so she could tell her own.

Except for a few teeth shifting around, she came out okay, still a pretty woman, the twinkle in her eye, the ready smile. Bina loved people. Something Eddie didn't. Bina would explain away Eddie's bad moods and surliness.

"Leave him alone, he doesn't like people."

Gottlieb, the landlord, and Taub, his teacher, would ask, "Why is he so angry? So serious?" Eddie wondered if they knew what *they* looked like. When faces were given out, Eddie must have hid, because what you saw was what you got. Except it wasn't anger people saw. It was stuffed fear, confusion, loss, displacement, not knowing who he was, where he belonged, how he got here, a strange kid in a strange land, trying on new skins, daydreaming in a field of insecurities.

Or was it young Eddie's disdain for being paraded around by his mother? For Eddie had a great ear, could sing, mastering Frankie Laine's "Jezebel" off the radio in one sitting. An eight-year-old Russian-Yiddish-speaking immigrant singing "Jezebel." It was all so bizarre. But when you have nothing, you show off what little you have.

Bina looked both ways, saw it was safe, crossed the street , went upstairs, telling Eddie to stay put. Oh, if only Eddie would 'stay put,' if only he'd listen, if only *everyone* would listen! But then there'd be no books, no stories, no endings, for we would all listen, we'd all stay put.

Her words stuck in his ear, *'Gey nisht avek!* Don't leave!' Eddie leaves. For Eddie, it's less about curiosity and more about defiance. If you want Eddie to do something, say: "Don't!" For "don't" is the guarantee for "do," and "do" the guarantee for "don't." Oh, the thrill of not listening...

Another Irish kid wafts off the steamy sidewalk.

How the hell do they find me?

"YANKEE OR DODGER?"

By now, Eddie knows more than one word and, recalling his last *McVisit*, blurts out, "YANKEE." The kid hauls off to whack him, but this time Eddie ducks; the Mick breaks his hand on the brick wall and Eddie's gone. Eddie's quick. Has to be. For reasons unknown to him, Eddie attracts trouble or creates it, but he can't see that.

* * *

Watching Maddy from the window, Eddie knows he's wrong, but can't admit it, can't find a place to stick the blame without some self-protective adhesive sticking to his psyche.

They don't understand.

Eddie works hard at not being understood. It's not his fault. He has a knack for knowing what people want to hear, so he gives it to them. But then when an honest moment is called for it throws him off, and then he doesn't know *what* he thinks. All he knows is he's blind to himself. Otherwise he would have changed... maybe.

The truth is, Eddie's done irreparable harm. The moments, the seconds of uncontrollable fury in the early years of their marriage, which he shrugged off as brief and insignificant, lasted a lifetime, freezing emotions, suffocating cells of life. Maddy had enough. Too many years of trying to circumvent Eddie's internal landscape, finally vacating, deserting a piece of life best left undone.

Blocking any attempt to undo the damage done, she throws a deaf ear to pleas from the window, punched glass shattering around her. She would have fought for custody but for Eddie's temper, a vat of acid on a slow boil. It just wasn't worth it; he had his father in him.

* * *

Eddie idolized his father, a strong, silent type Eddie called "The John Wayne of Poland." Bina would complain, "*Er redt nisht*, your poppa don' talk. He talks like he moves his bowels. *Von vord* in three days *iz* a speech. The man's *farshtopped*. And *dat's wit* a glass of prune juice 'n' hot *vasser* every morning. But *ven* he goes, *VATCH* out!"

Sol never learned the "Art of Conversation." Fleeing Nazis will do that to you. Leaving your mother and sister behind will do that. His life cut out from under him, Sol never recovered. An emotional amputee, Sol fought survivor guilt all the days of his life. Eddie didn't know that. Eddie knew very little. Eddie knew nothing. So when Sol exploded, Eddie thought it was something *he* did, that it was *his* fault, that *he* deserved it. The explosions didn't last long, just the memories.

Worse than the belt were his hands. Sol's hands were brick, hardened by Siberian coal mines, but soft enough to thread a needle or hold a child's hand, or a pinochle hand, for hours, cigarette dangling, eyes squinting, tearing, eyelashes fanning streams of smoke upstream. It had to sting, but the Zionist Zen Master never moved. He could teach the Buddhists a thing or two about being still. He had Six Million to forget. That'll keep you still.

Chapter Two

Eddie kicks the classroom door open, points to The Kid. Kid jumps out of his seat, and before "Teach" can say, "Mister Parker, please!" they're off, sprinting down the stairway, past truants, over hydrants, into seats. He guns the Caddy down Delancey, bobbing, weaving, missing dogs, cats, traffic, old ladies.

The Kid, cool as a cuke, looks straight ahead, deadpan.

"How many?"

"Ten."

Eddie hits a pothole, spraying guck onto the shoes of a natty old dude who shoots Eddie a look that if looks could kill, Eddie would be dead.

"Holy shit!"

"What?"

"That *alte kaker* looked like Sol."

"But he's dead."

"Yeah."

* * *

Sol was a dandy. Bina wore four-dollar housedresses while Sol won and lost thousands. There was no Gamblers Anonymous then, so everyone knew Sol. Who could miss this card? He wore fine shantung suits, custom-made shirts, silk monogram hankies meticulously rolled and tucked into his left breast suit pocket, gold cufflinks reflecting off his clear, polished manicured nails, crisp slacks he ironed himself in service of perfection, afraid the cleaners would fuck up the crease, a centimeter off.

To get the crease just right, he spit sprays a cloth, laying it gently down on the pant, pressing hot steel over the damp dish towel, ensuring a straight line over the calf-high dress socks funneled into two-tone Bojangle spats for the Ashkenazi Jew.

Head to toe, pinpoint perfect, Sol could make the mirror jealous. The only thing that didn't match was his accent. That goddamn Yiddish accent.

"Where you from, Sol?"

"*Vat* do you mean?"
"Where do you come from?"
"*Frum* **here**, you *besterd*!"

As much as he tried, he couldn't get rid of that accent, the *hoyker*, the hump on his back, a dead giveaway for damaged goods, so unbecoming for an Elliot-Ness-wannabe look-alike.

"How *de* hell do *dey naw I nut frum dis cuntry*?"

And everyone would laugh and shake their heads, amazed at Sol's amazement. Yet he'd be the first one to tell you, "*Meh zeht nor dem anderens hoyker.*" You only see the *other* person's hump. Poor Sol, deaf to one's own tone, to not hear yourself, not know yourself, it takes time.

The accent embarrassed the shit out of him. An embarrassment passed on to Eddie. Not the accent, but the embarrassment, the embarrassment of an immigrant father who when Eddie spotted crossing Delancey, would run to the other side.

A thin man of slight build, Sol had enormous physical strength capable of bringing down Samson's Temple. Instead, he *shlepped* produce around the city, delivering fruits and vegetables in and around Manhattan.

He'd line up at Hunt's Point depot at three A.M., load up by four, finish by three, home by four, sleep till seven, eat, shower, prep, and be ready for the street by ten. Between four and seven no one speaks, for Sol, "The Lion," sleeps.

Dinner at seven was law. Quiet, civil, slurping soup, chewing soft flanken for soft teeth made soft by Nazi rifle butts. Sol took great care in pampering himself. A hot bath, a close shave, remove the yellow-caked wax inside his ear with a hairpin; a life-long obsession of ear-digging, you'd think he was trying to reach China. "Brylcream," he'd sing, "*a li'l deb vill do ya,*" then smack his clean razor-shaven face stinging from Old Spice After Shave. "'*Hold Spice means qvality,*' said de Keptin to de Botsmin."
A song for every toiletry, a tune for every chore, every song ending in, "*dye-dil deedle, deedle dum!*"

With the precision of a surgeon, Sol spreads out his clothing on the pimply white George Washington bed spread, a ritual worthy of dressing the Torah. Boxer shorts, wife-beater undershirt, suspenders, socks, pants, shirt, tie, hanky, shoes, jacket, ring, watch, wallet, money clip, cigarettes, lighter, he gives a final soft cloth snap to the mirror-shoes, side tilt to the Stetson, raised eyebrow, and he's off!

To say that Sol was a creature of habit would be a gross understatement. Order gave him security. Rigidity gave him control.

Sol never rushed. And forget doing more than one thing at a time. For Sol, thinking while breathing was enough. Anything else was extra. Slow, but thorough, he wouldn't bite into his rye toast until every corner, every square inch of the rye, was evenly spread. For Sol, it could be a day's activity. To watch him do it once was painful enough, you could lose your appetite. But year in, year out, the same slow, deliberate, excruciating, mesmerizing stroke could send you flying off the tenement roof screaming:

"I DON'T WANT TO LIVE!"

And yet, he could catch flies in his bare hand.

Quicker than the eye.

One snap of his hand and goodbye fly.

Then back to butter on rye.

All of Sol's clothing lived in their own separate closet under lock and key, a lock you could snap open with a toothpick, but it was Sol's and Sol's alone. Bina would watch him approach the Cherry Wood Grail, eating up the entire wall of their stamp-size windowless bedroom.

"I should charge your *shmattas* rent," she'd fume, which is what the clothes did when Sol opened the closet, releasing a scent of many sinus-opening occasions. When Sol stepped out on the street, he'd say:

"*Now* I can breathe."

When he left, Bina would throw in some mothballs and say:

"Now *I* can breathe!"

Sol didn't bend. He broke. But rarely did he break. Once, Eddie caught him weeping into his huge hands on Yom Kippur, but that was it. Otherwise, he could endure anything. For Sol's forte was his strength. Behind a flat poker face he'd say:

"No one wants to hear your *tzures*."

How many times growing up Eddie would ask himself,

"How would I have done? How strong would I have been? Could I have survived?"

The father's test inside the young boy, envisioning himself hiding in the woods, running from Nazis, crawling at night, crossing borders deep into Russia, hunted, haunted, hungry, frozen, ending up on the floor of a stranger's home, the cousin of a cousin of a cousin's flat housing ten — Malke's home.

Malke, a widowed mother of six (two starved to death), with Bina at her side rocking dying babies, keeping infants alive, nursing siblings. Bina, seventeen, nowhere near ready for marriage, but Sol so grateful, so grateful for a piece of bread, a floor to sleep, a family, any family, they married; then children, the war, picking up the pieces...

Eddie would often think of what had to happen for him to survive. The events, the combination of seemingly unrelated but connected events that explained his life. The answer was always the same: Six Million had to die.

***

Eddie hits the brakes, jerk-stopping at an abandoned schoolyard off Grand, neighborhood toughs hanging on a rusted fence, leaning on a pole, rim bent. Eddie pops the trunk, flips The Kid the ball, takes a shovel, and heads for the wastes. A few words, quick transaction, and Eddie's chopping ice, clearing chunks from the basket to the winner's circle, twenty feet out, Kid's waiting. Eddie's exhausted, but keeps shoveling.

"Fuckin' ice!"

The Kid asks for the shovel.

"Save yourself, Kid, the helicopters should be here soon."

Chin resting on shovel, his mouth foaming, Eddie's gaze is skyward blue as he waits for a fleet of synchronized khaki helicopters to suddenly zoom in out of nowhere, swoop down on the abandoned schoolyard, rotating blades hovering over wet spots, whipping the cracked concrete dry. Then Eddie gives the pilot thumbs up. "Well done, son!" And off into yonder disappearing faster than Roseland's UFOs.

Back to chop 'n' dry. Some puddles collect at The Kid's feet, so Eddie removes his brown bomber jacket and lays it down, sopping up the water, leaving a dry spot for The Kid to stand on.

Shivering in his short-sleeve, red striped Banlon, Eddie cradles The Kid's hands, rubs them, warms them, blows on them the way Sol did for Eddie on cold winter days at Golishoff's counter, waiting for the hot Nestles to arrive under a pile of dissolving whip.

Teeth chattering, Eddie stations himself under the basket, catching each shot before it hits the ground, tossing the ball back cold, but dry. The Kid sinks ten in a row from twenty feet out. No rim, no net, no nothing, swish! Just ten in a row from twenty out.

Hustle done, Eddie settles up, flips The Kid the shovel, the ball, back in the trunk, back in the Caddy, back to school, up the stairs, down the hall, in the classroom, back to Max, scrambling eggs, dressing tuna, tossing salad.

"*SHMUCK'S* BACK!"

Counter roars.

"Have no fear, Eddie's here!"

Counter cheers.

"You know, Eddie, one day you'll run into yourself, but you'll be late!"

"Don't scrub your guts out *Max*, take it easy."

"If it wuzn't for your mother, I'd get rid of you!"

Eddie's lightning-quick, relieving the back-up in record time. He takes orders, cooks, serves, clears the counter and four tables in ten minutes flat.

"See, Max, nuthin to worry about."

Steadies applaud, Eddie curtsies, lights a cigarette, leans across the counter, schmoozing with the customers.

"We're not a community center, Eddie!"

But it is. Golishoff's is the place to be on cold winter days for locals who come in to warm up in the toasty luncheonette, radiator steam mixing in with the aromas of home-made soups, salads, sandwiches, eggs, fries, bagels, bialys, danish 'n' coffee.

Phone rings. Eddie grabs it, drops it, and gets his coat.

"Where the hell you goin' *now*?"

"Gotta go!"
"But you just came back!"
"Be right back!"
"Eddie, I can't run a business like this!"
Eddie's gone.
"SHMUUUUCK!"

* * *

"Who the hell do you think you are barging into my school like that?!"
"Listen, prince—"
"I am not prince! My name is Dr. Boyles and I am principal of this school!"
"'N' I'm the king of France."
Boyles sits down hard in a swivel seat behind a steel, grey desk.
"You have some nerve!"
"Chill out, Boyles. I took my kid out for lunch, what's the big deal?"
"So why was he cold and hungry when he came back?"
"Got me."
"Because *you* didn't feed him!"
"Hey—"
"What kind of father are you?"
"Fuck you, Boyles! Did your wife walk out on *you*?"
"What does that have to do with anything?"
"I raised that kid alone! Ten years! Think it was easy?! Takin' 'em to the schoolyard every day, perfect his jump shot, dribble with both hands, teach defense, I—"
"How you use your son is despicable!"
"Oh, you think sinkin' ten in a row was too much?"
"Five!"
"Five?!"
"Suspended for the week."
Eddie bolts from his chair.
"WHAT?!"
"You heard me!"

"But he's got a game tonight!"
"There'll be other games."
Boyles is scribbling a note. Eddie puts a clamp on his hand.
"Don't do this to me, Boyles!"
"Good day, Mister Parker."
"Heartless fuck!"
"Good day."
"And *you* work with children?"
"Good day."
"You wanna teach me a lesson, so you use my kid?"
Boyles hands him a pink slip and escorts him out.
"Pick up your son, and the next time you pull your shenanigans, you'll hear from D.Y.F.S.!"
"Is that like typhus, D.Y.F.S.?"
"No, Mister Parker. It's the Department of Youth and Family Services. You keep this up, you won't *have* a son!"
"I had typhus as a kid in Russia."
"Really."
"I got it from eating moldy bread."
"Too bad."
"There was nothin' to eat."
"Tsk, tsk."
He pushes Eddie out the door.
"We starved."
"Good day."
"They were droppin' like flies."
"Good day."
"But *I* lived."
"GOOD-BYE!"
Boyles slams the door.
Shit! Starving immigrant card didn't play.
Eddie's lost count the number of times he got laid with that one story.
But it doesn't work with men. What works with men? Ah!
Eddie puts his face to the door and whispers, "How's Dennis?"
Door opens.
"How do you know Dennis?"

"Everyone knows Dennis."
"What does he owe?"
"Want me to shout it out in the hallway?"
Boyles lets him in, the way you let a Jehovah's Witness in. Reluctantly.
"What does he owe, Mister Parker?"
Eddie walks past Boyles and parks himself in the swivel seat.
"It's not the *what*, it's the *who*."
"*Who* does he owe?"
"The world."
"World?"
"According to Ollie Calamari."
"Shit! How much?"
"It's not so much the how *much*, as the how *long*."
"How much and how long?"
"Twelve hundred for three months."
"Jesus!"
"Jesus is the only one he *doesn't* owe."
"I am so sorry for my brother."
"Afraid an apology won't do it, he's on the cusp."
"Cusp?"
"Between patience and collection, between trying on a pair of pants and having his legs broken."
Boyles scrambles for his wallet.
"Don't rush, Boyles. Ollie just wants to see some good faith, he's religious like that."
Eddie smells Boyles's armpits. He's got a nose for that. It sickens him. No animal stinks as much as men in fear, not even skunks, maybe women in decline.
"Fucking Dennis! I should let him rot!"
He hands Eddie ninety dollars.
"What's this?"
"It's all I have."
"Well, if it's okay with Ollie—"
"I can write you a check."
"How much?"
"Two hundred."
"Make it three."

"Can I pay out the rest?"
"Sure. When's the next payment?"
"I—"
"When do you get paid?"
"Friday."
"Friday's good... Kid plays?"
Boyles nods.
"You're a good brother, Boyles, a prince."
Eddie knows Boyles is in for a piece of the action. Dennis told him so.
Boyles holds the door open for Eddie.
"Good day, Mister Parker."
"Never know do we? If it's gonna be a good day? I bet you woke up this morning and thought it was gonna be a good day."
"Anything else, Mister Parker?"
Eddie's struck by Boyle's bulbous nose.
Where have I seen that shnoz? Could it be? The Irish Blimp? That anti-Semitic Sheeny, McSheeny Blimp?
Eddie returns the pink slip.
"One more thing, Boyles."
"Yes?"
"Yanks stink."

* * *

"*SHMUCK'S* BACK!"
"That's me."
Steadies were waiting for Eddie to return. Sometimes he did. Sometimes he didn't. This time he did. They applaud. It's Eddie's show.
"Where'd you go?"
"Nowhere."
"What's wrong?"
"Nothing."
"For nothing they called?"
Counter nods. Max draws first blood. Eddie counters with silence. Good move when a relative's breaking your balls.

"Don't break my balls, Max."

"It's *baytzim, putz*!"

Only Max could get away with calling Eddie names. From Max he could take it, because it was delivered with love. Max is the uncle every kid should have. Max forgave Eddie so many times, he made Yom Kippur obsolete.

"Is *Boytschick* in trouble?"

"No."

"*Boytschick's* not in trouble?"

Max always knew to ask Eddie twice, because the first time Eddie lied.

"What did he do?"

"Nothing."

"What did *you* do?"

"Can you let me serve my customers?"

"They'll wait."

"Max, don't be a *nudnik*."

"What happened?"

"I'm sure the customers aren't interested."

Counter nods, "Yes we are."

Harry walks in. Save-the-day-Harry.

"Soup 'n' salad, Harry?"

"What happened, Eddie?"

"Soup 'n' salad, Harry?"

"What happened?!"

"Soup 'n' salad?"

"You forgot how to talk?!"

"Soup 'n' salad?"

"Okay! You don't want to talk? Good. We'll talk later at *Momme's*!"

Counter's stunned. "That's it? Fight's over? This is what we came for? A nothing? A *shpritz*? Chickens get more angry!" Counter's deeply disappointed. They were looking forward to a fight, a good razz-a-ma-tazz between Max and Eddie, and now *this*?!

"Didn't pay to leave the house."

For sure this was one of those days just itching for a good scratch, a good fight, a good day to get under someone's skin, *tsheppa*, *tsheppa*, pick, annoy, get annoyed—a cold, dreary Monday, blue Monday, can't-trust-that-day-Monday, miserable people in a miserable mood on a miserable day, everyone sporting a hair on their ass, as close to the moon being out as you can get, and still nothing, a nothing with a nothing, a fizz, good for an egg cream.

The crowd stands to get their coats, more noise coming off their arthritic knees than the action between Max 'n' Eddie. They came to see a fight, they saw nothing. They came to witness and got *bubkes*.

"Soup 'n' salad, Harry?"
"Can I hang up my coat?"
"Soup 'n' salad?"
"Mind if I sit down?"
"Soup 'n' salad?"
"Can I read the menu?"
"Soup 'n' salad, soup 'n' salad, soup 'n' —"
"No soup, just salad."
Blood drains from Eddie's face.
"No soup?"
"No soup."
Eddie's day is ruined.
"Why?"
"I don't feel like it."
"You don't *feel* like it?"
"That's right Eddie. I don't *feeeel* like it!"
Oh, this is good! This is good! Crowd's coming back. There's hope.
"Soup's fresh."
"I give a fuck."
Who could have guessed it? Harry, straight-laced Harry, a miserable human being in his own right, a lifetime member of Golishoff's Miserable Counter Brigade, a Steady.

Who knew he had it in him? This most unlikely opponent, a stuffer who stuffed his food and his feelings, going up against Eddie.

You take a look at Harry and you see what's wrong with America. He's let himself go for so long that even if he wanted to, he couldn't find himself. It's a bitch when you lose interest in yourself.

Fat and ugly, he looks as if he's lost his best friend, but you don't necessarily want to help him. He doesn't invoke pity, or sympathy. It's something else. Maybe distance. But Golishoff's stools sit eight across , so you can't avoid him.

Harry sits and breaks one as "Lord Flatulence's" toneless *toches* swallows up the poor naugahyde stool, engulfing the remains of Harry's hanging ass, leaving the indentured imprint of a cylinder fudgie on his stained Hanes, causing his wife to wonder if Harry wiped. Well, at least she knew where he was.

"Soup's delicious, Harry."

"*You* eat it."

Harry, fuckin' Harry. Harry 'n' Eddie, the undercard better than the main event. Max 'n' Eddie, a dud. But Harry, Harry 'n' Eddie?! You see, you never know. People will surprise you.

"You all right, Harry?"

"I'm fine."

Harry buries his nose in the menu.

"What are you looking for, Harry? It's the same menu for the last fifty years. The Dead Sea Scrolls."

Harry's picking his teeth.

"What are you picking, you haven't eaten anything yet.

Order the soup 'n' salad, then you'll have something to pick."

Harry peeks over the menu.

"Shut up, Eddie!"

"Why no soup, Harry?"

"Gives me gas."

"Hey Max, does soup make you fart?"

Max farts. "Just the lentil." Crowd goes nuts. Who says Max can't tell a good joke?

Eddie says, "You're in luck, Harry. It's mushroom barley."

"I don't want no fuckin' mushroom barley!"

Oh! This is good! This is good! *This* is what they come for. The Golishoff Men, young and old, *far-haakd, tz-kaakd, tzekrochn n' ba-kaakd*—bewitched, bothered and bewildered, depressed in the middle of the day, staring at the ceiling, sitting in a fog.

Meanwhile, Gomez Siegel "The Illegal" is on skates, pouring coffee. Gomez has three names: "Gomez, The Illegal," reduced to "Legal," then "Siegel," 'cause "Legal" don't go with "Gomez" as good as "Siegel."

"More Sweet 'n' Low, Siegel!" they yell. Crowd roars.

This! This is what they come for. This is the stuff men are made of, needling, sparring, inciting, egging. "A good fight, that's all we ask." About *what*? "Doesn't matter." About *who*? "Who cares?! Just a fight, a good fight! Two guys beating the shit out of each other." *Three*? "Even better!"

"Soup's good for you, Harry."

"I don't give a shit."

"And you won't for a week!" chimes in Max. Crowd goes wild!

This! This is what they come for. Laughs, jibes, get the blood goin', save these poor suckers from themselves, from wives and girlfriends, hookers, bills, bosses, get 'em into the act, take sides, no sides, win, lose, allegiance, no allegiance, comebacks, come downs, put downs, and laughs, laughs, it's all about the laughs.

"Give 'em the salad, Eddie."

"Stay out of this, Max."

"Give 'em what he wants."

"But, Max—"

"GIVE HIM WHAT HE WANTS!"

You could hear a spoon drop. Max whispers in his undertaker voice, "What do you want, Harry?"

"Salad."

"No soup?"

Golishoff's explodes. Pots fall off the wall, Steadies fall to the floor, laughing. Max can't help it. When caught between a victim and a joke, it's no contest. A sucker for the rim shot, his loyalty is to the joke. Fuck the butt of the joke as long as it's not him. It's how Jews survived. How else do you come back from pogroms and slaughter? You make fun.

But not Harry. Poor Harry, suffering from an interminable lack of humor, hasn't laughed in years. A former beat cop, he went on permanent disability after his wife left him. With no children or wife to support, "there's no reason for me to work.

Let the City support me, like the addicts I chased."

So he faked a heart attack chasing a junkie down the block, holding up his pants over a mass of Jell-O intersected by a belt worn on its last rung.

"Do I get my salad, Eddie?"

"Not without the soup."

Harry stands. Max yells, "Sit down, Harry!"

This is drama at its best. Small men arguing about small things.

"Let him go, Max."

"He's a customer, you *putz*!"

"You lose money on him. All he does is drink coffee."

"I make my living off coffee!"

It's true. Max charges a quarter a refill. Doesn't sound like much, but it adds up. Three hundred cups a day comes to a hundred bucks a day; that's thirty grand a year for grinds, not bad. Max hit on something. For Max, a coffee-drinking customer is an annuity.

"You give up your seat, you lose it," warns Eddie. You'd think Harry was forfeiting box seats at Yankee Stadium.

"Sit down, Harry. Eddie's sorry."

"No, I'm not."

"Give 'em the soup!"

"SALAD! SALAD! SALAD!"

Harry breaks down.

"What's wrong, Harry? Mets lose?"

"Max... I... "

Harry's sobbing.

A sobbing man among men in a luncheonette on the Lower East Side during lunch hour is not a good thing. If a man's gonna sob, there should at least be a woman around, otherwise it makes things very uncomfortable for the other men.

In the company of men, sobbing is *verboten*! Unless it's the Ukraine, Middle East, or Golishoff's. A moist eye, a quivering lip, even a quiet, throbbing body shaking at low vibration is permissible. But not loud crying. The risk being that feelings are contagious, and a good group cry among men runs the risk of getting out of hand. Wet feelings hung out take forever to dry, and then you don't know if it's genuine or not, if you're crying for yourself or the other guy. Either way it hurts business.

"I have cancer."

Steadies moan, "Oh, my God!"

Max turns to Eddie, "You're happy now?! GIVE 'EM THE SALAD!"

Then the obligatory silence followed by the inevitable query.

"What kinda cancer, Harry?"

"Not sure."

"It spread?"

"All over."

"Are you dying?"

"Sooner or later."

Eddie mumbles, "Sooner's better."

Max rips into him, "*You* should get such good news!"

"I don't want him to suffer."

"How much time do you have, Harry?"

"I gotta be home by three."

"What?!"

"Gotta take the dog out."

"Told you Max! He's full of shit! He don't have cancer, he just don't want the soup!"

It's true. When cornered, Harry will say or do anything.

Max asks, "Why did you lie, Harry?"

Harry smiles. "Why not?"

Eddie can relate.

Chapter Three

Back in High School, Eddie had a friend, Larry, who he spoke to about sex. Anything dealing with girls met with the same response: "Feel 'er up."

Larry Shmuckler, son of bagel maven Hy Shmuckler, hated his name and later changed it to Smith. Smith Shmuckler was the rightful heir to the Shmuckler Water Bagel Dynasty, on the condition he kept the family name.

Larry's Yiddish nickname was "*Yoynee*," suggesting a wrinkled, unwashed, sleep-gunked, yellow-toothed kind of Jew. But Larry was anything but.

Hip, sharp, and fey, he called himself "Hot Stuff," the go-to guy for trends and fashion in High School, the first in his group to wear lanyard wristbands made at Camp Boiberick where he reigned as Head of Arts and Crafts. Larry had a look, a style, spiffy and current. Constantly campaigning against the *Yoynee* look, he modeled himself after his hero, "The King," Godfather of Cool, Elvis.

Back then, "Little Elvises" were sprouting all over America, running roughshod over Ozzies and Harrietts. Even little Ricky Nelson took up guitar with no voice or talent, emulating his equally talentless white bread hero Pat Boone, busy writing "Love Letters in the Sand."

Almost overnight, Little Elvises were running rampant over this great land, turning their backs on parents, facing the mirror. Cute little pecker boys falling in love with themselves, standing in front of the mirror for hours, puffing pomade pompadours into finely sculpted ducks' asses, seamlessly overlapping the groove down the back with spit-lubricated black tooth comb, shaping the shiny "do."

Then they'd slip the black tooth comb into their back pocket, top row of teeth showing—next, a slow glide of the palms along the sides of the "do," a tap on the "burns," pat on the head, swiggle-twist curl, and off to the corner candy store, window stopping at every shop. It took Larry an hour to walk a block.

To complete "The Look," Larry wore tight white t-shirts showing off twig-stick arms in rolled up sleeves holding filtered Kents, one in his ear. T-shirt tucked into twice-rolled cuff dungarees, black leather belt, argyle socks, desert boots, a peacock of a man, strutting around like he had a broom stuck up his ass.

As painfully shy as Eddie was with girls, that's how relaxed Larry was. He had this ease, this gift, to talk about *nothing*. A real schmoozer, Eddie watched Larry *buzhee*, breeze, glide, make small talk, laugh, giggle, swing his hips, lift his leg, hide his farts, shift his weight, pretend to listen, on the lookout for anything that moved.

There was talk that Larry hung with girls to get to the boys, that Smith Shmuckler was not the man he said he was. But who knew? In those days "gay" was happy, and *"faygele"* was just a bird. But looking back, all the signs were there. A love of musicals, poodles, Judy Garland, Tab Hunter, thin arms, white teeth, captain of the cheerleading *and* debating team, gossip columnist, head *yenta*, treasurer of G.O., a fondness for Charlotte Russe, great dresser, dancer, baby-sitter, and winner of the Frankie Avalon look-alike contest! All there!

Eddie wondered if Larry also walked around with a boner all day, stealing not so occasional glances at his crotch, unaware that Larry returned the favor, but for other reasons. Eddie confided in Larry and told him about a girl he liked, Pulkie Petrosia, who sat next to him in choir, how she inspired him, taking up her seat and most of his, thighs touching, a tenor's muse.

"I think I love her."

Chirping for his chick, Eddie hit notes a canary would envy. He sang on pitch with a clarity rarely heard in Brooklyn. Legend has it that the heat coming off Pulkie's thigh could thaw a frozen bialy, instant toast if she sat on it. By far the most popular girl in class, all the boys wanted to sit next to her, or on top. Pulkie had a pretty moon face and a body shaped like a *hamentash*, but without the three corners, more like a prune danish, with plenty of prune to spare.

What to do?

"Feel 'er up."

"But—"
"Take her to Brighton, buy her a papaya, 'n' feel 'er up."
"I—"
"Cost you a quarter."
"I—"
"Do you *have* a quarter?"
"Yes."
"So, what's the problem?"
"I—"
"It's what men do, Eddie! It's our job!"
"I know, but—"
"Scared?"
"No."
"Want me to set it up?"
Eddie pauses.
Biggest decision of my life.
"Well?"
"Can you come with me?"
"She doesn't want me, she wants you."
"Why?"
"'Cause you're the only one who hasn't felt 'er up yet. And she's a senior, so you don't have much time."
"Oh."
"But first you need to know some things."
"Did you feel 'er up, Larry?
"Many times. Come with me."

Larry leads him out of the basement, into an alley. He pulls a Kent from his ear and puts it in Eddie's lips. Larry strikes a match, Eddie leans in for a light but gets Larry's lips. Eddie pulls back. Larry leans in. Eddie pushes him.

"Get the fuck outta here!"
"Afraid to kiss a man?"
"I don't kiss men."
"Then give me back my Kent!"
Eddie tosses Larry back his Kent.
"Here, you homo!"
"Forget Pulkie."
Eddie panics.

"No Pulkie?"

"If you can't prove you can kiss a guy, how you *gonna* feel up a girl?"

Larry lights up, his back against the brick wall, blowing smoke to the side, very injured, very Joan Crawford. Eddie's boner is raging.

Is it worth kissing a guy to feel up a girl?

"Will she let me touch her... there..."

"Possible."

Eddie's mouth is dry, his knees weak, eyes glassy, heart racing, dick throbbing, and it's only nine A.M. Busy day ahead. He takes a deep breath, removes the cigarette from Larry's lips, and kisses him quickly.

"Again."

"AGAIN?!"

"Tongue."

"No!"

Larry looks at Eddie's boner. "Then take it out."

"What are you gonna do with it, Larry, put it through a bagel?"

"Take it out!"

"No!"

"Then I'll..."

Larry puts his hand on Eddie's zipper. Eddie smacks it.

"No!"

Larry runs his palm over Eddie's mound.

"It's practice for Pulkie... Close your eyes and think of her."

Eddie closes his eyes and gets his first blow job at fourteen, a feeling he'll remember and try to repeat the rest of his life. Eddie's an addict.

"So, here's the thing, Eddie."

"Shoot!"

"She's got big tits."

"Big."

"Huge."

"Huge."

"Hides 'em under her sweater, but trust me, they're big, *really* big."

"Bigger than Maddy's."
"Who's Maddy?"
"Someone I used to know."
Larry nods, a newfound respect for his apprentice.
"So you know what to do?"
"Oh, yeah!"
"Good. So her left tit's bigger than her right."
"Right."
"Don't let it throw you."
"No."
"Stay on her right."
"Right."
"Don't fake right, then go left."
"No."
"She'll let you stay on the right forever."
"Why?"
"To build it up."
"Build it and they shall come."
"What?!"
"Herzl."
"What hurts?"
"Israel, Herzl. He said, 'Build it and they shall come.'"
"I'M TALKING NIPPLES! BOOBS! KNOCKERS!"
"Sorry."
"LIST-EN!"
"Okay!"
"What a knucklehead!"
"Continue."
"Nipple on her right is an 'innee.'"
"Innee?"
"Don't try to get it out."
"No."
"Won't come out."
"Why?"
"I DON'T KNOW WHY! IT'S SHY!"
"Shy?"
"JUST DON'T DO IT!"
"Okay."
"Don't even think about it!"

"Okay! Okay!"
Larry's mouth is a rubber mallet.
"She'll freak!"
"OKAAAAY!"

Larry puts the back of his hand across his forehead and fans himself. He's having a moment. "I can't do this anymore!" Pulkie's pompadour pimp has had it. "That's it, Eddie! You got it?"

"Got it."
"Good, you're set."
"Thanks, Larry."
"Good luck."
"I don't need luck."
"Oooh…" Larry lets out a long whistle. "Look at you! 'I don't need luck.'"

Eddie has no clue where that came from. He must have picked it up at a movie or something. He tries on new lines so when a macho moment is called for he's ready. Larry, always needing to get the last word in, offers Eddie a sage piece of advice, "Remember what the Rabbi said." Eddie, not about to be outgunned by Smith Shmuckler, shoots back, "Don't eat pork?"

"No, *putz*! Today you are a man!"

Chapter Four

Pinned against a rock under Pulkie's kilos, face smothered in tit, Eddie's breathing through one nostril. Blinded by the light streaming through the boardwalk slats, Eddie's the recipient of heavy-footed, varicose-popping, *p'deshve*-aching pedestrians raining sand on his *kepee* from above. Pulkie's got a fist hold of Eddie, cutting off his blood supply. *Should I tell her I love her?* He would, but then he'd risk losing the nipple, and, as Larry warned, "A nipple dropped is a nipple lost." But he's so grateful.

"I love you," he says from the side of his mouth.

"Fuck you!" she says banging his head against the rock, stuffing her right tit back. Eddie's not sure if it's blood or sweat running down the back of his neck. He doesn't care. Going against Larry's strict admonition, he goes for it. He believes he can pop Pulkie's right nipple out, and save her from a tortured life of inverted nipple, by sucking as hard as he can. She whacks him across the head.

"What the fuck are you doing?!"

"I love you, Pulkie."

"Pam! It's Pam!"

"That's what I meant."

"And don't think I don't know what you boys call me behind my back."

"I'm sorry."

"No, you're not. You just say that. But you're not sorry. If you were sorry — blah-blah-blah..."

Larry's right. He should have listened. Now the moment's passed, the mood broken. She won't shut up. He can't get back into it. He can brave the sun, the wind, the sand in his eyes, the rock up his ass, but the talking, the talking. He realizes then that nothing kills a moment more than talking.

"Want a B.J.?"

B'YOYNG!

And before he knows it, she's got Eddie, cubes 'n' all, suctioning harder than a Hoover Upright. Eddie's head's

popping, as if stricken with Parkinson's and Tourette's.
"Like that?"
"Oh! Oh! Oh!"
"Then you'll love this!"
She bites down on his balls, not hard, just enough to break the skin.
"Ow! Ow! Ow! Ow!"
"You have to be gentle, Eddie," she says, licking the blood off his balls.
"Ah! Ah!"
"Know what I mean?"
"Yes! Yes! Yes!"
"What did you say?"
"I—I—"
Eddie's not much up for conversation at this point. Neither should Pulkie, dribbling from a mouth full of Eddie.
"Oh, Eddie, you could fill a cup." Eddie's spazzing. "No one's ever filled my mouth like that! Oh My God, it's coming out my nose!" she shrieks, her face a geyser of come, "Oh, Eddie, you're unbelievable! What'd you eat clams or somethin'?"
"Please, pleeeease, be quiet."
"All you guys are the same. All you wanna do is come. You never wanna talk."
"Pulkie, my balls are bleeding!"
"Come into the water, I'll jerk you."
"I can't."
"Yes, you can."
"No, I—"
"Come on, Eddie! Be a man!"
Eddie hears Larry:
It's what men do.
"I'm empty."
"No, you're not."
"I am."
"I'll let you finger me."
B'YOYNG!
Eddie's joint jerks right up, volunteering his involuntary muscle.

"Told ya."

Eddie's in shock. No one's ever spoken to him like that.

I'll let you finger me? My God, she's so, so, free, so cool. Pulkie's got her shit together, she's honest and free and hot, and maybe, just maybe, Pulkie's no slut, that she's an... angel... and all the guys are her servants, serving <u>her</u>! Sure they all talk about her behind her back. So what?! She's popular!

Pulkie takes Eddie's hand and runs into the ocean. Eddie screams, not so much from the freezing cold, but from the salty ocean eating the teeth marks on his balls. That and his tush made raw from the runs, right after Larry sealed the deal with Pulkie.

Eddie's weak spot is his stomach, although you'd never know it from the outside. The more placid, the more acid. Excitement didn't do it, anxiety did. He could deal with any discomfort as long as he didn't have to feel. Any pressure, any tension, any circumstance with some-*thing*—and he was fine. But throw in a mother, a child, a wife, a girlfriend, some-*one,* anything emotional, personal, anything that smells of affection, giving, receiving, anything mutual, a simple weave of feelings—and his stomach tanked.

Eddie can't believe how cold the water is. His asshole's numb, so that's good, but his dick's retreated in a shroud, a shriveled, dried out *kishke* case holding the shrunken sausage. But with each shake 'n' bake, Pulkie's bringing it back to life. Eddie hears fans rooting, "Bring it back! Bring it back!"

My God, she's doing it, amazing! Pulkie's a machine, resurrecting his dick, his half-dead, frozen dick! Bringing it back to life! It's growing, growing, forget walking on water! He's coming in the ocean! The Papaya paid off, a miracle in Brighton! Whoosh!

Slumped over her shoulder, one with the world, he watches the tide, the seagulls, pearly whites floating lazily out to sea...

Will a fish be born?

Now it's her turn. She takes his hand and slips it inside her. She giggles, letting his fingers do the walking, squishing, pinching, fishing around for what, he's not sure. But just the idea makes him hot. Inside her patch, she's got that grated Macintosh feel, reminding him of Bina's apple streudel. He wonders if she's as tangy down there. He dives to find out and almost drowns. He pokes around.

How many holes are there?

Eddie's transported to a class trip to the Hayden Planetarium, lost in the Milky Way, no idea of where he is, his fingers inside her, scaling walls, ridges, folds, feeling small, feeling lost, feeling... a stub.

He flicks it... once... twice. She shudders. He keeps flicking. She's going nuts.

"Oh! Oh!"

Eddie's paying back. He's so happy.

"Oh, oh."

Like the coin game in cafeteria, he keeps flicking, aiming for imaginary goal posts, waiting for a field goal. Pulkie's cheerleading.

"Don't stop. Dooooon't STAAAAAAAAP!"

"I won't!"

"Shut up, don't talk!"

"Okay."

"Keep doing it, keep doing it!"

"Okay!"

"You stop, I'll kick your balls in!"

"I love you, Pulkie."

"Oh, Eddie, where'd you learn this?"

"Cafeteria."

"Oh, Oh, Oh!"

What a great class trip. What's next? How long is he supposed to stay? Is this it? He's bored. He wants to go home, be with his friends, play stickball. He wonders what they're doing? He'd rather be with them, instead of being stuck here in the cold Atlantic flicking Pulkie, her tongue in his ear, giving him a good roto-rootering, blocking his hearing on one side, so he can only hear half the seagulls.

"I'm coming! Oh God, I'm coming! I'M-COM-ME-ME-ME-MIIIING!"

Women come?

"Oh, don't stop! Dooon't STAAAAAP-P-P-P-P-P-P-P-P!"

Oh she stutters.

Larry never told him about women coming. Eddie thought

that for women, it starts and stops with a moan. That's all he ever saw in movies or on TV. Just before commercial break, you'd hear the woman say, "Yes! Yes! Please, yes!" not, "I'm coming!"

What the hell is that? And where does the "come" come from? What's it look like, smell like? Is it invisible?

"DON'T STAAAAAAAAAAAAAAAAAAAAAP!"

He doesn't know what she's talking about. Until an hour later when his hand's about to fall off. He switches hands, but he's a "righty" so his fingers cramp. After a while, he can't feel his own fingers, let alone her pussy.

This is crazy. You can waste a whole day here. Satisfying women is hard. You gotta stay hard and your fingers can't cramp. Will I still be able to throw a good curveball?

Later on, he realizes that the whole thing about sex is the idea, the possibility, the anticipation. But once gotten, it's over. Next. Eddie sees gambling and chasing women as one in the same. All the action's up front, the set up, the moves, the planning, the conniving, the not knowing. The not knowing is what turns Eddie on. He loves not knowing, it's what pulls him in, keeps him going, thinking he knows, but knowing he doesn't, and he is willing to bet on it.

Routine and repetition, though comforting for most, kill Eddie. He sees it as life sucking life out of itself. If forced to line up with the rest of the Universe, he'd rather shoot himself. Eddie's about mystery, uncertainty, letting the world surprise you. What's the worst that can happen? *You'll be surprised.* At least you won't be bored. That's the worst. So hold off. Hold off coming as long as you can, no matter how long and steady Pulkie's stroke. Don't give in, be strong, be brave, be daring, for you know not what awaits, and isn't that the fun?

Eddie's amazed at how warm she is, how giddy.

"What's so funny?"

"I'm peeing in your hand."

He leaves his hand there, enjoying the vinegary stream. His laugh joins hers, and with mouths open and pee flowing, she gives him his first tongue kiss, consuming his mouth. He can't believe it.

Why didn't Larry tell me about this?!

She can't go deep enough into his mouth, sucking and chewing his tongue like a hot pastrami. Eddie thinks, "Can you come from the tip of your tongue?" A Talmudic question. What would the Rabbis say? "You bet, if Pulkie's got anything to do with it!" She's jerking off his tongue. The woman's incredible! Her mouth-to-mouth could resuscitate the Gowanus, Brooklyn's very own homecoming oral queen performing the Brighton Beach Water Dance.

"LET'S HEAR IT FOR PUULKEEEEE!"

The tides erupt in thunderous ovation.

That's twice in five minutes, has to be a record.

Tongue and fingers removed, he looks at her, sees her differently. *She's pretty, really pretty.* They kiss, allowing tenderness in — he begins to cry.

* * *

Goose-stepping behind Principal, Eddie passes Larry, giving him a thumbs up. They step into the office. Eddie stands on trial while Dr. Kostas sits reading a report. Kostas is a large man who looks like he enjoys frightening little children. He has fierce brows connected by a center mole, resembling tire tracks screeching to a stop. Eddie can smell smoked rubber coming off his forehead.

"Where were you son. It's the eighth period and you've been gone since the first."

"My father died."

"Oh, my God!"

"Heart attack."

Kostas grabs his chest. "When?!"

"Tuesday!"

"*Today's* Tuesday."

"Sunday. It was Sunday."

"Sunday?"

"I ran back for *Shiva*."

Eddie quickly scans the office. *No Mezuzah, picture of the Pope, a cross — good! He's a goy!*

"Sir, *Shiva* is when —"

"You're mourning, I know."
"My mother, she—"
"No, I understand."
"Can't leave her."
"Of course not, poor boy."
 In those days teachers still liked kids *and* believed them.
"Why didn't you say something?"
Eddie parrots Sol's signature sign-off for matters close to the heart, "What's the use?"
"So people can help you."
Principal pats Eddie's head. Eddie ducks under kindness. He hates being touched. *Unless it's Pulkie.* His surliness is seeping through. It happens after he comes.
"Why is your head so damp?"
"I sweat through the head."
"Yes, but—"
"I ran back to school."
Recoiling under Principal's pat hand, Eddie spots his suspicious brow.
I better do something.
Summoning up all his sincerity, Eddie gives it his best "refugee" just-got off-the-boat-feel-sorry-for-me Look. Eddie has many Looks.
The Look used to extract extra loaves on bread lines.
The Look taught by Bina, mastered by Eddie at five.
The Look head down, eyes up, mouth open, slight drool; manipulation riding the back of survival.
The Look guaranteed to win over strangers and kind hearts, eliciting underserved sympathy from unsuspecting patsies.
"Your head's *really* damp *and* sandy."
"We go to the beach after Kaddish."
"Why?"
"To throw our sins in the water."
"Isn't that done on Yom Kippur?"
What the fuck does he know about Yom Kippur? He's a goy!
"Isn't Yom Kippur when you throw your sins away?"
"Uh... yes, sir, but in Russia, when someone dies, you go to the water to cry... *in* the water, you go *in* the water... to cry."

"Like baptism?"
"What's that?"
"When did you say your father died?"
Why doesn't the prick leave me alone? Believe my lie and leave me alone!
"When?"
Fuck! I'm losing him! Gotta do something! What... WHAT?! ... CRY! That's it! Cry! Cry! Cry your kishkes out, cry your heart out! CRY, YOU FUCK! CRY!

Fuck! It's not coming! Hold, hold your breath, hold, choke, cry, heave, think! Think Sol, comin' at you, his belt beating you, whackin' away, back-front-back-front- IT'S COMING!... I'M, I'M COMING— back-front, back — CO-MIIIING! I'M CO-MIII-NNNNG! I can cry! I can cry! Instant cry! Bring in shit memory! To shit thought! Shit feeling! Shit cry! CRY! MOTHER FUCKER! CRY!

Eddie's turtle head is dipping into his shoulders, revving it up, churning tears, Sol-smitten tears.

Yes, Ladies and Gentlemen, this is a young boy crying on his knees. Praised be the Lord.

Principal kneels down beside Eddie, puts his arm around him.

"Let us pray."
"Okay." Eddie crosses himself.
"You know, son, I lost my father when I was young."
Good.

Eddie feels revulsion for any offer of help. The revulsion is self-disgust. He can't tolerate his dishonesty to himself. Later on, he deals with it much better. But at this stage, he's still too young to bullshit himself, and, of course, the fear of getting caught looms large. That, plus the compassion. He can't take it. Invites it, uses it, but can't stand it. It's not that he's such a *shtarker*, but any caring offered and he shuts down. That's how much he needs it.

Maybe if he let it in, allowed himself to be cared for, nestled his face in Sol's hands...

"It helps if you talk about it, son."
"We don't talk in my house."
"It's good to talk."

Shut up!
"Expressing your feelings is good."
I better kick it up a notch.
"It's helpful."
Eddie's wretching.
"Useful."
Heaving.
"Healing."

And with each suggestion, Eddie revs it up to the point where he's ready to be admitted, if not committed. Principal's scared. He's got a hysterical teen on the verge of a nervous breakdown thrashing on his floor. He thinks they must be hearing it outside. They could be hearing it downtown. He could be accused. He could be... fired.

"Want to go home, son?"
Yes, you fuckin' idiot!
"Yes, please."
"Okay, then. I'll write you a slip."
"Thank you."
"You've been through a lot."
No shit!

Principal stands up. Eddie's survival instincts kick in.
Do more! Hug 'em, squeeze 'em, love 'em! Seal the deal!

Eddie lunges and wraps his arms around Kostas's fat ass, stuffing his face into his crotch, blowing his nose into the pants, smelling the urine, feeling the love.

Oh, how I'd love to do a "Pulkie" on you!
"How's the family taking it?"
Bite your cock off.
"How's your mom?"
Eddie invokes Sol's Socratic method.
"How could she be?"
"I understand."

Hanging on to Kostas's leg, a forerunner of future legs he'd hold on to, Eddie thinks of Pulkie's soft folds, coming in the ocean, all the fish bathing in his come, Kostas swelling against his cheek.

"It's very hard, son, when it happens so suddenly."
"Terrible."
"How long will you be sitting?"
I better let go of his leg or else I'll have to buy him a papaya.
"It's the last day."
Eddie swallows hard, letting the lie slide down his throat, a sweet chocolate malt.
"I'll offer my personal condolences to your mother next week on Open School Night."
Fuck!
That's the thing about lies. They never stop. One lie begets another and truth is always an orphan.
Uncle Max will bail me out. I'll tell him about Pulkie and how I gave myself a late Bar Mitzvah present, and Max will laugh and go to Open School Night.
"Can I stay home tomorrow, sir?"
"Of course."
"Thank you, sir."
Funny how bold Pulkie made him, how strong, how arrogant, how *chutzpadik*. Eddie backs away slowly, bowing, leaving a trail of sand.
"My best to your family, son."
Once outside, Eddie throws his head back and breathes a huge sigh of relief. His head's spinning. The salty air, the sandy nipple, the hurried smokes. He smells his fingers. If he could just do *that*—suck nipple, smoke, lie, smell his fingers—he'd be fine for the rest of his life. Eddie's got a future.
The next day, flowers arrive.
Bina asks, "*Vats dat?*"
Eddie gets up from his "sick" bed.
"Flowers."
"From who?"
"I don't know."
"Is it a *simcha*, a *hasseneh*, who got married?"
She takes the card from Eddie.
"For your loss." Who got lost, Eddie? Who's *farblondget?*"

* * *

"GIVE 'EM THE SALAD!"
"But, Max, you don't understand."
"Understand what?!"
"I made a bet in my mind."
"Your *meshugeneh* mind?"

Eddie's mind is where he makes most of his bets, a turnstile of events. "Soft" bets are what he calls them, games he plays with himself, but takes as seriously as any "hard" bets at the track, ballpark, or crap table. The evidence being the reaction of strangers watching him fret, or the sudden expletive in a crowded elevator. It's not Tourette's. It's just Eddie talking to himself. You'd think with all the people in New York City you wouldn't have to do that, but...

The fact that he only has himself to pay off doesn't make it any easier, 'cause Eddie will not cut himself a break when he loses to himself. Eddie bets on anything. Anything and everything. He figures God made a bet bringing him into this world, so what's another bet?

Eddie sees a guy running for the bus and bets he misses it. That's fairly safe bet in New York because bus drivers are cruel, unless it's a woman driver, then he bets the other way. He bets the weather, the number of steps to the F train, the number of pigeons in the coop, the number of stops in the elevator, the age of the whores he bangs, the change in Bina's purse, a dropped coin, heads or tails, soup or salad.

Eddie whispers in Max's ear, *"I bet that Harry has soup ' n' salad twenty days in a row."*

Max whispers back, *"What's today?"*

"Twenty."

"Harry, my friend, for Shalom, for Peace, have the soup."

"I'm Albanian, Max. No peace! Revenge!"

"Okay, Eddie! That's it. Give 'em his salad!"

"But I made a bet."

"You **lose!**"

Crowd goes nuts. Great fight! Close! Harry by decision. Eddie serves Harry, but not before a parting shot. "Fuckin' Harry can never make up his mind."

Steadies fall off their stools. *This* is what they came for, *this*, someone losing, someone getting fucked, someone *else* getting fucked, the ultimate enjoyment. Even better is *you* getting fucked, if you can enjoy it. Problem is, self-pity isn't a spectator sport.

Eddie felt good. Boyles, Max, 'n' Harry in one afternoon. Great action, great fun.

Chapter Five

Eddie got his start gambling at Trios. Three hoods owned the joint; one ran it, Pete. Mild-mannered Pete, until he cracked a cue stick over your head. Trios. Ten tables: eight regular, two billiards. Few play billiards, because it has no pockets. A game with no way out, just a tiny red dot separating two white balls from the red. Hit yours, hit his, then the red one in any combination, sliding off the other, caroming off the cushions, a higher art form requiring lots of "English," spin, or "massé," but never a direct hit. A direct hit to dead center gets you nowhere, just a lot of noise, but no action, finesse, or spin, good for Neanderthal Nine Ball but not billiards.

To make it work, you had to be slightly off. Aim high, low, wide, side, but never right on, never the obvious. It was a game worth giving your life for at sixteen. It's all Eddie ever wanted to do—shoot pool morning, noon, and night.

Long before cinemas, supermarkets, casinos, and poison castle McDonalds, there was Trios showing the way to a longer, more fulfilling day. Get through the night and you get through the day, eighteen hours a day, seven days a week.

Trios, smoke-infested Trios, faded green felt on slate, chalk, wood, a slight tap of the cue on the floor signifying "Good Shot, Kid," was all the affirmation Eddie needed.

Trios, long, narrow, ten tables in a row leading to the john, jukebox, quarter a song crankin' out Skyliners, Platters, Ella, Tony, Frank, Frank, fuckin' endless Frank, but the best, the best according to Pete, was Darren, Bobby Darren—not necessarily best voice or best song, but pound for pound, match for match, singer to song, Bobby Darren, "Beyond The Sea." Oh, man…

Somewhere beyond the sea, she's there waiting for me…

Eight quarters, eight fuckin' quarters in a row, and Pete would still fuck it up.

"Somewhere *over* the sea, she's there *watching* for *us*."

Well, at least he got the melody right. Pete would croon, and Trios would cringe. No one played country. You play country,

THE FIX

you get shot. "Fuckin' Conway Titty!" After all, this was Brooklyn where tough guys sang like fags, harmonizing on street corners, freezing their asses, holding their nuts, seeing who could hit the highest note. "Big Girls Don't Cry." Frankie Vallee made men of us all…

Trios, Eddie's sandbox, a world within a world where, where where you stood, how you stood, how you looked, what you played, what you said, said everything.

For Eddie, it was the beginning of cool. The coolest guys said nothing. Eddie assumed their silence was by choice. Only years later did he realize that they were idiots, not a brain between them. Eddie was looking for something that wasn't there, empowering them with a strength, intelligence they did not have, a habit of putting people on pedestals, talking them up in his mind, searching for heroes, a young man's obsession that won't quit until you get burned, and then everyone's full of shit.

Trios, ten guys hung over ten dim-lit tables while another ten watched.

Trios, land of *Gavones*.

But whatever they lacked upstairs, they more than made up in street smarts. They knew enough to know that when in doubt, keep your mouth shut.

"Nothing good comes from it anyway. 'Cause the minute somethin' floats out of your mouth, you wanna pull it back, sayin' things you don't mean, or don't know why, words lookin' for ideas, a chase not worth pursuin'." So waxed Pete, self-appointed sage of the Silent Majority, who took young Eddie under his perforated wing.

"Listen, kid, if you can keep your mouth shut 'n' keep 'em guessin', why open it 'n' let 'em know for sure?"

"Know what?"

"That you're an idiot."

"What?"

"We're all idiots. The trick is not lettin' them find out."

"Who?"

"The *other* idiots. Don't make it easy for them. *You* be the canvas."

"Canvas?"

"They'll paint a picture of you better than you can paint yourself. I mean what's the worst they can say, that you're a mute? At least they can't accuse you."

"Of what?"

"Havin' an opinion."

Following Pete is a crossword puzzle.

"Just remember, if you wanna speak, don't. You won't believe how much heartache that will save you."

"Okay."

"Even if you see somethin' terrible happen right before your eyes, say nuthin'."

"Not even call the cops?"

"I didn't say don't *do,* I said don't *talk.* You talk, you don't do. Talk takes the air outta doin'. Talkin' tricks' you into *thinkin'* you're doin', but all you're doin' is talkin'. You keep talkin', you never do nuthin'!"

"Right."

"It's the one mistake God made."

"What's that?"

"Not rippin' our tongues out."

"Oh."

"But it's too late for that now. So don't look at what people say, look at what they do. If you wanna see where people are goin', look at where their feet are pointin', not the shoes they're wearin'."

"Right."

While Pete's talking he's making impossible shots. On some shots he doesn't even bother to look down.

"Get me a smoke." Eddie runs to get Pete's smokes. "Where was I?"

Seems no one finishes a sentence at Trios.

"You said if you can't do something, then shut up."

"Right! Right!"

"No one wants to hear it, you said."

"You're learnin' kid, you're learnin'!"

No one wants to hear your tzures.

"Especially from the young. I hate the fuckin' young."

"I'm sorry."

"Thinkin' you know everything! Meanwhile you know shit! You shouldn't even be allowed to talk before you're forty."

"Why?"

"Cause you don't know shit till then!"

"Oh, right."

"You open your mouth before forty, you should get smacked."

"Right."

"DON'T SAY 'RIGHT.'"

"Okay."

"DON'T SAY 'OKAY!'"

He finally misses and throws the cue against the wall.

A distinguished member of the "Loose Cannon Club," Pompei Pete would erupt just like that, anger out of nowhere, then wait for it to blow over, feel bad, say nothing, then continue as if nothing had happened. Eddie found that to be true with a lot of the older guys, sitting powder kegs, ready to go off, then gone, a stranger passing through... anger out of the blue.

Eddie gets Pete's cue and goes on a run of his own. By the time he was sixteen, Eddie could outshoot anyone except Pete. That he did at seventeen.

"If you're quiet, they'll think you're strong 'cause strong goes with silent, deep goes with silent, so deep goes with strong."

"Right."

"Ever hear of strong, silent types?"

"Uh—"

"Deep water runs still?"

"Sure."

Eddie hears birds chirping.

"Tall helps, too. Very few short, silent types, maybe short 'n' strong, but not silent, short, 'n' strong."

"Right."

"Short guys yap a lot, machine gun spatter, rata-tata-tat! Tall guys don't do that, don't have to—their tallness speaks for them."

Eddie's dyin'.

"So the less said, the better..."

"Yes."

"Better to listen..."

"Listen."
"You learn more..."
"More."
"I mean, what can you learn from yourself?"
"Nothing."
"Nothing you haven't heard before."
"No."
"Contrary to public opinion, all the wisdom in the world does not lie within you, King of Kings."
"Kings."
"So listen."
"Listen."
"Cause if you talk, you can't listen."
"No."
"It's not like walkin' 'n' talkin' or chewin' gum."
"No."
"And if you're gonna listen, listen to music."
"Music."
"Good music."
"Good music."
"Not country."
"No."
"It's all in the music anyway, anything you wanna know is in the music."
"Right."
"Stay in the passenger seat, Eddie. There's power in that, there's power in silence."

The Power of Silence, the greatest game of all, the hardest one to figure out, the gnawing obsession to know what the other person's thinking, the one you never win, witness Pete. How do you really know what someone's thinking? You don't. All the clues are there, the facts, the feelings; put 'em in some order, what do you get? Pete. May as well go fishin'.

"Game's over, Pete."
"Nice run, kid."

* * *

THE FIX

The guy with the biggest mouth in Trios was Chaalie, a tall, skinny dufus no one messed with because Chaalie was connected. Chaalie Calamari, reputed son of hit man Ollie "The Third," that is, the third partner in Trios. Chaalie would drop by 'round midnight, spot Eddie, break his balls, take cigarettes, money, smack Eddie back of the head.

At eleven, Eddie would start checking the clock, tightening up, anticipating Chaalie's arrival. Some nights, midnight came and went, no Chaalie. Then Eddie relaxed and racked up some good money. Money he'd need to put back under Sol's mattress before he discovered he's short. Sol kept thousands under the mattress, not trusting banks.

"I give the *Goniff* thieves money, the *Goniffs* loan me back *my* money, then charge me! It's a good business—for *Goniffs*!"

Eddie lines up the shot, bends down to shoot, and Chaalie walks in trailed by "Dufus Entourage." Eddie freezes, catching "Silent Majority" shrug, as if to say, "Sorry, kid, you're on your own."

Eddie re-grips the moist cue between middle and forefinger, scooped web to the thumb, forming the "flying asshole" circle sign through which the twenty-one-inch blue-tipped nipple cue plays peek-a-boo.

His stroke steady *before* midnight, Eddie's cue is now a fish stick, the roof of his mouth a cave. He takes a whiff of his pits. As if that's his biggest problem, but for a sixteen-year-old it is. His body's betraying him, betraying "cool."

Fuckin' sweat!

Sweat will kill "cool" quicker than a hose to a match. Balls, asshole, armpits, okay! But fingers? *Between* fingers? How do you sweat between fingers?

I mean, what the fuck? Did Sol's surgeon sweat?

No. He cracked Sol's rib open and replaced a leaky valve with a pig's, making Sol whole but *trafe*, adding years to his fucked up life, no sweat.

Eddie sprinkles Johnson & Johnson baby powder onto his chicken pink palms. Eddie's sweat, mixed with the talc, cakes into Bina's braided challah dough of egg, flower, sugar, yeast, and butter. Eddie extends his flattened body across the table for a long shot, his chin dripping sweat balls, a nauseating "choke" coming on, failure's opening act, the failure before you fail.

Get ready. Get Set... Chaalie bumps Eddie's elbow on the way to the john. Eddie misses. First game he's lost all night, courtesy of Chaalie's elbow. No apology, no excuses, just pay up. Pay up doesn't ask, "how?" or "why?" Just pay up!

Eddie sticks his hand in his back pocket, feels a leg, pushes his hand in further to remove a roll of Jewish bills, a ten over a five, folded over twenty singles. Chaalie's chin is resting on Eddie's neck, watching him count. Eddie settles up, calls it quits, turns to hang his cue but can't. Chaalie's announced his arousal, backing Eddie up against the table, wedging his joint up the crack of young Eddie's sweet cheeks.

"Where you goin', cupcake?"

Eddie squirms back only to receive another inch of Chaalie.

"I gotta go."

"But it's early."

"I got school tomorrow."

"It's Saturday."

"It's Yom Kippur."

"Yo *what*?"

"Holiday."

"What holiday? I ain't off."

"Jewish holiday. I go with my old man to Shul."

"Shoe?"

"Synagogue."

"Sin-a-gog?"

"I'm Jewish."

It's a hard thing for a Jew to say. It's easier being accused. The Nazis understood that better than anyone else. A shame, the shame of knowing everyone's got a little Jew in them.

"You're a Jew? I didn't know *dat*!"

What else don't you know, you stupid fuck?! "Go away! Go away!" Jews' constant refrain: " *Go away, I'm just trying to make a living!*"

"Pete, we let kikes in here?!"

"Leave the kid alone!"

"He killed Christ!"

"Get the fuck away with that shit!"

"He's a Jew." He turns to Eddie. "You're a Jew! Right?!"

Say it! Say it! Sol said, "Don't be afraid. They know anyway. Ask the German Jews."

"Yeah. I'm a Jew."

How could Sol have known that one day Chaalie Calamari, reputed son of hit man Ollie The Third, would start with the Jew stuff?

"You don't look Jew. You look I-talian."

"Thanks."

"*Eddie* a Jew name?"

"It was changed."

"Changed?"

"By my uncle."

"Uncle?"

"Father."

"Father?"

"Yeah."

"Why?"

"I don't know."

"You ashamed? Ashamed of your name?"

"I, uh..."

Good thing they don't start with last names.

"What's your last name?"

Oh, fuck!

No one has a last name in Trios unless it's something like "Calamari"—used less for recognition and more for extortion. Certainly not "Pyatiegorskia."

"Putty Wha? Putty Who?"

"Pyatiegorskia."

"What kind of a fuckin' name is *dat*?"

"I, uh."

"Is *dat* your first or second?"

"Second."

"Middle?"

"No middle. Jews don't get middle names."

"Why?"

"I don't know."

"So it ain't Parker."

"No."
"It's Putty-*wha'*?"
"Pyatiegorskia."
"So what's *Eddie*?"
"My name."
"No, your *real* name!"
"Aryeh."
"R. U. w*hat*?!"
"Means 'Lion' in Hebrew."
"Like Leo the Lion?"
"Yes."
"Hey! I'm Tony The Tiger." Chaalie's cracking himself up.
"Leave the kid alone."
"Shut up, Pete! Where you from, R.U.?"
"72nd 'n' 18th above the bakery."
"No, no, I mean where you *from*?"
"Here."
"No Jew's from here. You hebes always from some other place."
"Russia."
"Rush-eh!"
"Tashkent."
"Tash-wha?"
"It's in Russia."
"Where's *dat*?"
"In Russia."
"Ain't *dey* our enemy, Rush-eh?"
"Leave the *fuckin'* kid alone!"
"How much money you got, R.U.?"
"Not much."
"How much?"
"I don't know."
"What'd you come in with?"
"I didn't count."
"Well, why don't you count, you little cunt!"

Spooned between Chaalie and the pool table, Eddie feels the hard wooden edge dig deep inside his locked legs and soft groin, pickled in by Chaalie's homemade dry hump sandwich,

all that's missing is the mayo.
How the hell did I get here?
Sooner or later it's a question everyone asks themselves. All the way from Russia, an uncircumcised dick up his denim ass, wedged up against a pool table, jukebox playing "Big Girls Don't Cry."
Everything happens to me.
"Wanna play Ar-yay?"
"No, I—"
"Billiards, straight pool, eight ball, nine ball, ball ball?"
Eddie knew Chaalie sucked off most of Trios. One time Chaalie was interrupted four times because the guy he was sucking had to break away to shoot. But Chaalie was patient, sitting on the toilet seat, smoking weed, filing his nails, applying Chapstick, waiting to pick up where he left off. If Chaalie wasn't Ollie's son, he'd be just another fag. But family name made him a made man.
"Come on Ar-yaaaay!"
"No."
"I don't like, 'No.'" Chaalie's lip-nipping Eddie's lobe.
"You killed Christ."
I don't even know him.
Eddie looks up at Pete with Pluto eyes.
"Change the fuckin' song or leave the kid alone!"
"SHUT UP PETE!"
There goes my hearing.
"Kid's half your age, for Christ's sake!"
"That's how I like 'em."
Reaching one hand round Eddie's front, the other on his back, Chaalie grooves his tongue into Eddie's ear, his breath a thick cloud of sausage 'n' garlic. Eddie comes from a Kosher home. He's very uncomfortable. Eddie wonders if all this is really about money. He's gotten offers before from lonely rabbis, old men, and starched women, delivering groceries, but this, this is... getting... hard...
"Somewhere, beyond the sea..."
Not the best singer or song...
"She's there, waiting for me..."

Eddie whirls and cracks Chaalie's knee, breaking the cue *and* the tension in their boners. Eddie walks out, holding half a cue, tapping cues trailing behind him...

"No more sailin'... bye-bye sailin'..."

It was the first time Eddie dissed consequences. First time he didn't think about what would happen to him. First time he trusted God without knowing God. Actually, it was the second time. The first was when he was ten.

* * *

Sol had come home late one night, not unusual, but later than usual, intoxicated, especially surly, and nuts from a bad night out losing craps or something. Bina smelled the "something" on his fingers and it wasn't "*Hold* Spice means *qvality*!"

She goes after him with a vengeance even the donkey-fucking Uzbekistanis would be proud of. Startled out of his sleep by shrieks not heard in hell, Eddie leaps to protect little Maya, crying, terrified. Neighbors are yelling for them to shut up. Sol holds off Bina with one hand, slapping her face with the other. Eddie runs and grabs Sol's arm, gets whacked and goes flying across the room, banging his head against the wall, bringing down the glass-framed family portrait on his head.

He screams at Sol, *"SVEENIA! CHAZER!"*

Not quite fluent in one language, Eddie gets his point across in two. Sol removes his belt. Oh, boy. Bina's pleading. Maya's screaming. Eddie's coiled in a corner. It's a small apartment. Bina runs to protect Eddie. Sol swings wildly, misses Eddie, hitting Bina shielding Eddie.

"Sholom, he's a child."

"*VAT* DID HE CALL ME?"

Eddie's hiding behind Bina's see-through nightgown, dizzied by the scent of the remaining day's remnants of cheap Jealousy perfume, plump *toches*, huge breasts, and the sight of her curly graying pubic hair.

"YOU FUCKING PIG!"

Eddie's added a third language to his repertoire and spits in Sol's face.

Oh boy.

Now it's the window. Window or door. Sol's blocking the door, so it's the window. Good thing it's summer. Good thing he jumps. Good thing they live on the ground floor. Right out the window, to the schoolyard, barefoot in his pajamas. The schoolyard's his friend. He'd always find someone at the schoolyard to play with. But it's midnight. Who'll get him? He's ten, he cries, he cries at the drop of a hat. He wonders, *will I ever stop crying?* Bina gets Max and they bring Eddie home.

Sol's name in Yiddish is Sholom, "Peace." On Holidays, Sol, a man of few words but many numbers, would toast, "*Zol zein mit Sholom. Dere* should be Peace." And everyone would smile and say, "Amen, let's eat."

Sol rarely got mad but the threat always loomed large. Brooding, simmering, there was no doubt a battle was raging inside him. It exhausted him far more than the boxes he *shlepped*. Bina would say, "From boxes you can rest."

You think the past is over because you lived it and it's behind you. But it's lived and relived many times over, a daily reminder that you're never really done with it, even when it's done with you. The telling and retelling, the involuntary repetitious recalling, a constant refrain not letting you live. The present owned by the past, a complimentary arrangement of accommodating connections, twin cities living side by side. Let sleeping dogs lie, but you can't. It doesn't take much to rouse old wounds fed by fresh feelings. They never really go away. You're lucky if the stitching holds.

* * *

Yes, it was the second time lights went out on Eddie. And when lights go out for Eddie, it's over. The wall goes up and Eddie checks out. He doesn't, or can't, see what waits on the other side, nor does he care. He just doesn't give a shit.

No longer in need of protecting himself from himself, he reacts violently, releasing the present, no longer held captive, no longer the frozen bounty between past and future, no longer caught between window and door. Power's on, lights out, trigger down, regulator out, and all bets are off. Eddie's not to be fucked with.

"Funny thing about fear," Eddie thinks, "It only works when you're afraid. Not a good enough reason not to crack a knee."

On his way home, Eddie steps into an alley, unzips his fly for a whiz, and smells something funny. He bends down, lifts his shoe to his nose.

Chaalie must have smelled it too.

Eddie wonders how many tough guys shit in their pants, how many unsoiled heroes were out there? Did John Wayne shit in his pants? Superman in his leotards? Tarzan in his loin cloth? Or was it always a diaper?

Eddie and Sol arrive home about the same time, two in the morning. Sol from his game, Eddie from his. They both reek from smoke and know to put their clothing in plastic bags, for Bina had the same rule for both: "They can stink as long as they come home."

They didn't ask too many questions of Eddie, knowing any attempt to sit on him and he'd fly, for he had a bad case of *shpilkes*, needles in his pants.

Sitting in Shul with Sol on Yom Kippur, was *Shpilkes* Supreme. Eight hours of Shul breath, so that by four P.M. all the short, well-dressed congregants turned into hellacious, fire-and-smoked-fish-eating dragons.

Conditions got so bad it made the Spanish Inquisition a cruise on a tropical isle. Air was cut off, windows and doors shut because someone complained about a draft coming from the women's section upstairs, probably expelled from beneath the rotund ladies' pleated skirts.

The smelling salts were not so much for the fasting but for the bad air. By sundown, you can't distinguish between breath and fart, they all blend. It made Eddie sick and gag. He'd go to the bathroom, but it was worse down there.

What are they doing, reliving The Camps? Jesus Christ! Open the fuckin' windows!

Eddie liked to curse. Spit and curse, it made him feel American. Balling luggers, he'd spit for distance, an American in Shul fighting Shul breath, Shul smell, disgusting but familiar

Shul smell, the smell of the S.S. Blatchford.

* * *

The S.S. Blatchford, a converted World War II cargo ship, lugged war-torn refugees from Germany to New York, carting stuffed human sardines across the Atlantic through August storms, ten straight harrowing days and nights, fifty-foot waves licking Blatchford, washing over the stench. You come out of this one, it's a miracle. Eddie's a miracle. An emancipated, emaciated, vomit-wretched miracle. Hunger was a snap compared to that trip. He survived that, he could survive anything. He should have died many times over, but didn't. Years later, high rollers would invite him onto their luxury boats. "Sleeps ten," they'd say. "Oh yeah? Well, mine slept five hundred. Problem is, no one slept." To this day, Eddie looks at a glass of water and gets nauseous.

* * *

Sol sits in Shul, a stone, a true blue Commie, tested to the core, devastated by Julius and Ethel Rosenberg's execution, betrayed by Lenin, Stalin, the Gulog, the Party, the Lies, the Lies he believed in, the Lies he trusted.

"Everyone's equal," the Lies proclaimed, "except some are more equal than others."

Comrades in Poland, Russia, Workers' rights, Liberty and Justice, men and manly women hold rakes and shovels, sing *partizaner* songs — and then the disillusionment, the betrayal.

The Nazis killed his people. The Commies killed his faith.

But still he came to Shul every Yom Kippur. Why? Probably to tell God to go fuck himself or something. Not quite in those words, because there's no such words in Judaism.

Although, given everything he's put us through...

While Sol's sending his subliminal messages upstairs, Eddie's doodling football formations in the Siddur for Sunday's schoolyard football game at Shallow Junior High. Why would anyone name a school *Shallow*? That's Brooklyn for you.

Eddie was a pretty good schoolyard jock. A good split end, quick, fast, with great hands. But his real contributions were his plays. The plays were intricate, and, if executed properly, were a thing of beauty. But rarely were they executed properly, and even more rarely, were they a thing of beauty. Seems the opposing players got in the way. But the exercise kept Eddie occupied so he could get through the eight-hour service without crawling out of his skin. All the Jewish kids played their best football the Sunday following Yom Kippur. Bottled up from food, services, company, and family, they shot out of the holiday canon with a ferociousness inexplicable to their Italian counterparts. It was the only Sunday the Jews beat the Guineas. Every other Sunday, the Jews got creamed.

As Eddie's diagramming his gridiron notes in the prayer book margins, Sol glances over. He knows nothing about football, but it doesn't stop him from putting his two cents in. The only football Sol knew was the football the rest of the world knew: hitting the ball with the foot. Not some three-hundred-pound behemoths crushing each other over a stitched leather ball. He knew football, the football Americans call "soccer," a lousy brand name given by Americans for the world's most popular sport.

After a few *American* football seasons in the pew, Sol got the hang of it. It's how Sol got started in sports, through Eddie. It started with the '55 World Series when the Dodgers first beat the Yankees, then the Knicks, Rangers, and Giants. Sol picked up the games quickly. He listened, learned, his concentration razor sharp. He went beyond the peripheral, peeling away layers, analyzing, strategizing. He knew strategy. His chess games with Eddie could attest to that. If he had you by a pawn at the beginning, you lost by a pawn in the end; a knight, you lost by a knight. Whatever you gave up in the beginning, you lost in the end.

Eddie wouldn't think of using a pen for his sacred plays, only a pencil. A pencil with an eraser to erase the sacrilegious scenarios, although by this time, everyone in the congregation knew *The Shema* wasn't a quarterback sneak.

Sol accepted Eddie's desecrations, knowing it was the only

way to keep Eddie in Shul. The one day Sol needed Eddie beside him, Yom Kippur, the anniversary of his escape from Poland, leaving his mother and sister behind.

Sol also concluded that, as inappropriate as it was for his son to mark football plays in the Holy Prayer Book, it was just as wrong to glue donation labels inside the prayer books.

This Siddur donated by the Shmucklers, Edie and Hy, The Bagel Mavens.

"Who *de* hell are *dey*?!" Sol would complain to Rabbi.

But what could he do? As disrespectful as it was, marking plays in the Siddur, Rabbi knew Sol wasn't entirely wrong.

With this Rabbi no one was wrong. No one was right, no one was wrong. All you knew was that every Yom Kippur his sermon would end up with:

"And that's why we need a new roof!"

He wouldn't dream of confronting Sol, for Sol would give him a, **"What for!"** Rabbi can't chance it, can't chance anything, that's why he's a Rabbi.

"Leave it to God," he would say.

Sol didn't have a very high opinion of American rabbis. He saw them as talis-wearing businessmen with large mortgages.

"Rabbi, just because *de Shmuck* buys a few hundred Siddurs, he sits in front?"

"*Shmuckler,* Sol, *not Shmuck.*"

"Shmuckler, *Shmuck, vats de* difference?"

"*Der-cheretz,* Sol, *respect* for your fellow Jew."

"Respect? *De* rich sit in front and *de* poor sit in *de beck*?"

"Weeeeelll..."

"*Vat,* are *vie Blecks*?"

"Weeeeelll."

"Did Moses do *dat*?"

"Weeeeelll..."

"God *vud* give him a *k'nack* over his head *wit de* tablets!"

"Weeeeelll..."

"Is *de* Bagel *Shmuck* better *den* Moses?"

"Weeeeelll..."

Rabbi always starts off with "weee-eeelll...." It gives him a chance to squirm out of giving a direct answer to a simple question. It's a matter of survival for this silver-tongued Shul savant, a bulbous warrior of pulpit politics who's learned that no matter what answer he gives will be the wrong one. So, he sticks to his credo: "avoidance at all costs."

"Weee-eeellll...."

"*VEELLL, VEELLL, VAT?*"

"They're *machers* Sol!"

"You mean *dey* pay your salary."

Rabbi wants to knife Sol in the heart.

"Weee-eeelll..."

But he only has a pen knife.

"Weee-eeelll..."

He bides his tongue, which by now is hamburger meat.

"Weee-eeelll..."

He takes a deep breath to ward off a stroke.

"Weee-eeelll..."

Breathe... breeeeathe...

Rabbi's learned how to breathe. A survival technique he learned on Sabbatical at an ecumenical retreat in the Catskills where he studied "What Judaism can learn from Buddhism."

"Yes, Sol, they pay my salary," *aaaand... breeeeathe...* "fix the roof, repair boilers, support Sisterhood, Men's Club," *aaaand... breeeeathe...* "buy Torahs from Hungary, call bingo cards for smoking *goyim*, contribute ventilators, defibrillators," *aaaand... breeeeathe...* "Shmucklers do a lot, Sol."... *aaaand one last time... Namaste.*

"So *de* big shots sit in front."

"They don't have to, but that's where they like to sit."

"Because *dey* give."

"Yes, and because—"

"They're *machers*, big shots—"

"Sol, please—"

"So everyone kisses their *toches*!"

"It's Yom Kippur."

"**They can *kish mine*.**"

"Shhh!"

"I gave. I gave in Europe."

"We know."

"Lost my family."
"Shhh...."
"Murdered!"
"Shah!"
"My *madder*, my sister.
"It's Kol Nidre."
"On Yom Kippur!"
"The choir's singing, Sol."
"Nazi *besterds*!"
"Kol Nidre, Sol, Kol Nidre."
"*Det's vy* I'm here, to say Yiskor, to remember!"
Rabbi looks up to the ceiling for divine intervention to whisk this *nudnik* away.
"*Oder-vise* you *vould* never see me."
"God forbid."
"I come to Shul *vonce* a year."
Once may be too much.
"Out of respect."
Spare them.
"For them!"
And me...
"Even though in my heart I'm a **COMMUNIST!**"
"Shhhhhhh!"

The congregants don't even bother to turn around. They know Sol's Annual High Holiday Harangue as well as they know Rabbi's Roof Refrain, a code for keeping a roof over *his* head.

"Big deal, *dey* donate Siddurs. Let *dem* donate *de* Shul."
"Sol, would *you* like to make a pledge?"
"A pledge? A pledge is like *de* bank robbery in Tel-Aviv, *dey* came away *wit* a million in pledges...and ten dollars cash! Pledges you got plenty. *Gelt* is *vat* you need."
"Okay, then, would you like to send us a check to help burn the mortgage?"
"I'd like to burn Shmuckler!"
"I think you should go home."
Sol and Eddie fold their prayer shawls.
"A *shande*! A disgrace! Advertising bagels in *de* Siddur! *Vat?*"

De Siddur doesn't have enough names? *Dey* need *dat shmuck* Shmuckler's name?"

"*Gut Yontif*, Sol, I wish you a good New Year."

"Let me ask you, Rabbi, didn't Maimonides, *Der Rambam*, *de great* scholar say... *dat* de highest charity is *ven* no *von* knows de *shmuck who gave de gelt!*"

"Yes, but that's Maimonides, not Shmuckler."

"*Gut g'zogt, vell* said, Rabbi."

Having taken his annual pound of flesh, Sol's ready to go home.

"I *vish* you Peace, Rabbi."

Fuck you, Sol.

"Same to you, Sol. Hope to see you next year."

"God *villing*."

You should drop dead.

"My best to Bina."

Rabbi looks at Eddie and shakes his head.

Poor kid.

Eddie's thinkin', *Poor Rabbi*.

* * *

Sol rages all the way home, a roll call of religious hypocrisy. He kicks garbage cans and throws bottles.

"Pop, if Shul makes you so angry, why do you go?"

"I like it."

"But why are you so upset with Shmuckler?"

"Shmuckler's a *shmuck*."

"You don't even know him."

"That's why he's a *shmuck*."

"What?"

"What kind of way is that to introduce yourself? 'Hi, I'm Hy Shmuckler, I made a big donation!'"

"Still, he gives money."

"So he's a rich *shmuck*! America's full of *dem*. They call *dem* millionaires. *Vit* a name like Shmuckler, I *vouldn't* be so *qvick* to make a donation."

"Why doesn't he change it?"

"A name is all you got, *Boytschick*."
"So why did you change yours?
"It's America, you don't like *someting*, you change it."
"So why is Uncle Max 'Golishoff'?"
"Golishoff's *de* name of *de* crook who sold him *de* luncheonette. Max paid a lot of money for his name, so *vy* not use it?"
"But you're still Sol."
"I'll *alvays* be Sol, but you don't have to be."

Sol frames Eddie's face in his rough hands, kissing his *kepee*.

"Okay, *Boytschick*, no more *qvestions, Momme's vaiting* for us to eat."

It's what confused Eddie, that tenderness, those hands...
"But why 'Parker'?"
"*Vy?*"
"Why 'Eddie'?"
"*Vy anyting?* Blame your Uncle Max."
"For what?"
"*Everyting.*"

CHAPTER SIX

The day Max found out his brother was alive was the happiest day of his life. "The Joint," as in Joint Distribution Committee, notified Max in the spring of '46 that a lantzman from Sol's hometown in Bzezin, Poland, rode with Sol, Bina, and the children in the same cattle car for thirty days through Russia, Poland, Germany, landing in Bergen-Belsen, no longer the Final Destination to the Final Solution, but a way station for the lost and found.

Bergen-Belsen, where Anne Frank, the most infamous of all martyrs, perished, was now a displaced persons camp, a temporary relocation center. Temporary, meaning several months to several years for the several thousand fractured families living day-to-day in converted barracks, organizing, working, building schools, nurseries, clinics, factories, waiting for news on who lived, who died, the last time so-and-so was seen or heard from, every day raining hope and sorrow, each transport a trampoline of joy and despair.

Vie-a-heen zol ich gayn… Tell me where can I go?

So went the song and so went the unclaimed, the unwanted, to Israel, the one country that would have them. The one country they did not want.

"Where are they sending us? From one oven into another? A desert? Into a *mish-maash* of Bedouins and tailors, hashish-smoking merchants and teachers, masons and artists, shepherds and scholars. Who made this match? Allah? Yahweh?"

But they went, made lives, fought wars, taught their children not to be afraid. The "lucky" ones, those sponsored, went to Canada, Australia, South America. The luckiest went to The States. Some stayed in Europe. Even fewer stayed in Germany, reclaiming homes, businesses, possessions, taking back what little was left in the very place their lives were destroyed, choosing to stay in a cesspool of a country, confounding not only Jews but bewildered Germans scratching their dummkopfs.

"What is it with these people? Why don't they go away?

Isn't killing them enough?"

Juden in their midst sticking it to the Krauts, reminding them of their defeat.

Didn't we suffer too? Go away. Leave us alone. We were only trying to conquer the world.

Juden in their midst, witness to their shame, their shame of failure. That's what *grizzhes* the shit out of them—not the genocide, the atrocities, the mindlessness of a sick nation gone amok, but that they *lost*—again. That's twice in a century, make that half a century. What is it with them? Fuckin' Germans are on a losing streak. They should lay low for a while, let the Americans save them. Americans like to save. First destroy, then save. But even with the Marshall Plan, the Americans couldn't save the Krauts from the inconvenience of their own guilt. 'Cause no one hates failure more than Germans... maybe Americans, but that was before Capitalism made failure an industry, before the flowering of victimhood.

So they stayed, "The Yeckes," the German Jews, cutting themselves off from the rest, creating enclaves, mixing only when necessary, understanding each other when no one else did.

So how do they explain it to their children? Why they stayed? Can they say that staying was better than leaving? That starting over for some can be the end for others? Was it for money, comfort, knowing your oppressor... or maybe just no place to go?

Certainly they had it easier than those tossed and scattered to the wind, letting others choose. Why is it even necessary to justify? So that what? Children will know their history, their culture? Be proud? Of what, unanswered prayers? What's the point? What's the point of history, if it's a bad history? To learn from it? Learn how cruel people can be? What animals they can turn into?

Events teach nothing. Events record. Besides, who knows why anyone stays anywhere? Maybe the Yeckes knew that once you lose your home, you'll never find another, so why bother looking. Germany's as good a place as any.

Max tracked down "The Cattle Car Lantzman" in Cleveland

and found out that his sponsor was David Kaplinsky, the union *macher* a distant cousin of the Lantzman, which automatically made Max a relative. He went to the Lantzman to get his advice on how to deal with Kaplinsky to get his brother out.

"*Brek* his *bolls*, Max. *Dat's de* only *ting* big shots understand. Remind him how good *he* had it. Ask him what *he* did during the war while millions died. Make him guilty. He's already guilty, but make him more. I can't do it, cause I'm his cousin, 'n' he already did me a *toyve*, a favor, *farshtayst*?"

Max understood.

"Put *de shmear* on *de* bialy, Max."

"*That* I can do."

"Let him choke on it."

"Don't worry."

"And *don't* tell him I sent you."

"As God is my witness."

"That's the problem. God's a *vitness*. He should do something."

*　*　*

Max knew no *shtick*. He blew right past the receptionist and a room full of people.

"Mister Polinsky —!"

"Get out and wait your turn!"

"Regards from your cousin."

"What do you want? And make it quick."

"Golishoff. Max Golishoff. Call me Max."

Max extends his huge paw, establishing territorial rights, bringing Kaplinsky to his knees.

"That's not necessary!"

"Oh I'm sorry, *antschuldik*."

Max releases his grip... slowly.

"Mister Polinsky —"

"Kaplinsky! David Kaplinsky!"

"May I call you David?"

"No."

"David, I came here to help my brother."

"There's nothing I can do."

"If *you* can't, then who can?"

"I don't know."

David, you're a *macher*, a big-shot, I'm a nothing. I own a small luncheonette. But *you*, you're the President of the International Garment Workers' Union! You elect Senators! Presidents! You can't do nothing for my brother?"

"I'm sorry."

David, he has a sick wife, two small children, *pitzelach*."

"Max, there are hundreds of thousands trying to come to America."

"He's the only one I have left from a family of twelve."

"I'm doing my best."

"Do better, Doveedil."

Reducing David to *Doveedil* turns the *macher* into an infant.

"I'll try."

"I'll *try*? Did the Nazis say, 'I'll *try*'?! He could drop dead waiting for you to try."

"Put in your application."

"I did! Three years ago! The war ended three years ago! Why is my brother still in a refugee camp?"

"He's a refugee."

"But you're not."

Max stuck a hundred dollar bill in Kaplinsky's palm.

"That's not necessary."

"What, they pay you so much money for this *farshtunkene* job? You don't have a family and children to support?"

Max reads Kaplinsky's eyes. "See what you can do, Doveedil."

"I don't take bribes."

"It's not a bribe. It's a favor."

"Favors you re-pay."

Max pinches Kaplinsky's cheek.

"You're a smart boy."

Months went by and nothing. Max received a one-word letter from Sol.

"NU?!"

From that day on, Max was relentless. Every Monday through Friday, he showed up at Kaplinsky's office demanding action while Gomez Siegel held down the fort back at the shop. Max left right after the luncheon avalanche and returned before the dinner brigade. Kaplinsky's staff saw him coming from their window, a large mustachioed, heavy flesh-faced walrus rising out of the 14th Street subway station, lumbering toward them.

"A Golishoff Sighting."

More than capable of carrying the world's *tzures* on his broad shoulders, he held a small stained brown paper bag of leftover donuts and danish from the morning. Max timed his visits right after lunch because he knew that's when the body most craves sugar and sleep.

"You want the head, go to the stomach."

"FEED 'EM, KEEP 'EM" was the sign over Golishoff's door. "First words, then bribes," Max would say, "because words mean nothing. Maybe to poets, but not *fressers*. So whatever you do, if you ask a favor, don't show up empty-handed. It doesn't matter what it is, a cookie, a Cadillac, bring *something*."

"They'll always say, *'No, I can't take it,'* then take it, and if caught, deny it. *'I don't know what they're talking about!'* Couldn't they say, *'No,'* and not take it? No, because that wouldn't be nice… insult a briber? *'Take it – it's only a cookie, a Cadillac…'* *'Oh well, if you insist… it's only a cookie, a Cadillac.'"*

Max understood the whole world runs on bribes, otherwise nothing gets done. In America it's a big deal: they catch you, you go to jail. But in the rest of the world they kiss your *toches* and say, 'thank you.'

Years in the food business also taught Max the Power of Pastries.

"Sugar will get you what vinegar can't."

It got so bad that Kaplinsky and staff would start salivating at two o'clock. Unable to work, they'd congregate by the window, waiting for Max, dreaming of danish. For who could resist those soft-on-the-inside, crusty-on-the-outside, honey-glazed pecan coffee rolls baked with tons of butter and sugar, the best in the city, baked by Max's best friend Adi, the baker.

Max wasn't the only one badgering Kaplinsky, but not until Max showed them the way did the other applicants even think of bribes, and before long, Kaplinsky's waiting room smelled like Ratner's Kitchen, full of clamoring sponsors demanding visas. To top it off, every Friday at three, Max stood on a soap box in Union Square sounding off against Kaplinsky and The Joint Distribution Committee, accelerating not only immigration papers for his brother and others, but also landing a part in a film documentary on the Marshall Plan.

* * *

Sailing into New York harbor, early morning, August 23, 1949, the S.S. Blatchford stood tall and proud, surviving storms the likes of which only the human cargo it carried could appreciate. The last hundred yards, tugboats on either side escorted the weathered ship to its destination, capping off a many thousand mile journey with a little help from some friends.

Cries from the deck, "Statue, Statue," and they all came running from below to see The Statue of Liberty, no longer a statue, but a Lady, arm raised to the heavens, giving off light to those coming out of darkness. It takes a Lady to give off such light. It takes a Lady to welcome you into her home, and for that alone America shines.

No one can know the feeling of a displaced person. One given up for dead, never to be seen again, then being reunited with family, the kissing, hugging, crying, and engulfing each other with such love and intensity. It is, after all, the greatest of all human experiences — being found.

Joseph, having risen to Viceroy of Egypt years after being abandoned by his brothers, on the eve of being reunited, dismisses his servants for fear they will watch him break. It is this story more than any other in the Bible which breaks your heart. Every time. We are, after all, sad, lonely creatures in search of our own, animals who walk on two, but animals nevertheless, even more so when torn from the pack.

"MOISHE, MOISHE!" Bina knew Max by photo and spotted him instantly. Sol, always a step behind, yells "VIE?! VIE?" Bina shouts, "DORT! DORT!" Max screams, "DU! DU!" Sol yells, "VIE? VIE?" Bina blares, "DORT! DORT!" It's mayhem, everyone screaming, "VIE? DU! VIE? DORT!" Finally, Sol sees

Max. "BRIE-DER...BRIEEEEE-DEEERRR..." And with the recognition, a surge of power drives through Sol's wiry body into his arms, and with each arm he lifts his children to the sky, two shields, two life posts:

"DIS IZ VAAT I LIVE FOR."

If he had had a third arm he would have lifted Bina as well, for this was his family, his life. He hadn't eaten for days, giving up his ration to Eddie, but the adrenaline pumping through his body was so strong he could have held up his children forever. For as long as Lady Liberty held up her arm, so would Sol his. Sol the Statue, fist pumped in the air, more an act of defiance than deliverance, hoists Eddie on one shoulder, Maya on the other, Bina at his side looking out in wonder: a new land, new city, new life, one built on top of the other, the new built upon the old.

More than anything he saw that morning—the tugboats, the pier, The Lady, the City skyline—Eddie remembers being in his father's arms. And little Maya, wide-eyed cherub-cheeked Maya, she too, safe in her father's arms, unlike Bina, thinking of her father, black eyes watering. It was, after all, August, December not far away, the Dybbik on his way.

CHAPTER SEVEN

Shabbbes at Bina's was a weekly event. It started on Monday, putting in the order with the butcher; Tuesday, the baker; Wednesday, Waldbaums; Thursday, chickens; Friday, cook and clean; Saturday, collapse; Sunday, vacuum; Monday, start all over. All this before and after a full day's work. The hardest part was *shlepping* full shopping bags two long blocks, so that by the time she reached her apartment, Bina's arms were out of her sockets hanging down to her toes. One last heave plops the bags onto the kitchen counter, a foot below her double chin. She sinks into a club chair, her angina heart pounding, placing two nitroglycerine pills under her tongue while Sol's peeling an apple.

"*Oy*, Sol, *mein* vagina's *killink* me."

"You *vant* help?"

"*Vat* can you do, cook?"

"Okay." And he crunches down on the apple.

Eddie, Sol, and Max gave little thought to how hard Bina worked, or for that matter how hard any immigrant woman worked in the home, *der koch*, the kitchen. It was their six-by-eight-foot domain, off limits to men, a rule probably made by men whose value to the home was *outside* the home. But in the home, removing dishes from high cupboards and "Find the Brioschi" was it.

The women worked, cooked, cleaned, and served. The men ate. Not a bad distribution of labor—for the men. Bina called Sol "*Pooritz*," the Prince, when she was *tze-tootsed*, pissed, which was often. But when Sol offered to help, she refused. She liked him to ask, but not as much as she liked to decline, her knee-jerk response to Sol's empty offer.

Friday evenings started out pleasantly enough with the Lighting of the Candles, the *Motzi, Kiddish*, eat in silence, tea with *rugelach*, a huge fight, then sleep for the three while Bina was climbing up a tree, cleaning up. You could script the fight. Bina accuses Sol of whoring, Sol denies it, Bina threatens to leave, Sol threatens to leaves, she threatens suicide, he threatens suicide, she makes him tea, he reads the paper, she watches TV, complaining there's nothing good to watch. *"Noch a bubbe meise,"* she says, another fairy tale.

The "Friday Night Fights" had long since lost their power over Eddie who could shut them out as white noise, a hum above the fridge. With Sol gone it was quiet—quiet, but no peace, just absence.

***

Eddie finishes scrubbing the grill, Steadies have gone, Siegel takes his tamales, Max and Eddie close the luncheonette, pull the steel gate down with a crash, lock up, and pick up The Kid after basketball practice to go to the *shvitz* on 10th Street. Then on to Bina's for a good *Shabbes* meal, a Friday night ritual after Sol's departure. Although terribly heartbroken, Bina said: "You still *hev* to eat."

The Three Musketeers march along East Broadway, past the Garden Cafeteria, hardly a garden; the "Edgie's, "Educational Alliance Center kids, spilling over onto the sidewalk; Spanish grocery stores manned by Chinamen; The Jewish Forward Building, a haven for mousy, sunken-eyed reporters, dank cellar Yeshivas shooting out buckshots of black hatters, bug-eyed Hassids mumbling, *"Gut Shabbes, gut Shabbes,"* running and rushing to Shul before sundown.

Shabbes on the Lower East Side is intense. You can feel it in the air. Merchants who would haggle over a penny for eternity close their stores in mid-breath on Friday afternoon to run home and get ready for *Shabbes*. There's a saying that "more than the Jew kept the Sabbath, The Sabbath kept the Jew."

All this craziness around getting ready to pray and rest. Why can't they just pray and rest?

Eddie didn't get it. He should have 'cause he would have made a good Hassid. He had that frenzy, that drive, that passion. But for *another* God. You pick your God, you don't pick your passion. Passion picks you. Passion picks its purpose. Passion *is* God. What it embraces is passion's choice.

There are many things wrong with gambling, but an absence of passion isn't one of them. It's what pulled Eddie into the life. Nothing quite got his blood going like gambling: the rush, the urge, the urgency, it was a feeling unlike any other he experienced. The only other thing that came close was copping his first feel of Maddy. But by the second or third feel it didn't feel the same, unlike gambling where every bet's a new tit, the *first* tit.

He knew he was hooked early on when he couldn't sit in the classroom for more than a minute without falling asleep, but could play cards 'round the clock. Bored out of his mind, he'd hold his breath for interminable minutes, then explode with a gasp, scaring the shit out of everyone, grabbing his chest and dashing into the bathroom, splashing his face in the toilet bowl because the sinks don't work, then running down to the boiler room to hook up with Al, the Puerto Rican janitor, and other "hyperventilaters" for a fast game of gin. Ducking out of wherever became commonplace in the workplace for Eddie who always found a game within a game.

One game he found was a desk job one summer filing papers. Sol said, "A doctor he *von't* be *anyvay*."

Sitting across from Lou Palomino's desk, sales manager for Goldman Textiles, Eddie files invoices nine-to-five for $60 a week, $48 after taxes. First Friday, Lou gives Eddie the nod at noon. Eddie goes to the water cooler, takes a sip, and slips out the back window onto the fire escape, joining Lou, the Goldman brothers, and other clerks, cashing in his first paycheck which he promptly loses in ten minutes, needing to borrow a fifteen-cent token to get home. That night, Sol asks for the money. Eddie tells him that Goldman pays every two weeks. Sol doesn't believe him but knows Eddie will come up with the money, which he does, making it up at Trios—and then some. In those days, Sol held Eddie's money for him, each keeping tabs on the other, Eddie's security blanket under the mattress, Sol's nowhere to be found.

They get to the *shvitz* and walk under the sign above the building reading "10th Street Russian and Turkish Baths," though no Turk has been seen since Constantinople.

The Fix

The Three Musketeers walk up a long flight of tenement stairs into the musky reception area of the *shvitz*, a world where time simply stops. For at least an hour.

A gooey display case shows off the same sausage every week, taking on the season's colors. The Russian clientele eat sausage, kraut, smoke cigarettes, down shots of wheat grass and vodka while watching soccer from Bulgaria on a big screen. Life expectancy: 36.

The three check in at the desk and drop their valuables in a lock box provided by the uncommunicative Russian, Felix, called *Fay-Looks*. They're issued a matching lockbox key hanging from a frayed slimy rubber band they slip around the wrist, arm, ankle, or balls, whichever fits.

On their way into the locker area, they pick up an inverted tunic with two holes posing as boxer shorts, a ripped paper thin towel, one to a customer, and a green hospital gown, probably discarded as medical waste by some psychiatric institution, one size fits all. *Fay-Looks* never has to worry about missing inventory.

Fay-Looks knows the three and gives them lockers right next to each other in the section where the boiler sits underneath, heating the linoleum floor above so hot that they have to hop while changing or stand on the bench. Eddie changes quickly, hopping on his heels, refusing to put on the wet flip-flops, afraid of whose feet they last infected. The Kid follows suit as they both look at Max, standing flat-footed, pulling off his *gatkes*, revealing a pot belly so large and loose his dick gets lost.

"What are you hiding there, Max, a porcupine?"

"Wait till *you* get old and fat, Eddie."

"Never happen."

"That's what *I* said."

Eddie throws a stinky jock strap out of his locker."Look at this shit, Max! It's fuckin' filthy in here."

"What are you talking about? In all the years, have you ever seen *one* cockroach?"

"They won't come, Max. It's too dirty."

"I know. You're such a *cleantshick*."

"I'm sloppy, Max. Not dirty."

"Come, *Boytschick*. Bring your father, Mister *Cleantshick*."

The Kid laughs. Max makes him laugh. He gets a kick out of Uncle Max, who loves him as he did Eddie when he was young, but now it's different and whenever he gets angry at Eddie, he'd say, "*Boytschick* is God's gift to me. For not killing **you!**"

When The Kid was young, he'd run to Golishoff's after school to wait for Eddie to pick him up.

"Uncle Max! Uncle Max—"

Max saw The Kid running towards him, scooped him up, and squeezed the life out of him.

"Uncle Max, I can't breathe."

"You hungry, *Boytschick*?"

"YEAH! Can I have blintzes?"

"You can have anything you want! Your father, I wouldn't give shit, but *you* can have anything you want."

"After I eat, can I fix up your boxes?"

"First, eat."

The Kid loved to organize Max's stock room. He'd go down into the cellar, squeeze between large cardboard boxes, climb over others, put them in order, then take a nap on top of the highest box, drifting off waiting for his father, his little chest a bridge for scampering feet.

Bina called Max "a *mentsch*," a good person, especially after Sol left, or was thrown out. Either way, he was gone. Since then, Max made it his business to do the biblically correct thing and look after his brother's wife and children. Not that Max was so religious, which he wasn't, but he felt very bad for Bina and the kids and how they were left—and maybe he had something to do with it. Because it was right after a big blow up between the brothers that Sol left.

"I sponsored you, Sol! I gave you a new life with fruits and vegetables! I gave you suppliers! I gave you my truck! And you behave like a *chazer*, a pig!? You gamble, hit your wife, your son. What kind of man are you? Do you know how many visits I made to Kaplinsky? How many danish that *zhlob* ate for free, so that I could bring you over?"

The fight continued for days, weeks, months, years. One lost count, just another one of the many millions of re-united families' unfinished business. Max enlisted in the Polish army and was the oldest brother to leave, instructing the eighteen-year-old Sol to protect their mother and sister. The Nazis invaded, Sol hid in the woods with resistance fighters, and when he returned to get his mother and sister, they were gone. Max and Sol never talked about it. What was there to say? Everything. But no one knew how to start the conversation.

Max joined the Polish army and, after the war, came to the States by way of Poland, France, Spain, and Cuba. A warm, good-natured man, Bina called him a "*gute neshomeh*, not a bad bone in his body."

Finished changing, they weigh themselves in. Max weighs in first, gives a *krechtz*, a *zifts*, and they're off, downstairs into the subterranean tombs. Wet heat, dry heat, steam heat, and then "Big Momme," The Ruskie Room. Big Momme could easily be mistaken for a medieval torture chamber, hissing heat off stonewall spigots so hot you have to douse yourself with buckets of freezing water to jump-start the heart. "Oh! That's good!" If you survived, it's good.

The Russians are not a subtle people. Kicking the shit out of Napoleon and the Nazis requires a certain toughness unknown to these shores since the Puritans landed. The Puritans had that toughness. That's what Puritans are, Russians with manners. Napoleon and Hitler didn't know what hit them when they got to Russia, "It's *fuckin'* freezing!" No brie or bratwurst to be found in the tundra.

Sol had two favorite tundra stories: stories of toughness, Russian toughness, where "men were men." The first was of a Russian soldier captured by Napoleon, ragged and hungry. Napoleon mocks the Russian prisoner, questioning his 'toughness.' The prisoner removes a piece of frozen black bread from his pocket, pisses on it, and eats it. With that one move, Nappy knew he was fucked. No amount of *fois gras* could save his ass from the Ruskies. Bring on Waterloo.

The second story of exaggerated toughness was real to some extent. Certainly somewhat embellished, but what good story isn't?

Ask a child if they want a good story or a true story. No contest. Listening to stories, as a child, one doesn't question. It would take the joy out of the story, because children need heroes, and for heroes to spin their magic, they can't be questioned, just heard. There's plenty of time to fall off the pedestal later, but for now let's hear the story. It's a simple story. All of Sol's stories are simple.

After escaping from Poland to Russia, Sol worked in Siberian coal mines. The sleeping quarters were a good distance from the mines, and by day's end his shirt was drenched with sweat, turned black. The temperature, relatively mild during the gray fall day, dropped to freezing at night, so that by the time he walked back to his quarters, the shirt iced to his skin, forcing the men to pound his back, break his ribs, and tear the skin to get his shirt off. A good story.

The *Shvitz*, not necessarily in the same category as the Siberian coal mines, was in its own way a test of one's manhood. The manliest of men took the greatest heat. Rumor has it that *Fay-Looks* challenged his original business partner, Alex, to a "*Shvitz* Off" after he was tipped off by a former KGB friend that Alex was stealing.

"And it wasn't towels!"

Fay-Looks accused Alex, Alex denied it, drew a line in the *Shvitz*, and laid his sickle down.

For years *Fay-Looks* and Alex fought as any good Russian cousins would. It was fine until they started losing customers, a merchant's tragedy. They cursed each other, talked behind each other's back, threatening to kill each other. Who could sit and *shvitz* in such a hostile environment? Something had to be done. But neither had the money to buy the other out, so the towel delivery guy suggested they alternate weeks running the business.

"It's what we do with the towels."

It was a brilliant idea until they each started giving deals, extra towels, gowns, throw in a pierogi. It had to end this way, in true Chekhovian style, with all the angst, trauma, and drama one only finds at the *Shvitz*. Every *shvitz* has a story.

The Fix

Fay-looks and Alex sat through the night in Big Momme's tomb, stumbling out at five in the morning, wrinkled skin and flesh hanging off their bones. If placed in a crock pot, they would have made a tender brisket. Alex resembled a crushed lampshade, *Fay-Looks* a dried prune.

Fay-Looks was the younger and heavier with a stomach that put Buddha to shame, so it wasn't really a fair *Shvitz* Off. *Fay-Looks* had more to lose, and Alex was an old man of seventy-five, a good twenty years older than *Fay-Looks*. But something happens to old men when challenged by the young. The body's begging, "No!" but sick pride kicks in.

Fay-Looks, the vanquished, crawled out first on his hands and knees, followed by Alex. Although he wins, the old man's too exhausted to raise his arm for a victory wave to the crowd of three insomniacs. He gives a feeble wrist wave to no one in particular and drops dead on the spot, falling on top of *Fay-Looks*, crushing his nuts. They say *Fay-Looks* never looked back. He pulled his sack back and walked on, proclaiming victory: "Whoever lives, wins."

Alex cursed him with his dying breath and one final wish: "Don't screw my wife." Which *Fay-looks* heard as "do." After which *Fay-Looks* took over the business, screwing Natushka twice — once out of her share.

Oh, if only the benches could speak. Tiered planks receive tired *tocheses*, the highest tier for the hottest *toches*, so close to the ceiling that one must slip in sideways to spread out for the *playtzeh*, the weekly purification for daily intoxication.

Customers spread out on a slab of concrete, lathered, bathed, beaten with palm fronds, extracting the week's poison by creepy attendants working feverishly while hunched-over ghouls watch from below, sitting gingerly on splintered wooden benches, moving their *tocheses* around to avoid the occasional hot tip of a sprung nail popping into flesh, eliciting a fart, an "Ah! Ooh! *Oy! Vey!*" Biofeedback.

"All this for ten bucks," Eddie says. "But it's worth it, 'cause as soon as you walk out into the street, you feel renewed and refreshed."

But shortly thereafter, Eddie feels dizzy, nauseous, faint, ready to pass out, clinging to parked cars and telephone poles, hoping to make it in time for Bina's *forshpeiz* of pickles, cole slaw, sour tomatoes, and sauerkraut, her four food groups to replenish the salt lost at the *Shvitz*. You get your salt back, but you also lose your bowels. You know you're better when you can get up from the toilet seat without holding onto the towel rack. A weekly colonic event, Bina has it down, her system of checks and balances for *Shabbes, Shvitz,* and Dinner.

You can smell her food from the street. Once inside, the whole building is rife with *Shabbes*, but you can always sort out Bina's. If the three were blindfolded, they would still find their way to Bina's kitchen, as others would find theirs. Amazing how some extra celery, parsley, dill, and parsnip can separate one chicken soup from another, or fried onions in the chopped liver, or the homemade *g'beks*, cookies, and cakes, the *challah*...ummm.

The closer they get, the quicker their steps. You'd think they were running to meet Malke, the Sabbath Queen. No, it was Bina and her food. Always great, always delicious, always the same, always too much. Every Friday the boys ate with a gusto as if they'd never seen food before. And Bina would *kvell*.

"*Oy*, look at *dem, dey* eat like *enimals!*"

Nothing made her happier than watching her boys inhale her food, but always asking, always unsure, "Is *someting* missing? In *de* soup? Chopped liver, *knaydlach*? Was it better last week?" When asked for her recipe, she'd say, "*shit a heen, shit a herr*, a sprinkle here, a sprinkle there..."

Bina cooked by instinct, knowing what's missing and what isn't. If cooking's an art, she's an artist: free style, no recipes, no cards, no aids, no measurements, just her touch, her feel for food. The only thing she has no feel for are salads, vegetables, or meat other than chicken or brisket. As good as the chicken is, that's how awful the steaks and hamburgers are. You know when the meat's done when you're served ash on a plate. The problem is that you could actually get to like it, tasting the onions and garlic, thinking it's the meat. You always knew when Bina made steak: it smelled like a house burned down. Eddie would remind her, "Mom, they're *minute* steaks, not *hour* steaks!"

Bina would smile and top off the meal with a fresh bowl of Del Monte fruit cocktail, right out of the can. Everyone had their favorite fruit chunk to push aside. Eddie's were cherries.

Bina lived on Pitt Street off Delancey, under the Williamsburg Bridge connecting Manhattan to Williamsburg. From her bedroom window, she could almost touch the tracks of the distant train, forewarned by early vibrations, then the screeching sound of grinding steel slowing to a stop, pulling into Delancey Street station.

The sound's excruciating, but the rent's cheap. During the week she doesn't care because she works, and at night she's too tired to care. On Saturday the trains run less frequently, and Sundays even less so. But Friday night's a challenge. You have to time your conversations in sync with the oncoming train. Bina's the official resident signal conductor. A vibration maven, she's the first one to feel the train coming. Then she puts her forefinger to her lips, "Shhh." The conversation stops in mid-sentence. If you don't heed Bina's warning, you find yourself yelling at the top of your voice way after the train passed. So in Bina's home, the ebb and flow of *Shabbes* went far beyond the heavens and the stars. There was the D train.

After Sol left, she moved back to the Lower East Side from Brooklyn to be closer to Max, whom she needed to help control Eddie, who turned into a *"vilda chaya,"* a wild animal. Eddie took Sol's leaving very hard. They had long since stopped talking beyond essentials, but just knowing he was around gave Eddie a sense of comfort and security, less for himself because Eddie didn't really need anyone, but with Sol gone he was now "man of the house." Big fucking deal. As it was, he didn't have a childhood, and now to suddenly be responsible? A Man? He *was* a Man. Drinking, smoking, gambling, whoring, how much more of a man can you be at sixteen? Sol's boot off his neck, he was now on his own, no one to answer to, no shadow to walk under.

Eddie dropped out of school and turned to hustling. Bina worked on Orchard Street selling bras and girdles to hairy, unwashed orthodox women, and little Maya was a good little girl who got stuck with her mother, an incessant talker obsessively reminiscing about the past, its hardships. Bina was happiest when she talked about her misery.

Bina's favorite bedtime story was telling Maya how she tried to abort her with a coat hanger. She said it matter-of-factly. That's what was done during the war. No shame, just reality. She didn't intend to hurt Maya with the story, but knowing of the aborted abortion plagued Maya, and yet she knew it wasn't done out of lack of love, but lack of food. Babies died in Bina's arms. She could barely keep Eddie alive, how would she feed Maya? And, of course, Eddie was her favorite. He got the good tit, what little of it there was. He was the son she gave Sol, the grandson she gave her father, the father who didn't return from the war. Eddie always sensed that when Bina looked at him, she saw her father.

The shock of Sol's abandonment broke her. After Sol left, Max checked in on her every day. One day he called but no one answered. He ran over to find little Maya cleaning cold cream off the mirror while Bina stood in front of the mirror berating Sol, scooping globs of cold cream, flinging it, whiting him out.

Bina loved Sol, needed him, needed her family. They'd been through so much together and now that things were finally "normal," he leaves? They had work, a place to live, food; what more can a person want? What more does a person need? They never fought like this in Russia. They were too busy struggling to survive.

What is it about this country that invites such acrimony between people, families, and friends? It must be in the air. America's a troublemaker. It's so good and wonderful in so many ways—nothing you can't have, nothing you can't buy—but you won't find peace. There is no peace, just sales, always selling something. When you think peace should be the order of the day, you find it's not. You have to work at it, negotiate. How do you negotiate peace?

An absence of conflict isn't peace, it's space, still-born space, artificial lines drawn between people, a dead zone demanding distance while desperately trying to connect. Borders without walls, America makes up rules no one can live by.

"So what if he gambled, so what if he whored?" Bina cried. "At least he came home."

How small big things become, how small large indiscretions become, when the house is empty. Such is the force and power of abandonment, flinging cold cream at a cold mirror reflecting back the image of a woman she did not recognize, did not know.

She was admitted to Bellevue and Max took little Maya home. Eddie wasn't to be found for days, so when he finally showed up, no one was home. He ran to the girdle store—no Bina. He didn't want to deal with Max, but got frightened and ran to the luncheonette. From then on, Eddie made sure to check in, as much for Maya as for Bina. She needed to be protected: with Sol gone, Maya had no one. For as much as Eddie was Bina's favorite, Maya was Sol's. He adored her, loved her, and she loved him, lifted his sadness, the only one he spoke to, opened up to... and now he's gone... who would he speak to? Who would she speak to...?

There are people in our lives who you can speak to... and when they're gone, no one can take their place.

From the time she was a little girl, they took long walks together on Holidays, Sol with Maya, Eddie with Bina behind them. Sol sang Yiddish lullabies, telling her stories of his childhood, the difficulties and joys before the war. Maya was the love of his life and it killed Bina, put her right over the top, lashing out at Maya, jealous of Sol's love and tenderness. A love and tenderness she would hunger for but never get. And Maya—sweet, soft-spoken, soft-hearted, little Maya—caught in Bina's fury, wiping cold cream off a cold mirror.

* * *

"Mmm, soup's delicious, Mom."
"*Vat* it's missing, Eddie?"
"Nothing."
"*Pheffer, zaltz,* greens?"
"Nothing."
"Max?"
"Nothing."

"*Boytschick?*"
"Nothing."
"*Nahting*, Eddie?"
"Mom, I'm eating your soup forever. It's the same every week."
"Last *veek vas* better."
"Last week's always better. Next week *this* week will be better. With you, the past is always better, everything's better."
"Not *everyting*. Just *de* soup."

Unsuccessful in getting far enough under Eddie's skin, she turns her attention to The Kid.

"How's *de* soup, *Boytschick*?"

It's not that she's looking to get a rise out of Eddie as much as a few words, a response, something to make up for the long lost years with Sol, a man Bina dubbed *"Der Shtimmer,"* the mute. Sol dismissed conversation as *narishkeit,* nonsense. A conversation to Bina was gold, especially *narishkeit*.

"You like *de* soup, *Boytschick*?"
"Delicious, Bubbee."
"Is it missing?"
"No, all the soup's here," he laughs.
"Oh, you like to *kitzel* your Bubbee?"
"Just joking."
"*Dat's vat* a *kitzel* is, a tickle, a joke—*farshtayst* Yiddish, *Boytschick*?"
"A little."
"*Vy* should you understand? Your *fader* don't teach you. And he could, *vent* to Workmen Circle, Yiddish School; he hated it but his *fader* made him go. But you, you don't go to Hebrew School, Yiddish School, *nahting*. All you do is play *besketball*."

Kid says, "I love you, Bubbee," and she melts.

The Kid knows how to finesse Bubbee with a slice of the love knife as smoothly as a seamless behind-the-back pass. She receives the pass, drives to the basket, a *glet* of her hand over one cheek, a kiss on the other. Bingo. He scores!

"So *nahting's* missing."
"Perfect."
"See, Eddie, *vit* your son I can talk, not like *you*."

"Good."
"You know, you're just like your *fader*."
Silence.
"Is it my fault he left?"
Silence.
"Are you in a *behd* mood?"
Silence.
"You *voke* up on *de* wrong side, *epes*?"
Silence.
"You forgot how to talk?"
"Leave me alone!"
"So *vat's* wrong?"
"Nothing."
"*Vat's* – "
"I'M EATING!"
In a Yiddish household, that's it! "I'm eating" is Law!
HEAR, O ISRAEL. THE LORD IS GOD. I'M EATING!

Who can argue with that? Bina. That's because she knows something's up, sees it in his face, feels it in her bones. It drives him nuts how he can poker-face his way through life, but can't fool Bina.

"Can't fool your *mah-der*."

It's true. Mothers are fool-proof. He can't escape, can't escape her doubt, her probing, pushing his buttons, knowing exactly where they are. That's cause she put 'em there.

She goes straight for his *kishkes*, the examination, cross-examination, interrogation, questions, questions, endless barrage of repetitive questions. He can't take it. Can't take her questions. Actually he can't take *any* questions. From anybody. She doesn't stop. He thinks it's because she watches too much Perry Mason.

"You see your *fader*, *Boytschick*?"
"Yes."
"See how healthy he looks now?"
"Yes."
"He *vasn't alvays* so healthy."
Eddie mumbles, "Oh, no."
"Five years he starved."
"I know, Bubbee."

"*Der Malchome.*"
"The war, yes."
"It *vas* cold, freezing."
"Yes."
"No food."
"I know."
"People die."
"Yes."
"Drop like fleas."
"Flies."
"*Vat's* de difference?"
"Well, Bubbee, fleas are—"

She's not interested. It's Bina-speak. If *she* understands what she's saying, *you* don't have to.

"Fleas, flies, all dead, dead in *de* street."
"Mom—!"
"Bodies on bodies."
"Mom, we're eating."
"Rats!"
"Eeee-ting."
"*Dey ver* eating good too."
"Stop!"
"Better *den de* people."
"STOP!"

Forget it. Bina's on a roll. Under this kind of tenacious *tschepping*, there's only one thing Eddie can do. He sticks his head in the bowl.

"*Boytschick,* you hear how your *fader shlurps* his soup?"
"Yes, Bubbee."
"*Dat's* how he sucked on my *tzitzkes.*"
"MOM!"
"Hard."
"Stop!"
"Don't *tink* it didn't *hoyt.*"
"Jesus!"
"Who invited him?"
"Just stop with the stories!"

"*Vy*, you're ashamed?"
"Yes!"
"You *vasn't* ashamed *den*? You ate very good *den*."
"This is nuts!"
"I *noyced* him, *mein* cousins, *and* mein broder."
"I'm never coming here again!"
"A *rahmones*, a pity, a *pitzeleh* baby, so hungry, but *vat* could I do?"
"You could be quiet."
"I cry for him, but he no cry, a little *shtarker*."
"Finished?"
"Not so good-looking *den*, looked like a mouse, but a neighbor told me he'd grow into a handsome man—and she *vas* right, look at him."
"Yeah, look at me!"
"Look how handsome he is, *short* but handsome, but *you*, Boytschick, are tall and handsome—*de* tall I don't know *ver* you got, maybe your *mah-der*, but *de* handsome you got from me."
"Right, Mom, everything good I got from you."
"He *vas* such a good boy."
"I was good, okay?"
"Not like today."
"Can you stop?"
"He never complained."
"Max, do something."
"You see Boytschick, your *fader* keeps it all inside like his *fader*; it's not good to keep *tings* inside, it *hoyts*, like *mein tzitzkes, oy!*"

She hoists them up from her knees to demonstrate, as if the stories aren't enough. She may as well have been talking to herself. The Kid's retreated to the bathroom, and Max and Eddie are deep in their soup. She could care less. She simply raises her voice, adjusting her volume and pace to the speed and vibrations of the oncoming train.

"*VIE* LIVED TEN IN A ROOM!"
"Who cares?"
"NO *PLUMBINK*!"
"So what?"

"*VIE* MADE IN *DE* WOODS!"
"Good."
"*VON* TIME—"
"No one's interested."
"*VON* TIME—"
"MOM!"
"Shhh..."
"What?"
"Shhh."

She puts her finger to her lip... the train slows... grinds... stops... waits... leaves... good. Now she can finish her story before the next train comes.

"*BOYTSCHICK!* COME OUT!"

The Kid sheepishly goes back to his seat.

"So *von* time your *fader vas* crawling around on *de* floor—"

"Oh, God!"

"Maybe he *vas* two or three, who remembers, and he found an old piece of *bleck* bread *unter de... de...* Eddie, *vie zogt min,* how you say, *shaank* in English?"

"Closet."

"Right. *De shaank, mit de shmutz, n' de vantzes,* mosquitoes—"

"Spiders."

"*Vat?*"

"*Vantzes* are not mosquitos. They're spiders, spider webs."

Why am I even correcting her?

Whenever he came home, Eddie found himself speaking Yiddish more than he'd like to...

Maybe I should cross the street.

"*Vantzes,* mosquitoes, *vat's de* difference? He cleaned *de shmutz fram de bleck* bread, put it in *vasser,* and ate it like a steak, you remember, Eddie, you remember?"

"No."

"Of course, who can forget hunger? Only a child."

"Finished?"

"It' a good *ting* to forget, only sick people remember."

Bina lets out a long *zifts,* grateful for the courtesy extended by the D train to finish her story.

"Finished, Mom?"

"Finished."
"Thank God!
"**TWICE HE LEFT THE SHOP!**"
"Max, don't start."
"*Twice* he got called to school!"
"For *vat*, Max?"
"Ask him!"
The Kid retreats back to the toilet.
"Eddie, *vat* happened?"
"Nothing."
"*Boytschick* got suspended from school."
"Thanks a lot, Max."
"**GOTT, OY GOTT.**"
When it came to her children, Bina panicked. When it came to her grandson, she went apoplectic.
"*Vat heppend?! Vat heppend*?!"
"He didn't get suspended, Mom."
"Almost!"
"Almost doesn't count, Max."
"*Vat heppened*, Eddie?"
"I took 'em outta school, big deal."
"For *vat*?"
"Lunch."
"*Dey* don't eat in school?"
"Awright, I took em' to shoot some baskets, big deal."
"In *de* middle of *de* day?"
"It was nice out."
"Izzy, it's *tventy* degrees."
Whenever she had it with him, Bina called him "Izzy." Izzy was an uncle Bina hated for a hundred years. "Izzy, you *Paskudnyak! Boytschick* could get sick!"
He doesn't even know what '*Paskudnyak*' means, but it can't be good. Something the Bolsheviks might have said to the Czar.
"It was fine, Mom, I gave him my jacket."
Max says, "You think we're all stupid, Eddie?"
Eddie's head is down, clipping matzah balls floating in a yellow lake.

"The whole world's stupid but you... you learn nothing from A.A.?"

"*Vats Aleph Aleph*?" Bina asks.

"The low lives he hangs around with, the *shkutzim* he hustles at the schoolyard. He uses *Boytschick* to bet, then he goes to his A.A. meetings and takes *Boytschick* with him!"

"Let's go, Kid."

"*Ver* you *goyink*?"

"Kid's got a game."

"Finish *de* soup."

"I'm not hungry."

"I pack you a container?"

"No! And just for the record, Max, I was warming up The Kid for tonight's game."

"*Ligner*! Liar! As bad as your Poppa was, he never used you."

"Nothing for him to use, Max. I had nothing he wanted. So, fuck you!"

"Who talks like *dis*? You don't talk to your uncle like *dis*! *Vat* he did for you—"

"That's right, you no *goodnik*. What I did for you, you should be kissing my feet!"

"Kiss my ass."

"You lost your wife, you'll lose your son, just wait!"

And in a flash, they're gone. Batman and Robin off to school.

Leaving Bina's apartment after a fight (usual method of departure) was a bit like leaving the *shtetle*, but without Cossacks breathing down your neck. Only your mother and uncle.

In any post-Holocaust home, a certain kind of oppression hangs in the air, the silence burdened with a heaviness, a suffocating stillness settling in the joints... too much history, too much *g'knipped 'n' g'bindled*, too much intertwined family shit. So getting out was great. Going in was good, leaving was better.

"I'll call," he says. But doesn't.

Eddie's allergic to accountability.

"I'll call" means he won't.

"I'll be there" means he won't.

"Trust me" means don't.

"It's the best I can do" means he can do better.

Eddie knows these things about himself. But it stopped bothering him a long time ago. Just when, he's not sure. But he saw early on that something was terribly wrong with the world. People cheated, stole, lied, killed... left. Under that kind of umbrella, what are you supposed to do? Keep up, make peace. Make peace with yourself and all its opposing parts.

Can you love and kill? Absolutely. Usually the same person. Makes people nuts, the inconsistencies. But Eddie loves it— the look of surprise, the exasperation, the unfairness of it all.

"But, but, but you said... "

"I did. Probably meant it too... at the time."

Eddie knows life's a gun to your head. You say what you say when you need to say it. That's it. Get yourself out of the corner you paint yourself into. Two-face becomes one as the head turns. You don't have to be a ventriloquist to speak out of both sides of your mouth. Just be honest.

"You're lyin', Eddie!"

Everyone lies.

Eddie's thinking, why can't we all get along? Why can't we all live peacefully in a world full of contradictions, a vertical world turned on its side, a horizontal world where good, bad, truth, and lies lie together side by side, no one held responsible for anything, a world where changing your mind isn't a felony, where the best of intentions remain just that, where memory's a fossil, accountability a relic. It all shifts anyway, this fucked up life of squirming around.

"You're lyin', Eddie! Those were not the numbers you gave me!"

"I don't remember." This coming from a man with an encyclopedic memory for numbers.

"You don't remember?!"

"I don't remember *lying.*"

"I don't fuckin' believe you!"

"Kitzee, you don't think if I said it, I wouldn't remember?"

"What?"

Eddie can twist a sentence better than a pretzel.

"I have a great memory. I remember everything. It's my sickness."

"Those were not the odds you laid Eddie! Those were not the numbers!"

"Don't tell me I screw up numbers, Kitz! I screw up everything else. But numbers I know."

"No, no, Eddie. You said *this,* then, and you're saying that now!"

Pretty soon, Eddie could get you talking and thinking like him. The truth, oddly enough, comes out when he's threatened. Like the time Ollie Calamari summoned Eddie to his Staten Island mansion, right after Eddie cracked Chaalie's knee. Then Eddie straightened right up and could pass any polygraph test.

* * *

"Drop *de* pizza in *de* Kitchen."

"What?"

Ollie comes out of the living room, a bottle of Chianti hanging from his arm.

"Who the fuck are you?"

Eddie's shivering and it's summer.

"Eddie s-s-s-sir, Eddie P-p-p-parker."

"*You're* Eddie Parker?!"

"Y-y-y-y-yes sir."

"*You* broke Chaalie's leg?"

"Y-y-y-yes sir."

Ollie's laughing.

"You're a fuckin' shrimp! Chaalie said *dis big* guy broke his leg."

"S-s-s-s sorry sir."

Ollie takes a swig. "Good job, kid."

"Th-th-th-thank you, sir."

"Next time, do me a favor, whack his dick. I'd do it myself but his mother won' let me." He puts the bottle to his lips.

"What is it with women 'n' fags? *Dey* got *dis* bond..."

He takes a long swig and an even longer look at Eddie. Eddie's trembling.

"*Youse* a fag?"

"N-n-n-n-no, sir!"

"*Youse* got a cold or *sumtin'*?"

"No, M-m-m-mister Calamari."

"Call me Ollie."

Ollie lights up a fat cigar and goes into a coughing fit so severe his bowels could end up in a candy dish. Eddie's terrified, watching the whale erupt. Ollie's convulsing. He stands up and puts his arms out, freezing Eddie to his seat.

"*De* broom! *De* broom! Get *de* broom!"

Eddie runs to the kitchen.

"Whack my back!"

Eddie pounds Ollie's back, reminding him of Bina beating rugs on the fire escape. On one swing, he misses Ollie's back and whacks 'em in the head, stopping the cough.

"Fuckin' embarrassment! Cosa Nostra fag, my son. But anyone else call 'em a fag, I kill 'em."

I'm dead.

"If I knew he *wuz* gonna be a fruit, I woulda neve christened 'em 'Chaalie'... I woulda named 'em... " He raises the Chianti . "Blanche!"

Now he's laughing and crying. He takes another swig but misses his mouth and half of the wine ends up on his white shirt.

"But she knew, she knew! First feeding, she knew, starin' in his eyes, she says, 'He's different, Ollie.' No shit! But she knew. How do women know?"

"My mother's like that, sir."

"Fuckin' witches, I tell ya."

"Yeah."

"*Weze* in a losin' horse race, kid. Once *dey* give *birt*, it's all over. *Weze* useless. I once asked Vicki if she had to choose 'tween Blanche 'n' me. 'Bye,' she says. Yeah, *dat's* how much women love *dere* kids. Could be midgets, fags, two heads, one arm, skinny, fat, stupid, don' matter, *dey* love 'em just *de* same. We men don' even come in second. I *tink* we come in *aftah de* dog."

Swigtime.

"Yeah, once kids come along, forget it, forget blow jobs! Kids kill blow jobs. *Dat's* what kids are! Blow job killers! Fuckin' murderers! Killed my love life!"

Swigtime.

"I remember when I first met Vickie, on a pole, man could she suck! No, really, how's a girl from Altoona, P.A., learn to suck like *dat*?"

"I, uh—"

"Must be *de* coal mountain air or *sumtin'*."

"Uh—could be."

"I find *dat* girls from small towns suck *duh* best."

"Yeah."

"*Dat's* how much *dey* wanna get outta town... can you blame 'em."

"Not me."

"But no one came close to Vickie. Real *afro-desiac*. Once, twice, *tree* times a day, a *tousand* times *dat* year, dirt 'n' dishes pilin' up to *de* ceilin', couldn't see out *de* fuckin' window, we never left *de* motel... You know how many dishes can pile up when you're happy?"

"Uh..."

"Stay out of a clean house, kid."

It occurs to Eddie how spotless Bina's home was.

"You know how many guys go through the day, thinkin' nothin' but blow jobs?"

"Uh—"

"Millions. Fags, straight, don't matter. Life's all about blowjobs... I mean gettin' 'em, not given 'em. 'N' since Chaalie... Vickie stopped... retired... forced me to go outside the home... very few pleasures in life, kid..."

Eddie spots a tear.

"I mean, *dere* I is getting head from hookers, dreamin' about Vickie, when it should be *de udder* way around... if only she dusted off her *mout* 'n' came outta retirement. Now all she does *wit* her *mout* is eat... eat 'n' talk... wasted talent... Ever get one?"

"Sir?"

"Head."
"Head?"
"Blow job."
"Oh! Yes, sir!"
Thank you, Pulkie! Maybe Ollie won't kill me.
"Sister Mary gave me my first at eight, Father Flannery watched from *de* confession booth. *Den dey* switched. Sick bunch a fucks. Years later, I had 'em whacked. Dozen guys lined up for *de* honor, but *dat* one I saved for myself. Her I couldn't find. Probably out in *de* Congo doin' God's work. Amazin' how many perverts is out *dere*."
"...Yes..."
"Ever happen to you?"
"NO!"
"Woah! Slow down kid... jus' askin'..."
Rabbi Moshe Aaron... the refugee camp... loved Torah, loved God, loved... children... loved to show pictures of Jerusalem... 'Oh Jerusalem, If I forget thee, let my right hand...'
"NO!"
"*Wuzn't* your fault, kid."
Eddie can't speak. Doesn't take much to rouse fresh wounds fed by old feelings...
"But do you know what *was* your fault?"
"No, sir."
"Crackin' Chaalie's knee."
"I'm sorry."
"Broken, shattered, giblets he walks, I hear dice."
"I am so—"
"Now I gotta buy 'em a new knee."
"I'll pay."
"Got two grand?"
"No sir."
"Just stay away from him."
"Yes, sir."
"*Dat's* what I do."
"Yes, sir. And again, I'm so sorry."
"No you ain't."
"I'm not."

"*Youse* kissin' my ass to save yours."

"Yes, sir."

"I understan' *dat*, but never be sorry for *tings* you do, only for *tings* you don't do… or mighta done… just never be sorry, regret don't pay, not in my business… not in any business."

"Yes, sir."

Eddie wonders how conversations like these end.

"I *taut* Jews don't fight."

"Yes, sir, but sometimes—"

"When Chaalie told me a Jew cracked his knee, I got mad, but it's *mulyans* I hate. Jews are easy. You don't *bodder dem, dey bodder* you."

Eddie laughs.

"You hate niggers?"

"Uh… no sir."

"Of course, you Jews love everyone."

"Not everyone, sir."

"Who don't you love?"

"Germans."

"*Dat's* funny."

"Thank you sir."

"You know when *sometin's* funny?"

"When *you* say it is."

"When everyone laughs, ten outta ten."

"Ten outta ten."

"Not nine."

"Not nine."

"Cause if nine laugh, it ain't funny, not for *dat one* guy."

"Yes, sir."

"Jews would understand *dat*."

"Yes, sir."

"If you Jews *wuz* Sicilian, all *dat* bad shit *woulda neve* happened. *Neve* see *mulyans* in *my* neighborhood."

When Eddie first came to Trios, he saw baseball bats in the back room.

"In my neighborhood, *I* get smacked, *you* get whacked."

"Yes, sir."

The Fix

"Yeah, can't take no shit, *udderwise* people *tink* you like it... yeah what *dem* Krauts did your people, ' n' no one did shit... know what happens to anyone hurts *my* family? My Sicilian family? My **FA-MEEL-YAAAH!**"

Now Ollie's totally loop-di-loop, hovering over Eddie, swaying, all five feet, three hundred and fifty pounds, measuring Eddie with those dead fish eyes, that look forever etched on Eddie's forehead. Eddie's saying goodbye to everyone. Ollie falls back on the couch.

Swigtime.
"What's your 'ol man do?"
"Truck driver."
"Jew truck driver."
"Fruits and vegetables."
All of a sudden, Eddie's proud of his father.
"Hard workin'?"
"Yes, sir."
"Honest."
"Yes, sir."
"Gambles?"
"Yes."
"So how can he be honest?"
"Sir?"
"No one who gambles is honest. It's what sucks you in, thinkin' you can put one over on *de* rest of us."
"Oh, no, sir."
"Pete tells me you're a pretty good pool shark."
"I just play the game."
Swigtime.
"What's *his* game, your 'ol man?"
"Pinochle."
"Yeah, Jews love pinochle. Is he good?"
"Very good."
"Does he know you hustle?"
"I don't—"
"You don't hustle?"
"I uh—"

"I say you do. I say you're a snake. You look innocent, but you're a snake."

Eddie offers his head for a bullet.

Yisgadal, v'Yiskadash.

"*Weze* a small group us snakes, but we can spot each *udder*."

Sheme raba.

"Raise your head kid. *Dere's* a future in crawlin' on your belly."

He's nailed. No one ever nailed him like that. Ollie put a mirror to Eddie and stopped him from shaking. What a relief to finally get called on your shit.

"So I ask you again, does your 'ol man know you hustle?"

"No, sir."

"Plan on tellin' 'em."

"No."

"Good. Fathers and sons shouldn't say much to each other, life's hard enough without knowin' what's goin' on."

Eddie's shirt is soaked, expelling nerve gas through the hole in his crewneck, larger than the hole in his story. For Sol was gone.

"Yeah, we all got problems, you *wit* your 'ol man, Chaalie *wit* me, me *wit* mine, 'n' so it goes..."

Swigtime.

He offers Eddie.

"No, thank you."

"Italian blood."

"No, thank you."

"Take it."

"I'm sixteen."

"Wanna see seventeen?"

"Sir—"

"TAKE IT!"

Eddie lunges for the bottle and finishes in one gulp.

"Take it easy, kid, take it easy."

Eddie belches and promptly expels chunky Chianti on the woven burgundy carpet, complementing the wine.

"Holy shit!"

"I am so—"

He's not finished.

"De batroom! De batroom!"

Running down the hall, Eddie catches most of the vomit dribbling through his fingers, marking the plush white shag red. Eddie cleans up in the bathroom, sits on the bowl, and cries. He looks in the mirror. Not then, or since, has he ever seen a more pathetic, frightened figure. If there were a window, he'd jump out, run to the schoolyard... *but who'll get me, it's midnight.* He walks back. Ollie's on his knees pouring seltzer on the rug.

"It's Chianti ! Not Mana-Jewitz, you little prick!"

Eddie got a new name: "You little prick".

"Time you Jews stopped drinkin' *de* sweet shit! Life ain't sweet! Jews should know *dat*."

"Yes, sir."

"*Youse* people ain't stubborn. *Youse* stupid."

Eddie bends down to help.

"It's okay, you done enough damage."

Eddie yanks the towel from Ollie and starts scrubbing. Ollie can't get off the floor. He keeps rolling over from one side to the other. Eddie puts his arms around him, but Ollie's body is shaped like a toilet bowl so he can only reach half way around. Eddie grabs hold of his belt and gives one last heave, falling on top of Ollie, the human dreidel, lips touching.

"Get *de* fuck off me!"

And throws up on his face.

"JEEEZUUUUSSSS!"

Eddie bounces off Ollie, Ollie crawls to the john, and Eddie resumes scrubbing. Ollie comes out of the shower, in his bathrobe, holding one bottle of Chianti in one hand and scratching his balls with the other.

"I like you, kid."

You do?!

"You clean up *afta youself*."

"*Tank* you, sir."

"*Tank* you?! What *de* fuck is *dat*? I give you a job 'n' you start talkin' like me?"

"Thank you, sir."

"*Dats betta.* You got plenty *a* time to talk *de* Pope's English later. Meanwhile, I got plans for you."

You're gonna kill me?

"First you run errands, *den* deliveries, *nuttin'* too heavy, but more *den de* Post Office can handle."

A fuckin' job! Just what I need!

"When Chaalie told me you cracked his knee, I was expectin' someone olde'. I didn't *tink* a young kid would crack a knee *dats connected.*"

"I wasn't thinking."

"Keep it that way."

"Yes, sir."

"Any violence comes from *de* heart is earned."

"Yes, sir.'

"And you tell Pete, anyone else *bodder* you, let me know."

"Thank you, sir."

"Now get *de* hell *outta* here, for *de* nun comes home."

"Please tell Mrs. Calamari how sorry I am."

Ollie's amused by Eddie's sucking up technique.

"*Youse* good kid. Full *a* shit, but good. A mother's dream, a father's nightmare."

Eddie exits, bowing.

"*Whatcha* doin'?"

"Leaving, sir."

"What's *wit de* bow?"

"Respect."

Eddie reaches for Ollie's hand to kiss it. He's seen one too many mob movies.

"You kiss my hand, you suck my dick."

Eddie pulls his hand away.

"*Neve* bow to no one. Not even to a midget. Unless they're dead."

"Yes, sir."

"'N' Eddie?"

"Yes...?"

"Every dollar you hustle, I get half."

"Yes, sir.'

"Know why?"
"I don't have to know sir."
"To pay for Chaalie's knee."
"Yes, sir."
"Next time, break *sumtin'* cheaper."

* * *

Driving up Calamari Road, down Calamari Lane, into Calamari court, a cul-de-sac wider than the Horn of Africa, the standing goon in black greets Eddie. Goon tries to open the door, but Eddie jumps over.

"Don't *bodder*. Jammed from birth!"

He rings the bell of the massive mansion door. An aproned "gooness" peeks through the peep hole. Eddie shows off his award-winning smile.

"Eddie Parker for Mister Calamari."

Gooness yells, "He's expectin' *youse*?"

"No, I *wuz* in *de* neighberhod."

"LET *DE* JEW IN!" Eddie hears Ollie laughing.

Oh fuck, he's drunk!

Ollie opens the door. What a sight. Staten Island's finest. A wild crop of silver hair, a grey stubble, gold slippers, a huge gold "Yossel" hanging on a foot long chain around his fat neck, silver bracelets, a diamond pinky ring overwhelmed by the overgrown flesh around his little finger and a full-length red kimono.

And Chaalie's a fruit?

"EHHHH-DIEEEEEEE!" Ollie opens the kimono, totally naked, and engulfs Eddie inside. They just saw each other the day before, but Ollie's drunk, so every day's a new day.

"No kiss, Eddie?"

Eddie leans in and Ollie turns his cheek.

"Uh, uh, no *mout*! Remember you sprayed me?"

"Oh, come on Ollie, that was twenty years ago!"

They laugh and goose each other.

This is so much fun.

"Have a seat."

The three scariest words on Staten Island.

Ollie pours them a glass of Chianti.

They clink and drink. Eddie looks at Ollie and sees what the years have done on his face. Usually fat people don't get lines, but a couple of heart attacks and a hundred pounds lost will remove the natural oils.

"Love Chianti. Chianti n' Cumedin. Lifesavers! You know what else is good for the ticker? Aspirin. People say it's the wine. But the wine gives me such fuckin' headache that I gotta swallow a shit load of aspirins and that's what helps your heart."

"You need both."

"Cigar?"

"Sure."

"I like you Eddie. You're a good man. You make me laugh. We always have a good time together, shootin' the breeze, I can't do *dis wit* Chaalie."

Eddie nods, takes a sip, a drag on the cigar.

"Nice, right Eddie?"

"Very nice."

He blows a full smoke ring up to the chandelier.

"Cuban."

"Cuban's good. I like Cuban."

"Castro makes good cigars. I don't care what his politics is. You care?"

"I don't care."

A dish busts on the granite floor in the dining room.

"Time for lunch."

"I'd love to Ollie, but—"

"Stay."

"I'd love to."

"How's *de broder* Boyles's account?"

"Funny you should ask." Eddie gives him two bills. "*Two hunred* now 'n' *two* more Friday."

And one for me makes three.

"*Dat's* good Eddie, *very* good."

Ollie takes the bills, pulls out a bulge from his back pocket, slips off the rubber band, adds two C's to the wad, re-wraps it and stuffs it back. You get the feeling that if Ollie got a dollar back, he'd go through the same motion.

"Boyles should be even by next *munt*, Ollie."

"*Dat's* good, Eddie."

"*Dat's* if his lil' fuckin' prick *broder*, Dennis, don' make a bet 'tween now 'n' den."

Eddie automatically cursed around Ollie, fucking up his grammar to get in sync with Ollie, so he'd forget he's a Jew.

"Dennis not make a bet? Fat chance a *dat,* Eddie."

"Slim to none, Ollie."

Ollie laughs, Eddie follows.

"Hey, Ollie, you know what Dennis *tinks* Gamblers Anonymous means?"

"No, Eddie, what?"

"Means he *tinks* no one's watchin'."

"*Dat's* funny." He farts. Jokes make Ollie fart. And the funnier the joke, the bigger the fart. Weeks before a social, wise guys load up on jokes to get Ollie going. They love to hear Ollie laugh.

"Ollie, you know why Dennis bets?"

"Why, Eddie, why?"

"He likes bettin' on his life."

Ollie rips one off, melting the plastic off the sofa.

"'N' bettin' he dies."

"Stop, Eddie, stop."

"But if he wins, who's around to collect?"

"Eddie, you're gonna make me shit!"

Now Ollie's laughing and farting to beat the band, a noxious mixture of gags 'n' gas. Eddie stops before Ollie has an accident.

"*Youse* funny, Kid."

"I try."

"It's good to laugh, Eddie. Doc says it spreads out your life."

"If you don't shit in your pants."

Uh-oh. Ollie grows dark.

"Sorry, boss, didn't mean…"

Too late. Ollie's tone deaf to apologies.

"I'm really, *really* sorry, Ollie."

Ollie smiles, but no fart.

"Gotta go, boss."

"So *weze* all squared away?"

"Yeah."
"*Youse* doin' a good job."
"Tanks, Ollie."
"'N' don' worry 'bout your stupid joke."
"No."
"*Deze* tings don' *bodder* me."
"*Dat's* why I—"
"Like oil off a duck's back."
"Yeah."
"By *de* way, how *youse* doin' on *your* little debt?"
Eddie's sphincter locks.
"No problem."
"For who?"
"I got it. I mean, I have it."
"It's two *munts*."
"I wasn't aware."
"You wasn't *a-where?*... Don' fuck *wit* me Eddie!"
"I would never do *dat*, Ollie. I respect you too much."
"I don't want respect, I want cash!"
"Absolutely. When do you want it?"
"Yesterday."
"No problem."
"Better not be."
"My word."
"Your word?"
"My word."

That's as empty a word as Eddie ever felt come out of his mouth.

"Okay, see *youse* 'round, kid."

Eddie's no "kid," but Ollie still calls him that. It's what Italians do. They call ninety-year-old toothless men "junior." In the case of old Italian men, it's done with affection. In Eddie's case, it's to remind him of his junior status. And no amount of "dems" 'n' "dohs" will change that.

He leaves the fortressed mansion, driving down the cobbled lane under Santa's flying reindeer, along Ollie's quarry of cherubs 'n' swans, down to the spiked steel gates where another welching bookie was once speared.

No one can miss the joint. It's not just the blazing ornamental lights, but the unmarked F.B.I. surveillance van parked outside the property driveway, a quarter mile away.

Chapter Eight

Eddie takes his seat behind the home team's bench. His seat did not come uncontested. Only after The Kid refused to play did the administration concede, with the proviso that Eddie not speak to The Kid or the team during the game. They all hated Eddie — the coaches, teachers, administration — but the team loved him, loved his outrageousness, his generosity, treating them to days on Coney Island for Nathan's hot dogs 'n' fries, cyclone rides, Orchard Beach, Malibu Dude Ranch, Lundy's Seafood, pizzas, ice cream, tickets to movies, ball games, slipping them each a five on their birthdays. He became a regular at practice.
"What are you doin' here, Parker?"
"I'm watchin' my Kid."
"Practice is for players."
"Practice is practice."
"But when you're around, he performs for *you*, not the team."
"Got *that* right, coach."
"Leave!"
"Make me."
The Kid steps between them.
"Dad… please."
Eddie had his issues with everyone, but Coach Gordon he couldn't stand. A real "good guy," a "do-the-right-thing" kinda guy. The kinda guy you hate. A starchy motivator, he should have stayed in Nebraska. Strong on fundamentals, he lacked heart. And the kids knew it. When an explosion was called for, he remained calm. When a "Fuck you!" was in order, he'd gasp, "Oh, my Lord." If he really lost it, he'd say, "Damn!" and cover his mouth. The type of guy you wished would take a huge shit one day and clean himself out. Never happen. But the one thing they agreed on was The Kid, the genius of The Kid on the court. Eddie saw it early on. The Kid was maybe four or five, right after Maddy left. He took The Kid to Essex Street park and sat on a bench, reading the handicaps for the day, when he looks

up and sees The Kid bouncing a beach ball, twirling it on his little finger—hardly a finger, more of a stub most kids his age use to pick their noses. Some black guys playing a pick-up game stop to watch "Miniature Maestro."

"Hey looka' here! Squirt's gettin' ready for the Harlem Globetrotters."

The Kid puts his nose up against the fence and mimics one of the players trying a behind-the-back-pass, but the ball's too big or he's too small, and the ball gets stuck on his waist. The guys laugh, take The Kid inside the court, lift him up to the basket. The Kid hits three in a row with the beach ball. No rim, no net, no nothin', swish, the next Pistol Pete.

From then on, Eddie was sure that wherever he went, The Kid was never without his "beach" ball, a basketball Eddie deliberately over-inflated to make the shot tougher. The other kids would see The Kid coming with his "balloon ball" and run away, except when there was no other ball and they had no choice but to play with the monstrosity. But Eddie must have known something, because years of twirling and shooting balloon balls, mastering them in his young hands, made the regulation-size basketball a cinch. Initially The Kid cried, frustrated, embarrassed, swearing never to play with the outsized ball, but the pull of the street, the game, was too enticing. Eddie knew it: The Kid had "it," something special. He saw in The Kid something he felt in himself, but couldn't fulfill. Just one of the many millions of kids who think they're great until they step on the court and meet the other millions of kids who too are big on dreams and short on talent. In other words, ordinary. Those who have to settle for nothing more than just playing for the love of the game. And then there are those blessed *and* cursed by more than love of the game— their extraordinary talent. And the more talented, the more blessed, the more cursed.

Things came easy for The Kid. His hand-eye coordination was way beyond anyone's his age. It started innocently enough, going to the park, throwing a small rubber pink Spalding against a wall, then the backboard ten feet high, squealing with delight when the small ball went through the big basket. That was the beginning and the end.

Hours and hours, years of hours, spent throwing a ball toward a basket. In time, everything grew. The Kid, his hands, his height, his gift, everything but the rim. The rim, the pole, the backboard, the basket—they stayed. The one thing in his life he could depend on. And maybe that was the seed of the attraction—the pole, the rim, the backboard, the basket. They never moved.

You'd think the excitement would wear off with the mindless, numbing repetition of practicing shots, but for The Kid it only got better, never tiring of the same moves, the same motion, imagining stories and last-minute heroics. And as he grew, his array of shots grew, the stories grew, but the result was always the same. He won, hitting the winning shot at the last second.

"Ladies and Gentlemen! Championship game... five seconds to go. Seward down by one. Kid's got the ball. Mid-court. No time out left. Three defenders. He can't see. What's he gonna do...? He jumps! He shoots—

"OH MY GOD... IT'S GOING... GO-IIIIIING...**IN!** HE MADE IT! THE KID MADE IT! UNBEE-LIEEEE-VABLE!"

"Hey, hey, what's all the noise?"

"Oh, Mr. Gibbons—"

"Doin' your own play-by-play?"

"Yeah," The Kid laughs, a little embarrassed.

"Team practice over?"

"Yeah, waitin' for my dad."

"No problem."

"Look at this, Mister Gibbons."

The Kid shows off some new moves.

"Pretty good, kid, pretty good." Gibbons hangs around for a few more minutes and applauds The Kid. "Nice shot!" Then the janitor takes his broom and leaves. "Gotta get back to work. 'N' you keep workin' too, young man. You *sumtin'* special!"

"Ladies and Gentleman, championship game..."

Basketball was his life, the court his home, the players his family, the fans his friends. The Kid would dream of being locked up in the gym for days so he could practice. It wasn't a dream. Eddie slipped Gibbons a few bucks for the keys to the gym so on weekends, holidays, and nights, The Kid let himself in to shoot for hours and then went out looking for games.

Pretty soon he was playing with bigger, older kids, taken by Eddie to Manhattan Beach in Brooklyn, a sizzling hot bed of hoop action in the summer. They came from all over: Bronx, Brooklyn, Manhattan, Queens. Gym rats, hot shots, all-stars, pro's, semi-pro's, laughing, joking, elbowing, ankle's sprained, rib cages pushed in, an occasional tooth knocked out, hoop heaven.

In those days, everyone played for fun, and dehydration wasn't a word, you were just *thirsty*. They played in ninety-degree heat, and after each game, winners stay, losers take a dip in the ocean, waiting for their turn to avenge the loss. Meanwhile, thirsty jocks line up behind a leaky water fountain spigot encased by concrete, built for midgets by some sadistic park planners. The sweaty, six-foot-plus players stoop down, sweaty and naked from the waist, laying their head sideways on the concrete bowl, extending their tongue to lap up the dribbling stream of warm piss while impatient players sound off.

"I piss faster than you drink!"

"Oh yeah? If you piss like this fountain dribbles, you be pissin' the rest *a yaw* life!"

Bedouins treat their camels better than the City treats its jocks.

The Kid stands on the sidelines for hours watching the weekend warriors play. He holds Eddie's hand, squeezing it tighter and tighter with the flow of the game. Game over, high-fives all around, the crowd breaks. Then Eddie takes the "monstrosity" out of the bowling bag, steps out on the court, and feeds The Kid outside shots. The Kid hates the ball, but is thrilled just to be on the same court as his heroes.

No serious jock can ever forget the feeling of the first time taking stage on court. It's enough to bust you out of your skin. The guys laugh because The Kid's a squirt, but with each shot made, the laughs dissipate, replaced by, "Holy Shit!" Eddie leaves to take a nap by the water. He drifts off, smiling as he hears a chorus of "Holy Shit" off in the distance.

When you know you can do something, you just know. Bona fide artistry has no explanation. Put a bow in a child's hand, a book, a brush, a pen, a ball, you can spot genius, it isn't hard to do. Just look at the rest of us.

***

The crowd files into Seward Park Gym as the players do their warm-up drills in their shiny white nylons. Players love that part of the game. The tribal pride; being worthy of bouncing a ball off the high-gloss wooden floor, accenting the red dotted brown leather Wilson basketballs. The light-hearted joking, schmoozing with players, fans, reporters, announcers, cheerleaders — cocktail hour on the courts. Hitting long shots, short shots, jump shots, lay ups, hooks, fouls, twists and turns; loosey goosey, relaxed facade hiding the knot in the stomach, pain in the knee, joint, back and neck; shakin' it out, skin tight, tingling, needing to pee, sick with anticipation, ready to tip off.

Those would be ordinary feelings for any ordinary athlete about to compete. But not The Kid. The Kid's a phenom, demonstrating a calm, a deadness to the aliveness around him. In every other way, he's nothing short of ordinary, but on the court, he's from outer space.

No one wants Eddie there, but he needs to be close to The Kid, to protect his investment. Eddie's heckling, jibing, and chatter are a huge distraction to the coach and the fans, and a major irritant to the school administrators who consistently bar him from games for inciting free-for-alls for "bad" calls made against "his" team.

When "his" players are on the receiving end of a dirty foul, Eddie leaps out of his seat, leading his legions into battle with the battle cry, "Take No Shit!" In the middle of the melee, Eddie makes sure to remind The Kid:

"DON'T PUNCH WITH YOUR SHOOTING HAND!"

In a brouhaha, Eddie always goes after the "bad" guy, usually a mountain taller. He punches away at the tower, barely able to reach the young giant's chin. It's comical for everyone but Eddie. It takes six guys to pull him off the towering frame, but not until he brings down bony Goliath with a body slam.

"Get off 'em! Get off 'em!" Coach yells as he dives into the pile and pulls Eddie out. He'd really like to see Eddie pummeled, but it would upset The Kid. Gordon, a big guy, pulls Eddie out by the scruff of his neck. Eddie's bleeding from his nose, lip, ear,

mouth, a welt under his eye, missing half a shirt. Eddie doesn't need a purple star, his face will do.
"Why ain't *you* protectin' our guys, coach?!"
"'Cause I got *you*, Parker!"
"*You* should be out there!"
"When *you* sign my check, I will!"
"Pussy!"
Hometown fans explode.
"PUSSY! PUSSY! PUSSY!"
Eddie loves a crowd— loves being judged by the jury, the people's choice, a clown. He'll do things, outrageous things, anything, to win. He knows he has a winner in The Kid.

* * *

The Seward Park Tigers were on a tear that year of '75, winning twelve in a row, netting Eddie a nice chunk of change needed to make up for other losses. The more he won, the more he bet, the more he lost, the bigger the risk on his next bet. It's how Eddie does it, daring the inevitable, and inevitable does eventually becomes inevitable, putting him center square in harm's way when Ollie calls him to Di Roberti's pastry shop at three in the morning.
"I can't sleep, Eddie. When people owe me money, I can't sleep."
"I suffer from *de* same, Ollie."
"'N' *de* more *dey* owe, *de* less I sleep."
"I understan'"
"What's gonna be, Eddie?"
"I—"
"AY-YAY-YAYEDDIE? WHAT'S GONNA BE?"
"Listen, Ollie—"
"I'm goin' DEAF listenin' to ya."
"I'm good for it. You know *dat*."
"I *don't* know *dat*, Eddie."
"I ain't good for it?"
"*Weze* all good for it, but when, Eddie? WHEEENN?!"
"Two *monts*."

"It's **been** two *monts*! Now it's *tree*!"
"So what's two *maw monts*?"
"A fuckin' eternity! I could be dead by *den*!"
"Ollie—"
"You owe me twenty grand, you little prick!"
"I know, I know."
"You KNOW?"
"Can I pay it out?"
"You mean, *de* lay-away-plan?"
"Yes."
"Lay you away?"
"No!"
"Eggs *Benedicto*?"
"Oh, God, no, no!"

After one too many late payments, Ollie spooned Dennis's eyeball and served it on a bun.

"*Wit* coffee to go?"
"No! No! No! I promise, Ollie, I promise."
"Is *dat de* margarine, *Promise*?"
"Ollie, I'm beggin'!"
"Me *gots* me obligations, Eddie."
"I appreciate *dat*."
"You *appreciate* it?"
"What I mean is—"
"No *maw* fuckin' round, Eddie—"
"No *maw*!"
"*Dis* is it!"
"Make no mistake."
"Cause I'll kill you."
"No, Ollie, no."
"Even *doh* I loves *youse*, I'll kill ya."
"I'm not worth it, Ollie, believe me!"
"I will Eddie, I will, 'cause I can't afford to lose respect in *de* streets."
"Of course."
"Don' wan' no one sayin' I'm soft."
"I would never say *dat*."

Ollie takes a slow sip of his demitasse, his eyes on Eddie.
Fuckin fish eyes.
"So we understand each other."
"Perfectly."
"Is *dat*, 'yes'?"
"Yes, 'n' Ollie?"
"Yes, Eddie...?"
"If you can find it in your heart..."
"I better find it in my *hand*, Eddie. Twenty grand! Next week!"
"We go back a long time, Ollie."
"Yeah, we go back. You puked on my rug."
"I need time."
"It's twenty years I still can't get the fuckin' smell out."
"Two weeks."
"I bang *de* maid on *de* floor, I smell *you*!"
"Two, Ollie, two weeks."
"One."
"Be a prince."
"One."
"One 'n' a half?"
"Two *wit*. One *wit* out."
"*Wit out* <u>what</u>?"
Ollie holds up a teaspoon.
"I'll take one."
"*De* eye or *de* week?"
"*De* eye."
"Good. One *Capin'* Hook in *de* neighborhood's enough."
Cocksucker!
Eddie excuses himself, bowing out.
"Still bowing, you little prick? What are you, *Muslin*?"
Eddie bows out of Di Roberti's basement, waving bye-bye to Ollie, holding the demitasse cup, waving back with the two remaining fingers of his meaty paw, pinky in the air.
Eddie wasn't just playing on borrowed money. He was playing on borrowed time. Ollie's strings had strung. He had to do something. Like save his own life.

* * *

"Listen, Kid, I'm in trouble."

This wasn't the first time Eddie came to him. It started in grade school.

"Just hit three or four, or five... hit five," or "Beat 'em by six," or "Lose by two," or "They're so bad, let 'em win one... by two, not three! Three's disaster!"

He made it fun, a game with a kicker, the kicker being the point spread, the reward being Eddie's approval.

"Good job, kid!"

Kid loved it, the approval. So did the other kids. And after the game he'd slip them each a five or a ten.

"This is *'tween* you 'n' me."

They took it. These kids came from poor homes, broken homes, and not having to go to parents for money was a big thing. And of course the parents never asked, one less kid to worry about.

The kids took it, knowing it was wrong, but at fifteen, sixteen, it's *all about* doing wrong. The idea that one's too young to know right from wrong is bullshit. All they needed was a host for their disease, a ringleader, a thirty-eight-year-old ringleader for the sixteen-year-old kids, and The Kid. The Kid was key, the playmaker, point man, the go-to guy, the guy they looked up to, who did it all without saying much.

Most sixteen-year-olds have nothing to say anyway, their nerves do their talking. But not The Kid. He brought calm to their laces. They were a brash bunch with attitudes, arrogant, a gang of good-kids-gone-bad, made bad by Eddie.

When The Kid wasn't playing, he looked dead. A blank film formed around his face, a haziness, life sucked out of him by Eddie. He was clearly unhappy, overwhelmed by his father's intensity. With a *meshugeneh* father like Eddie, what's a kid to do but go inside, if only to survive? Who can compete with such insanity, a father out of control, a nut job. Kid's only defense was to remain cool, calm, collected, and depressed.

THE FIX

It's not uncommon for fathers and sons to be so far apart, especially during the teen years. As one goes up, the other goes down, and vice versa, the two never quite in sync. To get in step with Dad, you have to go back a generation, see what Dad's Dad was like. Then you get the picture. But you don't know that as a kid. All you know is not to piss off Dad, especially if he's the only one you got.

Chapter Nine

A bookie's life isn't a bad life. Mostly, you work on weekends, and it really isn't all that dangerous. You're more of a pigeon carrier, and there's nothing to worry about if you play it straight. That means place the money you're given on the bet you're told. Problem is, Eddie doesn't play it straight. To Eddie, the shortest distance between two points is a crooked line. Of course, he doesn't see it that way.

"I'm just borrowing some money for a little time to make the bet better for the bettor— just this one time."

But "just this one time" is one time too many if caught. Then, Eddie finds a way to reinvent himself into master con, master of deceit, deception, conniver, juggler, magician, artisto bullshit impresario, he can talk a lizard off a ledge. The bullshit just oozes out of him. The flow, a work of art if put to canvas, would produce a tangled tapestry of lies 'n' alibis. He *is* his best audience, the ultimate gratifier, jerking himself off.

Oh, man, am I good or what?! How the hell did I come up with that? Amazing how the bullshit just... visits me...runs through me... I'm... I'm a vessel for bullshit.

And then the *coup de grace*. A light pat on the shit-upon shoulder of the trusting sap. "Trust me," or, "we go back a long time," or, "if you can find it in your heart." And as the worm turns, performer and observer meld into one, making him whole again.

In Eddie's defense, being a bookie just doesn't cut it. He's no middleman, delivery boy, bodega guy, scalping a piece off the action. He's bigger than that, better, smarter, smarter than the rest, a legend in his own mind. The man's got dreams, plans, he's got... he's got... The Kid. And when Eddie's in a fix, The Kid'll fix it.

* * *

The Fix

High School games aren't even something the Mob would be interested in except that Eddie's made it a serious source of income, knowing full well the consequences of going so deep, so young, into a dirty game. Not that High School betting isn't done. High School football's already way ahead of the illegal betting curve, reaching deep into every city's corrupt underground pipeline, recruiting fine, blond, blue-eyed, square-jawed All-Americans to miss a block here, drop a ball there, a fumble here, a field goal there, not hard to do. Football's easy to fix, Baseball's hard, and Basketball has its own challenges, but Basketball only has to have one or two in on it. In Eddie's case, one.

* * *

Win number thirteen was close, too close. Eddie narrowly escaped Ollie's spoon. Seward won by six when they were overwhelming favorites over their brainy Stuyvesant opponents who win every science award imaginable, but can't put a ball though a hoop if their lives depended on it.

As bad as those teams are, there's usually one player who stands out and can make it uncomfortable for the favorite. The Kid's usually assigned to cover that player and has no problem shutting him down. The Kid's not only a phenomenal offensive player, but a brilliant defensive player, sticking to his opponent like flypaper.

Playing defense is a whole other game, much more difficult. You react instead of act, anticipate, be on the receiving end of your opponent's intentions. They go first and then you react with flailing arms, legs—it's chasing a mouse. Great defensive players are far and few between. That's because there's no money in defense. The money's in offense. The Slam Dunk, The Home Run, The Touchdown, The Goal, The Knock Out. The players know it, the coaches know it, the owners certainly do. It's what the fans pay to see: Offense. Showy, explosive, high-voltage, high-five offense: **SHOWTIME!**

But for the bookie, defense is his bread 'n' butter. That's because you can't control offense. A hard swing or long throw doesn't guarantee a home run or a touchdown, but good *or* bad defense can make or break a game. And easier to do, more difficult to detect.

Now, it's not uncommon for superior teams to hold back against much weaker teams, but this one had a strange odor written all over it. Seward's ahead by twelve with five minutes to go, running up the score. Eddie's having conniptions. He looks up at Ollie, Chaalie, 'n' Friends in the stands waving a bat and gets a stabbing pain in his eye.

"Slow 'em down, coach!"

"Shut up, Parker! Don't tell me how to coach!"

"Save it for the playoffs!"

"Get lost!"

Eddie whistles and The Kid goes down grabbing his ankle. The crowd gasps, Gordon glares. The Kid comes out limping. The hotshot player The Kid was guarding goes on a tear, reducing Seward's lead to a precious few... shall we say two?

"Hold the ball! Hold the fucking... oh my Lordy, what *did* I say?"

"Oh Lordy! Lordy! Coach Gordy, Gordy, said naughty! Naughty!"

"Fuck you, Parker!"

"I can't **heeeeeear** you!"

"FUUUCK YOU!"

Eddie blows him a kiss. Nebraska finally shows some passion. Too late. Stuyvesant makes the spread. Eddie salutes the stands. Chaalie salutes back with the baseball bat, escorting Ollie and Dufus Entourage to meet Eddie under the Verrazano Bridge.

***

Eddie hands Ollie a manila envelope.

Ollie smiles.

"I like *manila*."

Ollie opens the envelope, wets his thumb, lifts his leg, farts, and counts.

"You're short."

"There's ten grand here."

"Ain't twenty."

Chaalie standing behind Eddie whacks him across the back of the leg with the bat

"AAAAAAAAHHHH!" Eddie goes down like a shot.

"You know how long Chaalie's been waitin' to do *dat*?"

Chaalie raises the bat to smash Eddie's head.

"AAAAAAHHHHA-AAAAAAAAHHHH!"

Stops an inch short.

"I told you, I ain't fuckin' 'round."

Chaalie raises the bat again.

"AAAAAAAAHHHH!"

Then stops short.

"Ooh this is fun, Ollie."

Chaalie does it a few more times, like a check swing in baseball. Intermittent "swing 'n' scream," a Pavlovian move if there ever was one. Chaalie's become a Pavlovian. Eddie sees himself a seal being clubbed to death. "Shall we try again?" Chaalie raises the bat—

"AAAAAAAAHHHH!"

"Shut up!" Ollie screams. "You sound like a stuck pig."

"Playoffs, Ollie, playoffs...**Aaahhhhh**...I'll make it thirty! Not twenty! **Aaaaaahhhh!**"

"What do you *tink*, Chaalie?"

"I don't know, Ollie."

He raises the bat.

"AAAAAAAAAHHHHHH!"

Eddie can't believe the incredible pain. Only terror allows him to speak.

"I'm good for it, Ollie!!"

"You're good for it."

"I'm good! I'm good!!"

"*De ting* is, how can I be sure?"

"My word, Ollie! My word!"

"Your word?"

Ollie kicks his leg.

"AAAAAAAHHHHHHH!"

"But *dis* last game was close, too close."

"Coach is a prick, Ollie. Won't happen again! Promise!"

"Is *dat de* margarine, *Promise*? You gonna grease me *wit* Promise."

"I swear, Ollie."

"On whose life?"

Chaalie raises the bat.

"AAAAAAAAHHHH!"

"Shhhh, you'll wake *de* neighbors."

"I'll get it done!"

"'N' if you don't?"

"I will, Ollie! I will!"

"Will *youse* find it in your heart, Eddie?"

"I will! I will!"

"Cause *I* won't." And kicks Eddie in the head.

They drive off, leaving Eddie on a pile of cinder blocks and garbage. He sobs uncontrollably. It's caught up with him. His life finally caught up with him. The lying, the cheating, stealing, scheming, the cons, running, chasing, hiding, found... finally found.

It is, after all, the greatest of all human experiences... being found...

Sobbing on a heap of trash, he wishes he could die. Then he can join all the other seals who fucked up.

* * *

Eddie moves in with his mother. Max would have no part of him. Just as well. Eddie could never put anything over on him, anyway, so who needs him? Plus, Max is fucking his mother. The Kid, too, was getting difficult.

"Where you been?"

"Out."

"With who?"

"Friends."

"Doin' what?"

"Nothin'."

Fuckin' one word answers.

First rule when your unfinished adult walks in from a late night out: don't talk to them. Don't ask them where they've been, what they're doing, who they're with.

They need a few minutes to get used to your non-existence. Especially The Kid, whose father's been a no-show for so long his face belongs on a milk container.

"What's her name?"

"Who?"

"The *friend*."

"Tracy."

"What's she do?"

"Cheerleader."

"Slut."

"What?!"

"Dump her."

"No!"

"Bad influence."

"You don't even know her!"

"She a girl?"

"Yeah."

"I *know* her. She's a star fucker."

Kid turns to leave.

"She just wants to get into your shorts."

"And **YOU?!**"

He walks out and slams the door.

"GET BACK HERE!"

The Kid's back is up against the door.

"I'M CRIPPLED! GET BACK HERE!"

He returns.

"Look at me."

Blank stare.

"I said *look* at me!"

Lazy film forms over his eyes

"LOOK AT ME!"

Kid lifts his lazy eyes.

"They almost killed me! **YOU WANT THAT?!**"

"I want out."

It's the girl! I knew it!

"All right, listen, listen to me, I can talk to you now, you're not a kid anymore, I'm talking to you as your father, and, and, you know I want the best for you... so I'm gonna give you some advice..."

It's no fun when you're desperate trying to think of something

"... advice you can use the rest of your life... listening?"

Silence.

"Women can fuck you up."

Silence.

"Bet you didn't know that, did you?"

Silence.

"Look at what your mother did. Left me *and* you—*after* I married her! And I married her for *you*, so you would have a mother and she shouldn't look bad, being knocked up. *But*... she didn't care... women don't care, very selfish people, only think of themselves. I'm still not over it, but it was my fault, I didn't listen... Listening?"

Silence.

"Uncle Max warned me. Very wise man, your uncle, you like your Uncle Max, right?"

Silence.

"He said, he said this:... when I was first going with your mother, he said—and I'll never forget this—he said: 'Don't let her buy you with sex!' Is that fucking brilliant or what?!"

Silence.

"Is that not the wisest thing you ever heard, huh? Is Max not the wisest man on earth?"

Silence.

"But did I listen? No! I did not listen to the wisest man on earth, and look where it got me?! Two broken legs lyin' on Bubbee's couch. You want that?"

Silence.

"Broken heart, broken legs, all because of a woman."

Silence.

Now understand, I'm not blaming you, Kid, 'cause every guy goes with a girl for sex. We understand that. That's what falling in love is... for a guy... getting laid... but, then you get over it. Go on to the next one, but... for women, falling in love *is* falling in love, very dangerous... I'm not saying women can't make you happy. They can. They can make you very happy.

But then, they can also make you very *un*happy, they can do that, women can, they can tear your *kishkes* out, and trust me son, I've donated an organ or two... Listening?"

Yes, little boys 'n' girls. Women can fuck you up. They're not bad people...

"All I'm saying is, there isn't a miserable man out there who doesn't blame a woman. Don't take *my* word for it, ask the older guys, they'll tell you. Women are misery magnets. If *they're* unhappy, *you're* unhappy. But if *they're* happy, doesn't mean *you're* gonna be... which isn't necessarily bad 'cause unhappiness gets results, happiness makes you soft."

Silence.

"Listen, Kid... If you want a woman for the night, no problem, I'll arrange it. But *every* night, with the *same* woman is... is... **marriage!** You don't want that... you're too good for marriage, you're too good for anyone but me... Listening?"

Eddie's listening to himself and can't believe what's coming out.

I sound like an idiot. A combination of Sol, Max, Ollie, Rodney Dangerfield, Shecky Green, Henny Youngman, and Professor Irwin Corey.

"They can mess you up, Kid... mess up your head... make you take your eye off the ball 'cause trust me, she's got hers on *yours*."

"What?"

It eluded him. The joke totally eluded him.

"Her *eye*! *Your* ball! Get it?!!"

"No."

Eddie would have gotten the joke at his age. But The Kid, for all his savvy 'n' street smarts, was naïve, a good kid.

How did I raise a naïve kid, a good kid?

As bad as Eddie was, that's how good The Kid was. As many times as Eddie scolded him for helping an opposing player up from the floor, The Kid continued doing it.

One game, Eddie ran out on the court, grabbed the Kid by his jersey and screamed in his face, "You can help 'em up, but only *after* you knock 'em down!"

Eddie couldn't believe how likeable The Kid was. His fury on the court never spilled over. Eddie believed that to compete successfully required making an enemy of your opponent. The Kid's teammates were like that, but not The Kid. That's because there was joy in his game. A Magic Johnson joy—a foul, a smile, a pat on the back, an extended hand—he just loved being out there, he was that good. When you rise above others, wings will take you there, and since wings are attached to angels, there's no need to be nasty.

"I want out, Dad."

"Listen—"

"I want out!"

"LISTEN!"

"No more points. No more spreads."

"What's her name?"

"I just wanna play the game."

"WHAT'S HER NAME?!"

"I told you her name!"

"Tracy, Tracy, right, right! How long you know her?"

"I don't know, six months."

"Against what?"

"Against?"

"Me! Against **me**!"

"No!"

"Me who raised you, fed you, gave you everything, taught you everything, paid for everything, *did* everything, I worked my balls off!"

"Dad—"

"For **you!**"

Holy shit! Sol's eating his way through him—but it's not working.

What's that look on his face? Blank. Shit. Stop. Reverse.

"Awright! Look, Kid… I'm sorry…"

That's Eddie's genius. He can stop on a dime. Something doesn't work? Change. It's easy, 'cause he's not tied to anything. As stuck as he is in his outer life, that's how nimble and quick he is on the inside, as much a match for anyone off the court as The Kid was on.

"I'm sorry, Kid, really sorry."
WOW! APO-LO-GEE.
"I didn't mean it."

Eddie saves his apologies, he has so few to give. But even as he says it, the words come out loaded. He *was* sorry, *truly* sorry — but for whom? Lying there, two broken legs, a grown fetus curled on a coach, he looks for The Kid, but The Kid's long gone. His heart and eyes heavy with remorse, his body saturated with pain-killers, Eddie falls into a deep sleep dreaming of Sol coming at him with a belt.

"VAT DID YOU CALL ME?"

Sol raises the belt, Eddie pulls his knees up to his chest, waiting to be hit. He flinches, then feels Sol's hands, those huge punishing hands stroking his tiny face...

"*VAYK* UP, YOU BUM!"

Bina's holding a pot over his head.

"I ***brek*** your head!"

He cowers under the pot.

"Go to *verk* you bum!"

"Work?! I can't walk!"

"Can you talk?"

"Yes."

"Can you sit?!"

Eddie props himself up on a pillow.

"Yes."

"*Den* sit by *de* register."

"I'm not workin' for Max!"

"*Den* get out!"

"I'll leave tomorrow."

"LEAVE NOW! YOU BUM!"

Bina goes berserk, throwing pots, pans and dishes. Huh... and all this time Eddie thought he got his rage from Sol.

"BOXES, CANS, *DRECK*, *SHMUTZ*!"

He crawls under the kitchen table.

"YOU MAKE MEIN HOME A HEGDISH!"

He covers his head with his hands in case of a nuclear attack.

"YOU'RE A CHAZER! A SHMUTZ! AH SHLOCH!"

AH PUTZ! AH SHMUCK! AH NO GOODNIK! AH PASKUDNYAK!!"

And with each insult she kicks him under the table, until she's spent. She puts her hand to her mouth, trembling. Eddie climbs out from under the table and gimps over, putting his arms around Bina's stiff body.

"It's gonna be all right, momma."

"*Gott hot mir g'shtrofen. Gott pahnish* me."

"No, Momma, he didn't punish you."

"He took my *fader* and gave me *you*."

"Don't worry, Momma, everything will be all right." It's what he used to say as a child when Bina came home from the hospital. "You'll be fine, Momma." He kisses her forehead. "You'll be fine, Momma. Everything will be all right."

"*Ich vill shtarbin*... I vant to die..."

* * *

Next day, Eddie's back on the stool at the cash register, an unspoken truce between him and Max. He didn't want to be there, but no less than Max wanted him there. They did it for Bina and Bina did it for her *Boytschick*. She was watching him slide, withdrawing into himself. Bina watched Eddie slide the same way after Sol left. He was so smart, so talented, a good kid, and then he got caught up with the wrong crowd, his family.

Eddie reaches under the register for a roll of change. The rolls sit on top of a cigar box. He opens the box. It's stuffed with faded articles on The Kid: games, interviews, highlights. Eddie didn't know Max was such a fan. Max hated sports. But loved The Kid.

His one obsession outside his work was Israel, the survival of his people, the survival of The State. He was on every fundraising committee imaginable. During a crisis, he'd call his friend Adi, an expatriate who, when he wasn't baking, was fighting for Israel. He fought in the wars of '48, '56, '67, and '73. And with each war, Max asked:

"What can I do, Adi? How can I help?"

"Move to Israel."

"Besides that."

"Fight in the war."
"Too old."
"*Shnor* money."
"*That* I can do."

From then on, Max kept a "*pishka*" by the register, a light blue can for donations, supplied by The Jewish National Fund, whose mission it was to irrigate the land. Once a month, he'd declare, "Coffee for Israel!" where ten cents of every purchase was put in the can.

"Can I ask you a question, Adi?"
"Of course! What Jew doesn't come with a question?"
"It's not the question I want. It's the answer."
"If I know, I'll tell you. If I don't, I'll make it up."
"Good. So the money I collect in the *pishka*..."
"Yes?"
"Is it for water or bullets?"
"What's *de* difference?"
"For water, I don't give."
"No one does, Max."
"The Liberals do."
"They should all drop dead."
"Amen."

Eddie looks through the photos, reads the articles touting The Kid as the next Pistol Pete Maravich, the legendary scoring machine, out of Louisiana State. For Eddie, the similarities between The Kid and Pete were uncanny. Their feats on the court, their cool temperaments. They even looked alike: tall, stringy, knob-kneed, pimply scarecrows underneath a mop of flying black hair.

The clincher was that Pistol Pete's dad was also his High School coach, and, of course, Eddie regarded himself as The Kid's *real* coach, taking credit for everything, intercepting every compliment thrown The Kid's way.

"I taught 'em everything he knows."

Eddie puts down the articles and looks out the window. He sees a father and a young boy holding hands, crossing the street. It's been thirty years since Sol held his hand at Golishoff's counter, spoon-feeding him hot chocolate, blowing cool air on the hot spoon so Eddie won't burn his lips. Eddie watches the two walk by, licking his lips...

When you work in the same place for many years, staring out the same window, the same crack in the corner of the window, the same fallen shade, time has a way of standing still, bringing back memories, images, passages, feelings attached to those passages — coming to America, Maddy, the Blimp, The Kid, The *Shvitz*, Boyles, Trios, Pete, Ollie, Chaalie, Sol, Maya, Bina...

So many things happened. Nothing happened. Eddie looks around the shop. Steadies gone. Harry's ass no longer hangs off the naugahyde. Siegel's gone back to Puerto Rico to open his own coffee shop. Max gave him his first five grand to help get him started. Siegel burst into tears, kissing Max's hands, licking his face, climbing all over him with gratitude.

"May Jesus bless you, may Christ—"

"It's okay, Siegel. I *have* a God."

"I pay you back, boss, so help me Mother Mary."

"It's not a loan, it's a gift."

"Oh my God! Oh my GAAD! How do I thank you?"

"Just be healthy and work. Everything else takes care of itself."

Siegel crosses himself, Max, and kisses the mezuzah.

Max muses, "I guess from *one* God you can't make a living."

* * *

For Max, being generous is the most natural thing a human being can do. "Everyone needs help starting out. But the big shots forget." He had a special dislike for *knackers* who attributed their success to themselves, telling you how hard they worked to amass their fortunes. "Who doesn't work hard? Should I remind the *knackers* that hard-working *zhlobs* earn the least? That without cheap labor, you can close up!" When Max gets on his Socialist soap box, you'd never guess he's a Capitalist. "Every successful businessman is a *shlepper* , looking for other *shleppers* to do his *shlepping!* If the *shleppers* are good, the business is good. Otherwise the "genius" businessman is a *yutz!* That's why success stories are bullshit."

The Fix

Max recalled how *he* was helped when he first came over as an immigrant. For years he made the rounds on the Lower East Side, working for "Russ & Daughters: Appetizing," slicing lox as thin as cellophane to terminally dissatisfied customers, then "Yonah Shimmel," the knish joint, then "Gluckstern's," "Ratner's," "Second Avenue Deli," Jewish food joints run by surly servers. Max wasn't surly by nature, but being around so many malcontents rubbed off on him.

Especially "Ratner's," where you had to get on your hands and knees to beg for a glass of water. Although the customers didn't seem to mind. They liked it. Liked it or ignored it. Hard to say at the "Marquis De Ratners," where no plate found its way without a crash and a bang.

Clearly Max wasn't happy being unhappy. But he had no choice. He loved food and hated starving. Bad habit, eating. But the war spoiled his appetite for hunger. He knew, coming to America, that if worse came to worse, working in a restaurant he could always eat, and eat he did. When men his age and weight were keeling over en masse from clogged arteries, Max bellowed, "Quality Life!" stuffing a mouthful of blintzes, pierogies, cheesecake, schnitzel, franks, or whatever leftovers fit into that not-so-tiny hole in his face. Whatever the customer ordered, that's what Max ate. Max pushed the broiled halibut, his favorite and most expensive dish on the menu.

On his ten-hour shift, you could usually find Max hunched over in the pantry corner, resembling a bison, shoveling food into his mouth with his bare hands. Then he'd lick his fingers clean and wipe them dry on his stained apron. People thought he was a cook. Max called it "fine dining." But the waiters were always on the run, so they ate *what* they could, *when* they could.

And unlike his brother Sol, Max could do more than one thing at one time. He could eat *and* speak, which offered you a panoramic view inside his mouth, food pellets flying through the saliva, landing on your shirt and face. Max's white shirts were titled 'Stains of the Day' by the other surly nuts, and Max reminded them of the "freckles" on *their* faces.

Whatever money he earned was spent on rent, books, carfare, whores, Israel, whores, Israel, and whores.

"Pretty little *Tscha-tsch-kees*," he called them, meaning *Tscha-kee-tas*. "Big fat Max," is what they called him.

Of all the Spanish lovelies, Rosa was his favorite. A stunning miniature Puerto Rican mother of four, Rosa worked three jobs to support her family. Licking Max's balls was one of them. And, of course, he was very generous, thinking he was doing a *mitzvah*, a good deed. Rosa's *mitzvah* was performed in the walk-in-fridge, assuring brevity. One day it was too brief. Mister Ratner walked in on them and threw them both out. Max offered to marry Rosa, but she already had two husbands. Licking his balls would be fine and she credited him for the unfinished business in the fridge. Max only dealt with the finest.

He moved on to Ol' Man Golishoff's joint, a luncheonette with room for one waiter, and Max was it. He actually did better there than at Ratner's. Being the only waiter, he ate more and made more. He was doing quite well and saved his money in the freezer, although that's the first place *goniffs* and firemen go, after the mattress.

One day, Ol' Man Golishoff told Max he was retiring and selling the business.

"Why?"

"I'm tired of working."

"Where are you going?"

"The Jewish State."

"Israel?"

"Florida."

"You'll die down there."

"Let's hope."

"All you get is sunshine and *yentas*."

"Let's hope."

"But you're a young man."

"I'm eighty."

"Eighty's not old."

"You know what, Max? *You* live to be eighty, then I'll ask *you*."

"What about *me*? I still need to work."

"I'm sure whoever buys the store will let you stay."

"How can I be sure?"

"You can't."

Max does some figures in his head. "How much do you want for the store?"

"You can't afford it."

"How much?"

"Max, you're a *shlepper*."

"You won't let me make an offer? I worked for you all these years, I can't make an offer?"

"Max, if you have enough money to buy my store, I paid you too much."

"How much?"

"Five thousand down and three hundred a month. I keep the building."

"I'll be right back."

He needs money like I need a boil on my ass.

Max ran home, opened the freezer, but couldn't dislodge the bag encased in ice.

I should have defrosted.

He claws, he hacks, and bangs with a hammer. Finally, a large chunk comes loose. It's hot and the bag's heavy, so by the time Max runs back, he's clutching his heart, and the front of his pants are soaked.

"I have ice, Max."

"I know. It's in your heart."

Max cracks the ice on the floor, and gives the old man the plastic bag.

"Four thousand! Just like you said."

"I said *five*, plus the first month rent."

"Next month, I'll give you the rest."

"Max, I have a buyer. And I don't have to wait a month."

"Mister Golishoff, I'm a nothing, a waiter, a *shlepper*, but *you*, you're successful, kind, generous—"

"Max, please—"

"I love your store, I love your food."

"You love *any* food."

"Mr. Golishoff, you won't give me a chance? I'm a Jew, a fellow Jew, a *lantzman*, what I saw in my life, what I *lost* in my life, you shouldn't know, your children shouldn't know, your grandchildren—"

"No!"

Meanwhile, next door, Benny, the owner of "Benny's Toy Store," is watching the two haggle. He walks between them, pulls out a roll of bills, counts off thirteen one hundred dollar bills and gives them to Max.

Max is stunned. "But you don't know me."

"Max, I've gotten screwed more by people I know. At least with strangers, you never see them again."

Golishoff had a slightly confused and disgusted look on his face. Golishoff was a Jew. Benny DiMaglio was a *mentsch*.

Max never forgot that.

"Everyone needs a little help starting out, Siegel."

"How can I ever pay you back, boss?"

"Just be healthy and work. Everything else takes care of itself."

* * *

So Siegel's gone, Harry's gone, counter's replaced by bony-ass hippies and the Lower East Side is in a funk along with the rest of the country, run into the ground by that "Peanut *Shmuck*," as Max called President Carter. "I can't believe what America's become. A country of *shmucks* pissed on by the world. The whole country's *farkaaked*! The city's *farkaaked*! New York is dead!"

What kept the City alive those years wasn't Mayor Beam or President Ford, who told New York to drop dead, but its teams— the Yankees, Giants, Knicks, and Rangers. As long as they were doing well, everything was fine. In college basketball, John Wooden's UCLA Bruins were the national powerhouse and Joe Lapshick's St. John's Redmen were the local favorite. Other high-ranked teams included Louisville, Marquette, Kentucky, Duke, and the North Carolina Tar Heels, who became national contenders overnight by figuring out the key to winning: recruit the best players. Da!

So while other colleges limited their recruiting sights to west of the Mississippi, North Carolina raided the Big Apple, sending scouts to ghettos, parks, projects, and schoolyards, finding a candy store full of raw talent.

The Fix

There were more great players on one New York City block than in the entire state of North Carolina. Also more heroin addicts. But they played for nothing, expected nothing, ripe for exploitation. These kids played with a ferocity and desperation unknown to their white counterparts. For them it wasn't just a game. It was a way out of the ghetto, playing for their lives.

You can't teach hunger. You can't teach style. The kids from the streets hadn't been taught the "right" or "correct" way to dribble, run, pass, or shoot. Their skills grew from inside out, driven from the pit of their empty stomachs. No two players were alike. No Detroit assembly line here. No summer basketball camps, no summer leagues, no Police Athletic League, just warfare on the streets, behind chain link fences, hoping to ward off future chain link fences. Spirits not yet dampened by "organized" ball, the kids organized themselves. They knew each others' strengths and weaknesses, moves and counter-moves, head fakes and shoulder fakes. They knew the *real* fakes, sizing you up by the way you played, and although it's a team game, everyone knew it was every man for himself. Letting someone else down was first and foremost letting yourself down.

North Carolina's basketball success began, oddly enough, with a Jewish kid out of the Bronx, Lenny Rosenbluth, who led the Tar Heels to the NCAA Championship in 1957.

And if they think Lenny was great, wait till they see my Kid!

Eddie never thought the Jewish card could ever be played beyond the pity game.

The Kid's in his senior year and still no response from North Carolina or any other top school. But Eddie keeps writing and calling.

Maybe I'll tell 'em The Kid's black.

The mailman drops off the mail. Eddie sorts through the pile and notices one with a return address of North Carolina. His hands begin to shake, the room's spinning, he sits down, he can't breathe. He knows it always comes down to a letter or a call. All the great things in life come down to a letter or a call. Also the worst. His mind's a mess. The "what ifs" start marching in. He's afraid to open the letter. He smells it, holds it to the light. He rings up a customer for a fried egg sandwich and gives him twenty change for a five dollar bill.

"At this rate, Eddie, you'll be outta business by lunch."

He hobbles to the back on his crutches.

"Watch the front, Max. I'm going to the head."

Inside the stall, Eddie drops his pants, the pull chain resting on his head. He opens the letter and screams. A customer falls off his stool. The guy next to him says: "Well, Max, looks like your food finally killed someone!"

Eddie runs out, his pants around his ankles, waving the letter.

"Holy shit, Max!"

"You took a Holy Shit?!"

"Look! Look!"

"Pull up your *gatkes* and get some coffee filters."

"FUCK THE FILTERS! LOOK!"

Max reads the letter. "Who's from Chapel Hill? A relative?"

"They're coming! They're coming!"

"The Russians?"

"READ, YOU *SHMUCK*!"

"You're calling *me* a *shmuck*?"

Eddie hugs Max, grabs his crutches, and hops out the door.

"Again the *shmuck* leaves. My nephew's a *meshugeneh*. The whole family's nuts! Why did I ever bring them over? " Max is talking to no one in particular, nor is anyone listening. "You think you're doing a *mitzvah*, saving someone, but you can't save anyone from themselves. They don't appreciate it. What can I say? It's a *meshugeneh* life." He inhales a danish, Max's antidote to *aggravation*.

Eddie's on the corner of Allen and Stanton, on his crutches, waving the letter to strangers walking by muttering, "another socialist supporting a losing cause." New Yorkers have a penchant for ignoring people. They ignore themselves. He doesn't know where to go, who to tell. He can't believe it. The letter he's been waiting for his entire life finally arrives and there's no one to tell.

Bina? No. Maddy? Gone. Maya? Toronto. The Kid? Might throw him off.

The Fix

He's walking around in a daze. He sits down on a bench in Essex Street Park, the same park where The Kid was hoisted on black shoulders not too many years ago. Now other kids are playing. Chinese, Indian, Asian, Mexican. He looks across Essex on the other side of the street, shops selling *t'fillin*, *shmattas*, burritos, electronics, pickles...

Show the letter to Guss, the pickle man, show him I made something of myself.

A ball bounces at his feet. He kicks it back and screams, forgetting his broken leg.

I'm such a fuckin' nebbish... I'll just sit here and kvell, no one tell.

Chapter Ten

Eddie yells across the street, "Great news, Ollie!"
"You got my money?"
"Better!"
"*Betta*?"

Eddie hops over on his crutches and hands a letter to Ollie, who is sitting with a bib around his neck at Lanza's Italian restaurant down the block from Di Roberto's dessert shop. Ollie doesn't like Lanza's deserts, so the owner has the Lanza waiters wheel over the dessert cart from Di Roberto's along First Avenue, weaving between Sabrette hot dog vendors and trucks stuck in traffic.

The desserts look beautiful, but by the time they get to Ollie, they taste like Exxon. But he doesn't care. Once he's perched, he's down. The world comes to him.

"Sit down, Eddie."

Sitting at the sidewalk bistro, the Lower East Side as Ollie and Eddie knew it is no longer. Now it's the East Village, and although the Ukrainian restaurant, the Second Avenue Deli, and the *Shvitz* still operate, they're now overrun by NYU students, migrating back from the nations 'burbs. Dancers, actors, writers, artists, designers, filmmakers descend on the city, swelling the need for housing. NYU, once a small mediocre college for mediocre students, is now a mega-developer, posing as a higher learning institution, gobbling up every available inch of New York real estate, pushing out drug pushers, homeless vets, and the mentally deranged because of budget cuts in hospitals and shelters. Bag people roam the streets, AIDS is rampant, and window car washers outnumber cars.

NYU makes it all possible, surpassing the Church as the City's most powerful landlord, the ghost of Duddy Kravitz sitting at the table of Tisch. Now clean-skinned kids from Minnesota have the privilege of cramming four into a room for only two grand a month, trudging up six flights, the same six-floor walk-up Sol paid $18 a month some thirty-five years ago.

"We're gonna make a killing Ollie!"
"Who we killing?"
"Moolah Ollie! Moolah! Kid's getting drafted!"
"He's goin' in *de* Army?"
"North Carolina!"
"*Dey* raise pigs down *dere!*"
"They're coming!"
"Who?"
"The scouts! We're set, Ollie! Set! SET! SET! SET!"
"Slow down, Eddie. I *neve* seen you like *dis*."
"You know, I've been writing them about the Kid for years!"
"No, I don't know *dat*."
"So they finally wrote back and guess what?!"
"What?"
"They're comin' down for the Playoffs, Ollie, this is big! BIG! BIG! BIG! BIG!"
"Shut up! I'm readin'."
Eddie forgot how long it takes Ollie to read. Eddie's not sure if Ollie *can* read.
"*Dis* is good, Eddie. Very good."
"Phenomenal!"
"Don't use big words on me. When *deys* comin'?"
"Next week. Playoffs!"
"*Den* I get my money?"
"Absolutely! Just like I promised!"
"No margarine?"
"No margarine, Ollie. This is one *promise* I keep!"
"*Dat's* good, Eddie. Very good."
"Kid's gonna shine, Ollie! Gonna put on a show they won't forget!"
"*Dat's* why *youse* gotta hold 'em back."
"But... he's gotta do good... "
"He'll do good, but not *too* good."
"But the scouts, the bonus... "
"Let 'em score big first *tree* quarters, *den* let 'em get hurt or sometin' like *de* last game."

"Ollie, If he goes down, they'll think he's fragile, uh—gets hurt easily. They won't draft 'em."

"So?"

"Ollie, it's four years! We can fix games for four years! We'll make out like bandits! Let the Kid loose."

"Appreciate you comin' over, Eddie."

"It's for the future, Ollie, *de* future!"

"Future? *Dat's* the funniest word I ever *herd*."

"Ollie, I'm waitin' my entire life for *dis*, *everyting* I ever hoped for, *eveh* dreamed of —"

"What are you gonna tell The Kid?"

"...That if he wants his father alive..."

"*Dat's* good Eddie, very good.... and *true*."

* * *

"*Shmuck's* back."

"No more *shmuck*, Max."

"So what's all this mean, Eddie? We can retire?"

"Yeah, Max, we can *all* retire."

"What's wrong, you don't look happy?"

Eddie does a one-eighty.

"What the fuck is wrong with you, Eddie?! You come, you go, you stay, you leave! Do me a favor. Get lost! And don't come back!"

* * *

Eddie hobbles into Gordon's office in back of the locker room. The office smells of liniment and mold with lint in the air, coming from the vents off the washer and dryer in the laundry room next door. It's hard for Gordon to have a quiet moment with his players without the laundry guy walking in and out.

He sits behind a chipped wooden desk, not a paper clip out of place, X's and O's on a blackboard behind him. When he comes up with an idea, he posts it. If *he* doesn't come up with the idea, it's not a good one. Although, sometimes he'll wait until he thinks everyone's forgotten and re-introduce it as his own.

He files his notes in neatly stacked folders keeping records longer than the I.R.S. Although given his record, he'd be better off shredding the files. He's been coaching at Seward Park High for ten years and never won a thing. But his files are in order. An obsessive "open and close drawer guy," Gordon constantly checks his notes for ideas, afraid he won't get another.

Along the side of the file cabinets is a brag wall dominated by action shots of Gordon, an All-American, and one particularly oversized photo of Gordon holding the Big Ten championship trophy over his head. When coach reprimands a player, or is being interviewed, he makes sure to stand next to the photo op.

Old jocks never die, they just live off faded pictures hung on cracked walls.

"What's with the crutches, Parker?"

"I pulled a hamstring?"

"Sorry about that."

"I came to apologize, coach."

"For what?"

"Bein' outta line… I should just let you do your job. I mean, what the hell do *I* know… right? It's just that—I love the kids so much, and care so much about the team, the school, the kids, their futures. That's my problem, coach. I care too much."

"What do you want?"

"Can't I just say something without you thinkin' I want something?"

"Look, Parker, we both know what's up. The Kid'll do anything for you. You're his father and he loves you. But there will come a time when he won't love you so much."

"Wouldn't you just love that?"

"You got your hooks into him nice 'n' deep."

"And you want *yours* in."

"I'm just The Kid's coach, looking out for his interests."

"So why were you pilin' it on against Stuyvesant?"

"They're a crap team. The league showed us no respect, putting them on our schedule."

"But why did you pile it on?"

"Why did *you* have The Kid fake an injury?"

"They're a bad team and you were running up the score."
"So?"
"A good coach takes it easy on a shit team."
"Really?"
Eddie gives him the letter.
"Now, coach, you can stay in a shit city, shit school, make shit money, *orrrr* land a top job, top school, top money."
Gordon's listening, pretending he's reading.
"I can make it happen. Not the first time a coach sails in on the tail of his star."
"And...?"
"Like I said, a good coach doesn't pile it on... or does... depends... I'll let you know... *should* I let you know?"
Coach doesn't move.
"I'll let you know."
Gotcha!
He went in hoppin' 'n' came out bobbin'. Didn't think he'd get Gordon, but did. That's the thing about ambition, it's ambitious. Surprisingly, it lies dormant in the ones least likely to "do such a thing." But when it comes out, it's an ugly little fucker.

It's when you want something, *really* want something, that you know. Most times it's not even the thing you want but the *wanting*, a bottomless pit you never fill no matter what you want *or* get.

On a scale of one to ten on the "Wanting Scale," most people think they're at nine or ten, when it's one or two. And that's how they bullshit themselves their whole life through.

"I want it *soooo* much."
"No you don't."
The test being, what will you do to get it?

It inhabits those who want to win. Those who don't, forget. But those who want, truly want, are those who want to *win*. Not just compete, but win. Those who want the most get the most, and lose the most, for winning is a limitation in itself. Because after you win — then what? Win again? That's not a win, that's a repeat. Then it's expected. Winning's no fun when it's expected.

The Fix

Funny how you can do the same thing and at first be applauded, then ignored. Either way, once you win, it's done, over. Congratulations, you fed the beast, put ambition to rest, now say hello to the hole, the winning hole... sad, sad and boring. Winning is boring. Same old shit, no variety, just a lot of glad handshaking, backslapping, *champagnya* over the head, thanking God, smiling, laughing, jumping up and down, screaming, "I can't believe it!" Boring. No *schmaltz* in the herring, no *gribenes* in the stew.

I say, give me a loser, one who *almost* made it. The guy who came in second. Now *that's* interesting! Then you got something. Then you got a story. Then you got Eddie. Then you got *us*. Losers. Most people are losers. Why else chase shit all our lives, never satisfied, always coming up short?

If you're always after something, you must have lost something along the way, a childhood, a dream, who knows? To find it you have to look back. How do you keep moving forward if you're always looking back? So we dance to our own tunes, unconscious, a bunch of losers, looking for something, not quite sure what — but at least we're interesting.

* * *

Eddie heads straight to the bar on the corner of Essex. The owner pours Eddie two shots, opens the register, and gives him two hundred bucks.

"How's The Kid?"

"Good as gold."

"That's what I expect back."

"That's what you'll get!" Eddie downs the shots. "No problem."

Beware of anyone who says "no problem."

This is good, this is good! If it's a blowout, coach can dampen it. If they face Boys' High, Seward can't win anyway. Boys' High is too strong, even with The Kid. But the Kid can still show his stuff. Either way, I got it covered both ways.

Problem is, to cover both ways, Eddie needs ten grand. Problem is he's broke. Problem is he's on the balls of his ass, going down a razor slide.

WHAAAAAAAAAAAAAAAAAA!!!

"Hey, Freddy, bring over the phone."

"Is it local?"

"Of course."

Eddie takes out a slip and dials a shit load of numbers.

"Why you dialin' so many numbers, Eddie?"

"Don't worry about it, pour me another shot! 'Hey Maddy! Yeah, long time... what?!... No, no one died, no... no I don't want *anything*... I was just wondering... if... if I could have my wedding ring back…? Hello... hello?"

He tried it once before. A few years after the divorce he sent The Kid to Tampa for Christmas, telling Maddy The Kid missed her, that all the other kids in school had somewhere to go for the Holidays. He packed up The Kid and sent along an empty ring box from Tiffany for a ring he bought at Sears.

"Tell Mommy I really appreciate it, getting the ring back, and that Grandma would like it too, since she paid for it."

It didn't work then, but what the hell? Worth a shot, she mighta softened.

"You are some piece of shit!"

"So, it's no?"

"Fifteen years, Eddie! Fifteen years divorced and you want the ring back?!"

"I thought—"

"You tried that once before, didn't you?!"

"I don't remember."

"You sick fuck!"

"I didn't mean to upset you."

"Eddie, I am so, sooo happy I left you!"

"Sounds like you made the right decision, Maddy, but where is it? Where is the ring? Do you have it? Is it in a vault, safe deposit box, shoe box, do you wear it on sad occasions?"

Fuckin' Maddy, I'll shame her into giving it back.

"I'm havin' a rough time these days, Maddy, otherwise I wouldn't ask... shoes for The Kid, doctors, orthodontist, he's anemic, vitamin B shots; Bina sends her love."

"I'll tell you what I told you last time, Eddie."

"What?"
"GET A FUCKING JOB!"
"Hello... hello?"
Boy, when the Irish get mad...
"But where's the ring, Maddy? What happened to the ring?"
"I pawned it, Eddie. Things got tough, I was alone, I needed shoes, gum, mascara..."

* * *

"It's a lock, Kitz! Guaranteed!"

Kitzee's another bookie, a bit of a friend, a big guy, a *shlump*, a neighborhood agoraphobic, he never leaves the neighborhood. "Gotta stay close to my shrink." Kitzee suffers from clinical depression and blames his brain.

"Brain ain't your friend, Eddie. For some things it's good, like counting numbers or getting directions. Otherwise, it's useless."

"I need ten grand, Kitz."

"Brain makes you do things you don't wanna do, selfish little bastard! Fuckin' Pac-Man, gobble-dee-gobble-dee-guk! Eats everything."

"Just ten grand, Kitz. But only for a little while. Then it comes back to you *with* interest. So it's not really a loan. It's an investment! A sure-fire investment!"

"For what?"

"The future. You believe in the future, don't you?"

"I believe in pills."

Eddie shows him the letter, slightly revised, but with the same letterhead.

"Here it is in writing: ten grand signing bonus from North Carolina. Says so right here! You get it right after the game. Guaranteed!"

"Guaranteed?"

"Not even a question. So all I'm askin' really is an advance on the advance, but the good news, the *real* good news is — 'n' by the way, Ollie's in for a bundle — the *real* good news is that once The Kid's in, it's four years, four years of puttin' the fixins' on the burger. YEE-HA! How much is that worth, huh?"

"These the numbers?"

"Givin' me the ten grand."

"It's a loan."

"Right, right, an investment."

"No. A loan. You pay back!"

"Yeah, yeah."

"Ten grand, plus ten percent, plus late fee. And if you don't pay back—"

"I already got that offer."

"So these are the numbers?"

"Yeah, yeah."

"You won't be changin' them on me?"

"What are you worried about?"

"You!"

"I'm hurt, Kitzee, I'm really hurt, to think that *you*, my best friend—"

"Don't start cryin' on me, *awright*? 'Cause I'll smack you!"

"Kitz, we go back a long time. I'm the best friend you got."

"That's a problem."

"I need a chance, Kitz, everyone needs a chance."

"You don't need a chance, Eddie. You wouldn't know what to do with a chance."

"Kitzee. This is my opportunity, my golden opportunity, my time! Everything I poured into The Kid is finally going to pay off!"

"These the numbers."

"Jesus Christ! You don't trust me?!"

"You don't have the best track record, Eddie. Sign your name to the letter."

"I need the letter. It's the only one I got. I'll send you a copy."

"No, no, *you* sign it 'n' I'll send *you* a copy."

Eddie signs the letter. Kitzee gives him the cash.

"If you don't trust me, why you helpin' me out?"

"I like your Mom. She was nice to me on the ward."

* * *

The Fix

You have to wonder how Eddie gets away with this shit when everyone around him know what he's up to. He really doesn't get away with anything. People let him in. They like to play as much as he does. And without Eddie there's no one to play with.

We all need "Eddies" in our lives. People we don't love, trust, care about, but we keep 'em around. Eddie knows that.

Chapter Eleven

At Bina's funeral, Maya said a few words, Eddie sang, "*Yiddishe Momme*," and Max walked around like a lost soul.

"No more walks from the *shvitz* to Bina's, eh, Eddie?"

"Guess not, Max."

"Your mother was a wonderful woman, Maya."

"Yes, she was, Uncle Max."

Max drifts off to Gomez Siegel.

"I'm so sorry, boss. *Zolst zein g'zunt*, be well."

Working for Max all those years, Siegel became proficient in Yiddish sayings, most of them appropriate. And while Max wailed, Siegel sighed, his drenched island shirt blinding mourners.

After Eddie sang, Rabbi Horwitz invited family to speak. Eddie hadn't seen Rabbi in years and couldn't believe how terribly Rabbi had aged. When Rabbi saw Eddie he said:

"You don't look good, Eddie."

Eddie was out all night drinking, gambling, his legs were killing him, and he had a massive headache. Typical day.

" I know losing your mother is very difficult. Why don't you come to Shul to say *Kaddish*."

"Why, you need a new roof?"

Rabbi sighs. "Like father, like son."

"I don't have a father."

"You never heard from Sol, all these years."

"No."

"Weeell... it wasn't a good thing that happened."

No shit, Rabbi.

"I'm sorry for your loss. Your mother was a wonderful woman."

"You didn't know her."

"Good to see you, Eddie."

"Same."

"Let's hope we meet on better occasions."

"What are those?"

"When you're not so angry."

Responding to Rabbi's invitation for family to speak, The Kid, all six-foot-three, stood up and loped to the front. He unwrinkled a scrap of paper and read. Through sniffles and tears, this tall, shy, gangly, acned teen spoke quietly about how much he loved Bina and how she force-fed him. "Explains my height."

The Kid was funny, touching, and... surprising. The Kid hardly spoke. Ever. And to stand up like this, publicly?

Is this my kid?

It's like that with kids. You keep them fixed in your mind's eye as children, stuck in their lives as you are in yours. And then suddenly one day you look up and it's over. You notice that they've moved on and you haven't. Something they say or do, and you know that part of your life is over. Then you begin taking inventory. "How was I? Did I do right by them?" But, of course, all these questions come too late, which is why parents shouldn't ask. But the good intentions were always there as a reminder of what Eddie didn't do. He wasn't the best parent, but he did the best he could, or so he told himself, and within their distance, there was this attachment, this... feeling.

It wasn't all about point spreads, was it?

The Kid told the story of how Bina watched him play in the park from her sixth-floor kitchen window. When she saw him exhausted, she'd go downstairs, walk across the street, stop traffic, go onto the court, almost getting trampled to death.

"**BU-BBEEE! WE'RE PLAYIIIIIING!**"

"*Hev-a-b'ne-neh. Ess, mein kind, ess.*"

"I'm not hungry!!**LEEEEEEEAVE!**"

She's not leaving, won't budge. Not until he chews the Chiquita.

Everyone stands around and waits till he finishes. Players applaud.

"Okay, *Bubbee*?"

"*Haw-kay.*" She takes the peel. "Now you can play."

She tried to do the same thing in League play, but they wouldn't let her in the gym until she came in empty-handed.

They needn't have worried. With no food to give, she could care less about the game.

"Okay, guys, let's go!"

"*Vayt!*"

The players groan. She reaches into her apron and dispenses Tootsie Rolls.

"Looka here! Gramma's dealin'!"

For Bina, this was child's play. Only thirty-five years earlier, she was dealing for real in Russia's underground black market under Stalin's scrutinous eye. But then it wasn't for Tootsie Rolls, it was for bread. Sol was arrested for siphoning off oil in the munitions factory where he worked and selling it for food. Sol's foreman wanted a cut, Sol refused, and the foreman turned him in. While Sol was in jail, Bina saw the foreman, took Sol's route, gave the foreman his cut, the Judge his, and made enough money to feed her family and get Sol out of jail.

In exchange for the chewy fudge, the shiny young men gave Bina Gatorade which she gave her *Boytschick*—her nearest, dearest, and favorite grandchild of three, not letting Maya forget it. She never forgave Maya for leaving and refused to see Maya's two little girls. In Bina's world, daughters stay. Sons may come and go, but daughters stay.

"Just like your *fader*!" she spat as Maya's cab pulled away to the airport. It's always harder on those who stay. What do they have to go back to?

On her way to a new job, new city, new life, Maya should have been happier, but she sat in the cab numb, looking out the window on an overcast day. No more "Second-hand Rose," no more maid, servant, confidante, shopper, chauffeur, prescription filler... no more appointment maker, nurse, manicurist, hair dresser, social worker; no more Bina... no more... Maya.

In war-scarred European homes, women are shit and daughters are slaves. Just the way it is. *Traaa-dishuuun*! Especially if the men walk out, then the mothers take out on their daughters what's due their husbands, continuing the tradition. But this is where tradition ends. In America, land of the free, where children split the first chance they get, and no one holds on to anything or anyone for very long.

THE FIX

Parents never understand why children leave. "I was so good to her." Could it be they don't like them?

The day after Maya graduated Nursing School, she moved to Toronto, "New York without the *shmutz*." She worked, married, had two girls, a beautiful home, a good husband. Jewish holidays were spent with her in-laws, the Shlossbergs, prominent wine merchants, cousins of the notoriously rich, high-nosed whiskey men, the Bronfmens, in the *shtetle* of Toronto where everyone's a cousin of a cousin.

As she could do no right by Bina, she could do no wrong by the Shlossbergs. So when it came time to decide where to go for the Holidays, Maya went where the love was. She turned down Bina's annual invitations, who tried to bribe her with the sweetest gefilte fish this side of Poland.

"Fish like *dis* you *vont* find by your fancy *machataynim*."

Maya used different excuses, different years: work, distance, illness, schedules, anything to stay away from Bina on the High Holy Days, the Ten Days of Awe Bina called "Ten Days of *Och 'n' Vay!*" Ten days of food, prayer, reflection, recollection, indigestion, constipation: thank God, wash dishes, and apologize to your enemies.

As the High Holidays approached, the pitch of preparation rose sky high. There was always too much to do and not enough time to do it. The home was busy, frenetic, and somewhat joyous. But underneath the din lived a sadness no amount of holiday minutia could diminish. Keeping busy couldn't make it go away for Maya. For all its promise of renewal, Rosh Hashanah left in its wake a trace of sadness topped off with a slice of regret.

* * *

"That was nice, Eddie, singing '*Yiddishe Momme.*' Bina would like that."

"She should. I'm the only one who can sing it walking unaided."

"So what are the crutches for?"

"I got a little infection."

"Are you in some kind of trouble?"

"In, out, you know, *g'sheft*."

"*G'sheft*."

"Business, like any other."

They wait in the parlor for the hearse to return from the repair shop.

"Three times this week," the chauffeur tells Eddie, "Limos look good on the outside, but underneath they're like people, corroded." Chauffeurs, doormen, and cabbies can tell you more about about people than Freud.

Maya's angry. Eddie's disgusted. He thought he'd catch the last three races at Belmont.

"Uncle Max, at this rate, we'll never get to the cemetery! You mean to tell me all they have is *one* hearse?"

"They have three, but two are out."

"Why did you pick this funeral home?"

"They're good customers."

Eddie jumps in. "Well, they're not returning the favor."

"Relax, Eddie, you'll make the fourth race."

"Uncle Max, this is terrible."

"Mayele, they're calling all the *goyishe* parlors to borrow a hearse."

"With the crosses hanging?!"

"Crosses, mezuzahs, what's the difference? Two mezuzahs make one cross."

Maya and Eddie drift off to a corner; Maya hardly knows anyone and Eddie no one wants to know. The feeling is mutual. He's out of his element. All this pitter-patter parlor talk, well-meaning well-wishers laying down condolences. If he could just crawl out of his skin, leave it there, go smoke a joint, just get outta there.

"Eddie, can you believe we're waiting for a hearse!"

"Well, Sis, if you're gonna be stood up, might as well be a hearse."

"All the bad things in our family happen on the saddest day, Eddie"

"Yeah."

"Pop left on Yom Kippur, his family was killed on Yom Kippur, and Bina dies on Yom Kippur."

"That's one way of Bina getting you home for the holidays."

"God, Eddie, it's been so long since we've been together. Thank God for funerals or else we'd never see each other."

Eddie missed Maya's wedding, the birth of her daughters, birthdays, anniversaries. He missed a lot, actually, he missed everything.

"So, how's *mishpoche*, Sis?"

"Good."

"Girls?"

"Good."

"Barry, the Shlosses?"

"Shlossberg."

"Right, right, how are they?"

"Fine."

"And you, Maya?"

"Good... considering..."

"What?"

"Mom died."

"Right, right..."

"And how are you, my dear brother? How are you taking all this?"

"What do you mean?"

"Our mother's dead."

"Right, right... well, you know..."

"You seem preoccupied."

"No, just thinkin'..."

Can I make the fifth at Aquaduct?

"Can't believe she's gone, Eddie."

"Yeah."

"With Mom gone, we should try to see each other more."

"Sure."

"Reconnect."

"Yeah."

What is it about funerals that people want to connect, reconnect, promising connections? That's not something you talk about at funerals. That's Diner Talk. Good Greek Diner Talk where you can sit forever and the coffee keeps a comin'. A good place for reminiscing relatives to mourn the past, curse the present, catch up on each others' lives, and realize that these are the very same crazy fucks they ran away from in the first place.

Good Greek Second Chance Diners, stuck between lemon meringue, the clock, and the wall, listening to *bubbe meise* seaweed stories dredged up from the bottom, a good nostalgic *shmaltz* stop.

"Eddie, remember when—"

"OW!"

"What's wrong?!"

He pulls up his cuff, displaying calves the size of a house.

"Oh, my God! How did this happen?"

"On my feet too much. Rooting for the home team."

She barely touches his calf.

"Hey! Dr. Mengele! Don't play nurse."

"That's what I am."

"You're a *psychiatric* nurse."

"This is serious. You have a lot of fluid."

"Think they'll have to amputate my calves?"

"Don't laugh, you could get a clot."

My life's a clot.

"Did you see a doctor?"

"Nothin' they can do. Stage eight."

"Oh my God! Stage eight!! What's stage eight?"

"Strip club."

She squeezes his calf.

"OW!"

Eddie knows that in the face of fear, making jokes by the stricken shows courage.

"You must see a doctor."

"I hate doctors."

"You hate everyone."

"That's right. Everyone's full of shit."

"And you're not."

"I'm different."

"How's that?"

"I *know* it."

"Right, you're so honest. I'm sure the people who did this to you feel the same way."
"They're not into feelings."
"Are you taking aspirin?"
"Ice."
"Tylenol 'n' ice?"
"Smirnoff."
She gives him a *nuggee*.
"Hey!"
"You should do stand-up."
"I would but my calves won't let me."
She lets out a shriek of laughter and covers her mouth.
This is good, it's good, I'm taking her mind off our relationship.
"We used to be close, Eddie."
Shit!
"We were never close, sis. I mean *we* were, but—"
"Our family wasn't close?"
"Our family was fucked up like every other family."
"The early years were good."
"You mean when Mom was nuts and Pop beat the shit outta me?"
Oh, now she's gonna defend Pop.
"Was he beating you twenty-four hours a day?"
Now Mom.
"Was Mom nuts *all* the time?"
Friends and relatives.
"Were there no friends and relatives, holidays, walks in the park—"
Good times.
"Were there no good times? You played chess with Pop, watched ballgames, discussed politics—"
"This shit always happens at funerals, Sis."
"What?"
"Amnesia."
"Why are you so negative, Eddie, why do you always see things as—"
"They are?"

"As bad, Eddie, as bad. Was everything bad, was nothing good?"

"Uh…"

She looks at him, disgusted.

"What happened to you, Eddie?"

"What do you mean?"

"What do you mean, what do I mean?! Look at you! You're a waste! A bookie! A bum!"

"Can't have everything."

"And all you do is blame family! I come from the *same* family!"

"So?"

"Pathetic, Eddie, just pathetic!"

"We can't all be Torontonian Jews like the Shlosses."

"Don't you dare attack my family!"

"You're attacking my lifestyle!"

"Lifestyle?"

"I didn't even do anything."

"That's right, Eddie. You did nothing! Nothing in your life you can be proud of!"

"I raised a good son!"

"I wouldn't know, because I don't know him, he doesn't know me. You don't know my children, my husband, my family, my life. I made a life, Eddie. A life you know nothing about, because you don't care. You don't care about anything except your gambling!"

"Not true."

"What do you care about, Eddie? Family? Friends? How you look? How you come across to others?"

Torontonian Jews require that not only do *they* look all *far-pitzt*, but everyone around them does as well, or else it reflects badly.

"This is how you show up at your mother's funeral?! You're limping, you smell, your shirt's dirty, your jacket's ripped," she whispers, "piss stains on your pants, your breath stinks!" She gives him a mint. "Have you been drinking?"

"Only twenty hours."

"Oh my God!"

"I was trying to remember the good times."

"Always with the jokes, Eddie. As soon as it gets serious, here comes Eddie with the jokes."

Max comes along.

"Did I hear jokes?"

"Life's a joke, Max."

"True, Eddie. You don't laugh, you cry."

Max sees the steam coming out of Maya's ears.

"Everything okay, children?"

"Yes, Uncle (*fucking*) Max, everything's fine!"

"Listen, kids, after the cemetery, you'll come over, we'll sit *shiva* and eat deli."

"Perfect."

"You'll come too, Eddie."

"Sure."

"Mayela, you're as beautiful as ever."

"Thank you."

"Everyone good in Toronto?"

"Yes."

"When was I there last?"

"Never."

"I thought I visited…"

"No."

"Maybe in the future."

"That would be nice."

"Now that Bina's dead, we should see each other more."

"Sure."

"She woulda killed me if I visited then. She was so upset you left, but now I can visit. You'll come too, Eddie."

"Sure."

" Do you want to drive or go by plane?"

"Do I have to decide now?"

"I loved your mother, Mayele."

"She loved you too, Max."

"Better than your father, that *momzer*!" And he shuffles off.

"*Oy*, it's a hard life."

"He looks worse than you do, Eddie."

"He lost more."

Eddie gets into the hearse with Maya. Max follows in his Buick with The Kid and his girlfriend. Eddie looks back at Max. Max waves.

"Did you know about them, Sis?"

"Who?"

"M&M. Max 'n' Mom?"

"Sure. Why do you think Pop left?"

"Never said."

"The marriage was over."

"I thought she loved Pop."

"But he didn't love her."

"So why did they get married?"

"The war married them."

"So she 'n' uncle Max—"

"You get your love where you can, Eddie."

Next topic.

The funeral bill.

"Didn't Pop pay it off?"

"Yes, Eddie, but then he borrowed against it."

"Nice, using Mom's plot as collateral."

"You want to argue about it?"

"How much did this sh'bang cost?"

"Five thousand."

"Not bad."

"That's *your* share."

"What is she buried in a pyramid?"

"Simple pine was seven."

"What's wrong with simple? Mom was simple."

"I thought she should have more."

"*You* thought, or did the death shysters from the funeral home talk you into an expensive box?"

"*Me*, Eddie! It was *my* decision!"

"Goddamn funeral doesn't let you get out alive! Everything's a goddamn business!"

"If you can't afford it—"

"I can afford it, just not right now."

"Sure."

"Next week."
"Sure."
"By the way, Sis, is that 5K Canadian or American?"
"Why?"
"Canadian's cheaper."
Even the driver turns around on that one.
"You know what, Eddie? Don't pay!"
"Maya—"
"Pay **nothing**!"
"We never even discussed it."
"She was dead three days in her apartment! Where were you?! I'm in Toronto taking care of everything while you're *here*!"
"I'm sorry."
"You are something, Eddie, you really are!"
"I'm really sorry."
"Always sorry."
Not really.
"I was away, Sis, helping my friend Kitzee."
"Kitzee?"
"My best friend. Mom introduced us at the loony bin. He has no one."
"Now you're a visiting nurse. How many lies do you come up with in an hour?"
"I can't take care of a friend, my *best* friend who had a nervous breakdown?!"
Eddie can get quite righteous when he finds a hook.
"Did you forget what it was like for Mom?"
"I'm sorry, that was insensitive of me."
"I understand—you're upset."
"Forgive me."
He did it again! "The Victimization of Eddie."
"Truce, Eddie?"
"Truce."
They peck on the cheek.
"Sis?"
"Yeah."

"I still think ten grand's a lot of money."
You wouldn't by chance have another ten layin' around?
Next topic.
"The Kid spoke beautifully, Eddie, such poise."
"Yeah… strange… he's usually shy off the court."
"He got so big. I hardly recognize him."
"Well, you know, they grow."
"How tall is he?"
"Six-four."
"Wow."
"Actually six-three, but the scouts list him at six-four."
"Scouts?"
He shows her the letter.
Maybe she'll think it's a big deal.
"This is big, Sis, really big—"
"Was that his girlfriend sitting next to him, the pretty blonde?"
"They're after him!"
"So sweet, holding hands."
"Gonna make him an offer."
"She reminds me of Maddy."
"Big offer!"
"Ever hear from her?"
"Who?"
"Maddy."
They're crossing over the Verazzano Bridge and Eddie's thinking of Ollie and seals, broken legs, smashed heads, Jimmy Hoffa.
"Where does she live? Did she re-marry?"
"Huh?"
"Are you out of it?"
It's hard going to a cemetery with Ollie on your mind. For Ollie, it's one-stop shopping.
"Does he see her?"
"Who?"
"MADDY! His mother!"
"Yeah, yeah, yeah, in Tampa. Yeah, Kid spent Christmas there a few years ago."

Tried to get my ring back.
"Did she re-marry?"
"Pilot, four kids."
"Four kids, wow."
"Yeah, well you know *dem* Irish setters."
"And she never considered taking—"
"Nah! He's *my* kid."
"I feel so bad for The Kid, no mother, lost his grandma. He was crying so hard at the service."
"Well, you know he and Bina were… close…"
And as it's coming out of his mouth…
"What's that supposed to mean?"
I'm fucked.
"That I'm *not*? That I wasn't close with Mom?"
Definitely fucked.
"Maya, I—"
"I loved her!"
"I didn't mean—"
"**Loved** her!"
"Maddy—"
"As much as she loved me!"
"Maddy—"
"**More** than she loved me!"
"Maddy, I—"
"Maddy?!"
"I mean, Maya."
"What do you mean, Eddie? What *do* you mean?!"
Oh man! Is he really getting into this mud pile with Maya over Bina? He shoulda known. Don't ever get between a mother and a daughter. Before they kill each other, they'll kill *you*.
"Sis, we have a nice quiet funeral."
"Nice?"
"Let's not spoil it."
"Spoil a funeral?!"
"Let's not do 'Friday Night Fights.' I'm not Sol and you're not Bina."
"Then don't treat me like her!"

"What did I say?"

"I know, Eddie. You're such a good son. Fuck you! What did you ever do for her?!"

Now she's totally off her rocker. Maya never curses. It's amazing what a mother can do to a daughter who in every other part of her life is as normal as normal can be. But bring in Mommy Dearest and it's "Cuckoo's Nest" all over again. Even when they're no longer around, mothers can be difficult.

Maya's seething. They're standing at the grave. Family, friends, Steadies, all looking their way, especially Steadies: hovering hounds, smelling an eruption, begin frothing, white spittle collecting on their spotted ties. Who could have guessed it? Max 'n' Eddie? Maya 'n' Max? No! It's Eddie 'n' Maya! Brother and Sister! Bring It On!

LADIES AND GENTLE-MEEEEEEEEHNN!
FOR OUR MAIN EVENT!
RIGHT HERE AT BETH DAVID CEMETERY!
TWO ROOO-SKEEES FROM TASHKENT!
FIGHTING OVER A COMMON ENEMY!
LET'S GET READY TO RUUUUUM-BUUUUUULL....

In the right corner, wearing black, weighing 170 pounds, formally Aryeh Pyatiegorskia, now Eddie Parker, impersonating a human being, just barely getting by, by the skin of his teeth, rejecting his past, present, *and* future! his family, friends, *and* parents, a good son who didn't do enough while they were alive, and even less so now— he *used* to be the favorite— let's hear it for:

EDDIE "THE BAD SON " PAAAAAAR-KEEEEHRRR!

And in the left corner, all the way from Toronto, leaving husband, children, and in-laws on Yom Kippur, wearing a gorgeous teal sarong, bright red lipstick accenting her high cheekbones and Eskimo lips, weighing in at an undisclosed amount, she is here to do damage. Yes, Ladies and Gentlemen, this warrior, this *balaboosta*, primed, in the best shape of her life, but feeling dissed and un-a-ppreee-ciated, a condition passed on *by* her mother, who did everything and got nothing, a real *farbissener*, Maya's here to make Eddie pay for not caring enough. Let's hear it for:

MAYA "THE GOOOD DAUGHTER" SHLOOOOOSSSS-BEEEEERRGGG!

Sibling rivalry is the ultimate contact sport. Nothing beats it. Not Fathers versus Sons or Mothers versus Daughters... umm... maybe In-laws versus In-laws. But Brother versus Sister over parents is the best, the purest. So much to fight about, a blame game bonanza. Attack one, the other, then switch. It's endless, pointless, a match made in heaven, winner takes none. The best fights are about where to put the parents no one wants when they get old and sick. Not quite ready to die, but not letting anyone else live.

It's strange, being at a parent's funeral. The strangeness most sharply felt by siblings brought together in this non-galvanizing event. Whereas in life we go our own separate ways, in death we become one. Death binds us, demanding unanimity of good, positive feelings for the deceased, grateful for all the hard work and sacrifices, blah, blah, blah. After all, being raised in the same home, same parents, shouldn't all children feel the same?

In the death of a parent, all differences must be put aside; all that happened and mattered no longer matters. In one voice, all children must love, grieve, and suffer equally, and *most* importantly, say nothing bad, so that if the deceased happens to be listening, they won't recognize themselves. Just say, "They were great!" Let Dr. Death smooth out all the wrinkles, pay homage, line up all the little fucked-up duckies in a row.

Golishoff's vultures are caucusing. They were only going to stay for the funeral (as if they had some place else to go), but now they're glad they came to the cemetery for family feud at Beth "something or other." This could be good. All the ingredients are there: a pit, shovel, dirt, relatives.

Maybe she'll hit 'em over the head with the shovel? Maybe he'll push her into the grave.

"Oh God!"

"What's wrong, Sis?"

"Open the box!"

"What?!"

"I promised Mom she would have socks on her feet when she was buried."

Maya specialized in socks and shawls.

"I have to make sure they put them on."

"Are you nuts?!"

"She won't rest if her feet are cold."

"The worms won't bother her?"

"Tell them to open the box!"

"Maya, she's dead. You don't have to listen to her anymore."

"Yes, I do!"

"Maya, they're lowering the box."

"Make them stop!"

"Gimme a fifty!"

"What?"

"Just give it to me!"

And, as the casket's being lowered, Eddie shouts, **"STOP!"**

It occurs to him it's what he should have done at his wedding.

"I'm sorry, folks, but Bina asked that her feet be warm."

Eddie slips the Maitre d'Gravedigger the fifty.

"Open the box."

They pull it out, open it, but on the wrong end, so that wasn't pretty; they turn it around, but that wasn't pretty either.

"I knew it, Eddie! They didn't do it!"

She pulls a pair of red socks from her pocketbook.

"Red?"

"Her favorite color."

Maya puts them on to the shock of the horrified group standing around. Eddie squeezes Bina's toe.

"Cold."

"Told you."

"You should have them take something off the bill. Good thing you checked."

The Rabbi's incensed. He slams the Siddur shut, throws the shovel, turns to leave, and falls into the grave. He yells for help but pulls others in with him. The gravediggers come to the rescue with a hoe, pulling everyone out, when they could have easily buried the Rabbi and the mourners, proving once again that tipping is a good idea.

Final topic.
"He's sick, Eddie."
This is the longest day.
"Would you see him?"
"Maya, I haven't seen or spoken to him in over twenty years. I don't even know where he is."
"Israel."
"Of course. The unholy man goes to the Holy Land."
"Will you go?"
"What's wrong with him?"
"Emphysema."
Eddie takes out a smoke. Maya tosses it out the window.
"Go see him, I'll pay."
"No, thank you."
"Eddie, he's gonna die and you won't have a chance to-"
"What?"
"Make peace."
"You gotta be kidding! Still playing peacemaker?"
"Eddie, I don't want to see happen to you what I did to myself. I cut myself off. I'm very sorry I did that. I could have... should have worked at it."
"She cut *you* off! Get your geography straight."
"She was hurt. I have two girls and can only now imagine if they did the same thing to me... and who cares who did what initially. It doesn't matter... cause now there's nothing to work out with anybody."
"Who are you saving, Sis? Not me, cause I made my peace a long time ago."
"Eddie, you have no idea how badly he feels."
"Oh, *he* feels bad?"
"He loves you. He's your father."
"Well, I'm his son. And I don't love him. And what's he got to feel bad about? Beating me, wrecking our family? Leaving a sick wife and two kids?"
"He was sick from what he went through."
"Was *everyone* sick?"
"No, but—"

"Was he sick twenty-four hours a day?! Was he the only one who went through what *he* went through?!"

"I can understand how you feel."

"I don't want my feelings understood! I want them left alone. Don't do a head trip on me, okay?! I'm fine!"

"Yeah, you're just great. We're all great."

"I didn't say 'great,' I said 'fine.'"

"No one's fine, Eddie! No one who's been through the fire is fine! Not the first generation, not the second!"

"Oh man! Holocaust conversations. Hate 'em."

"It's a stupid life, Eddie, the whole thing—to be so split, so fractured, after all we've been through... I think I'm in a good place. Everything I ever wanted, I have. The things I dreamed about as a little girl, the things you told me—that everything would be all right, and it is... and it isn't...was it all for nothing? The struggles, the hardships....?"

He takes a locket from his pocket.

On her sixty-fifth birthday, Bina looked eighty. All the years took their toll. She was tired, depressed, obese, and sinking. Maya had just settled in Toronto, thinking she was finally free. Eddie asked her to come in and arrange a surprise birthday party. Maya took off from work and came in for the week.

As these things go, the idea is always better than the reality. They should be left as ideas. It was the slowest week of Maya's life, and she knew she made a mistake the minute after they hugged and kissed. The first few hours were fine, but the rest of the week was miserable. It rained all week, and all Maya did was watch the clock, so that by the end of the week, Maya was a worn out *shmatta*, listening to the same stories, the same questions.

"*Vat's* new...? You miss me...? Do I look *fet*?"

Maya cleaned the apartment, manicured Bina's nails, washed her hair, gave her teeth a good scrubbing, did her laundry, cooked, cleaned, and watched the soaps next to a snoring Bina. It's like she never left home.

For her birthday, Maya bought Bina a beautiful gold locket. She ordered an extra link for the long gold chain to fit around Bina's tree-trunk neck. At the party, Queen Bee was all dentured smiles sitting front and center, gold locket around her neck, a large piece of strawberry shortcake stuffed in her mouth. Maya laughed, fed Bina cake, and after all the presents were opened, it was "open locket time," saving the best for last.

"Open it, Mom."

Bina opened the locket showing a picture of Eddie and Maya with the inscription: "From your loving and devoted children."

Bina read: "*Vit* Love from Eddie."

***

Eddie opens the clasp. Maya presses the spring and the locket pops open, inscribed: "To Mom, with love and devotion, Maya."

"Where's your name?"

He shrugs, she laughs.

"If she were here, she'd still read your name, Eddie."

"Let it go, Sis."

"I'm trying... we both have to try."

"I never pushed you to make peace with Mom."

"You should have."

"Why?"

"Would have shown you cared. If you don't mind, I'm gonna skip Deli with Max. I want to catch an earlier flight home."

"Sure."

She doesn't really want to leave and gives him the strongest, most loving hug, piss stains, bad breath, 'n'all.

"What a life we had with them, Mom 'n' Pop."

"Some life."

"It's like they were our kids and we raised them."

"I don't know if we did such a good job, Sis."

"They did the best they could, they—"

"Sis?"

"Yes?"

"I can't see Pop."

***

"GET UP, YOU BUM!"
"MOM?"
Eddie's startled out of his sleep and covers his head. He breaks out in a cold sweat. It's three A.M. He dials Tracy. Eddie found the number on a slip stuck to a condom in The Kid's wallet. A worried voice answers, "Hello...?" Eddie hangs up and The Kid walks in.

"You know what time it is?"

Silence.

"You know, your grandmother's funeral was today. You think you could have stayed with me for a change, instead of her?"

"You went to the track!"

"Don't give me any lip!"

Kid rolls his eyes.

"And don't roll your eyes!'

Kid gets a disgusted look on his face.

"And wipe that smile off your face!"

"LEAVE ME ALONE!"

"Hey, hey, I was worried!"

"Well, I'm home. Okay?!"

"Okay, okay, settle down."

"Night."

"Wait, wait, what else is doin'?"

"Nothing."

"What did Max have? Corn beef, pastrami, roast beef, tongue—"

"Dad, I'm exhausted."

"We never talk."

"I need sleep, big game tomorrow."

"By the way, you spoke beautifully today, everybody loved it."

"I—"

"You made me very proud."

"Dad, I—"

" I don't mind. In a pinch, we use what we can, right?"

"I tried writing it and then I saw your notes in the trash."

"Don't worry about it, it sounded better comin' from you."

The Kid goes to open the Castro.
"Let me."
"I can do it."
"Sit, rest, you had a hard day."
Eddie hobbles around the bed, putting on the bedding.
"Dad, I can do this."
"No, no, it makes me feel good to do something for you. Open the fridge. I got us a little something."
Kid opens the fridge and breaks out in a huge smile. "TWINKEEEES!"
"Cold! Just like you like it. Bring the milk!"
So they're munching away, moaning, gobbling up the Twinkies, licking the chocolate off their fingers.
"Good, huh?"
"Oh, man! Thanks, Dad."
"Best late night snack in the world!"
"Thanks, Dad."
"You got it. My pleasure...so...eh...how's Tracy?"
"She's good, she's good."
"Sweet girl. A keeper."
"Thanks, Dad."
"How's her home? What do the parents do?"
"Her Mom's divorced. Nice lady. I like her."
"She on welfare?"
"No! She's a... she's in sales, computer sales."
"So she does well."
"Well enough. Pays the bills."
"You know, Kid, when you get signed and go off to North Carolina, you won't be able to see Tracy all that much."
"We'll make it work."
"It's good to make things work, but—"
"Dad, I'm really tired. Thanks for the treat."
"Come here, give me a hug."
Last time they hugged for anything other than a game-winning shot was when The Kid was a kid. Then Eddie used to *shmushkee* him all over. But it stopped.
"Night, Dad."
Kid slides under the sheet.

Eddie sits in the dark on the edge of the sofa bed .
"You know they almost killed me."
"Dad, please–" Kid puts his head under the pillow.
"I'm not asking–"
"No!"
"Have I said anything yet?"
"No, but –"
"You don't even know what I'm gonna say!"

Kid sits up abruptly. Eddie turns on the light and gives him the letter. Kid reads it and gives it back.

"You're not excited."
"No, it's great."
"It's what we worked for."
"Dad, I really need to sleep."
"Kid?"

The Kid sits up in bed. "Yes?"
"Like I said, they almost killed me. Know why?"
"You missed the point spread?"

He smacks The Kid across the face. The Kid swallows hard to keep from crying. Eddie looks for a belt, but he's wearing drawstring pajamas.

"They took the bat to me 'cause I refused to let them use you! I told 'em, 'Enough! It's over! You're not using my kid anymore! Even if you have to kill me!'"

Eddie sees the white imprint of his fingers come out against the reddening skin.

There are no words to describe the sensation of instant anger. It just breaks. Whatever it is, it breaks, from where, who knows, location's unclear. Does it start in the head, stomach, nuts, toes, 'tween the toes, ass, up the back, chest, neck, face, head, back down the shoulders, arms, palms, fingers—WHACK!

No one ever forgets their first whack. All whacks thereafter are simply commentary.

A good whack delivered by a stranger has a different feel than one delivered by a loved one, or not-so-loved one, say a close family member, say a parent. Whereas the "stranger whack" is an isolated event, the "love whack" is chock full of surprises. The forces breaking *that* wave are so much richer and deeper, the violation filled with so much more meaning, purpose, and history. The "love whack" is delivered with "it hurts *me* more than it hurts you," or "better *you* should cry than me." Things like that.

The "love whack" comes with guilt, love, disgust, and confusion, as mirrored in the eyes of the stricken child. It's a hell of a sight to behold: eyes widen, jaw drops, ears perk up. WHACK!

Pay attention, you're getting the shit beat outta you.
"Dad?"
"Yes?"
"Why did you signal me to go down last game?"
"Cause you don't bury a weak team."
"But if they're really bad?"
"Beat 'em by ten, fifteen, doesn't have to be twenty."
"Yes, Dad."
"Pros don't do it. Only small timers pile it on."
"Yes, Dad."
"Beat 'em, don't bury 'em."
"Night, Dad."
"Kid?"
"Yes...?"
"Just this one...last time..."

Chapter Twelve

The High School City Championships are held every year at Madison Square Garden on 48th Street. It's a treat for the kids 'cause the Garden's big time. Home of the Championship New York Knicks, Earl "The Pearl," "Clyde," "Dollar Bill," Dave, Willis — Wow! To be on the same hardwood as their heroes. Electric.

The Garden holds eighteen thousand and they're hangin' from the rafters. Every friend and relative of every eligible team is there. Toughest ticket in the city to get, and the action's intense. Scalpers are makin' out. The Garden promoters are smart, slotting the High School Playoffs right after the Knicks' season, before Ringley, Barnum & Bailey move their elephants in.

Seward moves up the ladder easily, eliminating their first three opponents by twenty and twenty-five points. The Kid's unstoppable and Coach Gordon makes sure to give Eddie a big wave after each lopsided win. The North Carolina scouts prepare the paperwork for a nice ten grand signing bonus (under the table), a car (under the table), women (under the table), plus a four-year scholarship, classes optional (above the table).

Eddie turns the ten over to Ollie as a deposit for the balance of the thirty, insuring his legs and head. Kitzee's ten he keeps to bet against The Kid in the Finals where he'll clean up, pay everyone off, then quit the game. Quit gambling. That's what he promised himself, a promise he made before, but this time it's for real. The "love whack" really shook him up.

I'm not Sol.

Seward's opponent in the final is Boys' High, winners of the past three years, heavy favorites. Boys' High has unbelievable talent, plus they're hungry and poor, an unfair advantage.

The Kid starts out cold. It's the pressure of knowing everyone's there. It's not the first time friends and relatives spoiled a great athlete's debut. That's because these are the very same people who didn't believe in you in the first place.

"Eh, he's just a local talent."

But when you prove them all wrong, you can stand up and say:

"I'd like to thank all those people who didn't believe in me..."

Ninety-nine percent of all success stories start right there.

So now they're all here: Eddie, Tracy, her mom, Pete, Chaalie, Ollie, Dufus Entourage, Max, Steadies, Harry's hanging ass, Adi and his son, Dennis one-eye, brother Boyles, *Fay-Looks*, Natushka, Prince, Piss-pant Principal, Second Chance Diner Support Hose Waitress, Rabbi Horwitz, Kitzee, Paul Headbanger, Pulkie, Hy and Eddie with *Yoynee* Smith Shmuckler's Village People dispensing raisin bagels. It was an event. The *gantze mishpoche* was there! What a crew! They all came out to see The Kid lead Seward to an upset victory over Boys' High in the Championship game.

Boys' High jumps to a half-time lead of twelve. Coach Gordon reams the shit out of the kids so loud you hear it in the stands.

The Kid comes out blazing in the third quarter, turning it around from a twelve-point deficit to a twelve-point lead, then fifteen, then twenty against the heavy favorites. Boys' High's falling apart, crowd's going wild, and Eddie is stabbing himself in the eye with the rolled up program.

What's the best way to kill yourself?

He looks up in the rafters and sees Ollie eating three hot dogs and Chaalie waving a bat.

Boys' High's embarrassed. Coach calls time out. He speaks quietly, whispering in each player's ear. Eddie's impressed by how cool the guy is. Now *that's* coaching!

Boys' High comes out and immediately cheap shots The Kid when he steals the ball, his defender tackling him from behind as he's driving to the basket for an easy lay-up. Say hello to the third row. Benches clear, Gordon leading the charge with "Take No Shit!" Eddie stays put in the catbird seat. Gordon comes out of the scrap bloodied, glaring at Eddie. Eddie nods and calls out, **"My Apprentice!"** It's good, it's all good. In a million years, you'd never guess they hate each other.

The flagrant foul lights a fire under Boys' High's *toches* and stops Seward dead in its tracks. As hot as Seward was in the third quarter, that's how cold they are in the fourth. They can't buy a basket, while Boys' High goes on a scoring spree. For entertainment value, you can't beat it. A great game for the fans *and* Eddie. Eddie bet a mountain against The Kid. The Kid twisted his knee in practice, but told no one except Eddie. Eddie told Ollie and Ollie bet the bank.

"Don't push yourself, Kid."
"Okay, Dad."
"Soon as you feel pain – "
"Dad?"
"You showed enough, scouts are happy."
"Dad."
"Yeah?"
"What's the spread?"
"Eight."

Fourth quarter, Kid's hobbling, but refuses to come out. Coach won't take him out, that's for sure. He cares about The Kid as much as Eddie does. With The Kid in, Seward's got a chance; without him, forget it. Gordon's got a better chance impressing the scouts by coming in close, even if he loses.

Late in the fourth quarter, Seward starts coming back with a little help from their striped friends, moonlighting racists, who complain, "They make you feel like you're workin' for *them*." But if a game's on the line, refs march arm in arm with Dr. King.

Seward narrows the gap. It's getting close, too close. Boys' High strikes back.

Fuckin' game's an accordion.

Boys' High was supposed to blow them out. It's not happening, go-go-mo-mentum, put your seat belts on, *weze* goin' for a fuckin' ride! Upset by Seward? Uh-uh! Not on your life. Not on Eddie's life. He stands on a chair whipping a white surrender towel above his head. Ref calls a timeout for "no reason."

Is everyone corrupt?

Of course, that's silly. Refs too? Especially refs. No one's more important in fixing games than refs, not even players. *They* should be the ones recruited and awarded the Most Valuable. Refs make no money, get no attention, no respect, so they're jealous, which makes them reliable.

Most refs are guys who couldn't make it playing. Those who *can*, play; those who *can't*, ref.

It has to be frustrating for these striped also-rans running alongside greatness, so close and yet so far, a painful reminder of not being good enough. So these high-minded, backhanded, flying giraffes flap rules and regs, chew their whistles, blowing for attention, the way a little baby cries for its *bottee*. Sometimes refs will make a bad call just to *get* that attention, and sometimes, because the game is getting away from them.

A questionable call by the striped fairy stops Seward's momentum, trimming Boys' High's lead down to seven. Eddie bet eight. Eddie's yelling for coach to take The Kid out. **"He's hurt! He's hurt!"** The fans are screaming for Eddie to shut up. Eddie stands on the edge of Seward's bench waving the white dish towel. But the Kid keeps playing, limping, grimacing, holding his injured knee after each acrobatic shot. Fans are eating it up. Eddie's eating his elbows.

"TAKE HIM *OUT!* TAKE MY KID *OUT!* HE'S *HURT!*"

Gordon sneers.

"Take him out?! What are you nuts?! Kid's a hero!"

Crowd chants:

"KID'S A HERO! KID'S A HERO!"

The fans' take on heroism is interesting.

If you're writhing in pain on the floor, they want you to get up. Not only get up, but play; not only play, but come out swinging; not only come out swinging, but all charged up; not only charged up, but score; not only score, but score the winning point; not only score the winning point, but score in the last second; not only score in the last second, but make an impossible shot; not only make an impossible shot, but fall down; not only fall down, but writhe in pain; not only writhe in pain, but get up; not only get up, but limp; not only...

Ten seconds. Boys' High: 66. Seward: 57.

Eddie screams:

"TAKE HIM OOOOOOUT!"

He bet *both* ways. The only way he loses is by nine... or seven... or was it six... ten? He can't remember...

Eddie screams:

**"AAAAAAHHHHHHH!...I CAN'T REMEMBER!!...
FUUUUCK!! TAKE HIM OUT! LEAVE HIM IN!"**
Crowd's lookin' at him like he's nuts, yelling:
"SHUT THE FUCK UP!!"
He's ripping his pockets looking for the crib sheet, his black hair turning grey. Gordon's crisp seersucker is sucking air, the side show's better than the show! It's mayhem! It's crazy! It's for the fans! It's all about the fans. It's about Eddie! He runs over to Boys' High's bench.
"PILE IT ON! BURY 'EM! CRUCIFY THE FUCKS!"
Boys' High coach calls time out. Eddie screams:
"WHYYYYYYYYYYYYYYYYYYY?"
Coach kicks Eddie in the ass.
"Get the fuck outta here!"
Eddie runs back to Seward's bench.
"PILE IT ON! BURY THE FUCKS!"
In all the craziness, Eddie lost track of who the fuck bet what. He checks his crib sheet.
"It's eight! It's eight! Anything over eight!!"
Coach bet under. Eddie bet over. Ollie bet under. Kitzee went over. No one knows anything. But Gordon knows his one-legged Kid is better than any of his other two-legged toys. The Kid hardly feels the pinch of the novocaine needle under the towel.

Ten seconds to go. Crowd's on its feet. Boys' High's up by nine. Eddie's frothing.

Seward takes the ball out at mid-court. Kid's surrounded by a swarming beehive of five.

10...9...8...

Eddie screams at the clock, **"HURRY UP, YOU SLOW PIECE A SHIT!"**

7...6...5...

Pass goes to The Kid. Uh-oh... Kid's eyeing the basket.
"NO! NO! PLEASE, NO!"
4...3...2...
Takes a bead...
"NO, GOD, NO!"
Lines it up...

"DON'T!"
Measures...
"PLEEEZE DOOOON'T!"
Get ready...get set...
"DON'T SHOOOOOOOOOOOOT."
Where's Chaalie's elbow?
"CHAAALIEEEEEEEEEEEEEEEEEE!"

Kid vaults, a white knight ascending out of darkness, a trajectory straight up. No white kid ever jumped that high, or stayed up that long. Certainly no Jewish kid, because it's a well-known fact that Jews don't jump. Ask any schoolyard jock. A "Jewish jump shot" will never see the light of day. No peek under the sneak for the weak. Jews must stay grounded in case any Cossacks show up for a quick pick-up game.

"UP...UP...AND...
AAAA-WAAAAAAAAAAA-YYYYYYY..."

The Kid pirouettes in mid-air from mid-court, releasing the ball in a high arc toward the basket. On this one move, The Kid could easily go one-on-one with Baryshnikov. With each backward spin of the ball, Eddie sees his life fly by, a series of rotations ending his life.

HE MADE IT! HE MADE IT! THE KID MADE IT!
HE FUCKED HIS DAD!

The Kid goes down, taking Eddie with him. No rim, no net, no bet, no spread, swish. Boys' High by seven. Eddie sees Ollie 'n' Chaalie comin' for him with the bat. It's vamoose! Eddie's loose!

Gimping for his life, Eddie spears his way through the crowd along Eighth Avenue, pitch-forking pedestrians with his crutches, knocking down an old lady for her cab. She fights him off, whacking his head with her Macy's purchase, a toaster. The crowd cheers. He jumps into the front seat of a police car, throws the crutches in the back.

"STANTON 'N' ORCHARD. HIT IT. MY MOM'S DYING!"

Escorted by two police cars, a fire truck, and an ambulance, sirens blaring, he gets there in no time flat. Sirens at night usually mean the bars are closing.

Eddie tips the cops, firemen, EMTs, and they vanish. He lifts the gate, unlocks the door, grabs a stale danish and hops downstairs to the basement, wedging himself between cardboard boxes, settling in for the night with a bottle of scotch. The whole city's looking for him. With that comforting thought, Eddie falls asleep, familiar feet scampering across his chest, a rat's reunion.

One night, as Max is closing, he hears a rustle. He goes down to the basement with rat poison and cheese. Eddie's curled in a corner, eating Muenster.

"I was wondering where all the cheese was going."

"No jokes, Max, this isn't funny!"

"You're telling *me?* Do you know how many bent noses come here looking for you?"

"Jesus Christ! What am I gonna do?"

"*Now* you ask me?! First you fuck up your life and *now* you ask me?!"

"Fuckin' Ollie."

"Fuckin' Ollie. Fuckin' D.A. Fuckin' F.B.I."

"What?!"

"It's in all the papers. They're going after the Mob for High School fixing."

"Holy shit!"

"They've had undercover cops for over a year."

"I'm dead."

"I told you! I warned you, didn't I?"

"What can I tell you, Max? You're a prophet!"

"Everybody gets theirs, Eddie. You're not always around to see it, but trust me, everybody gets theirs!"

"Believe how The Kid fucked me?"

"*He* fucked *you*?"

"Did you see that last shot?"

"Who didn't?"

"He buried me with that shot."

"Buried *himself*! Broke his knee."

"Broke his knee?!"

"Poor kid. No college, no scholarship, no nothing! And it's all *your* fault! You took a good boy and poisoned him, you *Momzer*! Now you can take that letter and wipe yourself!

Good thing your mother's not around to see this."
"Yeah, Max. That's the *one* good thing."
"What happened to you, Eddie? You used to be a nice boy."
"Shut up!"
"Just because your father left, you turn into a hoodlum?"
"Max! I don't need a lecture, I need help."
"You want a cheese sandwich?"
Eddie throws the Muenster in his face.
"I'm not fucking around Max!"
Max peels the cheese off his face
"Do what *Boytschick* did."
"What?"
"Cooperate. With the authorities. Turns out *Boytschick's shikse* girlfriend, her mother works for the D.A. Maybe you can work something out."

Eddie gets a stabbing pain between his shoulders.

No more points, Dad, no more spreads... I just want to play the game.

"Kid was wearin' a wire..."
"I don't know."
"You don't know..."
"No..."
"So how did they all know to be at the game?"
"Who?"
"Cops, undercover, D.A., F.B.I?"
"I don't know."
"You don't know a lot, do you, Max?"
"What can I tell you?"
"Tell me about Bina."
"I'll tell you about your father."

CHAPTER THIRTEEN

Eddie grows a long black beard, wears thick glasses, *tzitzes, fringes,* a long black coat, black shoes, black hat, white socks, and moves into the Hassidic community of Crown Heights in Brooklyn, a mixed enclave of ghettos and *shtetles*, Jews and Blacks, aware but indifferent to one another until the summer heat arrives. Then a Hassid gets knifed, Blacks get attacked, and the two are at war.

Max's friend, Adi the baker, a prominent member of the Hassidic community, arranges for Eddie to enter a Yeshiva, with Max paying the room and board. Eddie's only responsibility is to study and teach Torah. Adi passes Eddie off as a Russian Refusenik, recently released from prison for practicing his religion. The fact that Eddie speaks fluent Yiddish doesn't hurt. He used to speak fluent Russian as well, until Sol put a clamp on his mouth sneaking out of Russia. So *dasvidanya* to Russian, but Yiddish and English melded into *Yinglish*, and Eddie began to sound like Sol and Bina.

Eddie was welcomed into the Hassidic community with open arms and became something of a celebrity. Eddie joked he was "The Messiah." Some zealots took him seriously. That's what zealots do, take con men seriously. And there are no bigger cons than Russians, the most convincing people on Earth. So a match was made between Eddie, bullshit, and the Hassids.

Adi agreed to help Max with the ruse on the condition that once the heat died down, Eddie would make *Aliyah* and settle in Israel.

"Israel needs Jews, Max. Young Jews, not *alte kakers* like us."

"You're a real Zionist, Adi. One Jew who helps a *second* Jew send a *third* Jew to Israel."

The Hassids love Eddie. He jokes and sings, studies Torah, and drinks *schnapps*. He teaches classes in Yiddish on ethics and morality. Adi tutors him, legitimizing Eddie's claim as a bona fide scholar, tracing his ancestry to the Bal Shem Tov, "He Of The Good Name," the founder of the Hassidic movement in

THE FIX

Poland in the eighteenth century.

The Yeshiva smells like the eighteenth century. When he comes in from the outside, Eddie feels like a urine-soaked towel was flung in his face. He sits in the back on hard wooden benches, leafing through the Siddur, looking for Hy Shmuckler's bagel label. But these Siddurs are old, cracked, and yellow, and aren't even necessary for the Hassids, who *daven* so fast it comes out as gibberish.

An expert in Yiddish gibberish, Eddie mumbles his way through, and within one month he's leading services. The Elders sing his praises.

"To be so young, so gifted, so learned!" They smack their lips, "aye, yay, yay ! Ha-Shem sent us manna from heaven."

Eddie takes on his Hebrew name "Aryeh" and is quickly called "Reb Aryeh, The Learned One."

He's dying for a joint and, lo and behold, some Hassids oblige. Eddie rolls reefers in the 'cracked' and 'yellow,' and Torah stops being a drag. He's high most of the time, which the Elders mistake for "mindfulness." The reefers gain him popularity with the youth, and, in no time at all, he becomes legendary for his scholarship, his camaraderie, his joints, and his mood swings, blaming his erratic behavior on the mental anguish suffered in the Gulag where he claimed to have studied with Anatol Sharansky, the famous Refusenick-nudnick who later found a gig as an Israeli Pol.

Although secular books are strictly forbidden in Yeshiva, exceptions are made for Eddie's constant companion, Solzhenitsin's *Gulag Archipelago*. A scholar, storyteller, and singer, he sings, "*Yiddishe Momme*" on Mother's Day and "*Rummania*" on Purim, a popular Yiddish ditty Eddie learned as a kid when he and Maya were taken to Yiddish theatre during the "good years."

Sol and Bina loved Yiddish music and sang the kids to sleep with their favorite Yiddish folk songs "*Oyfn pripitschock*," about young children huddled by a fireplace, and "*Rozhinkes Mit Mandlen*," where a young widowed mother rocks her baby to sleep with a lullaby, singing of raisins and almonds, sweet dreams...

They were good years.

Eddie's having a ball in Hassidland. The only thing missing in his life is a wife. The Elders lament, "It's a *rachmones*, a pity, a shame, that such a beautiful human being, a handsome young man, a righteous Jew, a marvelous Yid, has no wife."

And as learned and as accomplished as Reb Aryeh is, he cannot truly receive Ha-Shem's full blessings until he consummates, observing God's First Law: "Be fruitful and multiply." Eddie just wants a blow job.

But he's under the microscope. The entire community mobilizes into one matchmaking service, and after each Shabbat service, the "Pick of the Week" accompanies him for his midday *shpatzeer*, a stroll along Eastern Parkway, a broad, tree-lined boulevard , almost making you forget you're in Brooklyn.

After *Shabbes* services, Eddie walks slowly, head down, arms behind his back, pensive, thoughtful— a good look, the downward look, a close cousin of "The Refugee Look." He's mumbling tracts of Yiddish even *he* doesn't understand, but he looks good. Authentic.

The truth is, he looks down because he's afraid to look up and see who the Elders chose for him. Trailing behind him are a column of Jews, a block long, on "The Long March to Marriage." He stops. They stop. He bends to pick up a penny. An Elder taps him on the shoulder.

"*Ts, ts.*"
"What?"
"It's *Shabbes.*"
"So?"
"Can't touch money."
"I just want to see if it's heads or tails."
"No."
"But in the Gulag—"
"Not here."
He looks at the "chosen" one.
Umm, not great, but not bad.
He gives her the penny.
Shoulder-tapper asks, "She's the one?"
"It's the dowry."

She smiles, showing off a row of yellow *farfoylte* teeth. Eddie takes back his penny.

Although some girls from *meeskeit.com* are pretty, he can only have one. Not enough. Plus, who the hell knows what's hiding underneath those pleated skirts? They don't shave, so strip landings are out. Forests in, landings out. He knows, because he's bangin' a few horny *rebetzins* whose husbands are off swaying somewhere.

Adi watches Reb Aryeh do his *shtick* and decides he's having too much fun. He'll have to get Eddie to Israel quick before God strikes both of them down. He has a heart-to-heart and Eddie settles down. He stops *valggering* around and turns his attention to Torah. He has no choice. Afraid to leave the compound for fear of getting whacked, he spends his days holed up in a room ruminating over some obscure interpretations of *Halacha* (not challah) Jewish Civil and Religious Law. The exercise sharpens his mind and, given his oppositional nature, Eddie's conversion from bookie *meister* to bible master isn't too far a stretch. After all, splitting hairs over *Rashi* or races…*what's the difference?*

What started out as weird and crazy settles into a comfortable lifestyle. He enjoys the camaraderie with his pious pals, despite their offensive B.O. For relief, he smells his own pits.

Most of the Yeshiva students are young men in their twenties, in terrible shape, with no body tone. Their pale flesh hangs off them like boiled chicken, loose *flaysh* hanging from thin frames that barely support their scant weight. Hunched over, *tzekrochen*, they look like old men, bodies shaped into question marks, old before their time, these kids make time look old.

These are terminal students, supported by the community, thankful that 'God will provide,' a code for being on the dole. Eddie knows because he delivers monthly welfare checks to the Yeshiva office upstairs, answering to a higher authority. In their view, the *only* authority.

* * *

"Yes, Torah Teamsters, I would say *all* religions believe *their* God is the *best* God. But *I* say, *our* God... *IS*... The Best God!"

Yeshiva breaks out in manic applause.

"*Emes! Emes! Emes!*"

"You ask, *how* I know?"

"Yes? Yes? Yes?"

"The truth is I know *nothing*, but have opinions about *everything!*"

"*Emes! Emes! Emes!*"

Eddie knows that with Jews you always start off with a joke. It could be a comedy, tragedy, doesn't matter. Your child could drown, and you'd say:

"Did you hear about the boy who *thought* he could swim?"

"Yes, my Torah friends, *iiiif* I had to lay odds, *meeeaaaning*, make a bet on the best God, I would make the Jews God's favorite, three-to-one."

"Yes! Yes! Yes!"

"If only because we survive!"

"YES!"

"Now *Chevra*, there are three ways our Yid God beats their Goy God."

"*Yeeeeee-eehssss?*"

"First of all, *our* God lets our Rabbis do it."

"*Oy vey!*"

"You know what I mean by 'doing it'?"

They nod.

"Truly an act of kindness."

Pimple boys respond:

"*Ha-Shem's* the best! *Ha-Shem's* the best!"

"Of course, my friends, for Rabbis to 'do it,' they must first be married. *Nisht g'ferlach,* not so terrible."

"No."

"But what's with the hole in the sheet?"

"*Oy-vey!*"

"I say! No! No to the hole! Save the sheets!"

"*Ay-yay-yay!*"

"The only hole you should know iiiiiis..."

They cover their ears.

"*Oy-Oy-Oy!*"

"The *second* thing, my friends, is that with *our* God, there is no hell."

"No!"

"Yidden don't do hell! So what's there to be afraid of?"

"*Gornisht!*"

"The third and most important thing is that *our* God is not a *sitting* God."

"No!"

"Wherever *we* go, *He* goes! New York, Cairo, Galicia, Auschwitz!"

"*Oy a broch!*"

"We don't need no Mecca, Bethlehem, *or* Jerusalem. We take our God *with* us!"

"YES!"

"We are a portable people!"

"YES!"

"On the move!"

"YES!"

"A knock on the door, grab the kids, take the sheep, 'n' vamoose! Run, run like *meshugenehs*!"

"YES! YES! YES!"

"But wherever *we* run, *HE* runs, wherever we go, *HE* goes!"

"YES!!"

"He's there! For *us*! His favorites!"

"*Emes! Emes! Emes!*"

"Our *sonim*, our enemies, can destroy our cities, our towns, our *shtetles*, but they can't destroy US!"

"NEIN! NEIN! NEIN!"

Boys bang their tin cups on the table. The Yeshiva's in a frenzy. They form a circle and lift Eddie in a chair singing and dancing around him.

"*Simin-tov-un-mazel-tov-n', un-mazel-tov-n'-simin-tov...*"

"From the Halls of Montezuma to the shores of Tripoli! From the Warsaw ghetto to the lakes of Galilee! From the Spanish Inquisition to Moshe's Red Sea! From Crown Heights to Boro Park, to Brighton to Brooklyn! He's here! He's there!

He's **EVERYWHERE!**"

Eddie can't stop. All the years of Yiddish school, Hebrew school, Rabbi sermons, United Jewish appeals, Max's jokes, Sol's tips, Bina's quips, all come pouring out of him. He didn't know he had it in him. All this useless information, buried for so long. Sol told him years ago:

"*Vit* Yiddish, you can go *anyvere*!"

"Pop! I hate Yiddish!"

"*Von* day you'll *tenk* me!"

Pontificating in his native tongue proved Sol right. They never heard such thought-provoking cockamamie logic, and in *Yiddish*, improvising in *Yiddish*, itself a casualty of improvisation.

A mongrel language, where nothing you say is your own. Born in Poland, written in Hebrew, stamped in German, a *mishmaash tscholent* of influences stretching over dozens of countries, hundreds of years, borrowed, stolen, adapted, adopted, until it hit the Holy Land. Then, Israelis wanted nothing to do with it.

"Old, ugly, disgusting," they say. Disgusting but catchy. "*Shmear* the bagel" and you're speaking Yiddish. "*Shmuck*" 'n' "*oy*" makes you fluent.

Heavy-duty Yiddish, that is, arguing, bargaining, praying, especially praying, requires "*shockling*," bending and rocking from the waist up, a dip of the knee, a simple choreography Jerome Robbins rejected.

Italians use their hands, Chinese their eyes, French their noses; Hassids *shockle*.

Eddie's a good *shockler*, which sets off a *shockle* circle jerk, and the stronger the argument, the quicker the *shockle*. Eddie's got it down. He can mimic a monkey. Using his entire body, he forms huge sweeping arcs with his accusatory finger, in and out of the argument, gesticulating wildly, the Yiddish evangelical *shockles* his ass off.

He's exhausted. The Hassidic life is getting to him. All that *shockling*, the studies, the prayers, the hours are just too long. It starts with morning *davening* and ends at night under fluorescents. He was never a morning person to begin with. Morning to Eddie was coming home from an all-night card game.

The Fix

Eddie's convinced all religions start their *shtick* early because it's when you're least conscious. And as bad as the week is, *Shabbes* is the worst. A "day of rest" it is not.

Shabbes dawn, Yeshiva awakes clapping, dancing, singing *nigunim*, lyric-less songs for old men with bad memories, picked up by *young* men who don't know *what* they're singing. The Hassids sing, dance, shower, and dress in clean, white, fresh underwear. For Eddie, it's getting ready for the electric chair. The demands of *Shabbes* far exceed what Eddie can tolerate, which is very little to begin with. Short on patience, long on action, Eddie needs more. *Shabbes* is just too draining, too long, too... spiritual.

He could have stayed back, feigning illness, but then he won't see the light of day or breathe fresh air for a week. Walking alongside hundreds of look-alikes mumbling, "*Gut Shabbes, gut Shabbes*," Eddie's become one of those long-necked, bug-eyed Hassids he passed on the way to the *shvitz* not too long ago.

On occasion, he'd pass a wise guy looking straight at him. Eddie looks right back. Underneath the black garb, thick glasses, and dark beard, his own mother wouldn't recognize him.

Eddie searches his memory if he ever met the passing goon.

No problem, he felt safe. Forever, if he wanted. He could live out his life as a Hassid and no one would know the difference. No one would care. And slowly he realizes that he means nothing to no one, that the meaning you have in your life is yours and yours alone, that the outside world is there for you to live in, and it doesn't matter to anyone but yourself.

Once a month, a *Shabbes* "*Farbrengin*," a Gathering, is held for the community to hear their leader, Rabbi Menachem Schneerson, speak from on "Mountain High," a circular hall attached to *Rebbe's* row house.

Old frail men in long white beards sit in a pit behind a long wooden table in a Coliseum absent Christians, lions, fools, and kings. Just Jews, a thousand in the round, locking arms, swaying in joyous delirium, sucking up *Rebbe's* every word.

Rebbe speaks in Yiddish sound bites, breaking every half hour for rounds of *schnapps* as a thousand men in black rise, holding out paper cups to toast their beloved *Rebbe* Schneerson who zeroes in on every disciple, gives a look, a nod, then down the hatch, breaking out in song, a full buzz on, reminiscent of a good German beer hall.

The voluntary confinement lasts until late afternoon when Hassids full of *schnapps* stagger out of the Coliseum onto the Main Sanctuary for a few *more* hours of prayer.

I can't take it!

Eddie's back is out, has a splitting headache, and is nauseous. *Shabbes* ends with a light meal of challah, herring, boiled chicken, potatoes, and contemplation of suicide.

Maybe getting whacked wouldn't be so bad.

Eddie's done. It's been a year and the fear of being found has long since passed. But now he finds himself in a world he can't understand, can't accept, can't live in. Once again he's adapted, and once again he has trouble knowing who he is. It doesn't matter that he's a Jew, or that the world he's in is Jewish. He's as cut off from them as the rest of the world.

The Yeshiva notices the change. They take him to see *Rebbe*. Every Thursday morning hundreds line up outside Schneerson's home and wait for hours seeking *Rebbe's* blessing and guidance. *Rebbe's* a small, pleasant man with piercing light blue eyes who listens intently, speaks sparingly, and quickly nails down the essence of the problem and the solution. Eddie doesn't have to go. He knows his essence.

I'm a fraud.

Chapter Fourteen

"You *aah* Jew?"

I can't escape!

Sleeping in the plane, Eddie wakes to another Hassid in his face.

As quickly as Eddie appeared on the Hassidic scene, that's how quickly he dropped out. One day he's in Brooklyn, the next he's on El-Al, clean-shaven, wrap-around shades, jeans, T-shirt, and a Yankee cap pulled down over his eyes, catching Z's.

"*Bist* a *Yid*? You *aah* Jew?" The Hassid asks.

Eddie's had four scotches and three sleeping pills. He drools back:

"Wha...?"

"I have *t'fillin, vant* to pray?"

"I'll have another scotch."

"Ha-Shem will bless you."

"*Shmuck*, do me a favor, get lost. And if you don't understand English, *tee mir a toyve, gey-a-vek!* Go away!"

"*Oy, ver* you *loyn* such *gut* Yiddish?"

"Catholic school."

Eddie crosses himself and the Hassid evaporates. A woman laughs. Eddie turns to a slim blonde at the window seat.

Trip just got shorter.

He thought he was in for a torturous fifteen-hour trek squished between the old pudge on his left and the "looker" on his right.

"Hi," he says.

"Hi," she says.

"Hi," she says, extending a pudgy hand.

Eddie turns towards the hot chick, reminding him of Cheryl Tiegs.

Cheryl Tiegs "light."

Straight blond hair, blue eyes, alabaster skin, small tits. Eddie's looking for her tits. Every man looks for tits. Some are easier to find than others. It shouldn't be hard to find Tiegs's tits.

She's not wearing a bra under her white linen blouse, fronting for lack of mound, open to the third button.

Why do titless women go unbuttoned to the third? Do guys with small dicks leave their flies open? What's the attraction?

Nipple.

Ah! Eddie's a nipple man. As long as the nipple is attached to the tit, the rest of the tit can take a vacation. It's the nipple that turns him on. It's why he loves women who come in from the cold.

As he's talking to "Cheryl" he's leaning into her, resembling an ostrich about to end up in her A cup. He gives up the safari.

"That was funny."

What? Not having tits?

"The Catholic line really spooked him."

"Yeah, it's how you get *wondering* Jews to stop *wandering*. You cross yourself—it's better than roach spray."

She cracks up. Eddie sees a twinkle in her eye. Or it may be nothing. He's quite horny, so he can make anything into something.

"How did he know you were Jewish?"

"C'mon, lady. I mean walkin' up 'n' down the aisle of a packed El-Al plane..."

"He didn't ask *me*."

"They don't speak to women, especially... pretty women."

"Oh?"

"But *I* do."

"Oh."

"You're not Jewish?"

"No."

"I didn't think so."

"What makes you say that?"

"I don't know. You're blonde, beautiful, blue eyes, straight teeth, you're not eating..."

"I'm Roman Catholic."

"I'm a fan of Roman Catholics."

"Really."

"Some of my best friends..."

He's not sure if that was funny or stupid. But he's got a good face, a handsome face. If he says something stupid, his face will save him. Handsome guys, like pretty girls, get a pass on stupidity. Unattractive people get a pass on nothing.

"Goin' to Rome?"

"This is a direct flight to Tel Aviv."

"Right... right... you pronounced Tel Aviv really well."

"I speak Hebrew."

"Impressive."

"Non-Jews *do* go to Israel."

"Why?"

"It's a beautiful country."

"That's what I hear."

"You've never been?"

"No, you?"

"Many times."

"What do you do?"

"Archeologist."

What do you say to an archeologist you want to bang?

"Interesting."

"What is?"

"Uh... looking for things?"

"They're only rocks, stones."

"Yeah, but stones in a pretty woman's hands."

Another Neanderthal line. He's rusty.

"Uh... I meant—"

She smiles. He smiles. He's a sap for a pretty face. She could weigh a ton downstairs, but a pretty face –ummm! He's eating her face.

She licks her lips.

He licks his lips.

Her lips protrude.

His lips protrude.

She applies chapstick.

A sign?

He imagines kissing her cracked lip, licking the blood, her lip moist, saving her from chafed lips.

"You have beautiful lips."

"Why... thank you."

I want to save them.

He hasn't had a "come on" conversation in years. He usually pays for it. But this is different. This is an intelligent woman. He loves fucking intelligent women. You get two for one: a fuck 'n' a critique.

"What do *you* do?"

"Oh, different things."

"Like?"

"I try to stay away from people."

"Why?"

"They're bad for you."

She laughs. Make a woman laugh and you're halfway home.

"I'm kind of a private person myself." She extends her hand. "Fran."

"Eddie."

Eddie expects a calloused hand, but it's soft, warm, and ivory, no veins; he likes that. A woman with low blood pressure.

"Eddie from?"

"Brooklyn. Fran?"

"From Minnesota."

"Nice."

"Minneapolis, St. Paul."

"Lakers played there."

"I don't follow sports."

"Neither do I."

"What brings you to Israel?"

"Family."

Eddie's skin is tingling. It's his psoriasis kicking in. He claws at the flesh under his socks, releasing snowflakes.

"Are you okay?"

"Air's dry."

"I have some lotion."

She takes out a small tube from her bag and squirts some into his palms, excreting a tiny fart. They laugh. He almost comes. He bends down, pulls his socks down and rubs the lotion onto his legs. If *she* did it, he'd definitely come.

"Feels good, Fran."

"Nivea."

He's pulling chunks of flesh from his legs.

And as long as I'm down there, might as well do some beaver shooting.

She crosses her legs and almost scissors his nose.

"I took Earth Science once."

"That's nice."

She straightens her skirt with a wiggle or two.

Wow! Look at this shikse!

Shikse! Just the word gets him hot. What a great word! *Shikse!* Saying "I'm fucking a *Shikse*!" will set Jewish men on fire. That's because they're forbidden. Didn't God warn Adam: **"Don't touch that *Shikse*!"**

Shikses will let you do things Jewish women would never. "Disgusting!" is what Jewish women would say. *Shikses* find nothing disgusting. That's why they make such great nurses.

Shikses — tall, blond, striking *shikses* from Norway beat short brunettes from Poland any day. Eddie would go so far as to say that bad sex with a *shikse* beats best sex with a Jew. *Emes*.

Eddie looks at her teeth. Perfect, white, even, big smile. Her smile's connected to his dick.

"You'll excuse me, Fran, but I'm not feelin' great."

"I have Tylenol."

Anything for a boner?

He goes to the bathroom and jerks off standing up. Holding on to the handle bar, he aims for the bowl, but the plane hits an air pocket and he comes all over himself, the cabin, the wall, the mirror, the floor. A loose fire extinguisher couldn't do a better job. It takes him an hour to clean up. When he gets out, ten people are waiting in line, wanting to kill him.

"Are you okay, Eddie?"

"Air pockets."

"Yes, it was quite turbulent."

"Not your fault."

"You look pale."

"I don't have any make-up on."

"Would you like some bottled water?"

"Bottled, yeah, anything bottled."

"You look dehydrated."
Just came.
"Spent."
"Spent?"
When sex is involved everything said takes on a new meaning, by the meaning you give to it.
I better shut up.
Eddie pulls his shades down over his cap and sinks into a fetal fold. Sometime deep into the night, he's flushed with fever.
Fuckin' flu! What a time to get the flu! Fuckin' air in these planes is polluted! Everyone's breathing in each other's shit! Hate fuckin' planes! Always get sick in these things!
Covered in blanket from head to toe, he's sweating, shaking, blanket's moving. He's so out of it, he's not sure if it's *his* hand, or... he looks to his right. Fran is sleeping. He looks to his left, Pudge is asleep. He peeks under the blanket. It's Pudge, her little pudge hand, barely able to wrap itself around his tubular.
Jesus Christ! The ol' lady fell asleep jerking me off! How boring am I?
She stops jerking. He puts her hand back in motion.
"Gentlemen! Start your engines!"
Make believe it's Fran.
An hour later, he's awakened by the blanket moving again. He turns left, Pudge is snoring, her breath so rank she could extinguish an acetylene blowtorch. He turns right, *no Fran*. He lifts the top of the blanket. It's Fran, sweet Fran, excavating, nesting his stones.
"Nivea?"
She nods.
"Ponds is good too."
He falls asleep, worrying that his shaft will crack. Eddie's prone to "cracking."
It happened during the "Pulkie" era, after she dropped him for another virgin. Depressed and aroused, all he could do was jerk off and sleep. It's not a life. Beating to the memory of Pulkie's drumstick, he beat his dick to a pulp. His pecker was no match for his hands, the thin membrane under the head was cracking, blood and come all over his hands. But he couldn't stop.

Pulkie lit his fire, stirred his pole, his soul, and left him with a perennial hard-on. He woke up with it, went to sleep with it, walked around with it, pushed it back, front, side against his thigh, tape, spit, glue, nothing helped. His dick stood at attention, loading and re-loading, ready to fire at will. **BANG!** But then it popped right back—a young man's malady only to be appreciated much later.

An adolescent's erection is like no other. It can serve as a key ring or coat hanger. Screwing in a light bulb can set it off. Eddie became a slave to his dick, jerking off with Bina's Ponds. His dick turned into a stick, but it never smelled so good.

Ponds is good, too, Fran.

An hour later, he awakes, alarmed. It's still night. Fran's reading a book about igneous rocks.

Did I... did she?

He dreamt about it, got it, and now can't remember. What good is it if you can't remember? 'Cause ninety percent of the fun is in remembering, and the other ten is in the telling.

He whispers, "*Did I...?*"

The next morning, Eddie helps Fran off with her luggage. He pushes Pudge aside, blocking the aisle.

"Move over, Mom. The gentleman's in a rush."

* * *

Landing at Ben Gurion aiport, Eddie's struck by the number of police, militia, and Uzi-toting security guards. He panics.

They're after me!

An obvious response from someone who thinks everything about them is about them.

The terminal's bustling, a hodgepodge of people from all over the world: different styles, dress, cultures, colors, languages; wearing suits, skirts, robes, jeans, jackets, heels, sandals, *birkhas* and *shmattas* on their heads. Eddie hears "We Are The World" blasting from speakers. Munich and Quincy Jones flash before his eyes. He's looking for terrorists, but sees Michael Jackson look-alikes moon-walking the polished airport surface.

It's Vegas.

For the life of him, he can't tell who's a terrorist and who's not. They all look alike, they all look like — people. How can you spot anyone in this *mish-maash*? Profiling stereotypes in Hoboken is easier.

Eddie's certain the Arabs must be holding back, because they could easily be setting off bombs every second if they wanted to in this seemingly safe and open society. Later on, Eddie hears that many more bombs explode than are reported. Nevertheless, life goes on, people go about their business of living and dying, the country in perpetual high alert, an undertow of anxiety driving the hectic pace. But, like everything else, once you get used to it, you hardly notice.

What Eddie *does* notice is the number of strikingly stunning, sexy young women. He forgets all about the Uzis, bombs, and terrorists. No trouble identifying *this* group! He feels old and horny, a bad combo. Eddie's only forty, but these cupcakes are barely twenty.

The sexiest are the women in uniform: cute beret, shiny boots, full booty, packing pistols. Eddie's drawn to the straining buttons on their flack jackets. He feels safe. They must know he's American. He's drooling. Israelis love Americans, love the States: the malls, the movies, Victoria Secret, Israeli's Statue of Liberty.

Since he's been on the lam, Eddie's sex drive has resurfaced. He was down to zilch, but now he's waking with bulges again. The *shikses*, the *Sabras*, even the yellow-toothed *meeskeits* of Crown Heights re-lit his oven. He's jerking off quite regularly, a sure sign of recovery, although he doesn't pull as hard or as often, a sign of the times.

As he's running from life, he's actually returning to it. He didn't realize how addiction kills sex, as it does everything else. You do one, you lose the other. You think and talk about it, but you don't do it, and as Trios's Pete said, "the more you talk, the less you do." Much like a relationship. If you have to always talk about it, you don't have one. Shades of Trios's sage.

"Talkin' makes you think you're doin', but all you're doin' is talkin'."

Eddie recalls his prime in his early twenties, the all-night card games, craps, horses, strip clubs, sex clubs, porn, pizza and girls ordered in, eating slices while getting sucked off two at a time, red sauce dripping, all his attention on the hand dealt. These days, Eddie's in the retread portion of his life. Everything seems like he's "been there and done that."

He steps out into the blazing Middle Eastern sun, looks up in the sky, the bluest sky he's ever seen. The sky, the people, the searing sun, get 'em all *farklempt*. He tears. The porters think he lost his luggage. "I'm in Israel!" He kneels to kiss the ground and singes his lips. He screams. People scatter. Now *he* could be a terrorist. Except he's wearing Bermuda shorts and a Hawaiian shirt.

At that moment, in baggage claim, Eddie's free of generational baggage. He's in Israel. *I'm home.* If not for Max, this is where they would have ended up. This is where his life would have been. How different it would have all been.

Eddie stands tall. That's because Israelis are short. Especially the *Sephardim*, short, dark, flashy, Puerto Rican types, reminding Eddie of Amsterdam and 72nd, where he did his young man's cruising.

* * *

He walks along busy Dizengoff Street with its trendy upscale shops, clubs, bars, hotels, cafés, restaurants, malls, the skywalk, just minutes from the Mediterranean. City's pumping, Dizengoff's hot, and Eddie's drawn to a cute waitress, skirt hiked up up to her *pipick*.

I think I'll stay.

He waits an hour for a table. Outdoor café's crowded with *youngees*.

No need to rush to Adi's Kibbutz, I'll just hang out here and watch the waitress.

He passes the time on line imagining them together, watching the movement of her popcorn tush under the skirt, rollerblading to customers, chatty and friendly. Eddie's finally seated, an ignored menu on the table. She glides over, short-stops, drops her pencil, turns around, and bends over.

"Eh, what you, eh, like?"
Huh, an order comin' outta her ass.
"You know, you could be a ventriloquist."
She turns around, "What?"
"Ice coffee."
"What, eh, else?"
"That's it."
"No, eh, *sahlaad*, no dessert?"
"No."
I just wanna watch you.
"No-theeng?"
"No-theeng, not hungry."
"Then you should stay home."

He likes that. A snippy chick in a tight skirt. She comes back with a coffee ice cream float.

"No, no, not float, coffee, *ice* coffee."
"Ma?"
"Ma *what*?"
"You want Café?"
"No Café! No Olay! Just coffee! ICE coffee!"
"This *is* ice coffee! Israeli *ice* coffee!"
"I don't want it!"

She stomps off. Customers glare at him.
Like I'm the problem.
Snip chick returns with a hot cup of coffee.
"Oh! Now you're really breaking my balls."
She spills it on his thigh.
"CUNT!"
Snip chick lets loose with a barrage of Hebrew insults.
"Same to you, bitch!"

She hurls another barrage and the rest of the coffee on his shirt.

Eddie throws a twenty in her face. She spits on him, picks up the twenty, and stuffs it in her cleavage, nipple visible.

"*Faaack* you, stupid American!"
"Fuck *meee*? Fuck **YOU**... *and* your nipple!"

"PEEEG!"
"STUFF A FALAFEL!"
"EAT SHEEET!"
"WHORE!"

Look at this! I'm in the fuckin' country for an hour, the "Nation of Peace," and she's fighting with me! So much for kissing the ground. It's more of a kiss my ass country!

It's hard. The people, the language, a fuck-you back-off kind of lingo, from short people with tall 'tudes. But comin' outta the ashes, what do you expect?

She smacks him across the face. It was not a "love whack." She does it again. The crowd cheers her on. He grabs her. Two Uzi-toting babes come running towards him. Better get outta there. He's here under a falsified passport. He has an arrest record going back years when he was picked up for running numbers. Now he really better start running. He pulls the twenty from her cleavage.

"Small tits!"

She grabs it back and rips it.

He sprints down Dizengoff, ducks into an alley, knocking over garbage cans, scaring the cats. Hidden from view, he watches the Uzi-toting babes run by.

Fuckin' chicks are quick.

He's up against the wall, wheezing. He takes his inhaler, gives two squirts, and lights up. He sits down on a pile of trash and looks around. *Looks familiar.* The garbage, the rats, cinder blocks... halfway around the world and it's Verrazano all over again...

What the fuck... you take yourself wherever you go.

He looks down at half the twenty in his hand... he's always leaving a half behind... half a cue, half a twenty, half a life... A drunk stumbles past him, to the alley door, into a titty bar. Eddie follows, smelling smoke, piss, booze, the sticky floor.

I'm home.

A true Zionist.

He sits at a greasy table, lights up, belts a few, gets a buzz, Van Halen blaring. The stripper crawls over, shoves some silicone in his face.

Finally some tits.

Chapter Fifteen

"The largest brush factory in the Middle East, right here in Kibbutz Ruhama!" boasts Uzi Ranon, Secretary of Kibbutz, as he shows Eddie around the plant. "We make everything from industrial brushes to toothbrushes."

"Nice."

"Ship them all over the world."

"Uh huh."

Uzi might as well be showing off a linen closet. The assembly-line workers look just as interested, working next to churning generators, spinning wheels and machines.

"We buy our equipment from Germany."

Uzi says it matter-of-fact, as if it were buying from Canada. Eddie grew up hearing Jews swear they would never buy anything German 'even though they make the best of everything!' so it shocked Eddie to see so many Volkswagens and Mercedes in Israel.

"So much for not buying German products."

"*That* war is over."

"How quickly we forget."

"I didn't say we forgot. I said, 'That war is over.'"

They walk up and down the aisles.

"Everyone looks so happy, Uzi."

"Work is not to make you happy, work is to make you secure."

"Uh huh."

"Besides, people are people. Happiness is a cause, not an effect."

"I don't know what you said, but it sounds good."

"No one makes you happy. You make yourself happy."

"Oh."

Eddie's been around enough Israelis to know they all want to sound relevant. The only one who didn't was Adi. But then Adi wasn't a *Sabra*. And when he prepared Eddie for his trip he said, "Remember, Jews are difficult. But Israeli's are impossible."

"You got a lot of workers here, Uzi."

"Over a hundred. Third of the Kibbutz."

"What are you doing makin' toothbrushes, shouldn't you be makin' guns?"

"The money we make from toothbrushes pays for the arms we buy."

"Israel's very own Iran-Contra."

"Except we have no scandals here."

"Are you criticizing Reagan?"

"A terrible actor, a worse president."

"I thought Israelis like him."

"We like him. We like him just the way he is, handsome and stupid."

"*Thar* you go again."

They both crack up. Eddie senses Uzi's enjoying him. If Eddie could choose a brother, Uzi would be it. Strong, handsome, rugged, smart, he could have easily stood in for Paul Newman's Ari in Exodus.

Eddie feels important being given the V. I. P. treatment. Walking down the center aisle of the factory, Uzi beside him, Eddie feels a little "Hitlerish."

Don't salute.

In Kibbutz, outsiders are considered prize plums, a status upgrade by association for the clannish crowd. Israelis are natural show-offs.

No twenty –one gun salute, Uzi?

"How do you know Adi?"

"My Uncle Max buys his pastries."

"Good desserts make good friends."

"How do *you* know Adi?"

"Adi was one of the founders of Kibbutz in 1948."

"Really?"

"He smuggled in arms for the Hagganah against the British, fought alongside Menachim Begin during the War of Independence, and fought every war through 1967."

"Huh... and I thought he was just a baker."

"No, he wasn't just a baker... "

***

A member of the visiting 1936 Czech Olympic gymnastics team, Adi vaulted for the golden hills of Jerusalem, deserting his team and country for Zion, vowing never to leave Israel. A vow he broke three times, returning in '48, '56, and '67.

To fight, he went to Israel. To live, he stayed in Brooklyn. With each war he got more disgusted with Israeli politics, the bickering, each military victory bringing on more internal division, a sure sign that Jews can't stand success, invoking Zion's first Commandment:

"How can I fuck up this joyous occasion?"

Jews, like Arabs, if you leave them alone, will finish the job the other starts, which is destroy themselves from within with no help from the other, thank you. So the best military strategy by one is to leave the other alone.

Adi saw it coming, felt it building, the obnoxious arrogance, the flaunting superiority, the self-aggrandizement, the fictionalized Sabra characterization of its own people, metaphorizing itself into a shit desert fruit.

"Is that what we are," Adi asks, "a cactus? Prickly on the outside, sweet on the inside? Who makes up this *chazerai*?!"

Madison Avenue. Of course. Bring on Madison Avenue's point man for Jews: *God!* Didn't God promise Israel to Jews, even though Israel was founded by Godless Jews who brought their God-less passion over from Russia and Europe? But if Madison Avenue says it works, use it. For it is written:

"Israel *for* Jew, *by* Jew, as *written* by Jew! Defended by ACLU — Thank you!"

Jews invented *Him* first, so first leads off. The Jews' Right of Return to the Promised Land, as promised by God two thousand years ago, statute of limitations intact.

Israel has the law on its side, a pretty good legal team, God and Alan Dershowitz, a strong legal — if not moral — case, plus guilt and suffering, the strongest of all arguments. And, boy, do Jews like to argue...and suffer.

"We suffered enough!" Jew says, "God wants us to have Israel."

Disappoint God? The U.N. didn't think so. Maybe in his next universe God will include others. But for now it's the Jews' turn to return. Their turn to prove themselves worthy of God's gifts, favors, and blessings.

It's become abundantly clear that God's picks may forever be fucked. God may be many things to many people, but for Jews he's not too good. So whenever the question arises, "Is it good or not good for the Jews?" Adi replies, "not if it's God!"

"Isn't it hard enough? Does He have to make it harder? Fight the Arabs, the world, *and* God? What is this a joke?! Jacob's ladder wouldn't reach!"

But it doesn't stop Jews from trying. They're an impossible people, drawn to the impossible. They like banging their heads against the wall. A stubborn people, they feel for the *wall*.

But there are times when stubborn is stupid, when strength is a weakness, when you're expected to be stronger than God, and even *stranger* when you are.

"But what's the choice?" Adi would ask, "Give up? Die?"

When you're taught not to be afraid, or too afraid to be taught, a piece of your humanity dies, your *mentschlichkeit*. You become hard. You "diss" consequences. It's what Adi didn't like about himself. Becoming hard. But living in Israel, there's no way to avoid it.

To escape, he made peace with God and moved to Brooklyn. He became orthodox, a pious Jew, not so much for religiosity, but for community, "for a Jew without his people is not a Jew."

So he opened a small bakery, lived above the store, and settled in between wars.

With each conflict, the prelude became more difficult. He read everything he could get his hands on, listened to all the reports, called everyone he knew to find out the latest news. His body may have been in Brooklyn, but his heart was in Israel.

Living so far away made it especially difficult, hearing of the alarming terror, the threats, saber-rattling madmen vowing to annihilate, destroy, burn, drown, kill, massacre Jews.

"What kind of way is that for nice Arabs to talk?" Adi would say to his customers, lined up behind the display case in his bakery showing off the most delicious raspberry cookies, rugelach, twists, danish, strudels, babkas, macaroons, 7-layer cake, each mocha layer lined inside the chocolate brick loaf casing draped with dark semi-sweet frosting.

They all came to hear Adi, the Scholar-in-Residence, and *nosh* on his free samples.

"All the Arabs are missing is the umlaut. They're trying to finish what the Nazis started! The Nazis couldn't do it *then,* and the Arabs can't do it *now*! Not in '48! Not in '56! And not now in '67! That's why they yell like *meshugenehs,* these *balagulas,* so loud and obnoxious, almost like Jews in Brooklyn." Customers laugh. "What kind of homes were they raised in? Who talks like this?"

And while he jokes, he waits for the call.

"Don't worry, Israel will win. Everything will be okay *during* the war. *After*, I'm not so sure."

So while Jews *kibbitz,* Arabs kill, Israel shrugs. They've seen it all before, heard it all before. Once again *Zahal* calls up reserves. Men and women drop their rakes, books, microscopes, leave universities, businesses, homes, cafés, to climb into cockpits and tanks.

Adi gets the call, and against his wife's and son's wishes, he returns to his post in the Negev, no longer Adi the baker, but Captain Adi Eizekovicz. The Danish will have to wait.

* * *

Adi's last vow broken was his most painful. Broken at the height of Israel's greatest modern-day glory following the '67 Six Day War, a stunning military victory which would have made Patton *platz.*

Israel struck at dawn and before dusk it was over. The recipe of sunrise surprise, and *chutzpah* caught the world by storm. American Jews responding to the call did what they do best: raising money, soliciting millions from minions, writing checks, cash, change, mounting pride bouncing off each coin tossed on sheets spread on city corners collecting money.

It was a victory the world was unprepared for. A victory Israel was unprepared for.

Fearless patch-eyed Moshe Dayan, sober somber Yitzhak Rabin, leading Israel Defense Forces; a *cholent* of *Hassids, Sabras, Ashkenazi, Sephardim* racing through the gates of Old Jerusalem to The Wall, The Western Wall, The Wailing Wall, soaking in thousands of two-thousand-year-old tears, spilling floods of longing, "How long we have waited..."

A short-lived victory, it was just too good to be true. Too much too soon. The Mouse That Roared, lightning in a *Mogen Dovid* bottle, striking with force, precision — targeting installations, sparing infants, raining bombs, saving innocents, villages.

Who fights like this? Where is it written? War with a conscience? Bombs with apologies? Minimizing human casualty at the expense of one's own. The math doesn't work. Death by selection, but a different kind of selection. Not by Jew, Arab, Black, or White, but bad guy. Get the bad guy. What an innovative idea to fighting evil.

Fuckin' Jews with their brains. They always had brains, but now balls, too? A military? A new breed of Jew? A Fighting Jew? Who knew? What *chutzpah*. The nerve! To fight back?! Millenniums of cowering in corners reversed in six short days. One day to rest, a thousand years to glow – evoking shock, respect, admiration — morphing to envy, hate, disgust.

Once again the world disappointed, once again the world denied.

For weeks prior to the outbreak, salivating spectators the world over stood on the sidelines, relishing the Second Coming of Semitic Slaughter, rooting for one hundred million Arabs to slaughter two million Jews.

The Arabs, heavy favorites, will finally make up for two humiliating losses, a Middle East-Versailles backlash, the two things Krauts and Arabs have in common: they hate Jews *and* they're losers to Jews. But '67 will turn it all around. The Arabs will, once and for all, finish the job the Germans started thirty years ago.

So what's the World to do? What's America, Israel's "best friend" to do? Send in troops? *Chas-v' ha-li-la!* God forbid. Maybe *after* the slaughter, send in troops, mop up. America's steadfeast excuse of protecting the "Only Democracy in the Middle East" will no longer be necessary. America can now openly drink the oil with the Sheiks, such stylish gents in flowing white robes, secret sufferers of inner-chafed thigh. All agree: Killing Jews will restore Arab pride at the pump, humility following humiliation.

Arabs humiliate so easily, so sensitive, so easily bruised. How can they hope to get ahead being so thin-skinned? Take a page from the pasty Jews: Jews don't get humiliated, they get insulted. You can work with insult. You can't work with humiliation. Humiliation breeds contempt, insult breeds apology. Insult's a headache, humiliation's a migraine. Insult's an aspirin, humiliation's a machete. One you apologize, the other you kill; one is embarrassment, the other shame; one gets you over, the other puts you over.

* * *

"Give them back! Give them back their land!" Adi shouts in the packed hall.

Every Saturday night was vent-your-spleen night at Kibbutz Ruhama. Kibbutz members would stand up and pontificate, voicing frustrations from anything and everything. Some for five minutes, some for an hour. The best part of the "Churchill Chimes," as Adi called them, were the frequent interruptions and side comments reducing prepared remarks to verbal gang bangs, so that by the end of the night it was a *balagan*, a free-for-all, with no one listening to anyone.

"That's Democracy," Adi would say. "It works for a few, but not for many—the machine clogs. You can't go fast, you can't go slow, you hurry, you wait, everyone has an opinion, everyone speaks, eventually, nothing gets done until a war breaks out."

But tonight is different. Tonight Kibbutzniks must put their differences aside (itself a miracle) and decide what's best for the country. This is what weighs heavy on Adi's mind as his wife and son stand beside him, closing the bakery to be with Adi at this pivotal moment in Israel's history, a tiny nation artificially created, transformed overnight, conquering anti-heroes occupying vast lands and people; two million rejects controlling a hundred million other rejects in a territory a thousand times the size of their own.

Rolling up his sleeves, he walks to the podium and stands there, looking out, locking eyes with each member. Adi watched The Lubovitcher Rebbe speak and learned that there's more to speaking than words, that if the eyes don't meet, then the heart has no chance; that for the voice to be heard, one must be seen.

"Lift up thine eyes," Scripture says. Not easy to do, all those eyes staring back at you. Adi looks down, aware of the buzz all around him. He waits. A master of discomfort, he says nothing; people squirm, fidget, chatter, chatter giving way to voice, then no voice. He knows that as long as he's quiet, they're all in his tent, but once he opens his mouth, he better say something good or else he's fucked.

He lifts his eyes.

"*Chaverim*, friends! I made *Aliyah* thirty years ago."

This they heard a million times.

"I settled in the Negev to work the land."

This they heard a million times.

"There is enough land for everyone."

This they heard a million times.

"We don't need everything we won."

This they never heard.

"We must return what we won."

This they certainly never heard.

"We paid for everything we won, Adi! In blood! Jewish blood!"

He knew Uzi would come at him. A veteran of two wars by age thirty, the steel plate in Uzi's head hadn't tempered his combativeness.

"You don't have to remind *me* of Jewish blood, Uzi! But if we don't give them back their land, then you'll first *see* blood!"

"Adi, for the first time, we have the power, we have—"

"Nothing!"

"We won!"

"What did we win? The right to imprison millions of refugees?"

"Were we not refugees?"

"Yes, but this is *their* land."

Uzi pounds the table. "It is **OUR** land!" The place explodes with applause and whistles. Adi waits until it dies down.

"Let me ask you, Uzi. What will you do with all this land?"

"Keep it!"

"Jordan, Lebanon, Syria, Gaza?"

"Yes!"

"Golan Heights, Sinai?"

"YES!"

"Uzi, we don't have enough Jews to populate Haifa!"

"It's a good problem."

The members laugh and cheer.

"At least give up The Sinai!"

"Return The Sinai?!"

"Yes, The Great Sinai! The only land in the Middle East with no oil. Our *mazel*. At least if there was oil, we keep the oil, and give them back the sand! Let them make windows! But all we have now is their sand and their misery."

"Better *they* should be miserable!"

"But their misery is now *ours*. We did the Sheiks a big favor, controlling their people, right in the middle of all this *great* desert land. This *farshtunkener* land!"

"Whose fault is that, Adi?"

"What?"

"You brought us here! You and your *partizaners*, to this *midbar*, this desert!"

"Where should we go, Uzi?! Uganda? Alaska? Sweden? If Jews settled in Sweden, the Swedes would become terrorists! The world hates us!"

"And giving back the land, they will love us?"

"No, but—"

"The world respects one thing, Adi! Power! We must teach the Arabs a lesson."

"How many lessons do you want to teach?"

"As many as it takes."

"You know what they learn from our lessons? They learn to hate us more."

Uzi walks from his seat and stands in front of Adi.

"I see you have become Americanized, Adi. Even when you win, you think you lost."

Uzi scores. Kibbutz applauds.

"No one wins, Uzi. No one wins in war. History will teach you that."

"We make our own history, Adi. *History* taught us that."

Adi's bristling. "Let me tell you something about you *Sabras*, the younger generation."

"Yes, Adi, tell us."

"You have no grace, a good Christian word you should know."

"Now you're a Christian, Adi. *Mazel tov*! Your conversion is complete!"

The crowd roars. Adi waits. In public debate no matter how badly you get stung, wait it out. If you wait it out, you can take back control. But if you wait *too* long, the audience thinks you're weak. And then the power shifts, so the best way back is not to defend or attack, but take the hit, speak softly, make it a lesson learned.

"Uzi, the world is not black and white, and if you see it that way, it is our fault we did not teach you well."

"No, Adi. You taught us well, *too* well."

"No, Uzi. You have no heart, no compassion for anyone else but your own."

"*We* have no compassion, but *you* do?"

Silence.

"Where did you learn that compassion, Adi? Marching to the ovens?"

The scab's ripped open, the repressed resentment of the younger generation against their elders, a place no one wants to go, and yet, it's the central issue in every Jewish home.

"Of course, Uzi – why, we went like sheep — Is that your question?"

Uzi's eyes fill. "I have no question."

"You watch too many American movies, Uzi."

One person laughs. Probably the other filmmaker.

"When spirits are broken, bones, not people, but bones, walk to ovens, ending lives that already ended... But I'm not here to talk about the past, Uzi. I'm here to talk about the future.

The past is dead. That's why we have Israel, not Palestine. But if we want a future, a future for our children, we must return the land or else *their* children and their children's children will hate us forever."

"So we will beat them forever."

Thunderous applause. Three hundred strong stand.

"We'll beat them with everything we have, Adi! We will not go down. We will not be defeated! They want peace? They'll have peace. They want war, that's what they'll get! Whatever they want, we'll give them!"

And that's the difference between old Jew and new...a point of view.

"Uzi, you think all wars will be so easy?"

"When is it ever easy for Jews, Adi?"

"They can lose many wars. We can only lose one."

"And where will you be when that happens, Adi, in Brooklyn?"

Visibly stung, Adi's heard it before, but this time it really hurt. The young matador finishes the old bull.

"You can't dance at two *chasenehs* with one *toches*, Adi. It's not enough to come here to fight. The fight for us is in the life *here*, not Brooklyn! We need Jews. More Jews!"

"Not more Jews, Uzi. Better Jews! Jews who understand that the time to treat Arabs with dignity is *now,* in their hour of greatest shame."

"You're defending Arabs?"

"Our fight is not with the people, Uzi, it is with their leaders. They suppress their own people! So for a piece of bread, the people swallow every lie. Their people want peace, they don't want to fight any more than we do. The only chance we have is if we give them back the land, if we show them we want peace, if we —"

The crowd boos.

"Are you so naïve, Adi? After three wars?!"

"Uzi, please, don't let them feel what we know all too well. Every human being has a heart — a heart which opens and closes depending on how it is treated. So in this hour of joy, don't be a *shtarker*, don't be arrogant. Yes, we performed a miracle!

We showed the world a strength even *we* didn't know we had. But the greater miracle is not victory, it is peace."

Adi's eloquence rose like his yeast, only to be punctured by the overwhelming sentiment against him, and for good reason. The victory did not come without a price. The Kibbutz lost a dozen of its young and many were injured. Not high numbers, but for a small Kibbutz of three hundred, it was a lot. In those days, everyone knew everyone in *Kibbutzim, Moshavs,* cities, villages, and towns, so every loss was personal, every loss felt.

"You would let our soldiers die in vain, Adi?"

"No one dies in vain if it's for the right reasons."

"That's right. We fight and die for the land."

"We did not come for land, Uzi. We came for a home. Give them back theirs."

Some smirks, some smiles, no applause for Adi's speech. He always got big applause for his big speeches. A small man known for big impassioned speeches, they came from miles around to hear Adi. A quiet man, a modest man with a gift, this genius for moralizing, keeping the faith, doing the right thing… not one applause.

Kibbutz Ruhama, stuck in the middle of the Negev, the Negev itself stuck in the middle of nowhere. Kibbutz Ruhama, the Kibbutz he helped found with a handful of pioneers, sleeping in tents, working the land, protecting the borders, fighting three wars, losing a leg… not one applause.

So at the height of Israel's greatest moment, Adi took his wife, son, and left.

***

"Tough nut."

"Yes he was. Come."

They cool off with a cold bottle of Coke back in the factory office. The paneled office is strewn with papers, invoices, desks and phones, boxes, file cabinets, a fridge, and some folding chairs. Along the walls are photos of the early pioneers working, always working.

Arbeit macht frei!

One picture shows Adi in a hard hat guiding cranes, installing heavy machinery into the brush factory when it was being built. Eddie steps up to take a closer look at the picture.

"Look at him here with his hard hat. He didn't need a hat. His head is hard enough. All these guys look the same, like Ben-Gurion, wild white hair coming out of their sides."

Uzi laughs.

"What is it with them , they can't afford a comb...or a brush? Is that why Adi started a brush factory? To brush his hair?"

He's got Uzi going.

"How did he get into brushes?"

"Everyone asked the same thing. They thought Adi was *meshugeh*. A brush factory in the Negev? But he heard about a brush factory in Cologne which was very successful, and was bombed by the Allies, but much of the machinery remained intact. He said the Germans were in a reparations frame of mind and would ship the machinery for practically nothing."

"He took advantage of the Germans."

"It was on sale."

"What Jew turns down a sale. Not even a Communist!" Eddie smiles. Uzi doesn't.

"Adi had vision, he saw the future. Not just with machines. Now we have our hands full with young terrorists, as he predicted in '67. We were too caught up in the moment, and it's cost us. We should have listened."

"Jews don't listen."

"No, we don't."

Uzi finishes the Coke and gives a *greps*.

"So, Eddie, where do you want to work?"

"Work?"

"Yes. The fields, factory, kitchen?" Eddie looks puzzled. "What's the problem?"

"Adi never said anything about work."

"What did you think you would do here?"

"Hang out."

"Hang out?"

"Yeah. He said you had a nice pool."

Uzi laughs so hard he can't stop. Doubled over in stitches, he stumbles into the main area. Workers turn down the drone of their machines to hear Uzi tell them what Eddie said. Now they're all laughing, pointing at Eddie.

"What's so funny?"

"Hang *out*?"

"Till the heat dies down."

"No, no, no—"

"I got a couple a bucks."

"We're not a hotel—"

"How's three hundred a month?"

"Three—"

"American."

"Eddie, we're a *Kibbutz*! Communists! You're offering Communists money. The Bolsheviks would be turning over in their graves."

The laughter's reverberating louder than the machines.

"Commies don't take money?" It gets quiet instantly.

I shut them up!

Uzi grabs Eddie under his arm and escorts him out.

"Let go of my arm!"

Uzi's hot and doesn't let go. "Listen, you jerk! This is a favor to Adi. He said you wanted to make *Aliyah*."

Eddie pulls his arm back. "Whoa! Whoa! Whoa, Uzi! I said I'd *think* about it. I never said I'd *do* it. You know my situation."

Uzi grabs Eddie's arm again. "I know the Mafia wants to kill you. You are a Jew, a friend of Adi, so we take you in. Otherwise, I don't care *who* kills you."

"Get the hell off me!" Eddie breaks free and throws a punch Uzi blocks. The two square off. The workers stop. Eddie looks at Uzi and decides he doesn't want to die on Kibbutz.

"Stay or get out! If you stay, you work!"

Eddie takes a time-out, examining his palm, and looks at all the "happy" faces in the factory.

"What time's lunch?"

"So you're staying."

"I'll leave after lunch."

"How would you like to eat a cactus?"

"What *kinda* work?"
"It doesn't matter. We rotate."
"Where do you get paid the most?"
"Pay's the same."
"How much?"
"Nothing."
"Nothing?!"
"Technically, you're a volunteer."
"Doesn't sound technical to me. Sounds like being used."
Eddie checks his watch.
"Do you have an appointment?"
"Yeah. When's the next bus *outta* here?"
"There's no bus till tomorrow morning, but you can leave now."
"In the middle of the fuckin' desert?! Where am I gonna go?"
"Hitch a ride. Maybe some Bedouin tribe can pick you up and you can 'hang out' with *them*."
Eddie examines his other palm. He weighs toothbrushes against Ollie's bat.
"I'll stay."
"Good. You'll be safe here."
"I feel it already."
"After a year, if we like you, and you like us, we vote you in as a full member."
"Wow. Up for election in a year. I'll tell you, Uzi, some days it just pays to get up."
Uzi laughs and the tension's broken. That's Uzi. One second angry, the next laughing. He laughs easily, a defense to keep his head from blowing up, which didn't stop a grenade from trying.
"It's a good life, Eddie, the Communist life. 'From each according to his ability, to each according to his need.' Karl Marx."
"From each I don't give a shit, to each I don't care much. Eddie Parker."
A whistle goes off.
"Ah! Lunch!"
"Who's cooking, Karl Marx?"
"Norma Rae."

"You sure know your union leaders, Uzi."
"Great movie. Good union film."
"So you must love *Reds*."
"And *Waterfront*."
"I once saw a documentary on Samuel Gompers."
"Don't make fun, Eddie. We take our films very seriously."
"I see."
"Every Friday night, the whole Kibbutz watches movies."
"What if you wanna watch another night?"
"Can't."
"Another movie?"
"Can't
"Who picks the night?"
"Committee."
"Who picks the film?"
"I do."
"No committee?"
"You know what a camel is, Eddie?"
"A broken horse?"
"Close. A horse created by committee."
"Very good, Uzi. I like that."
"That's what happened to Communism. They took a beautiful idea and gave it to the Russians, then Poles, Germans, Chinese, who made it worse, then Cubans, Koreans, Central America; only in Kibbutz do we practice it right."
"I'm not into politics, Uzi. I'm just out to save my own ass."
"That's what all politics is. Local."
Uzi's one of those rat-a-tat guys who loves to scrimmage. He found a partner in Eddie.
"So, what's *your* favorite movie, Eddie?"
"I like *The Hustler* with Paul Newman 'n' Minnesota Fats."
"Correction. Minnesota Fats wasn't an actor. He was the character played by Jackie Gleason."
"How do you know so much about movies?"
"I studied film at the University of Southern California."
"I was wondering why you had no accent."
"I left it in L.A., but then the wars interrupted.

I went back and forth. After a while, I couldn't do it. I had to be here. So I studied engineering, got married and settled here."

"I like happy endings."

"Where did you graduate?"

"Trios Pool Hall, School of Hard Knocks."

"No college?"

"No."

"High School?"

"Dropped out."

"Family problems?"

"Yeah. My pop split and my mom went nuts. What's for lunch?"

* * *

The blistering noonday sun hits hard as they head toward the huge dining hall on the hill. Kibbutzniks converge from all sides, reminding Eddie of a Pennsylvania steel mill belching out blue-collar workers for their one-hour lunch pail break in the mess hall.

"Uzi, this is a scene out of *The Deer Hunter*."

But that's where the comparison ends. The dining hall is a magnificent, modern, multi-functional, split-level structure featuring a theatre, banquet hall, meeting rooms, offices, health club, and dining facility serving three hundred members plus another hundred volunteers, three meals a day, seven days a week, for this small, tightly-knit, highly-organized little city in the desert.

"Uzi! This is like the Concord in the Catskills!"

"Not bad, huh?"

"I thought you guys were poor."

The imposing structure made of granite, glass, and steel forms a symbolic fortress, true to its history as Israel's southernmost outpost, its first line of defense against interior renegade attacks from surrounding hostile villages. That was in the forties, following the Second World War. For generations before, Jews and Arabs lived in peace.

THE FIX

Outside the patio leading into the dining hall are brilliantly colored mosaic floor tiles crafted by Kibbutz artisans, Jews from Italy who chisel away, jabbering in Italian and Hebrew.

Artists are revered on Kibbutz. Especially painters, sculptors, craftsman — anyone who works with their hands. For too many generations, the Commies argued, Jews made their living off the backs of others. They relied on bartering, playing middleman, sliding in and out, surviving with their brains. Brains they knew they had. Hands are what they needed. Hands to build and create. Sol always talked about how good he felt *shlepping* boxes. "Honest *verk*." He said that in many ways he regretted coming to America. That he would have wanted to go to Israel and *shlep* along with other Jews.

"In America you *shlep* alone."

A long food station splits the center aisle, containing chafing dishes filled with fresh fruits and vegetables; choices of chicken, beef, fish, vegetarian dishes; pastas, cheeses, breads, spreads, desserts and beverages. There was a soup *and* salad station, pizza, an assortment of dressings, choices of teas, coffee, and fresh milk straight from the cows. Eddie never tasted milk so delicious.

"Any Twinkies?"

Kibbutzniks eat like horses. They work like horses and eat like horses. Some *look* like horses. Thorough-bred horses, young *Sabras*. Healthiest, most beautiful human beings Eddie's ever seen. They load their plates, then go back for seconds and thirds. But no one's fat— *zaftig*, but not fat. Fit. Fit and healthy. Fit, healthy, and quiet.

Considering the many hundreds of people in the dining hall, it's eerily quiet except for the ten tables of volunteers in the back, boisterous and loud, buzzing with activity.

Coming from all over the world, different cultures and backgrounds, gives the young volunteers plenty to talk about. It's what it must have been like for the early Kibbutz settlers when they first arrived. A mix of youth and purpose offers an excitement like no other. Scanning the other thirty round tables of ten, there is no such life, just the sound of chewing.

Knowing too much about someone — living, working, and eating together day in, day out, year in, year out, brings a certain malaise. Like in one's own family. And not having to struggle on a daily basis, having every physical necessity taken care of, takes the bite out of survival. No one wants to suffer. But then no one wants to feel empty either, especially around so much food.

"Who died, Uzi? It's like a morgue in here."

"When we eat, we eat. When we talk, we talk."

"I mean, I'm not a *yenta*, but this is ridiculous. Feels like I'm home."

"What new can happen between breakfast and lunch?"

Eddie looks over to the corner tables of volunteers chatting away.

"They don't seem to have a problem."

"They're young, idealistic, and fuck a lot."

"That'll do it."

"They stay three months, work, eat, fuck, and leave."

"El-Al should advertise, 'Come to Kibbutz! Where the fucking is better.' You'll have no problem getting volunteers."

"How do you like the salad?"

"I like the salad. I like fucking better."

"There's plenty of both."

A piece of lettuce gets stuck in his throat. "Is this a swinging Kibbutz?"

"No, we just don't make sex a big deal."

Uzi must be banging lotsa women.

"It's part of life. As long as it's private, respectful, it's no one's business."

Definitely bangin' away.

"By the way, I'm married and faithful."

"I used to be one of those."

Salad consists of bowls of whole tomatoes, cukes, radishes, lettuce, onions, mushrooms, olives, artichokes, avocados, carrots, raisins, fruit, nuts. It's make-your-own, no servers, everyone responsible for their own, mindful not to waste. The rule is:

"Take as much as you want, but finish everything you take."

Kitchen crew hustles, filling and refilling chafing dishes; rinsing, washing, scrubbing dishes, glasses, silverware, pots 'n' pans, locking 'n' loading onto an industrial conveyer belt to a dishwasher so big, it could be a car wash. It takes a good two hours to clean up, just in time to start preparing for the next meal.

"I think I'll work the fields, Uzi."

"Good. The truck will pick you up at four."

"Afternoon?"

"Morning."

Eddie feels like crying. Nothing makes him sicker than the thought of waking early. Worse is actually getting up.

"But, I don't get up till noon."

***

A loud banging wakes Eddie.

"AAAAAAAHHHHHHHHHHHHHH!"

"Shh! You'll wake the Arabs."

"Jesus Christ! Don't come storming in like the Gestapo!"

"You should have been up already."

"I was having a nightmare."

"About what?"

"NAZIS!"

"Get dressed."

Eddie's slumped over the side of the bed, his head hanging. "What a fuckin' nightmare! What time is it?"

"Four."

"That's for gravediggers!"

"Apple pickers. Let's go, get dressed."

"*Gimme* a cigarette." Uzi pulls one from a green soft pack and the tobacco falls out.

"What the fuck is this, tissue with some tobacco in it?"

"Kibbutz cigarettes." Uzi lights him up. "So, Eddie, except for the nightmare, how did you sleep?"

"Great. The Sealy straw mattress was nice and firm and the bangin' bunnies on either side of me rockin' the boat, that was good too."

"Jealous?"

"May I have another shack *with* a girl, please?"

"I'll speak to the concierge."

"Kid on my left sounded like a stuck pig, and his twit girlfriend was screaming in her Queen's English, "*Hirt* me, *hirt* me, chap!""

"What were they saying on the other side?"

"Eat me."

Uzi laughs. "How do you like our cigarettes?"

"Now I know how Marlene Dietrich got her cheeks."

Eddie takes a deep drag and pierces his lip.

"What the fuck?!"

"Don't suck so hard. You look desperate."

"What's in here, shrapnel?"

"Chips."

"I smoked a *lotta* shit, Uzi, but I never smoked wood." He gives back the blood-stained cigarette. "Here, go make a cabinet or something."

Eddie puts on his shorts, but Uzi hands him Kibbutz gear: a pair of long pants, full sleeve shirt, boots, and a Kibbutz hat.

"I'm *gonna* sweat my balls off."

"You'll fry if you don't cover up."

"But what's with the stupid dodo hat? You can't tell the men from the women."

"Oh, you can tell."

He's gotta be fuckin' a lotta women.

"Let's go, princess."

Eddie boards the back of the open truck packed with young spirited volunteers.

"*Boker Tov*! *Boker Tov*! Good morning! Good morning!"

"Yeah, yeah, good morning (*fuckheads*)."

He's grown a goatee, a ponytail, drilled a stud in his ear, donned the largest shades, put his shirt collar up, wearing oversized pants and work shirts topped off with the dinky four-corned hat, toilet tissue hanging from his pierced lip, making Al Pacino look mild.

Uzi introduces him.

"*Chaverim*, this is our new volunteer, Aryeh. Can we call you Aryeh?"

"Call me Eddie!"

Youngees respond, "*Shalom*, Aryeh, *shalom*–"

"Yeah, yeah, *shalom, shalom* (*fuckheads*)."

One girl says, "Aryeh is such a beautiful name."

"Yeah, yeah, I'm beautiful.'"

Eddie's eyes are swollen, stinging, and hanging. He's got the runs, a migraine, his back's out and the bumpy half hour ride out to the apple orchard doesn't help, although it doesn't seem to bother anyone else.

I hate the fuckin' young. Pete was right!

Youngees jump off the truck and climb up the ladders stretched across several acres. The apples are picked in pairs. The one on top hands the one below who places them carefully in a basket round their neck so as not to bruise the apple for its many thousand-mile export to market. Eddie climbs to the top of the ladder and throws the apples down, bombarding his British counterpart.

"*Blitzkrieg!*" he shouts, "Run to your shelters!"

"Gentle, chap. It's an apple, not a hockey puck."

"'*Hirt* me! *Hirt* me!'"

At seven they break for breakfast in the field. A wide variety of juices, yogurt, cream, bread, rolls, bacon, eggs, muffins, cereals, pastries, cookies, coffee 'n' tea, served under a tent, as full and abundant as in the regular dining hall.

Eddie's off to the side smoking, holding a hot cup of coffee in the hundred degree heat, surveying the sumptuous spread and the young women, watching the *youngees* fill their plates to the top. Uzi walks over.

"Not hungry, Eddie?"

"Who eats at this hour?"

"Everyone."

"I'll wait for lunch."

"You'll like lunch."

He flicks the cigarette.

"Can't wait."

* * *

"Umm, you were right, Uzi. This fricassee's dee-lish, tender 'n' tasty, better than my mother used to make, and *she* was the *fricazee* queen."

"Every Friday."

"Sign me up."

Eddie goes back for a second helping behind the not-so-stiff Brit. He whispers in her ear: "*Hirt* me, *hirt* me."

"I see your appetite's back, chap."

"This fricassee is unbelievable."

"Fricassee? It's rabbit."

He drops the tray and runs for the toilet. He returns a half hour later, white as a sheet.

"If you want to kill me, Uzi, just do it. Don't serve me rabbit!"

"You said it was delicious."

"Before I knew what it was."

"See! It's better not to know."

"Call me Adam."

"And I'll be Eve."

When Eddie was a kid in Bergen-Belsen, he went to the bathroom at night and tripped over Peter Cotton Tail's slashed throat in the hallway.

"Scared the living shit outta me. Same reason I don't eat chicken. In Bergen-Belsen, every week they pulled chickens from the coop and chopped their heads off. Chickens ran around with blood shooting out of their necks; ummm, delicious."

"What did they do with the heads?"

"Not funny, Uzi." Although the whole table howls. "Not for the chickens *or* me."

Not funny. Not for that one out of ten.

"What were you doing in Bergen-Belsen? Were you in the concentration camp?"

"No, we were there after the war in '46 when it was turned into a refugee camp."

"Were your parents in a concentration camp?

"No. My father escaped Poland and met my mother in Russia, Tashkent."

"So you're Russian"

"Yeah."

"I didn't think you were American."
"Why?"
"You seem different."
"How?"
"You look like you suffered."
Eddie cracks up, but Uzi doesn't. He's got a steel plate in his head and an arm missing.
"Well, Mr. Uzi, looks like you haven't done so bad yourself."
Uzi picks up his plate.
"More fricassee?"
"I'll pass."
After lunch, communal fatigue sets in and all the members go back to their cookie-cutter rooms for a mid-day *shluffee*. Too hot to work, one to four is "*shluffee* time." Those three hours, the desert is as still as still can be, and can scare the shit out of you. The stillness brings in an eerie wind, lulling all to sleep. If he has to die, this is how Eddie would like to go, into the desert wind.

***

He fails at apples, so they put him on a tractor, which he drives into a ditch. Then to the kitchen where he drops dishes, to the factory where he jams the machines.
"What's wrong with you?!"
"I'm *gelaymt*."
"You're not *gelaymt*, you're lazy."
"My mother said I was a cripple with my hands. All I was good for was picking *kuzees* from my nose."
"You'll have to do more than that to stay on Kibbutz."
"What do you suggest?"
"I don't know. You've done so well in everything else. What do you think you can do?"
"I'm an idea man."
So they put him at the pool as a lifeguard. An Olympic-size pool no one swam in except the elderly for their early-bird swim at six and late afternoon at four. Weekends are busier, but for the most part he's just 'hanging out.' Just like he wanted.

He's learned how to clean the filtration system, balance the chlorine, maintain the pH level, remove dead flies, vermin, and a deer he tried to remove with a net.

To keep from going nuts, he swims laps under water. He's pretty good and can swim many lengths without coming up for air. The old people gather round the pool and cheer him on till he's exhausted. Then they drag him out of the pool and give him a cigarette. They take pictures of Eddie, doubled over, exhausted, a wood chip cig hanging from his lip.

Eddie credits the New York City Public School System for his lung capacity. All those years in class holding his breath prepared him for Kibbutz. What's even more remarkable is that he smokes three packs a day. It's the first thing Eddie gasps for when he comes up from the water.

"*GIMME* A CIGARETTE."

The old people get a big kick out of the crazy American they call "The Chimney." Eddie gets his inspiration from a Hungarian runner in the Olympics who broke the four-minute mile and smoked four packs a day.

"One for each mile."

Eddie boasts, "I could be the first long distance swimmer with lung cancer!"

Besides cleaning the pool, watching old people soak, and setting stamina records underwater, Eddie reads. He joins an English-speaking book club, invited by Uzi.

Eddie never read as a kid. The comic books he loved, Bina threw out. And from then on, he only read the back of newspapers. So, living in Kibbutz was an opportunity to make up for lost time. But he was also a notoriously slow reader, so he made up for it by becoming a prolific reader of flaps and jackets. He flipped from one flap to another, and made up everything else in between. One night after a vigorous book club discussion on Camus's *The Stranger*, Uzi lit into him.

"You read <u>one</u> paragraph, Eddie! Excuse me, one <u>sentence</u>! Excuse me, the <u>first</u> sentence, and you go off talking about existentialism!"

Eddie quotes Camus: "'Mother died today...or was it yesterday?' That's the first sentence, right?"

Uzi's seething. "Come on Uz, what else do you need to know?"

"Don't even *try* to justify your *chutzpah*! You're an idiot!"

"Uz, it's about Meursault, who's a clerk in Algeria who kills this Arab, so he can't be all bad... but then he's tried and the prosecuting Attorney says that he showed no emotion at his mother's funeral. I understand that. I didn't cry at *my* mothers funeral. I was drunk. It's when you're so fuckin' numb you don't give a shit. That's all existentialism is, right? Not giving a shit about anything... when you're *not* drunk, does that make sense?"

"YOU DIDN'T READ THE BOOK!"

"How do you know?"

Uzi grabs the *The Stranger* out of Eddie's hands.

"Because the pages haven't been cracked, and there's a smudge on the top of the first page."

Eddie takes back the book. "Okay, so I read the summary. Big fucking deal! Shoot me!"

"It's not a fashion supplement, Eddie! It's a classic! A modern-day classic! It deserves to be taken seriously, as you should begin to take *yourself* seriously!"

"You're just pissed because you can't beat me in chess!"

"I don't like fakes, Eddie."

"I'm not a—"

"You can't pick up a book, read the flap, then discuss it as if you know what you're talking about."

"I don't like to read."

"You can't pretend you read the whole book if you don't."

"I'm not pretending."

"How do you expect to be well read?"

"What are you talkin' about? I read five books today."

"One more joke and you're back picking apples."

"So, I'm not well read, but I'm well lived. Does that count?"

"No!"

"Am I saying anything out of line?"

"That's just it! I don't understand how you do it."

"It just comes to me. All God's wisdom <u>is</u> within me."

"Eddie, you can't skim books the way you skim through life."

"Why? I thought I skimmed the pool pretty good today."

Uzi shoves him Michener's *The Source*, a thousand plus page book.

"What do you want me to do with this?"

"Read it!"

"I can't lift it!"

"And if you show up to the book club having only read the jackets, I will shoot you."

"Sounds reasonable. Meanwhile I need a hand truck."

"For what?"

"This fucking book!"

Eddie reads *The Source* in a week, then on to *Hawaii*, Dostoevsky, Tolstoy, Marx, Engles, Nietzsche, history, philosophy, novels, magazines, anything he can get his hands on, making up for years of *flapomania*.

He continues in the evening at the Moadon café, reading, listening to classical music, discussing politics, playing chess with Uzi. A good place to get cultured after a full day of lifeguarding.

Not a bad life.

Their nightly chess duels become the highlight for café members. Eddie and Uzi take their seats in the corner of the café and sit for hours on hard wooden chairs peering over a chessboard. They're fiercely competitive and ride each other throughout the match.

"How many lives did you save today, Eddie?"

"One."

"How many rats?"

"One."

"Remove any deer with a net?"

Eddie attacks.

"Rook to Queen four."

"Ooh."

"The end is near, Uz."

"Whose end?"

"Check!"

"Ow! You play a strong game, Eddie."

"Taught by my Pop. If he had you by a pawn in the beginning, you lost by a pawn in the end. Whatever you gave up in the beginning, you lost in the end."

"Checkmate!"

"Fuck! What happened?"

"You didn't have me at the beginning, and you don't have me at the end. How you start is not how you finish."

"Do me a favor, Uz."

"Yes?"

"If you're gonna beat me, do it without a moral at the end."

* * *

Eddie fell into a routine. He resisted it initially, but order and structure settled him down. He liked knowing where he was going (nowhere) and what he was doing (nothing). He'd been on Kibbutz for a year and the vote was coming up. He long ago passed the test of likeability and productivity. People liked him. He liked them. He made friends, lovers, liked the food, Rabbit became his favorite dish. He worked in the fields, drove a tractor, became a chef, worked in the factory, the office, wherever they needed him.

He noticed a transformation in himself. Life slowed down and took him with it. He picked up the "ehh's" in his broken Hebrew, appreciating the pause giving his brain a rest. Sex stopped being a big deal. Fidelity was respected. And when it wasn't, it was worked out. The Commies got something right. They took the angst out of living. With nothing to get, nowhere to go, and no one around, any friction or agitation had little chance of fermenting. The desert, in its sobering vastness, brings home how insignificant the whole deal is anyway. Nothing more ridiculous than arguing under a huge desert sky.

Maybe it was living in Israel. Maybe he was the same and hadn't changed at all, and the country was more hyper than he was, every day aware that any day could be its last. A country on the run, sucking up every breath of life, traveling at the speed of light, and he, Eddie, in his space suit, traveling at no speed, noticing nothing.

No. He wasn't in sync with Israel. He was in sync with Kibbutz. Kibbutz isn't Israel, just like Albany isn't Manhattan. Kibbutz life is quiet, measured, tempered, and calm; his life, a set schedule, work six days a week, five to eight, breakfast at nine, lunch at twelve, *shluffee* till four, work to seven, dinner, then to Moadon Café, "Figaro East," with the best cappuccino, tea, latte, pastries, comfortable lounges, sofas, newspapers, books, chess, music; Friday flicks, Saturday off, Sunday work. And so it went.

The biggest change Eddie notices are his dreams, usually nightmares. A few bad ones in a row make him nervous, so he offers up a prayer to ward off the *kaynahorah*, the bad spirits. He gets into bed, watches the fan in the ceiling, and says the *Shema*, then drifts off...and the dreams return... as dreams.

He dreams of Sol and Bina, The Kid, Maya, and Max. The few nightmares he has are of Ollie 'n' Chaalie. But mostly he dreams of Sol. He doesn't remember the dream, but feels good in the morning. In the past, any dreams dealing with Sol were in the Ollie 'n' Chaalie range: terrifying and ridden with rage. But life on Kibbutz is a sedative, calming and peaceful, dislodging Eddie from his "twin terrors" and placing Sol in the "soft" dream group, emitting nightly endorphins lasting through mid-morning. He even allows himself the memory of *the few good times*.

To think well of your father, pleasant thoughts, loving thoughts of a man you hated, isn't easy. You could be having a nice lunch and suddenly it feels like you've been punched in the stomach. "Daddy's twitch" is what Kitzee calls it.

For years, it was impossible for Eddie to think of Sol without bile rising in his throat, triggering a cough which disappeared as soon as Sol died, or he killed him — in thought or memory. To allow Sol back in, Eddie would have to break his promise of hating him forever. A promise he made to himself as a kid when he was being beaten.

In the heat of abuse, the promise of eternal hatred for a child brings huge comfort, so Eddie clung to that promise. It gave him hope, something to live for. Revenge kept him alive, but it's the kind of revenge in which you ultimately kill yourself.

Not easy. Promising to stay angry forever takes a lot out of you. You really have to work at it, concentrate, because if you let go of the anger, what do you have left?

Right after a Sol beating, Sol would bring him a present, take him for a walk, tell him a story, sing him a song, and Eddie would thaw long enough to trust again, love again, then… WHACK. Smoked. Again.

How many ups and downs before you can't go up again? Better to hate, because love you can't count on.

***

"Talk to him."

"It's twenty-five years, Uzi."

"Just talk to him."

The "Talk." The mythical "Talk." The open-hearted exchange that will change everything, and never does. It changes *while* you're talking, but after? Forget it.

It's the thing people don't get. The impossibility of real change. Real change doesn't change. And if it does, it's so infinitesimal you hardly see it. One may feel it in themselves, but it loses something in the transition, so by the time it reaches the other person, it's gone.

Nothings changes but the pursuit of change. To keep it going, they give pursuit a name. They call it hope. Can't give up on hope, can you now? Where would we all be without hope? What would we do with our time? Hoping takes the pressure off change.

"I thought for sure he'd be dead by now, Uzi."

Maya wrote to Max, who called Adi, who called Uzi, who told Eddie.

"He asked for you."

"I don't wanna see him. It's not gonna work."

"You don't know."

"*I* know."

"Listen, Eddie, men of that generation, they saw things we'll never know; what they overcame, how much they lost, their sacrifices, their—"

"Where's *your* old man?"

"He died in the battle at Suez in 1954, the year I was born."

"Sometimes that's better, isn't it?"

"What?"

"No father."

"No, I would have wanted one."

"Not like mine."

"Yes, everyone thinks they have the worst."

Eddie's staring at the chessboard.

"Uzi, I'm gonna spill my guts and he's gonna look at me like I'm crazy. I don't want that Nuremberg face staring back at me like, what did *I* do?"

"If that's the face you see, that's the face you'll get."

"I hate the fuck!"

"Well, then you'll definitely get the Nuremberg look."

"Do you know what he did?"

"Whatever it is, I'm sure he's beating himself up much more than you could."

"Walked the fuck out! I was sixteen!"

Eddie closes his eyes and remembers coming home from Trios that night, an ambulance pulling away from the front of their building. He yells and runs after it, catching up, hopping on the back fender as the ambulance gets stuck behind cars waiting for a light. He holds on to the door handles and looks in the door window, waving to Bina who's lying inside, a compress on her head. Max is holding her hand. She sees Eddie in the window and looks away.

Eddie would have hung on the back fender all the way to Kings County Psychiatric, except he heard Maya calling him. He looked back and she was holding on to a neighbor's hand. He jumped off, ran back to Maya, thanked the neighbor, and took Maya upstairs to their apartment, greeted by a smell of smoke in the hallway, a smell of smoke and mothballs. He opened the door and the apartment was flooded, Sol's suits, shirts, shoes, Stetsons, on the bedroom floor, charred. Sol told Bina he was leaving and she set fire to his closet.

* * *

The Fix

"What should I tell him? That I love him?"
"Don't you?"
A teardrop hits the King.
"Why bother if you don't."
Queen.
"You talk about him, dream about him."
Castle, Knight.
"Do you know how long I waited for him to come back?"
Bishop, Pawn.
"Well, now he's waiting for you."

Chapter Sixteen

"*Hazak v Hazak*, Eddie! Come back strong! Come back safe! Next week, you become a full Kibbutz member."

Eddie revs up the Vespa and heads out. Riding desert roads for a year turned Eddie from a *shlemiel* rider into a fearless one. "**Put your helmet on!**" Uzi yells to deaf ears.

"**YEEE-HAAAA!**"

The Kibbutz gave Eddie a week and Uzi offered to go with him, but it was a trip he had to make alone. He wasn't coming back.

It came to him at the six-month mark. Up to that point, he thought Kibbutz Ruhama is where he would spend the rest of his life. But now it's six months later and they're gonna vote him in as a full Kibbutz member... and it's that commitment thing again.

As long as he knows he can leave, then he can stay. But as soon as the expectation, the pull, the lure of safety appears — then it becomes a problem. How can you trust if you never trusted? Believe, if you never believed? That once you give yourself over, you won't get smacked?

He can't tolerate security. It's too unsettling. He needs a piece of him to know that he can destroy himself, shoot himself in the foot, break a leg, fall off a bike, kill himself. He should be able to count on at least that much.

Being normal, civil, secure, and content isn't very comforting for a man on the run. And although it may appear to others and sometimes even to himself that he's changed, his sense of isolation hasn't. And nowhere does that isolation feel better than cutting through the granite mountains of the Judean Hills, exercising a controlled recklessness. Eddie speeds the straightaways, then slows around the treacherous turns, dismounting at times to personally escort the bike down the steep, narrow bend, knowing one misstep may ruin his reunion with Sol.

Eddie looks up the side of the sheared mountain, warning of falling rock zones. (As if you can do anything once the rocks start falling.) It's how he understands his relationship with Sol. Once sheared, the rocks start falling. The mountains were sheared a long time ago, but rocks still fall...

Although Arad is only a half-day's ride from Kibbutz, Eddie takes the longer circuitous route guided by interest, instinct, and avoidance. He needs time to clear his head to steel himself for Sol.

All these years and I'm still afraid of him.

A feeling reminiscent of the lull before the snap of the belt. Eddie's stomach is Jell-O. He needs a good pep talk, some airy reassurance.

It's gonna be good, gonna be good, all good.

Another myth.

Family reconciliation is a great idea. But the minute you commit to reconcile, say hello to doubt. It's a matter of getting past the past — the second-guessing, the first-guessing, still a guess, always a guess, you just don't know, don't know with family. You don't know if your best intentions will find a partner.

Still, Eddie has to make the trip. No doubt, doubt will wrestle him along the way, but the Vespa underneath will shore up his balls and take him there.

Using Michener's *The Source* as his guide, Eddie reads about biblical life in the Holy Land, thrilled to be standing in the very same spot of so many epic events, so much bloodshed, history, kings and gods, heroes and tyrants, a connection he feels here in the desert, on the *Tels*, in the hills, mountains, and valleys. This is where he belongs, with his people, his land, and for that brief moment, doubt takes a back seat.

Riding seventy miles east from Kibbutz near the seaport city of Ashkelon, descending to the Dead Sea, the lowest point on Earth, Eddie turns back toward Jerusalem, rising two thousand feet past Hebron, Bethlehem, Beersheva, back down to Jericho, up to the top of Masada, parking his Vespa and hiking the hairy snake path, forgoing the touristy cable car.

Trudging up the snake path brings him closer to imagining the Roman assault up Masada, held off by a small rebel force of zealots hurling vats of boiling oil on legions clawing their way up.

Couldn't have been fun.

In between his own labored breath, he hears screams of scalded men within the quiet suicides. When he gets to the top, he lies down on the ground on his back, and spreads his arms to hold hands and be with the 916 martyrs. He looks up at the sky, saying his last goodbye. He's not afraid, and it occurs to him that Death has no chance against Mass suicide. It's dying alone that's the problem.

Everyone! Jump into the pool!

Towards evening, as the sun is setting, he's so wired he stays up through the night for dawn's sunrise to next day's sunset. He's up thirty-six hours straight. He's sure the martyrs didn't sleep either. Nor were they as concerned with the view. But for Eddie it's a miracle. The 916 martyrs, the pact, the bond, the view. Sunrise to sunset at Masada, the most brilliant spectacular beginning and end to any day.

Burnt reds and oranges, yellows, and browns reflect off the dead black waters of the Dead Sea, giving way to the lush springs of En Gedi. Just too beautiful. Too beautiful a day to see Pop... it would go against nature.

Did you see your father, Eddie?
Nah, it was too nice.
What did you do?
I stayed in En Gedi and died on Masada.
What did you do after?
I went to The Wall.
To pray?
To bang my head!
What the hell am I doing? Why am I going? Waste of time, thinking I can repair something, it's stupid. What am I doing?

Eddie's favorite question.

It's noon and Eddie's bathing in a spring, a pool of fresh water falling from a cut ridge, washing off the remains of his body caked with black mush scooped from the Dead Sea, rich with life-enhancing nutrients and minerals. His skin's tingling and he feels better, much better, his joints and bones baking in the sun, ridding nooks and crannies in his neck and shoulders.

Leave in for twenty minutes at 350 degrees. Bina always said, to bake in the oven, leave in for twenty minutes at 350.

Was it the same for the Krauts?

Eh, don't think about that, it's too beautiful out here.

Being in Israel is being in a constant state of collision. How can it not be. And so all this natural beauty does is make it worse. Was the sun in the camps? Is the black mush, ash? Is the warmth of the ash, children's ashes?

Whether lying on Masada, or covered in black mush, if you're conscious, it's hard to take in the full experience, the physical beauty a distraction.

The crystal clear water is cold and refreshing, the waterfall pelting his head, making his eyes heavy. He moves back into a crevice in the rocks behind the waterfall, watching the shimmering curtain in front of him.

* * *

"Hi, Pop."

"*Vat* are you doing here?"

"I came to see you."

"*Vy*? So I should say, 'I'm sorry'?"

"Yes."

"Go home."

"You know *Momme* died."

"Go home! I don't *vant* to see you!"

"Can I sit down?"

Sol points to the bed. Eddie sits on the edge, Sol alongside him. Sol takes Eddie's hand and they look out the window. The sun goes down and the wind breezes in, taking over the night shift.

"*Vant* a cookie, *boytschick*?"

"With hot chocolate and whip?"

"Sure...*veel* go to Golishoff's."

"And would you warm up my hands, Pop, like you used to, sitting at the counter?"

"Sure, *boytschick*, give me your hands."

Eddie extends his hands and falls in the water.

***

"Who?"

"Sol. Short guy, big hands? Looks like Rabin."

The guy behind the desk was a sweet old man and Eddie was almost sorry he woke him. He looked more like one of the residents in the nursing home than the manager.

"Sol... Sol... Yes... He die."

"What?!"

"Yesterday, maybe Friday...?"

Fucking Camus!

"Monday?...No! *Eet* was Friday."

"He..."

"Sick...*veree* sick, can no breathe. He go to hospital, but die anyway...too *minny* cigarette." He turns his face to the fan on his desk. "*Veree* hot, *veree* hot in Arad."

"How long was he here."

"Here... two year."

"And before?"

"He work."

"What kind of work?"

The old man stops. "You KGB?"

"Relative."

"KGB relative?"

"Nephew."

Eddie was embarrassed for a stranger to know he wasn't a good son.

"Oh, *veree* nice you come from *Amereeka?*"

"Yes."

" Sorry you no see *heem. Deed* you know he was *seeck?*"

Eddie gets weak in the knees.

"You want water?"

"Yes, please."

Eddie sinks back on the couch, takes a long drink, and feels the cold enter his body.

"Was my uncle alone?"

"No, he had wife, but she die, then *hee* get *seeck*.

When women die, men get *seeck*. When men die, women dance."

Bina didn't dance.

"What kind of work did he do, before he got sick?"

"In market *wit* fruit and vegetable."

"What was he doing in Arad?"

"*Eet veree* good here, government want people here, so *dey geeve* apartment, car, money, job, *veree* cheap to *leeve* here, and life *eez* good, you no have to work *haard*, not like in Russia, where life *eez veree haard*." He fans himself. "Here is *better; better* hot *den* cold."

"Did you know him?"

"Oh yes. We friends. We play chess. Your uncle *veree* good player, he have you by pawn, you lose by pawn. You play *wit* him?"

"Used to. I was looking forward to playing with him."

"We always *tink* there's more games to play."

"What's your name?"

"Victor."

"I'm Aryeh."

"Aryeh Leib, like *de* Lion."

"Yes. Are you the manager?"

"I manage, but I no manager. Manager not here, had heart attack — or cancer, I no remember. Many sick people here, and *eef* you not sick when you come *een*, you sick when you die."

"Was he alone when he died?"

"His daughter come and take care. You know her, Maya?"

"I know Maya."

"She take *veree* good care. Daughters take better care *den* sons. I have daughters. You have children?"

Eddie steps out into the mid-day sun. There's something about the sun washing over you in your darkest moment...death should only come at night. But then you can no easier look at the sun in the day than you can look at death at night.

"Can I see his room?"

Victor takes Eddie down a long corridor. They step into an empty room.

"New man come tomorrow."

And then it starts all over again. New beginning, same ending.

There's a bed, a desk, a chair, a dresser, a closet. Eddie opens the closet which could fit in the corner of Sol's Holy Grail back on the Lower East Side in the six-floor walk-up apartment. Eddie sees Sol's pants and shirts hanging.

"You want to take?"

"I'll take the white short sleeve."

"Okay, we *geeve rest ah-way. Eez dat* okay?"

"Sure."

Eddie removes the belt off the hook.

"You want to keep belt?"

"No." And passes out.

He wakes up at night in his father's bed. Victor's smoking.

"*Fay-looks*?!"

"Who *Fay-looks*? I Victor."

"Pop?"

"No."

Eddie begins to cry. Victor pours a half glass of vodka for each of them.

"*Veree* hard, when *fadder* die... I cry for days...I still cry..."

Eddie jumps off the cot and staggers down the hallway, indifferent residents step aside for Eddie Parker—*The Golishoff Man! Short-order cook by day, fuck up at night...*

He jumps on his Vespa, head pounding, dry heaving, crying, spitting, screaming, racing eighty, ninety miles an hour, gunning down the highway. The desert's closing in, twenty-eight miles to Beersheva.

It's pitch black, except for the flickering lights of Bedouin camps on either side of the road. Don't stop, he was warned, or else he'll be some camel's lunch. It's freezing. All he's wearing is a ripped T-shirt, jeans, and sandals from the hot day, but once the sun goes down and stars take over, the desert temp drops forty degrees in an hour.

He's shaking, he wants to live, he wants to die. He hits a hundred.

Can't see a fucking thing!

He's blind, the sand, the wind in his face. He leans in, hugging the Vespa, his face inches from the broken white line splitting the asphalt, his life on the line.

Follow the fucking line!

Lifeline ends and he streaks miles without a marker, refusing to slow. A Fiat passes him as if he's standing still.

Good! Follow Fie-fie!

He stays on *Fie-fie's* tail, on top of the red tail lights. The broken white line picks up again. He swings out left to pass, but *Fie-fie* cuts him off. The Cat and *Fie-fie* game goes on for miles. *Fie-fie* won't let him pass. He screams into the wind "**FUCKER!!**" The white line breaks and he's back on *Fie-fie's* tail. Don't lose *Fie-fie*. Just he and *Fie-fie* make two and road makes three.

Whizzing the straightaway, he's clocking in over a hundred miles an hour. Several miles down, *Fie-fie* slows to a crawl, stops, makes a sharp left turn and continues. Eddie follows, slows, stops, makes the same sharp left turn. He looks right — a ravine. Eddie shits in his pants.

I woulda never seen it.

He looks up and *Fie-fie's* gone into the night, no tail light.

Eddie cleans up in Beersheva and heads north to Jerusalem. Getting to the outskirts of Jerusalem was a breeze compared to the traffic in the city. Meandering through the congested streets, Eddie parks his Vespa by Mandelbaum Gate and walks through the marketplace on the way to The Wall. It's nine at night and the ancient market square is *tumling* with tourists. A young shopkeeper pulls him in to buy a rug. Eddie's exhausted. He sits down on a stool in the shop.

"Sir, this carpet goes back generations—"

Who cares?

The merchant invites Eddie to the back for some tea with his family of ten sleeping and resting on the floor. Eddie sips, looking at the young merchant and his father sitting alongside him. Merchant says, "Sir, you are looking for your father?"

Eddie's stunned.

"How do you know?"

"All men look for their fathers."

Ain't that the fucking truth.

"You were not together when he died."

"No... I missed him."

"But he is safe and at peace, he wants you to know that."

Eddie nods.

"And he wishes the same for you."

Young merchant closes his eyes.

"Close your eyes, give me your hands."

Eddie closes his eyes and places his hands. Young merchant's hands are warm, and Eddie falls asleep on the floor between a few boys. He opens his eyes.

"How long have I been out?"

"A few hours."

Eddie stands up and gives the turbaned young man a hundred dollar bill.

"May Allah bless you."

The young man reaches for the rug to give Eddie.

"It's okay, I already had one pulled out on me."

Eddie's not sure if Allah's rugs are a come on, but whatever it was, it worked. He felt renewed and refreshed. Allah's a good merchant. He knows more men go looking for their fathers than a good rug. Come to think of it, Eddie didn't see any other rugs in the store. Some bongs, but no rugs. Only the one rug with the one frayed corner...

He should rotate it, like Bina did with her mattresses.

Eddie walks across the huge plaza to the The Wall. He writes a note, slips it in, joining thousands of note-slippers making The Wall a prayer-field of snow. Eddie's thinking, "God must be choking on his own prayers."

Eddie wants to help God, so he pulls some notes from The Wall. Eddie figures that at this rate God stopped taking messages a long time ago. But he'll take *his*. There's room and it's short.

"Dear Pop... sorry it took me so long..."

Chapter Seventeen

It's collect. It's always collect when trouble calls and it's always at night. Night gets one ear to the pillow, one to the phone.

"Yes, operator, I'll accept."

Maya almost forgot the years of Eddie's nocturnal calls from the precinct, the streets, the alleys, from being beaten up, drugged, drunk, or in jail, the card games, the bailouts. It was always collect, come collect Eddie. Bina wouldn't do it, so she sent Maya.

"Sis?"

"To whom may I direct –"

He's crying into the phone.

"Any messages?"

"I'm sorry, Sis, really sorry for not being there for you and Pop."

"Don't you think it's a little late?"

"What time *is* it?"

"It's four in the morning, where are you?"

"Jerusalem! It's only ten here. Sorry, lost track of time."

"What do you want Eddie?"

"Can I stay with you?"

"What?!"

"I've changed, Sis."

"Because *you* changed, means everyone's changed?"

"No, but — Maya?... Maya?"

As long as I call her name, she won't hang up.

"Maya? Maya?"

"Yes?"

"Can I stay with you... in Toronto? I cleaned up my act. I haven't seen Barry or the girls, never met the Shlossbergs... hello... hello, hello?... Are you there? I'll be good... hello?"

Once again, Maya got stuck burying a parent. Once again, she flew thousands of miles to Israel, disrupting her own life, to take care of business when he was right there and did nothing.

Once again, the furthest sibling shows up first. Once again, the responsible get stuck.

"I saw Pop like you wanted me to... hello? Maya? Maya?... Maya?... "

* * *

The ride back from Jerusalem to Tel Aviv, usually a few hours, took Eddie all night. Understandable given all the hashish he smoked with the young rug merchant — after he stuck the note in The Wall and woke Maya.

"Oh, Sir, how good to see you, again. Some tea?"

"Yeah, more tea 'n' bong."

On the ride to Tel Aviv, the broken white line on the highway turned into a long licorice stick, and *Fie-Fie* wasn't showing up twice, so he went real slow.

The sun was rising when he rang Dora's bell, the owner of the rooming house he stayed in when he first arrived in Israel a year ago. He hears *krechtzing* and breathing.

Dora's doing Yoga.

"Be right there!" she says sprightly, "Who could it be this early?"

She opens the door and Eddie collapses in her arms. He sleeps through the day and night, waking the next morning to fresh white sheets and pillows, feeling virgin. Waking is a slow process, feeling groggy. He wants to get up, but the smell of fresh linen keeps him there. It's like he felt growing up in Bina's home — clean, crazy clean — and he almost forgot how good it felt, how within all the household turmoil, the safety and warmth of clean sheets to crawl into at night would help him fall asleep and wake to a new day.

He puts on the white terry cloth robe hanging on the door, picks off the clean bath towel at the foot of his bed, and walks down the hall to the bathroom to shower and shave. He cleans himself up and returns to his room, his underwear, jeans, and Sol's shirt washed and folded on the bed, alongside loose Yoga pants and top.

Dora.

He slips on the Yoga togs and walks to the deck for some "down dog."

"Eddie! Come in! Join us. We're just getting started."

He joins Dora with some *alte kaker* tenants on the deck in back of the house.

"Are you all right, Eddie?"

"Better now that I'm here."

The rooming house has six rooms, communal kitchen, living room, a study, two bathrooms and showers in the hall, a garden, a deck in the back, and a bomb shelter in the basement. The house is made of Jerusalem stone, located on a quiet residential street lined with trees and bushes, flower beds in front of every home. Dora's tenants are elderly, retired, and alone.

Dora's a slim, attractive South African widow, well into her seventies, who looks unbelievably young and vibrant. If you view her at certain angles you'd swear she was a woman in her middle years. No make-up, sparkling hazel eyes, luminous skin, and stunning grey hair pulled back in a bun — beautiful, ageless, hot — ol' lady or not.

Dora made *Aliyah* to Israel with her husband and three young children in the early sixties. Her husband died the day they arrived. There was pressure from her family to return to Johannesburg, but Dora was upset by Apartheid and wanted her kids to grow up in Israel.

She stayed, raised three sons, and worked as a nursery school teacher until she retired at the age of seventy-five. She then purchased the rooming house. "More to be with people than being a landlord."

When Eddie said, "What's so good about people?" she replied, "People are good for you, good for the spirit – especially children. Children keep you young, but old people are like little children, so they need to be taken care of too."

Dora attributes her good health to working, stretching, fruit, seaweed, rice, not being alone, Yoga, her husband dying, not remarrying, and being regular.

"I had to rely on myself. Take care of my children. No time to feel sorry for myself. No time for silly things like men. Oh I've had my share of companions, but men aren't worth being taken seriously." "And," she'd laugh, "they just get in the way."

"Of what, Dora?"

"Breathe, Eddie, breathe—Ahhhhhhhhhhhhhhhhhh," as she reaches for the sky with her arms. "It's important to breathe, Eddie."

You would think breathing isn't something you need to be reminded of.

"Especially Yoga breathing, it's very good for you."

"And without Yoga you stop?"

Hmm...that's something Sol would say.

It scares him how as he's getting older, he's taking on Sol's mannerisms, his *shtick*, his looks. *Solisims* are creeping in. Sol the body-snatcher is snatching Eddie without his permission.

Gotta be careful I don't start buttering bread.

Could it be that by the time Eddie dies there will be no discernible difference?

"AHHHHHHHHHHHHHHHHHH!"

Now that's a breath.

Morning Yoga finishes at seven, and Eddie falls asleep on the sun-drenched deck lying spread-eagled on his Yoga mat. The sun on his face, he hasn't been this happy in years.

"Get up, young man!"

Eddie's eyes feel sand-papered.

"I need to sleep, Dora."

"Plenty of time for that when you're dead, young man!"

"Almost did that."

They had some yogurt on the deck and Eddie told her his story.

"So your sister is angry with you."

"Yeah."

"Well, give her time. She'll come around. It sounds like she's a very forgiving person."

"Yeah, I give her a lot of practice."

Dora closes her eyes and lifts her face to the morning sun.

"Glorious sun."

"It is."

"Go for a walk, Eddie. It's a beautiful day, and you've had a difficult night."

Why couldn't Dora be my mother?

Not that she didn't *noodge* — but it's a soft *noodge*, gentle Yoga *noodge*.

There are people like that in the world, soft souls who *noodge* softly, round out the edges. They come into your life when you least expect them. Usually strangers who understand you in ways no one else could. The kind of people, who, when you're together your blood pressure drops forty points, you start drinking green tea, sit with legs crossed, have slow conversations, and look at antiques. It works for as long as you're with or around them.

"Uh, Dora?"

"Yes?"

"Do you have any work for me?"

"You'll have to get up early."

In exchange for room and board, Eddie cooks, cleans, shops, and watches the house when Dora visits her children and grandchildren. On his first day off, after a month, he wakes at noon and takes a walk downtown. He misses the city. Kibbutz was great, but the pulse of the city got his blood going, reminding him of the Lower East Side. No two cities pulse the way New York and Tel Aviv do. Two high blood pressure cities heading for a stroke.

He walks along Dizengoff's hotels, shops, and restaurants, takes in the people, breathes in the fresh air, checks out the sky, as clear as clear can be.

My life is good.

Eddie buys *The Jerusalem Post*, sits down at a café, and reads while waiting for the waitress to come over. Every article he reads is the same. Depressing. Hostility, bitterness, fighting, quarreling in The Knesset, the U.N. dominated by a coalition of the unfeeling and unforgiving, new settlements, religious right, warring factions, bombs, bomb shelter assassinations, people blowing themselves up, killing infants in baby carriages. Fire extinguishers not putting out fires, but cleaning up the mess of flesh.

What the fuck, they'll never be any peace in the Mid-East. The world started here and and it will end here! But while I'm waiting for the world to end, why not have some ice coffee.

He motions for the server, snapping his finger in the air... He hears a familiar sound coming towards him. Not a very reassuring sound, the sound of rollerblades.

He hums, "I got a brand new pair of roller skates..."

Snip chick's standing over him, tapping her blade, cracking her gum. He keeps his head down. But she lowers hers smack in his face.

"What you want?"

"Israeli ice café?...Please."

"Anything else?"

"Uh...sure, humus, falafel, chicken schnitzel, soup, and a side of Israeli salad. I'll have dessert later."

She smiles. "You are hungry!"

She doesn't recognize him.

Why would she? I'm not the only ball buster in town, there's one right behind me.

"*Dese* ain't no fuckin' meatballs!"

Snip chick says, "It falafel, sir."

"I WANT MEATBALLS!"

Eddie doesn't know what a heart attack feels like. But this is close. His chest seizes and a memory cramp freezes his calf to the chair.

I could be calf's liver!

He shoves his face into the *Post* so close he can smell the ink.

He hears Ollie spit out falafel, disgusting everyone around him.

"Looks like meatball but tastes like shit! It'a trick meatball!"

Customers scat, including snip chick who knows not to give Ollie any lip. He's a little *too* American for her to start up with.

"What*chu* eatin', Chaalie?"

"Kebob."

"But what's *wit de* spear in *de* 'bob'?"

"Holds all *de* shit together."

"Maybe I'll use *de* spear on Eddie, 'stead *a de* spoon."

"If we can find *de* prick! Can't *believe* we come all *de* way to Jew-Land to take out a fuckin' eye!"

"Not just an eye, Chaalie."

By this time, you can read the print off Eddie's face.

"Let's get d*e fuck outta he*r, Chaalie" Ollie flips snip chick a fifty.

"*Feefty Dawllars*!! For **me**?"

"Yeah, *faw* you, you cunt!"

Snip chick gives Ollie a big hug.

"I *laaav* you!"

"Turn around. Let me see what you got."

Snip chick shows off her goods. Ollie eyes her ass and throws in another fifty.

"I'm stayin' at *de* Hilton unde' Ollie Calamari, *not* Chaalie Calamari. He wouldn't be interested."

She smiles. He laughs. Eddie's eating paper. He makes a break for it. Snip chick goes after him.

"YOU NO PAY!"

Chick chases check.

"OH YOU *DE* AMERICAN *PEEG*! **YOU** TOUCH MY TEEET!"

They see Eddie and pull their guns.

"GET 'EM, CHAALIE! GET *DE* SCUMBAG!"

Chaalie does the chasing, Ollie the yelling.

"GET 'EM, CHAALIE! GET 'EM!"

Eddie ducks into an alley, knocks over one garbage can, climbs into another, and closes the lid. His heart's pounding so loud it's a percussion instrument. He waits a while till it's quiet, lifts the lid, peeks out and sees an old familiar drunk stumble out a back door, pulling up his pants. Eddie starts to climb out.

"YOU'RE TOAST, EDDIE! MOTHER FUCKING TOAST!"

He leaps back into the garbage can. Ollie and Chaalie screech through the alley in a Mercedes with a bullhorn.

"YOU'RE TOAST! TOAST!"

I'm toast!

He could be a BLT wearing lettuce, tomato, onion, cukes, and radish on his head.

Israeli salad.
He waits for a while longer and climbs out.
Safe by a twat's hair.Whew!
The old drunk is sitting on the ground, his back against the titty bar door.
Eddie says, "Can you move, buddy, I'd like to go in."
The guy's three sheets to the wind.
Eddie puts the guy's arms around his neck, to lift him up, when the door opens and knocks them over. Two young punks laugh at them lying on the ground as they walk away. Eddie yells, "Fuck You, Punks!" They pull knives and start coming towards him. Eddie picks the garbage can up over his head and starts running towards them. The punks make a bee-line out of the alley. The drunk is laughing and kisses Eddie's hand. Eddie looks at the old man and wonders how he got this way. He makes up a story of a guy on the run, who ran so long that time ran out.
The two fallen soldiers hold each other up and stumble into the bar, celebrating their newfound friendship over several rounds of boilermakers in the middle of the day.
Life is good.
Eddie stuffs dollar bills in his mouth and nestles his nose between Miss Silicone, the drunk asleep on his lap.
Eddie wakes, nipple in his mouth, reflecting:
I'm toast! Fuckin' toast! They'll find me! Wherever I go, they'll find me! Fuck! One whack across Chaalie's knee and look where it got me!
Eddie's kissing the nipple, doing "life review," a regret riff. Ollie said, "Regret don't pay." But we keep coming back to the store.
Why didn't I let Chaalie blow me? What would have been so terrible? At least it would have saved my ass –not <u>that</u> ass, but <u>this</u> ass... I coulda had another crack at life—I mean it's only an ass... If I could do just <u>one</u> thing over, that would be it—whackin' Chaalie's knee, not lettin' him blow me—big mistake, biiiiiig mistake. Or... maybe... knockin' up Maddy. Yeah, that ranks high on the regret chart, leavin' Maddy. Wait! She left <u>me</u>. Or, maybe if I stayed in school. Wait! I hated school. Or—or, what if I worked at Golishoff's? Wait! I hate Golishoff's!... I hate <u>work</u>! Or—what if I didn't gamble, shoot pool... what if I took up bowling! What if I— didn't lie...?

Wait! I love to lie. Wait!— What if I... had other parents, wasn't born, wasn't a refugee, Rabbi didn't suck me off, if I sucked Chaalie, what if I—Wait! What if—?

That night, he finished "life review" between tiny dancer's legs, got stoned, jacked up on speed, and stole away into the night back to Kibbutz. Dora never heard a sound as he wheeled the Vespa out of her driveway at dawn and drove south four hours.

He's so fucked up, he can't ride. He stops off on the side of the road to sleep on a rock. A small caravan of Bedouins find him and take him back to their tents near a spring. Next morning, he washes up; they feed him fruits, dates and nuts. He mounts a camel and has pictures taken with his new friends. He gives the Bedouins his Polaroid and goes back on the road, recalling Adi's words to Uzi:

Our fight is not with the people, they want peace as much as we do.

* * *

He was only gone from Kibbutz two months, but it seemed much longer. He made the turn off the side road, then rode miles between fields of crops and water pipe lines. It was evening, sun falling rapidly. Each sunset in the desert brings its own colors, every sunset different, every sunset new, far more brilliant than sunrise... as it should be. After all, it's the end of the day, richer for all it's endured.

Eddie knows he's getting close to Kibbutz when he smells the tangy aroma of orange groves. He's taking it all in when he goes over a bump. He remembers the first time he went over a bump, and it wasn't a speed bump. Uzi pointed out the ten-foot black tube sliding across the road between the fields was not a loose rubber tire, but a snake, a "good" snake protecting the crops from field mice.

Not all snakes are bad.

Eddie didn't exactly feel like a snake. But close. He cut out on the Kibbutz without a word. They gave him a home, food, work, friendship, and this was his "thank you."

I'll just say I'm sorry.

He hangs out at the chicken coops, behind the Moadon, waiting till night. He doesn't want to see anyone or explain anything. He just wants to pick up where he left off, no questions asked.

He strides into the Moadon, past a café full of shocked members, and sits down at the chessboard opposite Uzi, who's playing another opponent.

Uzi's opponent looks at Eddie and leaves. Eddie sits down in his place.

"Set 'em up, Uz."

Uzi flips the board in Eddie's face and walks out.

To stay in Kibbutz, Eddie had to commit to another probationary year.

What's another year in my fucked up life?

The nightmares return with a vengeance. He's a seal getting clubbed to death, and the other seals don't give a shit. He screams and cries through the night. It's a problem. *Youngees* can't fuck. He's fucking up all the fucking around him. Wholesale migrations of volunteers leave Kibbutz to do their fucking elsewhere, depleting Ruhama's cheap labor pool. They put Eddie in a shack far away, but still hear him.

"DON'T KILL ME. DON'T!! OW!! OW!!!"

It's now three months since Eddie ran from Ollie 'n' Chaalie, learned of Sol's death, on top of The Kid's betrayal, Bina's death, Maya's anger — a lot to digest for a crazy fuck to begin with.

***

Uzi watches Eddie disintegrate. He's seen many men break — after wars, after sustained periods of stress, never the same. And although Eddie wasn't on the battlefield, he was suffering the same as if bombs were dropping around him. And they were. He checks in on him.

"How are you, Eddie?"

Eddie cowers in a corner.

"Don't hit my head with the pot."

Uzi's cleaning up the mess in the shack.

"You need a doctor, Eddie."

"It's only at night, Uzi. The seals only get clubbed at night."

"You need to be hospitalized."

"I'll stay up. That's what I'll do. This way they won't get me."

"No one's after you."

"I saw them, Uzi! At the Dan Café! Ollie was eating a meatball thinking it was a falafel and—"

"You're sick, Eddie, you need help."

"I'm not crazy."

"You need sleep."

"How can I sleep? They want to kill me."

"Eddie, it's over a year. These people don't even know you exist. They don't care, they're not interested in you." Uzi speaks in the mildest, most sympathetic tones. "You're safe here in Kibbutz."

"THAT'S WHAT *YOU* THINK! You don't know these fuckers! They're like the Arabs! 'Vendettas Forever!' They'll find me! They said so! Said I'm toast! They won't rest till I rest! IN A FUCKING BOX! WITHOUT MY EYES!"

"Eddie, why would the Italian Mafia come here?"

"You don't understand. I embarrassed them, made them lose face! They want their face back! I can't give them their face back, so they want *my* face!"

"Eddie, you're hallucinating."

"You don't understand. Dora understands."

"Who's Dora?"

"A Yogi, she's nice, very nice; you're not nice."

"Eddie?"

"WHAT?!"

"Did you see your father?"

Uzi takes Eddie to a hospital. He's discharged after two weeks, fully medicated, calm and lifeless, looking like Bina.

Like mother, like son.

Uzi drives Eddie back to Kibbutz. Eddie sleeps through the night and the nightmares stop.

"Be sure to take your medication, Eddie. And you must see the psychiatrist."

"Sure."

Eddie sees a shrink, gets new meds, overmedicates, and becomes a walking zombie. He lays in bed awake, days at a time, afraid to sleep. He stops eating, washing, shaving, turns into a recluse, erratic, making Howard Hughes look stable. No one comes near his shack. The *youngees* say, "There's a crazy man in the shack!"

A vote is taken and Eddie is asked to leave Kibbutz. Another good thing about Communism. Any other place, you behave like a nut, they throw you out. Here they take a vote: by a vote of nine to one Eddie has to go. "He needs a hospital, not a Kibbutz," says the committee. "A permanent one."

Uzi's on his way to deliver the news when he smells a noxious odor coming from the shack. He runs, kicks the door open, and drags Eddie out. The pilot flame on the kerosene heater was out and fumes were everywhere.

"WAKE UP EDDIE! WAKE UP!"

* * *

"Are you up?"
He feels a light hand stroke his forehead.
"How are you, honey?"
His mouth's pasty, nose crusted, and eyes weigh a ton.
"Thank God you're up."
"Who's this?"
"Maya."
"Who?"
"Your sister."
"Who? " He smiles.
"Oh stop it!" She laughs and sighs, buries her face in his neck. "Oh, Eddie, thank God! Thank God you're alive!
"How long have I been out?"
"Days."
He looks at her and sees the fear behind the smile.
"I'll be okay, Sis, don't worry."
"You'll be fine."
"I'm sorry, Sis. Sorry for a lot of things."

"Shush. It's okay, Eddie, I'm just happy you're alive."

He tries to prop himself up on the pillows. He's too weak. She helps him. A curtain track separates him from the adjacent bed. A TV's on the wall blurting weather, bad news, and traffic. He takes the remote attached to his bed and tries to turn down the volume, but the bed starts collapsing down the center. He pushes other buttons—the TV volume blasts through the roof and the bed expands and contracts. He knocks all the medication off his tray as doctors and nurses run in. Maya grabs the controls and steadies everything.

"What the hell are you doing, Eddie?! You're gonna give me a heart attack!"

"Still happy I'm alive?"

He looks at the mirror on the wall behind Maya. His cheeks are hollow, sockets for eyes, scarecrow neck, sunken chest, bones for arms.

Hello, Auschwitz.

"Jesus Christ, Sis! Do you see what I see?"

"Well, you took enough tranquilizers to kill a cow."

He looks back at the sunken figure.

"I look like death warmed over!"

"Why did you put out the pilot?"

"Huh?"

"The pilot light for the kerosene heater was out, gas was coming in all night. A crack in the window saved you, and then Uzi found you. You're very lucky Eddie."

"Yeah."

"Doctors say you're at risk, suicidal. Why did you do it?"

"I don't remember doing anything."

"Uzi said it was right after you imagined you saw the mob."

"I *imagined?*"

"You saw a psychiatrist?"

"Yes."

"What did he say?"

"He didn't say anything! He said, 'Take these,' and gave me a closet full of pills. So I took 'em! I'm not suicidal! I took a few pills! Fuckin' moron, calling me suicidal!

She pours him a cup of water. He sips slowly through a straw.

"Doctors weren't sure you'd come out of your coma."

"Can you turn down the lights, Sis? It's too cheery in here."

She dims the lights and removes a *yahrtzeit* candle from her bag.

"Who died?"

"Six million. It's Yom Hashoah."

Maya's big on milestones. Birthdays, graduations, anniversaries, births, deaths, she knows when the Jewish holidays come out, calls Eddie to remind him of Sol's or Bina's birthday, the anniversary of their arrival on the S.S. Blatchford — she's plugged in that way, and while she remembers everything, Eddie can't remember his own name.

"I guess this is what it comes down to, eh, Sis?"

"What?"

"Sipping through a straw in a styrofoam cup, looking out the window of a hospital bed. Is this what Pop looked like?"

"Worse, he couldn't breathe; the cold air from his oxygen mask was stinging his eyes. It was terrible, but the only way for him to breathe. It was so painful watching him."

"Could you do me a favor, Sis?"

"What?"

"If I get like that, put a pillow over my head. And I'll do the same for you."

"It's a deal."

"You stayed with him?"

"Yes."

"I went to see him."

"I know."

"Got there late... for a change."

"I'm sorry."

"He saved my life."

"Uzi?"

"And Pop."

Eddie told her about *Fie-fie*, the one solitary car, on the one solitary road, on the one solitary turn.

"Car wouldn't let me pass. I was headed right off the cliff... He was watching out for me. No other way to explain it, Sis."

"No."

"Did he ask for me?"

"Always."

"What did he say?"

"That he loved you and wished he knew you better... that he wished he would have been a better father... "

He turns away from Maya, his body shaking. She slips into bed beside him, wrapping her arms around him.

"Do you know you're a *zaydee*?"

"No."

"Little Benji, named after Mom."

"They had a *bris*?"

"Yes."

"Were you there?"

"Yes."

"You always show up, Sis."

"And this time it wasn't a funeral."

Eddie's quiet for a long time. He feels an infusion of something he can't describe, but it has something to do with having done something right in his life.

"And The Kid. How's The Kid?"

"Good."

"And your family, the girls, Barry?"

"Fine."

"And Max. How's Uncle Max?"

"Max... Max was tied to a chair, and the store was lit."

Six million — and one.

Chapter Eighteen

Eddie's sentence is reduced from ten to five, eligible for parole in three. Ollie got thirty 'n' Chaalie twenty, courtesy of *Benedict Eddie* cooperating with the Feds via Tracy's mom, the D.A. investigating mob activities.

He named players, coaches, refs, teachers, principals, bookies, wise guys, not such wise guys, he named names, he named anyone he could.

Payback for Max's execution... tied to a chair... burning... because of me... one Kristallnacht is enough.

Although not a very popular guy at the moment, the entire neighborhood comes out to see Eddie, lining up the courthouse steps to spit at him.

So this is what Sol tasted when I spit in his face.

Eddie remembered when he was on the corner of Trios with two other wise guys, when he turned his head and shot a glob right into the face of a man walking by. Eddie didn't mean to do it and was about to apologize, but the guy kept on walking, figuring whoever has the balls to do that, you don't fuck with. The two wise guys were impressed as well, and so the word got out that Eddie's crazy. Who else but a crazy man would turn state witness against the Mob?

* * *

They got Ollie 'n' Chaalie on corruption, fraud, extortion, gambling, and the mother of them all, tax evasion. In America, you can cheat, steal, bribe, extort, maim, embezzle, even kill. But ignore taxes?

Uh-uh. They don't call 'em *Uncle* for nothing. No one said he was a *good* Uncle. You get *yours,* Sam gets *his,* a pound for an ounce. That's how they get the big guys and anyone else who doesn't keep receipts.

"Receipts? You want *'hit'* receipts? *Lemme* check my bank statement."

Ollie laughed all the way to the penitentiary. Chaalie listed Trios as his only source of income. Father 'n' Son put away for thirty and twenty would make Chaalie sixty upon release, and Ollie a hundred. But even if he could get out, Ollie preferred to stay, saying the health coverage was too good.

"Doctors, lawyers, dentists, a guy checkin' my prostrate for free? Where do you get *dat*? Every man should have **dis**!"

Chaalie also preferred prison. "So many hunks." He became the official prison welcome wagon... "Hey, girlfriend!" Behind bars was the only place Chaalie could come out. And Ollie was okay with that.

"He's my kid, what am I gonna do?"

* * *

Eddie didn't do as well in the Father and Son category. The Kid wouldn't see him, didn't return his letters, calls. The Kid was too hurt, too bitter. In two short years, he lost his heart, his soul, his team, his dream. That's more than anyone should have to lose, but for a kid of twenty? He turned from a sweet, kind-hearted kid into an angry young man.

He worked as an electrician, the tallest electrician on site, but lowest man on the union totem pole, just a young sap with a limp and a cap, a "has-been" at twenty. He lived in a one-bedroom with Tracy, Mary, and the baby, not bothering to come home nights, staying out with the boys, drinking, gambling, and whoring. He'd be gone for days—and when he showed up, he was drunk and broke. He had his father in him.

* * *

During the trial, Eddie's quarantined in a hotel room, sole occupant on the twelfth floor, guarded in eight-hour shifts 24/7. He leaves for court at nine and returns at five. Mary visits to brief him, go over depositions. But that's it as far as contact with the outside world is concerned. Eddie spends most of his time staring out the window, watching the little *busy's* scurry below. He has no patience for TV or books; he's listless, sleeps a lot—a half-sleep going over his life, what happened — what didn't — the trouble he got into, his breakdown, his return...

"Can you take this letter to The Kid, Mary?"

"He'll rip it up."

"Give it to him anyway."

Throughout the trial, Ollie, Chaalie, 'n' friends stared him down, whispering death threats.

I have a fan club.

To get through the hearings, Eddie took on the role of a crazy Hassid, hissing at them in Yiddish.

"He's nuts!" the Mob said.

Eddie knows the only people the Mob's afraid of are the mentally deranged. No one can stare you down better than a nut, so they stopped.

Thank you, Bina.

The trial concluded, Eddie copped a plea and was sent away along with the rest of the "Crew," put in different correctional facilities.

Eddie figured he'd pay his dues, come out, and start from a new place. The day he arrived in prison, he called The Kid.

"Hello, Kid?"

"Fuck you!"

With "fuck you" stuck in his ear, he knew that place no longer existed.

* * *

Federal Correctional Institute in Texarkana houses low-risk detainees in its minimum-security prison. *Minimum* doesn't mean the inmates aren't dangerous. It just means the chances of violence are far less because inmates have far more privileges and won't risk blowing it for a maximum-security site with fewer amenities, i.e., computer classes, board games, health clubs, gardening, and quiet time. In penal terms, it's the difference between the White House and a crack house.

Seventeen hundred inmates live in cells around a quadrangle, encircled with a ten-foot aluminum chain-link fence. Except for the fence, it could be a campus. The dorms are immaculate and inmates take special pride in their eight-by-nine cinderblock coops. Most prisoners are young Blacks and Latinos in their twenties and thirties, busted for possession. They come from Mexico, Guatemala, Honduras, the Caribbean—illegals in the wrong place at the wrong time, lured to a corner by overweight undercover cops out to meet their quota.

The criminal justice system depends on poverty to keep it going. So, forget winning the War on Drugs. There is no war, just drugs and money, in a system dedicated to sustaining the greater good. Jobs. Too many folks addicted to making a living off drugs, hooked on the criminal court system for jobs and pensions: cops, lawyers, judges, vendors, bus drivers, cabbies, parking lot attendants, hookers, haberdashers, secretaries, and unemployed jurors.

Everyone stands to do good in this artificial business made to look real, as busybodies scurry around on marble floors in cavernous municipalities lugging briefs, accordion files, newspapers, coffee cups, tin cups, pens and pencils in mouth, driven and harried, little people acting big, pushing paper, pushing themselves, pushing shit.

Where else can they find such meaningful work? Where else, but in these vaulted containers, could they look so busy and important, stepping into huge union-operated elevators, men and women in civil uniforms pushing a brass lever up and down—twenty floors, eight hours a day, for fifty grand and benefits—in service of lawyers, defendants, clerks, judges, criminals, cleaning women, custodians— everyone going up or down, but equal between stops.

And where else could *zhlobby* men with large teeth and tight-ass women wear expensive clothes and suits and ties, wing-tip shoes, and spiked heels on glitzy floors in this most confidential of all arenas, where every little whisper bounces off hard benches and paneled walls, making it sound like one big joke. The criminal *in*justice system.

Druggies approach undercover cops (not hard to spot) offering a joint (not hard to get) *just* to get arrested. The addicts could care less about drugs. What they want is what most of us want: three squares a day, a clean bed, and smokes. It's a sad day when a prisoner's time is up.

"Good luck, Juan."

"The luck is in *here,* Eddie, not out *there.*"

Juan is Eddie's cellmate, a prison staple.

"But what about family? Don't you want to be with them?"

"Fuck family, they no good for you."

Eddie looks at Juan.

Siegel..? Gomez Siegel...?

"Do you have a brother, Juan?"

"I have many. Why?"

"You look like someone I used to know."

"You get old enough, Amigo, everyone looks like someone you *used* to know."

"Well, good luck on the outside."

"I be back."

"Back?!"

"Sure."

"How, by sellin' drugs?"

"No, no, I write a note."

"Note?"

"I give Banco Popular teller note. In note, I write, 'I **not** ARMED – give me money!' They scare. They only see 'Armed.' They give me money, ring bell, arrest me, I give lawyer note, and Judge send me back here."

"Jesus Christ, Juan! That's a funny way of paying off a Judge."

Juan laughs. "Good man, Judge."

"I was wondering why every new inmate looks so familiar. Explains recidivism."

"What's that?"

"Same people returning to prison."

"Did you know, Amigo, that it costs fifty thousand a year to keep me here? As much as an elevator operator! Who else would pay so much for an old man?"

"You know, Juan, they say those who live *inside* of institutions are those who cannot live *outside* of institutions."

"Who want to live outside, when *eet* so good inside?"

He's right. For the four grand a month the State pays, Juan gets an eight-by-nine cinderblock, including amenities. Four mega TVs, two pool tables, a gym, commissary, library, grounds, picnic tables, vegetable garden, cafeteria, snack bar, lounge, clinic—all within walking distance.

Eddie's Daily Schedule
6:00 A.M — — —- Wake up.
7:00 A.M. — — — — Breakfast.
8:00 A.M. — — — — Nap.
9:00 A.M. — — — — Gym.
11:00 A.M. — — — -CNN.
12:00 P.M. — — — — Lunch.
1:00 P.M — — — -Nap.
2:00 P.M. — — — — — *Shpatzeer.*
3:00 P.M. — — — — — Read.
4:00 P.M. — — — — — Nap.
5:00 P.M — — — — -Rest.
6:00 P.M. — — — — — Dinner.
7:00 P.M. — — — — — Evening activity.
10:00 P.M. — — — — *Shluffee.*

Eddie looks out the window of his cell, sees the desert, and for a brief moment he's in Kibbutz, except everyone's speaking Spanish.

You can live in many different places and they're all the same.

Forty-eight's the magic number. Twenty-four cells, forty-eight prisoners. Three times a day prisoners line up outside their cell for roll call. Guard does mandatory count, and, with no one missing, life goes on. Breakfast, morning activity, lunch, afternoon activity, *din-din*, evening activity, and *shluffee* at Kibbutz Texarkana. Read, relax, play cards, checkers, chess, shoot pool. Although no one plays with Eddie. He's too good. If you miss, you stand around for an hour until he decides to miss.

He runs racks, thirty, forty, fifty in a row, everyone leaves, he's shooting alone, a pool shark widow.

No fun.

So he organizes tournaments, gives lessons, prizes, has a waiting list. It becomes *The Event of the Week*. Lots of action, side bets, everyone into it. He shoots a video on the matches and sells it with an hour of consultation.

Always a game within a game.

He starts a monthly newsletter listing winners, losers, writing profiles and human interest stories, especially on those taking his cue.

Before each tournament, Eddie does his usual exhibition warm- up, wowing the crowd with trick shots, setting up angles and configurations *Rube Goldberg* couldn't figure. He makes the shot and collects his bets.

It's all done in good clean fun, except once a pool cue is in his hands, Eddie's eyes freeze. DJ's blasting "We are Family," but Eddie hears nothing. He isolates, muting the lawn mowers, generators, the hum of the fluorescents, the hush. He's ready. He's clear. Then "labels" appear:

"Sociopath — Antisocial Personality Disorder."

He blinks, and tries to shake it off, but can't. It's his "strictly confidential" psychiatric report from Israel which Maya gave him.

Why did she do that?

Oh, I asked her.

"I don't think you should read it, Eddie."

" What could they say that I don't know?"

"Manipulative, grandiose, narcissistic, con man, pathological liar, paranoid, reckless, callous, an incapacity to love, promiscuous ,irresponsible, not concerned about wrecking others' lives, parasitic lifestyle, criminal versatility, changes image to avoid prosecution, changes life story readily, no life plan, no boundaries, no remorse, rationalizes. For all these negative characteristics, Mr. Parker is glib, superficially charming, intelligent, and funny, using diabolical humor as a defense.

Psycho-Social Summary

Mr. Parker was traumatized as a child surviving the Second World War. Schizophrenic mother. Detached father abandoned family when patient was sixteen. Considering his rage and repression, it's curious patient exhibits no physical symptoms."

Eddie's eyes blur, trying to shake off the report. He takes a deep breath, bends down to shoot, makes the shot, but can't get up. His back seizes and Eddie lets out a *g'shry* heard in Tashkent. *Exhibits no physical symptoms.*

They peel him off the pool table and carry him to bed. He lays there for days, ingesting aspirin quicker than M&M's at a bad movie. Chief Cuckoo stops by. Cuckoo's the head of the prison pool tournament committee — *and* every other committee in prison.

"How you feel, Kimosabe?"

"No good, Chief."

Chief Cuckoo is "King" Cuckoo. A six-foot-five, four-hundred-pound Navajo, Cuckoo's named after Nicholson's friend in *One Flew Over the Cuckoo's Nest*.

Cuckoo's in cahoots with guards, inmates, doctors, and can get you anything you want, a sundry without walls: cigarettes, drugs, candy, lotions, blades, condoms, shoes, tattoos, whatever. You want to get blown, no problem. Up the tush? No problem. Cuckoo? No problem. Only rule is: he's the Bull. Too heavy to get on top, he gets you from the back. Eddie marvels at all the brawny guys he services.

"I know how to fix your back, Kimosabe."

"It's okay. I'm not the Lone Ranger."

"You play Saturday, right, Kimosabe?"

"I may have to cancel."

"What?!"

Eddie makes Cuckoo a lot of money.

"I'm in pain."

Cuckoo snaps back Eddie's head by his hair.

"No tournament this Saturday?"

Through puckered lips made possible by pincers meeting in the middle of his face, Eddie says, "Cuckoo... I'm getting... dimples!"

Cuckoo releases Eddie's head, turning his neck into a slinky. Eddie waits for his neck to stop bobbing. "Thank you Cuckoo. I didn't know I was an accordion."

Street business in prison is conducted as it is on the outside, except you can't escape, so consequences run much deeper.

"I break your legs!"

"Come on Cuckoo, I'm already a cripple!"

In prison, sympathy's in short supply.

"I want my stamps, motherfucker!"

In prison cash is forbidden, so stamps are the currency. Friends and family mail in *thousands* of stamps. You can do well at twenty cents a pop. Everyone's in on it: prisoners, guards, administrators, employees. If they're not in on it, they know about it, and let it be.

Eddie amasses a goodly sum of stamps, then has the *chutzpah* to ask a guard for a stamp to mail a letter.

"I'll pay you later," he says.

Eddie makes his stamps playing cards, placing bets, hustling pool, and smuggling chickens. Two Vietnamese brothers, the "Hung Bro's," hate rice and beans, the prison's staple diet for its mostly Tex-Mex population, and employ Eddie as their chicken middle man, a title he wears begrudgingly given his *fowlphobia*. But a buck's a buck, a wing's a wing, and a stamp's a stamp.

For Eddie the currency could be a noodle. He doesn't care. He just needs the action. So on "chicken days," Eddie goes up for seconds and thirds, wearing long baggy pants to hide the goods. On his way out of the dining room, he makes sure to walk sideways, disguising any angle for protruding chicken parts from his socks. At night, Eddie rendezvous with the Hung Bro's and the protein contraband is dropped off to the starving Bro's for stir-fry at midnight.

I'm in Chinatown.

Eddie showers, scrubs his ankles, and burns the socks.

The prison, although minimum-security, is not without its warring factions and periodic flare-ups. When caught, offenders are placed in solitary confinement in a cell called "The Hole," the most secure cell in prison.

The Fix

One Hole incident involved a gang member by the name of "Angel" who owed Cuckoo $500 in stamps, Postmaster Cuckoo was looking for his money. Angel didn't have it, so Cuckoo ordered his wings clipped. Angel went to another gang for protection, promising them $600. They agreed and charged him a grand. He got lucky, cause stamps went up a nickel, but still didn't have enough. He called his family, promising them an additional ten cents on the already overtaxed stamp. They were ready to do it, but it was the weekend and the post office was closed. Now both gangs were out to kill him. He went to Eddie. Eddie gave him $400, charging $200. "Short-term rates," Eddie said, justifying the rip off. The guy takes the $400, owing Eddie $600, $500 to Cuckoo, and a grand to the gang.

Angel had a month left before his release but won't last a day if he goes back to his cell. So he attacked the guard and served out the month in The Hole, thereby screwing two gangs, Cuckoo and Eddie.

No chance of recidivism there.

Eddie doesn't have to resort to such measures. He's flush and stays out of trouble. When not hustling he keeps to himself. He's called "The Weed," not for the reefers he smokes but for being cool. And why not? He's safe, Ollie and Chaalie a thousand miles away, nothing to worry about.

"I *keel* you! "

"No problem, Cuckoo!"

"This is business."

"I understand."

How do I kill a four-hundred-pound Navajo?

"If I have to, I'll use my crutch as a cue stick."

Eddie winces as he turns on his side, looking like an oscillating wave. Cuckoo licks his lips.

"You got buns like Chita Rivera."

Eddie turns over on his back; Cuckoo laughs.

"You see the doctor?"

"They can't find anything."

"Then you mental."

"What?"

"They no find nuthin', means you *loco*. It's in your head."

"No, no, I have a slipped disc."

"You have slipped disc in your head." Cuckoo taps Eddie's head. "*Loco.*"

"What the fuck you talking about?"

"You fuck your kid, your uncle, sister, friends, the mob, you fuck everybody. When you fuck alotta people, your back goes out."

Doctor Cuckoo.

"I know because it happens to me."

Cuckoo's got a conscience. A real "mentsch."

By this time everybody knows Eddie's story. How he fucked his kid, had a breakdown, beat the mob. In prison, everybody knows everything about everybody. What else is there to talk about.

"Go see Loco Doctor."

"Yes, Cuckoo."

"Tell him I sen' you."

* * *

Facing Dr. Stanton's door, Eddie's reluctant to go in. Eddie believes every doctor's door has an invisible sign:

"Walk in—you're fucked."

And if you weren't fucked before you walked in, you will be when you leave. It's called "The Patient-Doctor Relationship." No good news going in and worse coming out. And, if your doctor's not wearing white, well, it can only mean one thing:

He's gonna screw with my head.

Eddie gives a feeble knock. Dr. Stanton opens the door. Eddie's hunched over. A "Young Frankenstein," he hangs there.

"In? Out?"

"Not sure."

Stanton closes the door.

That was a good session.

Eddie knocks again.

Door opens.

Eddie gives Stanton the once over.
Thin, short, bald, droopy eyes behind droopy glasses, pipe.
"I can take you in an arm wrestle."
"Would you like to come in?"
"Not really."
Stanton's about to shut the door again when Eddie steps inside and takes a whiff. First thing Eddie does when he walks into a new room is smell it.

Umm, pipe tobacco. Good, it's not tuna fish .

Eddie runs his finger along the back of the worn black leather couch and takes in the rest of the office.

Wood chair, oak desk—likes wood; inscribed pen set, probably doesn't work; brag wall, bookshelves, pharmaceutical reference books— big on meds, that's good; table on side of couch, tissue box on table— makes patients cry, pishy shrink. Venetian blinds rolled up looking out on the village green.

He meanders into an alcove.

Kitchenette, half fridge, four burner stove— likes to cook, or warm up his oatmeal; Farberwear coffee pot— knows good pots — on a yellow-speckled Formica counter top—no taste in tops, Bina had the same top, hated it...

Eddie nods and gives it his Good Housekeeping Seal.
"Nice place, Doc."
"Why thank ya, glad you like it."
"Has that lived-in look. You live here?"
"Would you care to sit down."

Eddie *shleps* back to the living room holding a heating pad to his back, dragging a foot at a time, every step a wince. The right side of his back is swung out so far it looks like a second hip.

Stanton points to a comfortable club chair in front of his desk.
"If I sit there, I'll never get up."
"Well then, let me help you to the couch."
"I don't need your help."
"As you wish."
"What I mean is, I won't be here long. I came for a painkiller."

Stanton takes a puff of his pipe and Eddie hobbles over to the foot of the sofa, but can't bend down.

"Get over here."

"What did you say?"

"Uh—can you help me?"

Stanton helps lower Eddie onto the couch.

"You find it hard to ask for help, *Misteh Parkeh*?"

"I heard about you couch guys."

"Don't worry, I'm not an analyst, just a regular psychiatrist."

"There are no *regular* psychiatrists. You're all nuts!"

Stanton chuckles. "I see you're a student of our profession."

"Weirdest group of people I ever met."

"Where did you meet them?"

"I'm just sayin'."

Eddie stretches out on the couch, puts the heating pad underneath, and closes his eyes.

"Wake me in an hour."

Dr. Stanton moves to the head of the couch, sitting behind Eddie in his wooden chair, wearing a stiff white shirt, dark slacks, black shoes, straight jacket, thin tie, legs crossed, pipe in mouth, pad in hand, fiddling with his pipe.

"You gonna smoke that thing or make love to it?"

"So, *Misteh Parkeh*, what brings you here?"

"Percoset."

"Well, for that you don't have to see me. You can see a medical doctor."

"I did. He sent me to you."

Stanton looks down at a report. "The referral here says you lost your temper with him."

"Wouldn't give me meds. Little prick's a resident in Med School denying me my meds."

"What did he say?"

"I should take a hot bath, wait a few days. I don't have a few days. I'm in pain **now**!"

"Well, I'm afraid I can't prescribe anything either, until I know a little more."

"My back went out. What else do you need to know?"

"How did it happen?"

"I bent over to shoot pool."
"You shoot pool a lot, I understand. Why did it just happen?"
"I don't know."
"Why don't we find out?"
"You won't give me meds?"
"Not right now. I have to know more."
"Oh, I get it, I'm your prison ping pong ball."
Stanton laughs. "Oh, you think you're caught up in penal bureaucracy, for a bad *back*?"
"Can I get my meds?"
"Not without further evaluation."
"Okay. Evaluate. What's wrong with me?"
"Probably *you*."
"I mean what's wrong with my back?"
"Could be any number of things: stress, pressure, anger, you're upset, any number of things. It's complicated."
"Yeah, with you guys *everything's* complicated."
"*Misteh Parkeh*, there *is* a relationship between body and mind."
"Doc, I'm the most relaxed guy in the world."
"Apparently your mind doesn't think so."
"So you're one of them fruity k'zutti guys."
"What do you mean?"
"Everything's connected, we're all connected?"
"Obviously, you don't believe that."
"I don't believe in anything."
"What do you believe in?"
"Pills."
"Afraid not."
"Then, I demand to see a chiropractor."
"Dee-mand?"
"My Miranda rights were never read to me."
"You've already seen a chiropractor, and an orthopedist."
"I want a third opinion."
"*I'm* your third opinion."
"Then I want a fourth."
"*Misteh Parkeh*, your X-rays are negative, so no one's

prescribing anything until we know what's going on." Stanton sticks a piece of gum in his mouth.

"Tell me a little about yourself."

"I was born."

"And?"

"It's fourty years later and I'm in prison talking to a shrink about my back."

"Anything else?"

"That's it. I didn't come here to talk."

"But that's what we do around here, sir, we talk."

He's a yenta.

"Called the talking cure."

Talk makes you think you're doing, but all you're doing is...

"No meds?"

"Maybe, after we talk."

"Okay, let's talk! Have you been under a lot of stress lately?" Stanton writes on his pad, puffing his pipe. "Anything happen lately? Anything stressful? Anything I should know about?" Stanton continues writing. "How are you sleeping, eating, shitting? Does your heart race, do you have gas?"

"You're a wise ass, aren't you, *Misteh Parkeh*?"

"Doc, I'm *talking;* why don't I feel better?"

It's quiet. There are different kinds of quiet. This one's especially quiet. Silence is one of those invisible things you shouldn't be able to see, but it's as visible as anything said. Stanton's writing, chewing his gum, puffing away.

I'm getting to him, good. Keep bothering him, keep annoying him, tscheppa, tscheppa *the shit outta him till he writes you a prescription. Cough, cough. The squeeky wheel gets the pill.*

"Can I have some water, Doc?"

Make him my servant.

"Excuse me?"

"Your pipe, it's bothering me... I'm allergic."

Stanton looks at the pack of Marlboros in Eddie's shirt pocket. "You smoke, *Misteh Parkeh*?"

"Cigarettes, but pipe tobacco's too sweet, tickles my throat."

Stanton blows smoke in Eddie's direction and goes to the fridge. Eddie's coughing up a storm. "My, my, you are allergic, poor boy." He gives Eddie a bottle of water.

"Can you unscrew it?"

"Do you want me to drink it?"

"My back affects my thumb. It's a mind-body thing."

Stanton looks at Eddie like he wants to unscrew his head. Eddie looks at the bottle.

"Poland Springs. My father's from Poland, but I don't think he saw any springs."

Eddie unscrews the top, takes a sip, closes his eyes, and rests Poland on his chest.

"Tell me more about *yaw fatheh, Misteh Parkeh*. I gather there's some family history there."

Stanton speaks with a lisp in a slow Southern drawl.

"Mind speaking faster, Doc. Makes me think you're a little slow upstairs."

If I insult him he'll write me a prescription just to get rid of me.

"*Misteh Parkeh*, just because *Ah* speak slow, doesn't mean *Ah* think slow."

"*Ah* appreciate that, Doc, but prison shrinks ain't necessarily at the top of your profession."

Eddie points to the wall.

"Where'd you get your degree from?"

"University of Pennsylvania."

"Quaker or quack?"

Stanton puts down his pipe.

"Good day, *Misteh Parkeh*."

"We're done?"

"*You* are."

"Great!"

Wait! Cuckoo! The fuckin' tournament! I'll never make it without the meds! Holy shit!

"Uh, listen, Doc, uh— I'm really sorry."

"Get out!"

"Come on, Doc, don't be so sensitive."

"*Misteh Parkeh*. Don't waste my time. Get out!"

"Can I pee? I don't wanna pee on your couch."

"You do that, Misteh Parkeh, you'll be very sorry."

"Can you help me to the bathroom?"

"No."

Stanton goes to pee in the john behind the kitchen alcove. Eddie hears tinkle, tinkle.

Eddie yells, "You're making me jea-lous."

More tinkle, tinkle.

"You're not gonna make me suffer like this, are you?"

Tinkle, tinkle.

He pees like he talks.

"Remember the oath, Doc."

Tinkle, tinkle.

Eddie raises his voice above the slow waterful.

"NEITHER RAIN, NOR SLEET — DON'T HIT THE RIM!"

He hears Stanton say, "Damn!"

"WIPE THE RIM!"

Stanton walks back to his seat, trying not to laugh.

"Made you miss, didn't I?"

That sends Stanton over the top and he explodes into a huge laugh.

"Sir, you are worth the price of admission."

"Stay for the next show?"

Stanton unrolls another stick of gum, lights his pipe, and sips coffee.

"Okay. Let's try again. Tell me what's goin' on?"

"Well, Doc, between your pipe, coffee, gum, and talk, I think your mouth should charge you rent."

"Anything upset you recently?"

"No."

"Seen anything, done anything, anything anyone said?"

"Look, Doc, I'm getting out in three months. Can't you just write me a prescription?"

"*Misteh Parkeh*, symptoms don't just appear out of thin air."

"Well, this one did."

"Could it be that the prospect of anticipating your release has set off issues?"

"I have no issues."

"No issues."
"None."
"So what do you think your problem stems from?"
"Have no idea."
"Come on, *Misteh Parkeh*, you're a smart man."
Eddie feels the tide turn.
"Well, if it's not physical, *Misteh Parkeh*, then what in heaven could it possibly be?"
Let this one go. Not every question needs an answer.
"Could it be emotional?"
"Emotional."
"That's right, *Misteh Parkeh*, e-mo-tional."
"What's that?"
"I believe the cause of your discomfort is the repression of traumatic events in your early life."
"Would you care to rephrase that?"
"To?"
"Patient was shooting pool and his back went out."
"Oh."
"And sometimes a pain is just a pain, right Doc?"
"If you break your leg. But you don't have a broken leg, *Misteh Parkeh*. You have something else that's broken, far deeper."
I'm gettin' nowhere with this cracker!
"So to treat the symptom, you must first address the cause."
If I get crazy, he's gotta give me a sedative.
"So, what you're saying, Doc, is that my head is in my back."
"In a manner of speaking."
"Does that mean your head is up your ass?"
"There you go again, going on the offensive—"
"FUCK YOU!"
"All lit up because you can't cope."
"GO FUCK YOURSELF!"
"Tell me about Poland, your father."
"FUCK YOU!"
"Were you abused?"
"WERE **YOU?!**"
"No."

"WOULD YOU LIKE ME TO START?!"
Eddie pumps his fist.
"GIVE ME PILLS, YOU FUCKIN' QUACK!"
Stanton stops chewing, puts down his cup, pad, pencil, and pipe. He walks around to the side of the couch, standing over Eddie. Eddie looks away, afraid he'll laugh at this short, thin, effeminate, bald man standing in front of him, maybe one hundred and forty pounds, soaking wet. But then Stanton's voice drops an octave and gets very scary.
Oooh, Te-lu-laaaah...
"*Misteh Parkeh.*"
"*Yay-us?*"
"*Ah* would caution you not to threaten me."
"Or else what, you'll scratch my eyes out?"
Stanton opens the door to his office and calls in the beefy guard.
"*Officeh*, please escort *Misteh Parkeh* to the mental ward."
"Whoa! Whoa!"
"Let's go, buddy."
"What did I do, Doc?!"
"You're too agitated to go back to your station."
"C'mon, I was kidding."
"I'm not."
"Don't screw with me, Doc!"
"Or else what, *Misteh Parkeh*, you'll scratch me?"
"I was kidding, can't you take a joke?"
Eddie looks at the massive slab of Texas, legs spread, arms folded.
"What do you think, *Officeh*?"
"I don't know, Doc. Is he dangerous?"
"Not sure, he keeps threatening, but then apologizes."
"Then we gotta break 'em like our broncos."
"WHAT THE FUCK!"
Beef says, **"SHUT UP!"**
"Sorry."
"See what *Ah* mean, *Officeh*? Attack, then retract."
"My kids are like that, Doc."
"So, what's your recommendation?"

Doc's askin' Beef for his medical opinion... they're fuckin' with me.
Eddie shrivels up on the couch, thumb in his mouth.
"Well, sir—" He looks at Eddie, "from the looks of things, I would give 'em another chance, but if he sounds off again—"
"*Ah'll* be sure to call."
Stanton winks to Beef, who closes the door behind him.
"Where were we, *Misteh Parkeh*?"
"Look, Doc. Here's the deal. I gotta hold a cue stick by Saturday or my ass is grass."
"Yes, I hear you're quite good."
"I'm *no* good if I can't shoot."
Stanton takes a moment. "Okay here's *mah* offer. You come in for treatment, I'll prescribe medication."
Eddie's face drops. "How long do I have to see you?"
"Remainder of your time here."
"**THREE MONTHS?!**"
"Unless you want to extend your stay."
"How many times a week?"
"Three."
"Come on, Doc, you said this wasn't analysis! That's not fair."
"We got a lot of work to do in a short period of time."
Eddie rolls over on his belly.
"I can't, Doc. I really can't."
He slides off the couch and crawls on all fours to the door. He uses the doorknob to pull himself up, but when he turns the knob, a piercing pain brings him back to his knees.
I'll never make it by Saturday!
"Three times a week?"
"Yes."
"How many pills?"
"Enough to get you through Saturday."
"How's two times a week?"
"Three."
Two, Ollie, two.
"Two?"
"Three."
"Two and a half?"

"Three."
"For twelve weeks?"
"Yes."
"That's thirty-six sessions."
"Uh, huh."
"That's thirty-six hours."
"Yes."
"Is that a regular hour, or fifty-minute shrink hour?"

Stanton goes to the kitchen and rinses out his coffee cup. Eddie crawls back on the couch.

"Let's figure this out together, Doc. So, let's say it's a shrink hour, since you're a shrink, okay? Sooo… if we knock off ten minutes from the regular sixty-minute hour times thirty-six, I save three hundred and sixty minutes. That's six hours off."

"That's pretty quick calculations there, *Misteh Parkeh.*"

"So, if I save those six hours— That's six sessions."

Eddie hears the squeak of Stanton drying his coffee cup.

"You really like getting in there, don't you, Doc, wiping everything clean?"

Stanton walks back in the room with a fresh cup of coffee and lit pipe.

"So that's two weeks off…. are we talkin' a five- or seven-day work week?"

Stanton opens the window, sticks his head out, and blows smoke.

"Nice day out."

"Why don't we base it on a normal five-day work week, 'cause I'm 'normal' which means I get seven days credit, or a week and a half off, and if I'm sick a day a week—that's another twelve, plus the seven makes it nineteen; throw in another day, round it out to twenty." Eddie sits up on the couch. "So, why don't we say, I see you in a month; in the meanwhile you can write me a prescription."

Next day, Eddie gets to Stanton by two, walks past the sleeping mass guarding the waiting room, and walks in on another patient.

"Ooh, sorry, Doc, I thought I was your one and only. Didn't know you cheat."

"We'll be finshed momentarily."

At two o'clock the other patient walks out, a burly buzz-head with cut-off sleeves showing off arms as thick as pillars decorated with rows of heads on crosses.

His arm's a totem pole!

It's also a distraction, used by the guy to take the focus off his *hot* zone, his messed up head. Eddie 'n' buzz-head keep their heads down. In a shrink's waiting room, patients don't acknowledge each other. As if doing so is an admission of guilt into *m'shugeeland* — the land of the ashamed, a double whammy, sick *and* ashamed.

Eddie's feeling better, *thank you Meds*. He walks straight for the couch, lies down, crosses his arms, and takes a short snooze. A few minutes pass and Eddie's woken by Stanton's arm shaking him. Eddie's been crying in his sleep.

Veree, veree hard when fadder die...

"Are you all right, *Misteh Parkeh*." Eddie notices his psychiatric report on Stanton's lap. Stanton gives him a tissue. Eddie wipes his eyes and blows his nose. "Quite a history, *Misteh Parkeh*. Ah read here that you were hospitalized several times in Israel. Is that correct?"

"It's the Jewish Holidays. In between I'm fine."

"What happened?"

"I almost had a nervous breakdown."

Stanton's eyebrows meet.

"Almost?! You tried to commit suicide!"

"Suicide isn't something you try, Doc. If I wanted to do myself in I woulda done it!"

Eddie lights up a smoke, blowing smoke rings at the ceiling.

"The man who found you —" Eddie sticks his finger through the smoke ring. "Now, if he didn't come along?"

"We wouldn't be *talking*."

"So you did attempt to —"

"I attempted nothing! The goddamn pilot light went out!"

"So you were lucky."

"That's me. Mister Lucky."

"Your friend found you in time... fate."

"Yeah, fate always finds me."

Stanton unrolls a Tums.

Eddie puts out his palm. "Tums for the tummy."

"What led to your 'almost' breakdown?"

Eddie takes two and returns the roll.

"I saw my killers."

"The Mafia."

"Ollie 'n' Chaalie. They were after me. But no one believed me."

"Who didn't believe you?"

"Everybody. The doctors, Uzi, the guy who found me... they wouldn't believe me. They said I was making it up. It's like when I was a kid, no one believed me... but I saw them, and they said I *thought* I saw them. How do you *think* you see your killers?"

"Well—"

"Did I also *think* I saw the bat that broke my legs?"

"Well—"

"Well, well, WHAT, Rabbi?!"

"Rabbi?"

"We had a Rabbi who always said, 'Wee-eeehlll.'"

"Uh-huh."

"Even the paranoid have enemies. Isn't that what you shrinks say?"

"Doesn't make it any less distressing."

"Yeah, I'd say it's distressing! Getting beat to a pulp with a baseball bat *iiiis* a little *distressing*, wouldn't you say, Doc?"

Stanton makes a note. "Uh-huh."

"Stays with you for a while, don't you think?"

"Uh-huh."

"Damn straight, *uh-huh*! They tracked me down, Motherfuckers! In Israel! Fuckin' Mafia!"

"To kill you?"

"**NO! THEY CAME FOR MY *BAR MITZVAH!*"**

Stanton almost creases a smile.

"It's amazing how little you *goyim* know about Jews! All you know is bagels, lox, 'n' *Chanukah*! And if *Chanukah* didn't come out on Christmas, you wouldn't know shit!" Stanton empties his pipe in an ashtray. "You're not Jewish are you?"

"No, sir."

"So how'd you get into Med School?"

"So you fled to Israel, thinking you would be safe."

"Last place on earth I thought they'd look for me."

"Of course."

"I'll tell you, Doc, if Jews can't be safe in Israel —"

"And then you came back to testify shortly after your second hospitalization.

"Yes."

"That took some doing. Quite extraordinary, considering your vulnerable state. It took courage. What motivated you to do that?"

"They fried Max."

Stanton closes his eyes and puts down the pad. Eddie's sobbing.

"They were looking for *me* and killed *him*. *I* killed him, like I killed everything else in my life that's good..."

Stanton pours Eddie a cup of water. Eddie takes a sip.

"I'm done. That's it. Can't talk no more."

That night, Max kept Eddie's feet to the fire, strapping him to a chair, flames licking his toes. Next morning, the guard found him on the floor, sheets torn, and his back out, worse than the first time. Stanton gave him a sedative and shot of cortisone.

"Why couldn't you do this *before* you fucked with my head?"

"Keep in my mind, whenever you open up, you may feel worse before you feel better."

Exhausted from the night, Eddie falls asleep on Stanton's couch. Stanton lets him sleep the hour, smoking his pipe and reviewing his notes. He empties the ash from his pipe and Eddie awakes screaming:

"ASH! ASH! FIRE! FIRE!"

Stanton holds him down.

"It's okay, *Misteh Parkeh*, it's okay."

Eddie's dazed and terrified.

"Where am I?"
"In *mah* office."
"Oh."

Stanton gives him another sedative, and, combined with the cortisone shot, Eddie sleeps off his fatigue and his back pain, showing up on Saturday, straight as an arrow, shooting the eyes out of the ball. Cuckoo and Company give Eddie the week off, who also gives himself the week off from Stanton.

No need to see the yenta.

Until his back goes out again. This time he merely bent down to pick up a piece of paper.

Next session.

Eddie's lying on the couch, smoking a cigarette, staring at the ceiling. Stanton's scraping his pipe.

"Can you stop that?! Right in my ear!"

"*Ah'm* sorry."

"What are we in a movie? You gonna start eating popcorn, next?! Smoke a fucking cigarette!"

"*Ah* don't like cigarettes."

"Smoke dope! Jesus! How many other patients do you annoy like this?"

"Probably many. Thank you for pointing it out to me."

"And while you're at it, stop cracking your gum! Snip chick cracked her gum like that!"

"Who's snip chick?"

"This is bullshit! My back's out! I thought I was cured! Now I got another tournament comin' up 'n' Cuckoo's up my ass! Correct that... in my grid! This is fuckin' extortion!"

"Well, unfortunately, there are elements in prison life—"

"I'm talking about **YOU! Forcing me to be here!**"

Stanton shakes out the smoked ash into an ashtray, sprinkles fresh tobacco from a small leather pouch into the brim.

"*Ah* can understand your frustration, *Misteh Parkeh*."

"Fuck you! I don't wanna talk to you!"

"If we are to continue, then the profanity must stop."

"Fuck you!"

"You need to calm down."

Eddie points to the ceiling. "You got some 'cracked' tiles! Why don't you work on **them**!"

"*Misteh Parkeh*, you agreed to see me three times a week. I honored my end, you reneged on yours. You took the week off; that's not being a gentleman, that's not an honorable way of—"

Eddie takes the wooden ash tray and throws it against the wall.

Beef enters. "Everything all right, sir?"

"*Jest fahn*. Thank you, *officeh*." Beef leaves. "You'll have to clean that up."

"I can't, my back."

"Fuck your back. Clean it up." He gives Eddie a vacuum cleaner. Eddie looks like a disabled person cleaning.

"*Misteh Parkeh, Ah* believe *Ah* can help you, but not if you—"

The vacuum gets jammed, a whirring sound, and dust starts flying out. Eddie doesn't know what to do.

"Turn it off!"

"Where?"

Stanton grabs the vacuum discharging dirt and shuts it off.

"The bag was full. You must empty the bag."

"What bag?"

"The dirt bag. Where do you think the dirt goes when you pick up dirt?"

"I don't know."

"I'm not talkin' about the vacuum cleaner, *Misteh Parkeh*." Eddie gets back on the couch. "In psychological terms—"

"Not everything is psychological, Doc! You shrinks think everything is psychological!"

"It's called transference, transferring your anger—"

"Okay! That's it!"

Eddie pulls the heating pad from his back, swings his legs over to the side, tries to stand but keeps falling back on the coach, too painful to get up.

"Fuckin' co-dependent couch is a prison!"

Stanton's nose is in a pharmacological book.

"What are you checking? I'm a sociopath, okay?!

Suicidal, okay?! But before I kill myself, you'll kill *me* with these fuckin' bullshit sessions! So consider me done!"

"You realize, *Misteh Parkeh*, psychological clearance is required upon release. I'm not prepared to do that."

"Listen, Stanton! I didn't come in sick. And I ain't goin' out sick. I paid off my debt!"

"You haven't paid off anything! You owe, *Misteh Parkeh*! Big time!"

"To who?"

"Yourself!"

"THERE'S NOTHIN' TO PAY-OFF! I'M OKAY!"

"Yes, you're okay, *Misteh Parkeh*, like your father was okay, your son, your childhood deprivation, your terror, your dislocation, a schizophrenic mother, abusive father, yes, you're okay like the Holocaust is okay, like survivor's guilt is okay, the guilt you carry in you as much as your father did, trying to understand all the whys: why you chose a criminal path, why you broke your marriage, used your son, destroyed people's lives, including your own! Yes, you're okay! You're just *FAHN*!"

Eddie returns to his cell and removes a box from under his bed — the cigar box Max gave him the night he hid in his cellar.

He by-passes the articles on The Kid, plus the many letters he received from scouts, and pulls one letter in particular he reads every night before going to sleep. His psychiatric report, Eddie calls "The Shrink's *Shema*," or *How fucked up am I?*

Reading the evaluation reminds him of his report cards from elementary school, entering Kindergarten as an eight-year-old, sitting with four-year-olds, learning the alphabet. How humiliating, he recalls, singing nursery rhymes with little children. By the end of the year, he entered the third grade and, though he caught up in English, everything else in his life got stuck in Nursery.

He realizes that he's spent his life running up a down escalator, trying to catch up, going nowhere. He memorized his diagnosis, which drilled him to the core and pinned him down on the pool table that day, and the days thereafter with Stanton.

"Manic-depressive, suicidal, paranoid, compulsive, sociopathic features, addictive, destructive..."

Jesus, this guy needs help.

* * *

The next three months Eddie sees Stanton three times a week, never late or missing a session, most of the time spent on his childhood.

"So you survived the worst of the war in the very worst place, a miracle."

"I guess."

"Do you have memories?"

"I don't know if they're memories, or stories I heard or made up."

"Which ones?"

"Starving, cattle cars, the camp, the boat."

"Frightening."

"That was hard. But the scary part was being afraid all the time. From the time we arrived in America, from eight, nine, and on, my mother was sick, sick and loving, my father cruel and kind. Beating and protecting me all at the same time, smuggling me across borders, giving me his last food ration, his belt, a mixed bag."

"Not mixed for the child. You took the beating because it came with the love and the security you needed; you had no choice if you wanted to survive. You were traumatized."

"Wasn't everyone during the war?"

"Yes, but for children it was especially difficult."

"It happened so many years ago; it feels like yesterday."

"Yes, that's the mystery of it all. How the first five, six years of your life are so few in the span of a lifetime, but play out so significantly for decades."

"Don't kids get over things more easily?"

"It may appear that way, but children shut down to protect themselves. Once the danger's over, doesn't mean the fear leaves. In your case, I don't think the danger's ever left. You see the world as a very dangerous place, Eddie."

"It is."

"But not dangerous enough for you. You have to make it more dangerous."

"I don't understand."

"I know it sounds like a paradox, but that's your pattern, *Misteh Parkeh*. You do outrageous things, brazen things, hoping to be stopped, but no one does, so you continue, fighting authority, fighting your father, fighting yourself, all to stay away from your real terror, the thing you're most frightened of."

"My anger."

"No, *Misteh Parkeh*. Your sadness... your deep, deep, sadness."

Eddie feels the air inside him collapse.

"For a childhood that never was... you haven't allowed yourself to mourn the early years, or forgive yourself for the later ones... so you fight with everyone, cut yourself off from others, yourself, trying not to feel. But that doesn't work, *Misteh Parkeh*... you pay a price..."

"I waited twenty-five years to see him."

Eddie covers his face with his hands.

"Tell me about him."

If you want to see men cry, ask them about their father.

If you want to see them sob:

"Tell me about your son."

If you want to see them heal:

"Tell me about yourself."

When you're finally able to hear the truth, the rest comes easy.

"Can't mend a broken heart going to the one who broke it, *Misteh Parkeh*, nor can you make them pay for it."

* * *

The last week, they talked about ending therapy, what he would do once he got out, what he would say to The Kid. The last session, Eddie gave Beef a pack of Marlboros. He bought a pack for burly buzz-head... but he had committed suicide, and another patient walked out, passing Eddie, avoiding his glance. Eddie stood by the door, wiped off the invisible "you're fucked" sign, and walked in hopeful.

The Fix

"*Misteh Parkeh*! Last session! How does it feel?"
"Think you can call me *Eddie* by now?"
"Of course, *Mis*— uh, Eddie."

Eddie sits on the couch. Stanton comes around and they sit together for a long time, looking at the wall, saying nothing.

"Jesus, Doc, you got a lotta degrees hangin' on your big brag wall. Afraid no one will believe you're qualified?"

"*Ah'm* proud of my wall. Lots of work went into it." He stands to straighten out a framed certificate. "Might be something you would be interested in pursuing."

"Yeah, well, first I gotta finish High School."
"I would encourage you to do that."
"Gonna take me three years."

"Well, Eddie, in three years you'll be three years older whether you do it or not. Coffee?"

"Sure."

"New product on the market, Starbucks! Puts hair on your chest!"

"Wow, all these diplomas, licenses, certificates. Must have cost a pretty penny."

"Yup, my daddy. Put his trust in me."
"He did a good job."
"My daddy worked in a mill."
"Hard work."

"Yes, he worked hard, but he wasn't runnin' from Nazis, and we always had food on the table."

He brings over the coffee with two mugs from the hot pot.

"Farberwear pots make the best coffee."
"I've had mine for eight years!"

"My mother's lasted ten years, and the day it died she returned the pot to the same store she bought it and exchanged it for a new one, saying the one she returned didn't work."

"She wasn't lying."
"My mom could return a used pair of underwear."
They both crack up.

"See, Doc, I come by my conniving honestly. But you're the only one I didn't try to con."

"How come?"

"I trust you."

"How's that feel?"

"Foreign."

"Eddie, how do you live an entire life and not have one honest relationship."

"Sort of a success story, don't you think?"

"Well, now you can begin a new one."

Stanton gets up and goes to his briefcase.

"*Ah* got a little somethin' for you."

Eddie stops him.

"Wait! First, I got something for **you**!"

Eddie hands him a leather pouch full of rich tobacco.

"Why, thank you, Eddie." He smells the tobbaco. "Mmmm... how many racks did you have to run at the pool tournament for this pouch?"

"Many."

"Them other pool-shootin' boys won't be sorry to see *you* go..."

"Cuckoo will."

Stanton hands him a wrapped box. Eddie unwraps it and removes a leather bound book.

"Wow...soft, like *buttah*. Did you get this as a promo gift from a pharmaceutical company?"

Eddie leafs through the blank pages.

"You know, Eddie, every time you think something's funny or clever, you don't have to say it."

"It's a tick."

"Well, here's a journal you can put all your ticks in."

"You got a deal. Shut *mah* mouth!"

"This will help, keeping a journal, while you're getting re-oriented to civilian life. A friend you can tell anything."

"I don't have much to say."

Stanton almost swallows his pipe. He fills his pipe with the new tobacco, lights up, and pours them a shot of bourbon.

"To better days."

"Better days, Doc."

They stroll over to the wall of diplomas and pictures. One small picture shows a young man smiling, Stanton's arm around him.

"Who's the kid?"

"My son."

"Didn't know you had one."

"Yup."

"Never noticed him before."

"I just put up the picture."

"Where is he?"

"Killed a year ago in a car accident."

"Oh my God! Drunk driver?"

"No, *he* was the driver. Drove himself right off the road."

* * *

Eddie left Stanton on Wednesday, due to be released on Friday, the third anniversary of his incarceration. The next few days he brings flowers, cards, chocolates, expresses his appreciation to the board, the warden, and guards for helping him rehabilitate.

"F.C.I.'s the best thing that ever happened to me!"

Guards kid Eddie, "Loved havin' you. Don't return."

They were kidding, but Eddie understood. He understood what Juan was saying. He was leaving his home. A place he understood, which understood him. The most honest men he ever met were in prison. No airs, no bullshit. 'Cause inmates, tell it the way it is, live it the way it is. Down to basics. He gained enormous respect for the men he was leaving and felt sad for *their* lives. He felt a strong kinship and loved them. It didn't start out that way.

The first year, all he could think about was getting out; the second year, less so; and the third, he wasn't so sure. So it is with the power of confinement, and now it ends—the last day. He wakes his usual time at six and showers. He shaves off his full-length beard, looking twenty years younger. His cellmates whistle and Eddie grins. He grew the beard when he first entered prison to look crazy and threatening. A quiet man in a long black beard is not to be fucked with. He looks in the mirror and recalls the last time he was so clean-shaven. First day in prison, his "Mano-y-Mano" initiation.

It was evening. He just finished a long day of orientation, processing, physical exam, given his uniform, assigned his cell, deloused, and showering, the brown soap stinging his eyes. Two other guys show up showering on either side of him, feeling something lukewarm on his leg.

They're pissing on me.

Suddenly he's yanked by the arm and rammed up against the wall. The "yanker" is Galuck, a ball-headed, shaven animal, twice his size with a horse cock to match.

This could hurt.

Eddie sees that this is what it's going to be like. He'll become everyone's girlfriend. He can try to talk his way out, but the guy's too stupid. His cock's bigger than his head, twice as hard, and fully lathered.

Eddie feels a bar of soap about to pass up his highness. Galuck's cadre of "mini-Galucks" appear – cheering him on, waiting their turn. Eddie drops his head, turns and swift knees Galuck in the balls, spins out, grabs the goon's hair on his back and smashes his face into the wall. Mini-Galucks back off. Then Eddie helps Big Galuck up, bleeding profusely from his nose, and smashes his face into the wall again. He looks at the mini-Galucks.

"Next?"

Mini-Galucks applaud. Eddie finishes showering, Galuck's crumpled body in a heap beside him, the water flushing the blood down the drain.

The next day, Eddie visits the goon in the hospital with a bouquet of roses. Galuck sees him coming down the corridor and begins to cry. Eddie gives him a razor.

"Shave your back."

When he thinks of the times he struck out like that—the time he spit in Sol's face, cracked Chaalie's knee, fights in the streets, mashing Galuck's face—he can't believe it. He looks in the mirror.

I'm such a nice guy. Who was that?

He takes a deep breath, runs his hands along his clean-shaven face, and sings: *"Hold Spice means qvality..."*

Can't believe it. Three years. The days dragged and the years flew by.

He puts on the clothes he came in with: jeans, held up by a canvas belt, a T-shirt, and Keds sneaks. In his napsack are some books and a flight ticket to New York.

He looks out the window. Maya's waving, waiting in a cab to take him to the airport. He opens the window.

"MAYAAAA!"

"ARYEH! I LOVE YOU! COME HOME!"

It is after all the greatest experience. Being found.

The guys are outside their cells as Eddie high-five's them walking down the hallway. Cuckoo motions Eddie to the back stairwell. He gives Eddie a wrapped box.

"Don't forget to write."

Eddie weighs the box.

"Thanks, Cuckoo. You're first class."

He gives Cuckoo a big hug, Cuckoo lifts him off his feet, and Eddie feels a knife fillet its way into the soft part of his back, right below his ribs, careful not to touch the heart. Eddie collapses, Cuckoo pulls the knife, covers him in a blanket and carries him down the bloody stairs to the infirmary. Eddie opens his eyes briefly. "Thanks, Cuckoo, I was chilly." Cuckoo places Eddie on a gurney and says to the physician:

"Take care of my friend, Chief Running Blood."

CHAPTER NINETEEN

Winton Country Club boasts the finest nine-hole golf course in Bethlehem, New Hampshire, a popular resort for asthmatic millionaires. The abbreviated course built exclusively for women, by the men, is adjacent to the full eighteen-hole men's course. The course took four years and ten million dollars to build, only two years and five million over the original estimate. But the men are very pleased, giving the women a course of their own.

Eddie is now a caddy, a golf-carrying *shlepper, shlepping* clubs for blue-haired ladies and prissy daughters. He also drives a cart chauffeuring around women with new hips, and, on rainy days, he doubles as a waiter, turning in his green crocodile short-sleeve shirt and white shorts for a dark penguin suit. He cuts his hair and sports a pencil-thin moustache à la David Niven.

To complete the "Witness Protection Makeover Look," Eddie assumes what *he* thinks is a British accent taken from multiple viewings of Peter O'Toole's *Lawrence of Arabia*. Inflecting his own brand of sophistication, he goes off at times sounding a bit Russian and Yiddish, raising *wasp brows*.

"Where did you say you're from?" The club members ask.

From here, you putz! Ver vud I be from?

Eddie's transformation to elegance is startling — a total departure from his overgrown, woolly look in "Cuckoo's nest." Next spring he's up for an Oscar for his many character portrayals.

I'd like to thank the Academy for sticking me here in Bethlehem...

Sticking is how Eddie got to Winton, by way of Cuckoo's knife puncturing his lung, spleen, liver, kidney; worth ten thousand stamps. Cuckoo was offered twenty, but only took half, refusing to finish the job. Payback.

"Did good for me and played when he was hurt."

After eight month's recovery, Tracy's mom, Mary, set him up at Winton with a new name, new job, and new look.

Eddie's housed in staff quarters, set back in the woods off the 9th hole, sufficiently hidden from members. Twelve Mexicans share the four-bedroom facility. But it's clean, food is free, and no one knows him. He gets one day off a week, goes to the movies, reads, writes, plays poker, and hunts pussy. Three years in the can backed him up, so he's looking to catch up beyond his own hand. He falls into a routine with work and play, and checks in regularly with Mary by phone. He's excited to hear she's making a progress visit.

Maybe I'll get lucky.

From the first time he met Mary (in handcuffs) he was taken with her.

I could use a mercy fuck, but she's my in-law. But then who doesn't want to screw an in-law?

During the trial when she briefed him in the hotel room, he fantasized banging her. She was worth fantasizing over. Short, pretty, dark brunette, green spit-fire eyes, olive skin, full lips, curved hips, strong legs, tight tush, perky tits, big nipples and great personality, she reminded him of Dorothy Hamill.

Must be great on skates.

But with three F.B.I. agents, two guards, and two attorneys, he'd have to wait to make his amorous move until the evening when he was alone in the shower.

He makes dinner reservations for them at the Sinclaire Inn. The Inn is a rambling three-story Victorian structure with cozy New England features, right in the heart of town, a favorite for locals, friendly, inviting, with reasonable room rates. He goes there for the ambiance.

Eddie arrives early, has a lead-off scotch, schmoozing with Lee, the Asian Maître d'. Lee's family escaped from Saigon in 1975 when the government fell. Lee's cousin gave him a job working twenty-four hours a day in his 7-Eleven convenience store. Lee preferred working eighteen hours a day at the Sinclaire.

Lee's slim, cool, handsome, bright, should be getting laid 'round the clock, but he's Asian, and cursed with "Asian Man Hex." No sex appeal. The women, that's a whole other story. You wanna fuck their eyes out. But the men forget about. Maybe because they *look* like women — without the appeal.

Eddie feels bad for Lee, but—
Not my problem.
Lee's a natural—friendly, courteous, efficient. He loves giving advice, telling bad jokes, and jabbing Eddie about his 'cunt' hunt.
"Who is she?"
"A friend."
He whispers in his ear. "You have no friends, Harvey, your only friend is pussy. I never seen anyone so *hawny*. What, did you just get out of prison?"
"There she is."
They look towards the front door.
"Not bad, Harvey, not bad."
Mary's got the power look, wearing a blue and white seersucker suit with a white tailored shirt, pumps, and a black shoulder bag.
"I didn't know you go for accountants."
Eddie greases Lee's palm with a "Jackson."
"Table in the back."
"No problem."
Eddie takes his scotch and walks towards Mary in slow motion, giving him time to watch the fold in the front of her skirt ride up to her *knish.*
Stairway to heaven.
A handsome package in his own right, Eddie's wearing a light tan chino suit, blue shirt, beige tie, polished loafers; he's clean-shaven with shiny dark hair.
"Harvey, my, my, don't *you* look good."
She loves me.
"What a transformation! You look like a movie star!"
He shows off a dazzling five-hundred-dollar smile, whitening his teeth for the occasion.
She extends her hand, he goes for the mouth, she turns her head.
She's quick!
He kisses her on the cheek and pushes his nose down her neck, inhaling her perfume.
She gives him a gentle push.
"What are you doing?"

I wanna fuck your neck.
"We're civilians now."
"Oh, stop it!"
"What are you wearing?"
"Opium."
"I love opium."
"Down, Rover, down!"
Eddie spots Lee laughing at him. He walks up to them.
"I'm Lee, your host."
Lee bows and escorts them to their table in the back. Mary's walking behind Lee and Eddie's grooving on her ass.
What I could do with that!
"The waiter will be over shortly to take your order."
Mary says, "Thank you, Lee."
Eddie says, "Hey, Lee, why don't *you* take our order?"
"*Is* not my job."
"Don't you work here?"
Mary says, "It's okay, I can wait."
Eddie says, "You shouldn't *have* to wait!"
Patrons are looking their way. Mary grits her teeth.
"Don't make a scene, Harvey, it's not a big deal!"
 He palms Lee another twenty.
"Is it a big deal?"
Lee breaks out in a huge smile.
"No! No big deal, my good friend. What would you like Madam?"
"Gin and tonic, please."
"And I'll have another scotch neat, but don't cinch on the scotch."
"I don't do that."
"Yes, you do. You do it when there's no ice."
Lee leaves.
"*That* was rude."
"He's a buddy, we go back a long time."
"You're only here six months."
"So how are you, Mary? You look beautiful."
"Why, thank you."

"I miss you."

Wanna fuck?

He looks across the table and takes her in. He allows enough time for her to take him in. Eddie believes that if given enough time with a woman, he can make anyone. Just a matter of time...

I wear them down.

He once heard about a bigamist who had nine wives. The guy was a pilot, so he got around. When he got caught, all the women talked about how kind and loving he was. Eddie saw pictures of the women and they were pretty hot, ones *he* wouldn't mind banging. But when he looked at the guy, he couldn't believe it. Unattractive, short, bald, nerdy, no great shakes. When asked how he did it, the guy said, "It's all I ever thought about.. sleeping with *that* woman. I kept that thought in mind and never let it go, because I knew that if I treated them nicely and was a good listener, they would eventually find me attractive."

"The trick, in getting women," he said, "is *being* there for them at vulnerable moments and *not* taking advantage. That you do later *after* they trust you... with women, kindness and trust trump looks... and don't forget to compliment."

"Nice suit, Mary."

"Thank you."

"I really like it."

"Why, thank you."

"It looks very good on you, so stylish."

"Cut it out, Harvey."

"I'm offering a compliment."

"That's not the only thing you're offering."

"Lighten up, Mary. I'm a gentleman."

"I see."

Lee comes back with the drinks. She raises her glass and he meets it.

"Cheers."

He breaks out in a huge toothy smile. They sip.

"How's your drink?"

"Excellent. Yours?"

"Beautiful. Love single malt."

"Lee filled it up, just like you wanted."
"Want a sip?"
Get her drunk.
"Sure."
She takes a quick sip and stiffens up. "Wow! That's strong."
"Another sip?"
"No, thank you."
Well, won't get her that way.
"Glad you could come out, Mary.'
"It's my job."
"Right, right, so how are you?"
"The better question is, how are *you*?"
"Good."
"How do you like Winton?"
"Hate it."
"Oh?"
"Hate the people, hate the work, hate everything about it."
"But for the most part?"
"It's fine."
"*That's* the spirit."
 "I'm not big on golf, but it's a good re-entry. Like a fish outta water."
She looks around at the stodgy patrons.
"But you're safe here."
"It's not Egypt."
She looks at him with a grin.
She's digging me.
He grins back.
"I can't get over how great you look, Eddie, like a new man—handsome, sophisticated, debonair, totally unlike you."
"Interested?"
"No. How did you come up with this polished look?"
"My Pop."
"Dapper."
"Yes, he looked like a sharpie, spoke like a refugee."
"You never mention him in any —"
"How's The Kid, how's Benji?"

* * *

Eddie's convinced he's the only Jew at the club. The anti-Semitic jokes give it away. If he isn't the only Jew, you wouldn't know it because the other *Marranos* just laugh along.

Multi-talented, multi-dimensional, and multi-personalitied, Eddie serves the P.G.'s —Privileged Goyim (Goyim love acronyms)—in the club's elegant dining room housed in a 19th century mansion built in 1970—a knock-off of the one that burned down in *Gone With the Wind*, which is where Eddie wants to go—not the mansion, the wind.

He hates the place, hates the people, staff, functions, facilities, lockers, pro shop, snack bar, game room, health club, pools, tennis courts, driving range, rosebushes, tees, golf, hates golf, those who play it, watch it, talk it, eat it.

*Fuck **golf** and the people who **love** golf!*

He hates runways, woods, clubs, drivers, putters, irons, traps, sand traps, mousetraps, claptrap, squirrels, grass, greens, greens, fucking greens! Won't they ever stop talking about the **FUCKING GREENS?!**

"Hey, John. Did you see the greens, a sheet of glass. I woulda had a *birdie*, but the greens made it a *bogey*."

Eddie doesn't get it, doesn't get golf— its attraction, its culture, its language.

Birdie, bogey, tweety talk for chloroformed tweety-birds in polka-dot shirts and visors, thinking they're fucking pilots or something! Fuck you AND your greens!

This inner sanctum of misguided martyrs impaling themselves on putters over a missed putt.

"I don't get it, Mary! What the fuck is it with golf?! It's a fucking disease transported from Scotland! What do we have in common with the Scotch?! Single malt! *That's* what they should be playing."

"Shh, keep your voice down! They're talking golf all around us."

He whispers, *"It's for bored chazers who don't know what to do with their money!"*

"Shh..."

Lee passes by. Eddie says in a big voice:

"Hey, Lee. How are the greens today, Lee?"

"Fast, Harvey, fast."

After dinner, they're sipping Grand Marnier. Eddie's jacket is off, and Mary's shoulder bag is on the floor.

"Where you staying tonight, Mary?"

"Here."

"At the Sinclaire?"

"Yes."

"Wow!"

"It's only five miles from the airport, convenient for me to visit all my clients in the New England area."

"You have *other* clients?"

"You think I only came out to see you?"

"Yeah."

I'm in!

"Think again."

I'm out.

"And I thought I was special."

"You're very special, Harvey. Tonight I'm all yours."

I'm in!

"And tomorrow I'll be checking in with someone else."

I'm out.

"Well, Harvey, it's good to see you're doing well."

"Yeah."

"It takes time to adjust."

Umm... at this point, it's a toss-up if I score... I'd give it 8 to 5.

"I must tell you, Mary, this 'Harvey' name, 'Harvey Colter'? Very bad choice."

"You don't get choices."

"Where was 'Harvey' picked from, a losers lottery?"

Mary laughs.

Make a woman laugh and your halfway home. Now say something impressive.

"All you really have in this life is your name."

"Would you like to change it back to Aryeh Pyatiegorskia?"

"How are the rooms upstairs?"

"*You* tell me."

Eddie's mouth drops and Mary bursts out laughing. She's tipsy.

I'm in.

"Sorry, Eddie, slip of the tongue."

Tongue?

By midnight the place is empty, his eyes are a blur, and she's talking up a storm about Warren Beatty being her favorite actor — and did Eddie know he was Shirley MacLaine's brother?

Better make my move now before she drinks my week's wages!

She stands up straight as an arrow.

Fuckin' Mary's got a wooden leg!

"Get me a bloody Maryeeee! I'm going to the powder room."

Lee hisses, "We're closing!"

Eddie waves another twenty. Lee gives him the finger. She returns.

"Where's my drink?"

"They're closing, but I can take us some drinks upstairs."

"Well, Eddie, this was fun."

She puts on her jacket, picks up her shoulder bag.

"You know, Mary, Winton can be a lonely place, lonely and cold..."

"It's July."

"You know what I mean."

"I'll take care of the check. See you in six months."

"Where you going?"

"To sleep."

"Alone?"

"Harvey, come on."

"You called me 'Eddie,' just before."

"Well, now you're *Harvey*, and Harvey's a gentleman."

"A gentleman tucks a lady in."

"I don't think so."

"But I got all dressed up for you."

"For little 'ol me?"

"And whitened my teeth."

"Did you now?"

"Cost me five hundred dollars! I gotta tell you, Mary, you're not a cheap date!"

"DATE?!"

"And I don't appreciate being led on."

"Harvey, I can't believe—"

"I'm not **HARVEY!**"

Well, now that I'm not getting laid, I might as well let her have it.

"I hate this fucking place! With these Jew-hating white-bread wasps thinking their shit don't smell!"

"Shhhh!"

"There's no one here!"

"Fuckin' Bethlehem, New Hampshire! I've been to Bethlehem, Mary! This ain't no Bethlehem. I never thought I'd miss seeing Arabs, but after *this* fucking place—"

"Watch your language, Mister Debonair."

"You stick me here with these mannequins on grass when you know I'm a city guy!"

"You want city? You want to make it easy for them to find you? You want to be knifed or shot, your head bashed in, or tied to a chair set on fire, your eyes taken out?! You want that?! I can arrange that! No problem!"

"You could have told me this over the phone, Mary."

"Told you **what**?!"

"That I'm not coming home."

She walks up the stairs and waves.

"Be nice to the ladies."

"I tried and look how far I got."

"Goodnight, Harvey."

* * *

Eddie behaves for about a year (his max), until Winton's biggest fundraising event of the year, The Annual Eye Bank Luncheon, kicking off festivities on the 4th of July for its genetically reserved members.

Eddie's sweating like a pig, serving and clearing plates for Winton's finest. During the presentations, the clearing of dishes stops so it can be quiet, since microphones still don't work in this ten million dollar *tscha-tsch-kee* house.

This year, as *every* year for the past *hundred* years, the sponsor of the event is the Bank *Zhlob* (a handicap not *only* on the golf course), plus featured guest, a little nine-year-old girl with a lock of hair over her new eye – a shade off from her *other* eye. Doc fucked up, but Doc's lawyers say, "At least she can see."

The little girl says, "I don't want to see. I want my old eye back." Hence the lock over the eye and a settlement of a million dollars for the little girl's "eye gone wrong" acceptance speech. The parents take the check, saying, "No one's perfect."

As *Bank Zhlob* is slurring through his speech, waiters stand by their stations, hands behind their back, in white gravy-soaked gloves, Winton's "French Service."

Eddie stands at attention at his station studying a young woman's calf. He spots a *djagundo* shrimp under an old prune's chair, sitting next to the young calf.

Prune looks at Eddie, thinking he's looking at her, but sees him eying the calf. Jealous prune points to the shrimp on the floor. "Well, if you won't pick *me* up, then pick up the goddamn shrimp!"

She nods. He nods. She smiles. He smiles. She leers. He leers. She points. He points. She snaps her fingers. He snaps back. Finally, Grandma Moses slides her bony *toches* down the seat and kicks back the contested shrimp to Eddie. He kicks it back. She kicks it back. He kicks it. She kicks it. One last kick and Eddie drives the shrimp between her legs, splitting the goal posts!

"GOOOOOOOOALLLLLLLL!" He screams, raising his arms.

Fired on the spot, Eddie drops his gloves, walks from his station to the ol' bag, and walks her to the dance floor to waltz the Blue Danube to the great delight of the soused guests. Eddie finishes off the 'ol bag with a dip at the end, almost losing her. Guests try to stand for an ovation, one of Winton's finest moments.

Eddie bows, "bag" curtsies, almost falling over, but Eddie catches her, puts his arm around her girlish waist, escorting her back to her seat goosing her. The "goose heard round Winton," sets off goose gasp, shock waves reverberating to the *greens*.

Eddie then picks up the shrimp, walks to the dais, shrimp hanging from his hand, kisses the little girl on the cheek, bites half the shrimp, she eats the other half, and he walks out the guest entrance, dropping the shell on the floor, striding out to the soft applause of the dozen Mexicans hanging out by the garbage in the back.

* * *

"What the hell is wrong with you?!"
"It's a bad place, Mary."
"There is no good place, Eddie."
This time they meet in a bowling alley so Mary can ream him out without worrying about noise.
"They hate Jews, Mary."
"All you had to do was work!"
"Very anti-Semitic."
"Can't you just shut up and work!"
"Mary, I can work, I can shut up. I can't do both."
"Keep pushing it, Eddie! Just keep pushing it!"
"I'm sorry."
"Stop that shit! I don't wanna hear it! You're not sorry! You're never sorry! You couldn't do all those fucking things if you were sorry! I don't care if you are sorry! **YOU GOT THAT?**"
Definitely not getting laid. Not with Mary.
"Putting yourself and our program at risk! What an idiot! Grow the hell up! You're running out of places, Eddie! You pull this crap one more time, you won't have to worry about the mob! I'll kill you myself!"
"What's the score?"
Mary pulls off a bowling shoe and throws it at him.
Next stop: Lyonsville, Iowa.

* * *

"This time, check your personality at the door!"
"Okay."
"Don't draw attention to yourself!"
"Yes, Mary."
"If you get a traffic summons, pay it; if you stay out of work, call in; if you make friends, don't go out; if you fall in love…"
"Yeah…?"
"Don't!"
"Can I at least…?"
"Listen, smart ass, you're lucky you're alive. We were ready to kill you in Winton, except for the fact that you testified, which I have to say, took *cojones*."
"Yeah, look where it got me—Iowa. Can't wait for the caucus."

Lyonsville, Iowa, the most non-descript place ever, no way to describe it, words would get bored describing it, nothing to describe, it's the Gulog. Eddie looks around.

Solzhenitsyn would have never written his book here…

Eddie's with Mary at the Lyonsville Diner, right outside of town next to the Greyhound station. They're sitting at a wooden booth, smoking cigarettes, drinking coffee. He looks at the old men sitting at the counter, staring at the ceiling, depressed in the middle of the day, blowing smoke, waiting for the smoke to clear.

Lyonsville steadies.

He thinks of Max and Golishoff's. How he got from there to here, how it all started in Tashkent, with stops in Poland, Germany, Lower East Side, Bensonhurst, Crown Heights, Kibbutz, Texarkana, Bethlehem, ending up right here at the world-famous Lyonsville Diner, open 24 hours, when it shouldn't be open for one.

Max shoulda never left Poland. Hitler should have never invaded, and Stalin should have been a poet. But as shrink Stanton liked to say, "It may have started before you, but it ends with you."

The diner is greasy and grimy but comforting. The comfort of all food smelling the same no matter what the food is, no matter what time of day or night, the smell of "fried" permeates the place. It's Wesson gone wild. Grease imbedded in the paneled walls, wooden booths, ceiling, floor, makes everything smell fried. It emanates from the multi-purpose grill, grilling everything from harsh, overdone potatoes to brutal bacon, pulverized eggs , pancakes, burgers, grilled cheese, onions, peppers, toast, chicken, ribs—everything tastes fried. Even the beer tastes fried. But people like it.

"Food's not bad once you get used to it."

"Gotta go, Tom." Mary slides out of the booth.

"Where you running, you just got here."

If you have a problem, call *before* the problem erupts."

"Yes, Mom."

"Call from a booth."

"Yes, Mom."

"Don't call me *Mom*."

"Okay, Grandma."

She laughs.

"D.A.'s still laugh?"

"Yes, D.A.'s still laugh."

"You're not still angry with me?"

"Nah."

She applies lipstick.

"I like the color."

"Thanks."

"Mary?"

She takes a deep breath. "Yes, Tom?"

"I was really inappropriate last time."

We both drank a little too much."

"I didn't mean nothing by it."

"I know. You were just being yourself." She hitches her shoulder bag, takes her briefcase. "Okay, be good."

He jumps up and grabs her arm. "Wait, wait, wait! How's The Kid, you haven't said anything about The Kid, and how's Benji? Little Benji. And how's your daughter Tracy?"

She doesn't answer.

"Hey, maybe we shouldn't be mixing business and personal, but we got an eight-hundred-pound gorilla between us. For better or worse, we're family."

Mary sits back down.

"We're trying to get him into a program."

"What's he into?"
"Alcohol, drugs."
"Gambling?"
"No."
"Well, thank God for little favors, eh?"
"Yeah."
"Does he mention me?"
"No."
"Can I call him?"
"I don't think it's a good idea."
"If he won't let me be his father, maybe I can be his sponsor."
"Doubt it."
"I messed him up real good."
"At this point it doesn't matter. He has to take responsibility. I really have to go."
"Another minute, please." He signals the waitress for more coffee. "How's my little Benji?"
"Adorable."
She shows him a picture.
"Wow! Look at the little *pisher* on a two wheeler! How old is he?"
"Five."
"Five?! Who taught him how to ride?"
"Taught himself. He saw some older kids in the park and took off!"
"Just like that."
"Evel Knievel! He whizzes down the block, yelling, 'Look, Grandma, I'm a blur!'"
"Little *bahn-dit*, a wild one."
"Has no fear."
"That's good, Mary, not to be afraid... five, huh?"
"Going on twenty-five!"
"Smart?"
"Oh, yeah, the other day I told him I loved him, and he said, 'If you love me so much, can you buy me a truck?'"
Eddie stares at the picture.
"Who's he look like?"

"You, Eddie, around the eyes."

"My little *Uzbek*..."

Eddie presses the picture up against his lips.

"Keep it, I'll send you more."

"Thanks, Grandma."

"Only my grandson calls me that."

"Pretty good lookin', Grandma."

"When I get complimented as a grandma, it's really time to leave." She stands.

"Don't go."

"I have a plane to catch."

"I don't. Please, another minute."

He motions the waitress for a coffee refill.

"Tracy's got her hands full."

"She's fine, she's strong."

"Like her mom. Bet she's a great mom."

"Wonderful. Has the patience of a saint."

"She's home with the child?"

"No, he's in day care; she works part time, going to college at night. Very proud of her."

"She's making a life."

"She is."

"With or without him."

"With. She loves him. He's a good person. Has to find that out for himself. And she's there to help him do that. If he wants it."

Waitress pours Mary a refill, but Eddie waves her off.

"Coffeed out, Eddie?"

"Tastes like fried onions."

Mary laughs. "It does!"

"My Uncle Max made good coffee..." Eddie closes his eyes.

"You did a very brave thing, Eddie."

"Yeah, I was brave. I hid in my uncle's basement and got him torched."

"You were on the run."

"My father ran too. He ran from Nazis, and I ran for a plea bargain."

Eddie lights up, offering her one.

"I'm trying to stop."

"My father died from cigarettes... but I think it was the war."

He takes a deep drag. Sol's been coming to him, in his dreams, in his writing. The sessions with Stanton and his journal entries helped him understand, empathize, if not forgive, putting himself in his father's shoes and what it must have been like for him. And he wept. And the empathy washed over the rage, and he woke early, feeling Sol's presence around him.

I know you're here Pop, and I hope you're okay. Down here it's been rough, but I'm getting back to myself. You wouldn't believe where I am. In the shtetle *of Iowa. You have an* aynickle, *a great-grandson. He's a bahn-dit."*

He see's his father's face more clearly, a small handsome face, straight nose, strong lips, brown hair, hazel eyes, mournful around the edges. He recalled the "good times," and now that he was no longer angry, he remembered there were more than a few. And the stories, the sad, bitter stories of the war, the few he told.

"He didn't tell many, Mary, but there was one Max told me the night he found me hiding in the cellar."

Mary gives him a tissue.

"After the Nazis invaded, my father was beaten and his mother and sister begged him to escape before they killed him... he didn't want to go,he really didn't... being the last son... but he went, hiding in the woods in the outskirts of town. One night he returned to get them, but they were gone... the whole town was gone... he never got over that... years later he heard from another survivor what happened after he left. The Nazis separated the old women from the young, loading them on separate trucks. The young worked, the old were sent away. But my Aunt Rachel, only thirteen, kept jumping off her truck to be with her mother... my grandmother... Three times they threw her back, but she begged the officer, and he finally let her go."

Eddie looks up and Mary's wiping her eyes.

"Hard to understand how people survive all that, Eddie. I think of Tracy."

She takes a sip of coffee, goes to the bathroom, and returns.

"What time's your plane?"
"I missed it."
"Oh geez, Mary, I'm so sorry."
"I'll catch the next one."
"Can I buy you dinner... the burgers are actually good."
She pauses. "Why not, we're family."
"When do I get to see them?"
"Not for at least another year. Enough time to get you off the radar."
"That's tough, Mary, real tough."
"I know. Just hang in there, stay busy."
"Doing what?"
"I don't know, just don't smoke, drink, gamble, or goose old ladies. Why don't you play some golf."
They finish at the diner and Eddie walks her to her car.
"How long did he wear the wire on me?"
"A week."
"He buried me with that shot."
"No, I think he saved you."

Chapter Twenty

Eddie is now Tom Leonard, a goateed academic who works in the local library, lives in a boarding home, rents a room for six-hundred a month subsidized by the Feds.

Eddie works nine to five, Monday through Friday. On evenings and weekends he reads and writes. On Wednesday evening he attends a beginners' writing class at the local community college, taught by Dr. Chester Luskin, former chairman of the English department who just retired after fifty years of teaching. As a retirement gift, Luskin was awarded Professor Emeritus and a key to the President's private office suite, complete with hidden bar for "fundraising purposes."

To enroll for Luskin's class, Eddie submitted an outline of a short story about a young boy coming over from Europe with his family after the Second World War. He had been writing regularly since he left Texarkana, a page a day, absent a month allowing for Cuckoo's input.

Eddie kept in touch with Stanton and every birthday, November 27, Eddie received a new journal. This was his third, and Eddie made it a practice, on the day of his birthday, to re-read the journals from beginning to end.

Although quick in his writing, he's drudgingly slow in reading, averaging fifteen pages an hour, and many times he has to re-read sections because his mind strays, a condition Stanton labeled "ADD" and Eddie called "normal."

It took Eddie ten hours to read two journals, so he extended his birthday to two days, calling in sick, because he didn't want to interrupt the flow. Although slow, he can read continuously, sometimes twenty hours in a row, with a ten-minute break every hour to take a drink and a pee, not so different from his marathon poker playing days.

By his own calculations, in ten years he'll have to take off three months to read his journals and won't have *time* to work.

Maybe I'll go on Sabbatical. But I'm only working a year. Why would the library give me three months off? Maybe I'll become a writer, then I won't have to work.

There are ten in the group, three men, seven women, all in their middle years. They read sections to each other followed by Dr. Luskin's comments, who speaks in measured monotone, careful not to wake anyone. On the Luskin-Richter scale, there's no vibration, but the rumor is he's alive.

Luskin offers his critique as if handling a fragile work of art, careful not to hurt feelings of budding artists (mostly around the waist) who are in sales during the day where no attention is ever paid to hurting feelings. In fact, it's encouraged. But in Professor Luskin's class "We are safe."

Eddie can't believe how sensitive writers are, how easily writers bruise, until it's *his* turn to read. Then he does it with one eye on the page and the other on Luskin, ready to defend his work. It seems Eddie's not there to write, but to fight. But Luskin keeps it in neutral, giving hyper-sensitive "Tom" the same feedback he gives everyone else:

"Nice work. Keep it up."

The canned comment sets Eddie off.

*What are we a McDonald franchise, everyone's the same? I **know** I'm better than these chumps!*

Luskin's sensitive to his children vying for his praise, so he makes sure not to play favorites. Eddie's not comfortable with that. He believes all compliments should go to him and criticisms to everyone else—a fair distribution of critique, in *his* mind.

When he first attended Luskin's class, Eddie felt intimidated. But after hearing some chapters, there was no problem. In fact, he soured. To be among writers, or those aspiring to write, which he finds out is just about everybody, is slightly underwhelming. Who *doesn't* say: "I have a book in me."

"Good. Now write it."

"I thought you could write it, since I came up with the story."

And who doesn't have a story? Many, as Eddie finds out.

But most are shit...

Luskin encourages input. Not always a good idea among the "creative" who use their "creativity" to delicately rip each other apart. Luskin tries to keep the claws at bay.

"We're here to **EN**courage, not **DIS**courage. Be careful of not only *what* you say, but *how* you say it."

In monotone?

But much of the writing Eddie hears stinks, which Luskin calls "interesting." Eddie can't believe Luskin doesn't see it, how he finds *something* good in every piece, taking the most boring story and making it sound good by engaging the writer, asking questions about their process, what it is they want to say. Many times the conversations are far more interesting than the work.

And so, in Luskin's class, writers write another day, staying out of each other's way, while Eddie's losing his mind. He can't tolerate what he hears and can no sooner turn the other cheek than his other ear, every chapter an earworm.

Boring lives, boring stories. Ten pages describing a cupboard passed down from mother to favorite daughter, inciting jealousy. Who gives a shit?! Fuckin' Americans have no history, so they make up cupboard stories!

He's angry with Luskin, and believes teachers who take great pains to avoid hurting others are murderers.

They're killing honesty.

Eddie's no killer. He's an assassin with a vengeance, ripping into everyone. He gets like that when he's most insecure about his own work.

"Why are you so angry, Tom, so belligerent?"

"I didn't think I—"

"STOP LOOKING FOR THE HOLES IN THE CHEESE!"

"But it's such shit."

After a while, Luskin ignores Eddie's hand being up, so Eddie speaks out of turn and is chided publicly by Luskin, who's embarrassed by his own behavior. But that's what Eddie does. He brings out the worst in people.

But it's gotta be in there for me to bring it out.

They get into name-calling, calling each other "assholes," which to Eddie is mild, but in Iowa it's a capital offense.

Luskin suspends Eddie, calling him "rude" and "insensitive."

Insensitive? Let me introduce you to Cuckoo, or take a shower with Galuck!

"I find your behavior totally inappropriate, Tom. I want you in my office right now!"

Of course, all of this has nothing to do with class, his writing, the other students, or Luskin. It's his life in Lyonsville.

They take the elevator to the top floor and walk down a long corridor, directly into the President's suite.

Can't seem to stay out of the principal's office.

He walks behind Luskin remembering Smith Shmuckler giving him thumbs up after the sandy retreat with Pulkie.

They enter a large office with built-in bookshelves, floor to ceiling, oversized furniture, a huge mahogany desk, soft couches — a space large enough to host a small reception with an anteroom in the back for smoking cigars and shaking down alumni for endowments.

Luskin goes straight for the bar, fuming. Eddie strolls around the room, eyeing banquet photos, group shots of faculty, trustees, trophies, and awards on dark paneled walls "Donated by Panels Are Us," the large mahogany desk and chair set "Donated by Goldstone Furniture," full-length drapes "Donated By Barrie Linens," leather couches "By Jennifer," and a fully stocked mirrored bar "Donated by Lyonsville Community College Alumni."

His back to Eddie, hunched over like Max at Ratner's, Luskin guzzles a long amber drink, puts his glass down, and turns towards Eddie, a bit unsteady, full of anger and amber.

"It's bosh, Tom! I mean for a librarian, it's just bosh!"

Bosh? Never heard that.

"Shameful! Childish and shameful! You have absolutely no impulse control. Your mouth is a run-away stream — strike that! A filthy torrent of water!"

"Well put."

"Don't patronize me, Tom!"

"I'm sorry."

"These are my friends, my neighbors. I taught their children, and now they want a chance to express themselves. No one here is a finished product, Tom! It's a *beginners'* class, we're *becoming* writers, and if you discourage writers at the beginning, there *is* no end. Can you imagine if Mozart was discouraged?"

He had talent.

"Does it matter if the writing is good or bad?"

Uh — if you wanna publish.

"It's a process! We're all exploring! Do you know what exploration is?"

Pulkie's privates?

"So if you don't like or disagree with what you hear, well, that's just too goddamn bad! We might not like what *you've* written."

Unlikely.

"But no one stands up and says, 'that's shit!,' or 'it's boring,' or 'My grandmother from the Ukraine could do better!' That's appalling, Tom."

"In all due respect, sir, I — "

"You have **no** respect, Tom! For anyone!"

He's reaming me out pretty good. Must have problems at home...

"That's your problem, Tom! And I will not tolerate your kind of boorish city behavior!"

How does he know I'm from the city?

"I don't know where you come from, Tom, but we're a small town here, we don't run roughshod over each other! We're not cockroaches!"

Cockroaches, in Lyonsville?

"Your behavior is intolerable. I cannot bee-liiieve our public library hired you!"

Holy shit! This guy could blow my cover! Mary will kill me. **Ollie** *will kill me!*

"I hear what you're saying, sir — and you're right. It's just that — "

Eddie breaks down crying. Luskin's moved. You can tell, because he puts down his drink.

"What's wrong, son?"

This is so pathetic, at my age, but — a man's gotta do what a man's —

"I—I—can't anymore—"
"What is it, son?" Luskin kneels beside him.
Oh fuck! A Fundamentalist!
He puts his arm around Eddie.
Fundamentalists are no fun.
"Shall we pray?"
No, no, please, no!
"Let us pray to our Lord, Jesus Christ."
He ain't my Lord!
"Our Savior."
Sorry, Ha-Shem.

They're on their knees, Luskin's praying, his eyes closed, Eddie's eye is on Luskin, waiting for the criss-cross move at the end. Eddie's not sure of the hand-to-shoulder sequence.

Tap, right, left or left, right, head first, shoulders first?

Luskin finishes and Eddie does a good job criss-crossing after which Luskin helps him up.

"How do you feel now, son?"
"Better."
Glad I didn't have to blow my nose in your crotch.
"Prayer heals."
"Does it ever."
"So, what's wrong?"
"It's my new job, sir, the pressure; feels like I'm going to crack up."
"Oh my Lord!"
"New systems, files, computers, message machines, faxes, too much, too much."
"Yes, yes."
"Too many self-help books, no one helping anyone, we're in transition, sir. It's the Eighties, no one reads, they're addicted to those toxic boxes!"
"YES! YES!"

The few times Luskin loses it, it's over TV. How this great nation is being led to an "intellectual hell-hole by the dumbed-down media!"

"Toxic boxes, sir, poisoning our minds!"
"Terrible."

"Local news, fires, earthquakes, death, rape, embezzlers, greed, the world's going to, to — something in a basket—"

"Hell."

"That's it! Hell! Changing, sir, changing, the world's changing!"

Simon-Tov n' Mazal Tov! Back in Yeshiva!

"Barnes and Noble getting bigger, minds getting smaller; they go to bookstores for *lattes*!"

"Disgusting!"

"Libraries losing members, culture's dying, people don't return books anymore."

"I noticed that."

"They steal them, sir, or forget them; it's the younger generation!"

Blame everything on them!

"Unconscious, sir, a generation of unconscious, entitled morons who don't understand the meaning of life!"

"True."

"What *is* our future?!"

"None!"

"No future, sir, it's bleak out there, sooo bleak and those inside flaps don't stick, nothing's sticking, sir—we're coming unglued!"

"Oh my God!"

"It's a business, the whole world's a business; too much, sir, tooooo muuuuch!"

Luskin runs for the amber.

"That's the pressure I'm under, sir. That's what I bring to class every week."

"I understand. That's how I used to feel end of semester, marking papers. Exhausting and stressful. People think the academic ife is easy because of all the time we have off, but when we're busy, we're *really* busy."

Luskin knocks off his tumbler and pours the next two.

This guy doesn't want to go home.

Luskin raises his glass.

Neither do I.

"To Macallan 18!"
"Macallan 18!"
They clink and drink.
"Son, just because the world spins, doesn't mean *you* have to."
Although, in quick order they're both spinning tops, guzzling scotch like it's soda. Eddie wonders if he should leave.
And abandon single malt?
"But, sir, sometimes, my medication wears off, and with only one pharmacy in town, it doesn't always arrive on time, and that sends me off. I wait for postal every month."
"What are you on?'
"Prozac."
"My *wife's* on Prozac!"
People get so excited when they find out you take the same medication.
"So if I run out?"
"Absolutely! Come on over! She's got a closet full."
Eddie sings, *"Like a good neighbor..."*
"I'll drink to that, Tom!"
"Not **alone,** sir! Down the hatch!"
"Down the hatch, Tom!"
They loop arms, lock elbows, and close in for a clink and drink.
"I feel cursed, son...and blessed; she's a good woman, I mean I love her..."
No one who's drinking loves anyone.
"Don't bother with the glass, son, just bring the bottle."
Eddie's about to light up a cigarette.
"Put that away, I have something better."
Luskin opens a humidor, takes out two huge cigars, and runs them under Eddie's nose.
"Ummm."
Luskin lights them up and they take deep puffs.
"Sooo good, sir."
"Cuban."
"Fuckin' unbelievable!"

Luskin laughs. "My Lord, Tom, you sound just like one of the characters in *The Godfather*! What a great impersonation." Eddie forgot and dropped his standard American.

"What I meant, sir, is that this cigar is an extroadinary leaf."

"Well, that doesn't sound like you either, Tom. You seem to have a good ear for dialect, as is borne out in your writing. Do you ever wonder what your real voice is?"

"Not when I have so many others." And they both laugh and drink.

"Tom, should you be drinking and smoking when you're on medication?"

"Ab-so-lute-ly!"

"That's the spirit!"

They fill the room with thick cigar smoke. Eddie looks up at the ceiling.

"What are you thinking, son?"

"The fire alarm goin' off."

"Oh, don't worry, the Fire Marshall disconnected the smoke alarm."

"The Fire Marshall?!"

"An alumnus."

"Nice to be so dis-connected, sir."

Luskin blows out a big ball of smoke towards the smoke alarm, and turns on the ceiling fan.

"Alumni have everything covered."

"Yes we do, Tom."

Eddie raises the bottle.

"To alumni!"

"Alumni!

The next two swigs are followed by bottles of beer, scotch shots **aaaand... They're off!** Eddie flips his shoes, jumps on a couch. Luskin sits across him in a big club chair. They're in for the night.

"You'll keep all this confidential, Tom?"

"*I* will, if *you* will!" Eddie laughs.

Luskin puts up two fingers. "Scout's honor."

"And no one can know about this at the library. Not a word."

"Mum's the word, Tom."

"Mum-di-mum-dum-dumb."

"I'm here for you, Tom."

"And *me* for *you*."

Eddie pulls a pouch from his jacket. Luskin almost pees in his pants.

"Oh, my God! I haven't smoked pot since the Sixties, when I protested the war. What a nice surprise! But not here. In the bathroom! Bring the booze!"

Luskin's a little freaky. Oh well. What the fuck. Maybe I'll get an A.

Luskin takes a hit and says in a high-pitched voice.

"This is good shit."

Nothing's funnier than a high Presbyterian.

"And the scotch ain't bad either."

"We know good scotch in Lyonsville."

Eddie raises the bottle.

"To pot 'n' scotch!"

"Pot and scotch, Tom!"

Luskin giggles like a hyena.

That's the genius of pot 'n' scotch. You can smoke and drink it anywhere, think you're somewhere, be nowhere, and it doesn't matter.

They go deep into the night, plastered and wasted, confiding in each other, talking about themselves, the joys and difficulties of life, of dreams and goals, aspirations, disapppintments. Eventually they get down to their two favorite subjects: drinking and writing.

"Secrets are the key, Tom."

"To what?"

"Writing. Yup. Good writers don't write what people think, they write what people *say* to *hide* what they think."

"And readers?"

"Readers read."

"I think readers are afraid to say what they think, so they look for it in a book."

"So we agree."

"I think so Chester."

By this time they're slurring more than speaking.

"Stories come down to two things, Tom...someone coming and someone going."

Eddie passes the bottle.

"It's the in-between that's rough."

"True, sir, true."

Luskin starts to cry.

"It's the hardest thing, Tom, isn't it, to feel disappointment and failure, and loss. And yet, that's what good writers do—they remind us of loss."

"Cocksuckers!"

"Seems everything's about loss these days, Tom. Especially as you get older. Fucking writers don't let you forget about death!"

"No, they don't."

"It's unusual for me to curse, Tom."

"They deserve it."

"Bastards!"

"Sadists!'

Luskin takes a hit, a puff of Cuban, and a swig.

"But they do serve a purpose, Tom."

"What's that, Chester?"

"I'm not always sure... but there's gotta be something there... If not, I've wasted my life."

Eddie looks up at the ceiling and sees bituminous clouds forming...

"You think I've wasted my life?"

"You helped *me*."

"I *should* be more happy..."

I need an umbrella.

"Everyone should be, sir, but we have a lot to be grateful for."

"I guess."

"After all, we're after the same thing."

"What's that, Tom?"

"A good story."

"You're right, Tom, it's why writers write, isn't that so?"

"I don't know why we write."

"To tell our story, deal with our anguish."

"Sounds right."

The Fix

"Keep it up, Tom—the writing, not the anguish."
"Yes, sir."
"It's good, it's all good. Nice work. Keep it up."
Luskin leans foreward, turns off the faucet, and sinks back into the suds.
"Ahhh, isn't this nice, Tom?"
"Can I return to class?"
Luskin squeezes Eddie's balls.
"Of course."
Luskin slides down.
"Don't let me drown, Tom."
"Don't worry, sir, I used to be a lifeguard."
So they leave the questions of the universe to:
the novel,
the tub,
the pot,
n' the bottle.

Chapter Twenty-One

Iowa's getting on his nerves. He's swallowing pounds of M&M's to keep from shooting himself, all the while becoming a larger target. He's gained thirty pounds and all the women are bringing M&M's to class.

"We weren't sure if you like peanut or plain, Tom."

"Plain, Midge, plain."

Like you.

Midge is a pleasant looking, heavy-set, middle-aged widow who took to writing after her husband fell off the roof putting on shingles.

Eddie's waiting on line at the corner coffee shop during class break, minding his own business, a dangerous move in friendly Lyonsville.

"Where you from, Tom?"

"Minnesota."

"How lovely. Where in Minnesota?"

"Minneapolis, uh… St. Paul."

"Is that where you received your degree in library science?"

"I think so."

Eddie's counting the people in front of him.

Eight to go! Fuck!

"So you came directly from St. Paul to here?"

"Yes."

"I have relatives in St. Paul—"

Fuck it! Not worth it!

"I'm sorry, Midge, but this line is too long."

He breaks out, but Midge pulls him back.

"Oh, look, Tom! They put another girl on. Aren't we lucky?" He hesitates. "Stay, Tom, stay."

He gets back into line as Midge allows just enough room for him to squeeze in, grazing her ample boobs along his back.

Oooo-whaaa.

That's the magic of boob. Big, small, point, or cushion, it doesn't matter, boob awakens man and Eddie's a man under the influence.

Wearing a corduroy jacket, Eddie shouldn't feel anything on his back. Certainly not a brush of a boob. But he could be wearing a steel jacket and feel it. It's the power of boob.

Eddie's first brush with boob was with Maddy in the sixth grade, playing Seven Minutes in Heaven, a kids' game along the lines of Spin the Bottle, but instead of pecking the girl on the cheek, you went into a closet together. Eddie's hand ran over Maddy's boob, more of a button, setting Eddie's hair on fire.

The warmth on his back brings him back to the present.

"So what brings you to our little town of Lyonsville?"

"Starbucks."

"That's so funny, Tom. You're such a funny man. And your writing is so funny."

"Thank you."

Midge moves in closer.

"And yet it's serious, Tom. Which one are you?"

"Both."

His shirt is soaked.

Three to go. Line's moving too quick!

"A little too much profanity for *some* people, but *I* like it."

He feels her mohair.

"Because it isn't gratuitous, it's within context."

He looks behind him.

I'll let some people pass in front of me.

"How do you like our library, Tom?"

"Love it."

"We love our library."

"Hell of a library."

He never thought the word "library" could get him hot, but with boob on his back, every word is a drop of semen.

"Nice, nice, library."

He backs up into her "V."

Like getting into a tight parking spot.

"And our town. How do you like our little town?"

And might those be her sturdy little thighs on my toches?

"Love small towns."
"Me too."
Feeling her "FOMA" (Fat Over Mound Area).
"Been here forever, Tom."
Love hot "FOMA."
"I don't think I'll ever leave."
"Me neither. There's something to not leaving, Midge."
"Have no desire, Tom."
Eddie's balls are shvitzing.
If I take her on the floor, will the manager unlock the john?
"My husband died here."
"Good place."
"We were childhood sweethearts."
Midge gets teary. He puts his arms around her.
What a stack!
But then the girl asks for her order.
"Earl Grey, please."
Eddie says to the girl, "And I'll have Mister Bigelow."
"Oh Tom we're both tea *lovers*."
I'll drink poison if it gets me laid...
Eddie's been looking, but all the women look like younger and older versions of Midge.
Might as well settle for the original.
"You're a fascinating fellow, Tom."
"I'll pick up the tab."
"Oh, Tom, thank you sooo muuuch! You're such a gentleman."
"And you're a lady."
She almost passes out.
Look how little it takes to make a widow happy. Some nice words, fifty cents for tea, quarter tip, and Midge thinks I'm Aristotle Onassis.
"Would you care to move to a table, Tom? We have another twenty minutes."
"Sure, why not?"
"You're so easy to talk to, Tom. Can I tell you about Leon?"
"Leon?"
"My husband, he was the most wonderful man, and when he fell off the roof, that sound, *splat!* By the way, Tom, he left a brand new set of clubs, do you —"

Cut her off!
"How's your book coming?"
"Oh great, Tom, great. Thanks so much for asking."
"Tell me about it."

Ask a writer to "tell me about it" and you lose 'em for days. You don't even have to be there. They just keep going on and on until...

"Would you know where I can get my book published?"
"Why don't we discuss it over dinner."
"Oh, Tom. Oh, I'm so flattered! When?!"
"After class?"
"Nothing like the present."
"You're a Buddhist."
"Oh Tom, you're so funny."

Chapter Twenty-Two

Eddie's short story has turned into a novel. A five-hundred page novel! At first, he didn't think he could fill a notebook, but the story kept growing, using up three journals and more. He ran out of journals. His novel becomes his journal, dominating his life.

It IS my life!

Luskin cautions him, "Tom, you can't write everything you know in *one* book. Save it for the next one."

"I don't have a next one! I don't get another life!"

He's fucked. The writing life's got a hold on him, pulling him out of bed in the middle of the night; it doesn't stop, reams and reams of paper, it consumes him, stories written *by* him, *through* him, keep pouring out of him.

He writes furiously, unaware of time, five hours go like five minutes; he gets up at four, writes till eight, showers, dresses, gets to work by nine, writes through lunch, dinner, till midnight, going on four hour's sleep, stealing a few cat naps in the library. On weekends he writes fourteen, sixteen hours a day, forgetting to eat, sleep, wash.

He looks in the mirror and sees "writer's eyes," hanging hoods kissing the bulge under the slit called eye.

He can't stand to look at himself. He's turned from a sharpie into a *schlump*, which happens to writers. You can't sit on your ass for ten hours a day — your head a railroad station — and expect to look good. Writers are the most unattractive people in the arts, so they compensate by making their characters look and feel worse than *they* do.

Eddie's room is made for writing: a desk, a bed, a bathroom, a fridge, a window, a chair. When he isn't sleeping he's writing. Forget reading. He's too wired, in a constant state of agitation, mind run over by words, phrases, sentences, paragraphs, chapters, quotes, commas, ideas, *fucking ideas killing me*, new ideas, old ideas, no ideas, a feeling of not being in this world while still having to function.

The Fix

Eventually one of the two will have to go.

He delays his turn to read in class until Luskin insists. He's embarrassed, or afraid. He's begun to take himself seriously and it unsettles him. The jokes no longer save him, and the more he writes, the less funny things become. Luskin reads his first hundred pages privately and encourages Eddie to read in class.

Eddie finishes reading the first chapter and silence ensues.

Did I just kill someone?

In "writers' world," Eddie finds a silent reaction to your reading is not a good thing. It can be envy, indifference, taking a nap with your eyes open — it can be anything. One thing it isn't is comfortable.

"Anything you want to say, Tom?"

"I'm sorry I read it. I'm even sorrier I wrote it!"

It's why writers don't like to read their own works. They write so they *don't* have to hear their words. Otherwise they'd be writing plays. The beauty of fiction is the comfort of not knowing or seeing your audience. They can throw your fuckin' book out the window and you could still have a nice day. And if writers could read, they'd be actors.

Eddie wants to put his manuscript under his arm and sneak out. Midge is the first to applaud and the others follow with polite exuberance.

Luskin says, "Let's hear it for Tom." And a second round of constipated applause leaks out.

"You have a very fruitful mind, Tom, bubbling. Ideas just seem to mushroom out of nowhere; it's a jungle in there — you can certainly write, but — "

But WHAT, cocksucker?!

It's a terrible thing when they attack your little village of self-delusion.

"You should try to stay on track."

Which one?

"Commenting on your own comments, the disembodied voices — I don't know where this is going."

You think I do?

"It feels lost. Are you lost?"

Eddie's twitching.

"Lost in your novel?"

Not just the novel.

"It's not uncommon for writers to have difficulty separating themselves from their story, especially if it's so personal."

It's my story, moron!

"An interesting dilemma, needing to go as deeply as you can into your character, while keeping distance — much like when actors stay in character *after* the performance and can't come out, or the desire of the artist to dive into his painting while creating it."

"What?!"

"As a short story, Tom, we were able to follow, but now, it — I don't know — you free associate, but sometimes there is *no* association, it just goes *off*."

It's why it's free, Chester.

"But then you bring it back, but then I don't know where I am."

In a tub?

"I should be able to follow."

"Not necessarily."

"Excuse me?"

"Books should be confusing, hard to figure out."

"Really."

"Make the reader work. Let them work for their money. I mean we worked hard writing it. Why can't they work hard reading it?!"

Class breaks out in hives.

"Never quite heard it put that way, Tom."

" Sure! Writers try too hard to put things in order, as if trying to organize our lives in...chapters. Doesn't work in books and it certainly doesn't work in life... too tidy, might as well read a children's story."

Luskin scratches his head, and Eddie scratches his balls. Luskin rolls up his sleeves.

"All *I'm* saying, Tom, is —"

I don't give a fuck what you say!

"You must be clear —"

All I want are compliments!

"If you're not clear as the writer—"
Compliments! Compliments! Compliments!
"It confuses the reader and then—"
"You're on to something."
"You're on to *nothing*!" Luskin stops. "Tom—are you okay?"
"You mean *okay* okay?
"Yes?"
"We're having a discourse."
If we argue, I don't have to read.
"So, Tom, the writer must respect the reader."
"Why? Do they respect the writer?"
"If it's good."
"How do we know that, by *applause?*"
"The point of all this is your audience is intelligent."
We discussed all this, didn't we, Chester?
"You don't have to spoon feed them, but you must know where the spoon is."
Where we left the hashish?
"Good writing is clear, concise."
And your metaphors suck!
"Do you know what I'm saying? Can you relate? Can anyone here relate?"

Enter Midge, grieving tea-meister.

"Tom and I are friends, so I know he'll take this the right way, won't you Tom?"

When Eddie anticipates any criticism, he feels a heart attack coming on.

"Tom, I know it's hard to hear other authors comment about your work, but I'll try."

"I'm with you, Midge."

And she pauses.

"Confusion in writing is not good, Tom. It's not good in writing, in life, in anything."

I can't believe I started this.

"It's... confusing. I mean, just imagine, at the library, if a book comes in late and you're not sure what the late fee is? How does that make you feel? *Orrrrrr* you can't find a book and someone's waiting?

That would get *me* very anxious... *Orrrrrr* a book's been put back on the wrong shelf, miscategorized, and you have the darndest time finding it — finding it — in — the library of your mind..."

"Well put, Midge. You nailed it."

They're Christians. Don't say "nail."

"Stabbed it! Stabbed it to its essence, don't you think, sir?"

"Anything else, Tom?"

"Just that Midge makes a helluvah chocolate chip cookie."

"I do Tom! I do!"

Luskin asks, "Anyone else want to comment?"

Eddie looks out, a pained scowl on his face discourages further input.

"So, Tom, that wasn't so bad, was it?"

"Fun."

"That's what writing is — fun."

A scream.

"And we all appreciate you not being defensive, Tom."

"Thank you."

"It takes courage to be criticized."

I'm a hero.

"Last word, Tom?"

"Just that Midge stabbed it."

Midge has been stabbing "it" every morning at eight, coming by, taking a shower, getting boffed, and driving Eddie to work. He's begging her to stop, but she misses Leon too much. On weekends she misses him three hours in the morning and three hours in the evening.

Seems like everything these days is about loss.

Chapter Twenty-Three

"GET ME THE FUCK OUTTA HERE!"
"Eddie, what's that noise — are you bowling?"
"I need to get outta here!"
"So leave."
"No ! No! I need to get out of Iowa!"
"Eddie—"
"I can't, Mary, I can't. These people—"
Pins crash.
"All they do is throw strikes and cheer, and they're so *nice!* I have to be nice! I can't be nice! It's wrong! Not human! Everyone's so fucking *nice*! They're not *really* nice! They're faking it, but they've been faking it for so long, they *believe* it!"
"Listen, Tom—"
"I know about those things, Mary! I know how to fake it! I wrote the book!"
"Tom—"
"I'M NOT TOM!"
"Are you off your meds?"
"NO!!"
"Having a bad day."
"I'm not having a bad day! I know what a bad day is!"
"Everyone hits the wall, Eddie. Get a grip!"
"When do I see my Kid, my Benji?"
"Just hang in there."
"How long, Mary? **HOW LONG?!**"

Eddie's been in Lyonsville two years, and hasn't seen Benji or The Kid, or talked to him, received a card, a letter, a picture, nada.

He's forty-four and looks sixty. The ups and downs evened off, but with it went his passion, his drive, his energy, his life. He reads, writes, and drinks, finding things out about himself, but it doesn't matter. He has no one to practice on. He doesn't know if *he's* changing or his *characters*. But they seem to be doing better than he is.

At least something's happening in <u>their</u> lives. I'm fuckin' stuck here!

Eddie's writing has slowed to a crawl, staring at the wall, a glass of scotch next to a glass of milk to save his stomach from being eaten the way he's eating himself. Eddie realizes most of writing is staring at a wall with some hootch, or jerking off.

I need a lobotomy.

When you write and go through this kind of interior work, the self-examination, self-exploration, the digging, this metamorphosis, this seeming transformation, you need fresh waters to swim in, people to practice on, people to notice, people who knew you *before* to note the difference, to tell you, "You've changed, you've grown." You want to hear that. You want to know that all your experiences weren't for nought and that you've become a *mentsch*. Isn't that what everyone wants to hear? That you're a good person?

Days, weeks, and months go by. He doesn't even know what the hell he's waiting for anymore. He's in a constant knot, stops reading, writing, can't focus, doesn't care, nothing turns him on. He's dead above the neck and below the waist. The writing's not doing it anymore. The tingle's gone. He's sleeping, in a funk, hasn't shown in class for weeks, and Mary's not returning his calls.

"Knock, knock."
"Who's there, Midge?"
"Oh, Tom, you're such a funny man. Open the door."
"I can't."
"Dr. Luskin's concerned. I'm concerned."
"Thank you."
"You dropped out so suddenly."
"I have a cold."
"But you invested a year, and your novel is really good."
"I'm done with my novel."
"Why, Tom?"
"It beat me up."
"Don't say that. You're a wonderful writer."
"I'm shit."
"Was it something Dr. Luskin said?"

"No."
"Something *I* said."
"No, no."
"He may have been a little rough on you."
"No, no, he's fine. I'm fine, please go away."
"Were your feelings hurt?"
"No more than usual."
"That's why I brought you something."
"Leave the cookies by the door."
"How did you know?"
"Wild guess."
"They're delicious."
"By the door, by the door."
He hears Midge lean into the door.
"I want to give them to you in person."
Don't let her in!
"My cook-keees."
She'll never leave!
"Open up, honey, I want to see you."
Oh shit!
"Make sure you're fine, Mister Big-Below."
Oh God, I'm getting hard!
"Make you tea?"
"Get away from the door!"
"Tea for two?"
"No tea! No tea!"
His dick is pounding and he runs around the room.
She whispers in the peephole: *"Bigelow, calling Tom, Big-a-Blow for the Big-Below..."*
I— can't—I—
He drops his shorts, licking the door, putting his mouth to the peephole.
"I can't, I, I—Oh, Oh—"
"Tom? Are you okay?"
"Oh God! Oh God!"
"Do you have asthma?"
"Oh God!"

"Are you having a stroke?! Oh my God!"
"Sweet **Jeeee-zuuuus!**"
"How wonderful. You're praying to Jesus!"
Don't stop, don't staaaaaaaaap!
"Jesus will save you."
I'm coming, I'm co-miiiiiiiiiing—!
"Come to church, Tom. After, we can go for a long walk, talk, come back here... cuddle..."
"Wait right there."
He climbs out the window.

* * *

There's twenty rooms at the Lyonsville Skylight Motel and no vacancy tonight due to a snow storm expected, headed East, with a sunny thirty-degree morning forecast the next day.

Eddie checked in the day before after he hightailed it through the window away from Midge. He took a small suitcase and was prepared to hang out at Skylight for as long as it took him to reach Mary.

"Where are you now?!"
"In a motel."
"MOTEL?"
"Skylight across the Greyhound bus stop! I'm coming home!"
"Are you crazy?!"
"Mary, I, I'm dying, I'm—"
I'm having sex with a door!
"I can't, Mary, I can't anymore!"
"Eddie, you're asking for trouble; you leave, it's open season, you're in danger!"
"I'm in Iowa! You don't think that's dangerous?!"
"It's hard, I know it's hard."
"I'm living in Iowa, Mary. People **LEAVE** Iowa!"
"Be patient."
"I'm working in a library. A fucking library. I'm a librarian. In I-Oh-Wa! **What did you do to me?**"
"Kept you alive."

"You call this living?! I'm a joke, Mary! A joke! My name's *Tom Leonard*. Who the fuck is Tom Leonard? I'm not Tom Leonard. I'm Eddie. Eddie Parker. I'm not *even* Eddie Parker. I'm Aryeh, Aryeh Pyatiegorskia from Tashkent!"

"Listen to me—"

"My uncle's Igor Pyatiegorskia, a world-famous cellist! Did you know that?!"

"Don't be impulsive."

"I'm heading towards my nineteenth nervous breakdown!"

"That's not funny!"

"I'm so fucking bored, I'm doing family trees! I want to come home, Mary. I want to see my son. I want to see Benji, my little Benji. I don't even know him. My little *Uzbek*. He's gonna grow up and won't know me! I won't know him!"

"Be patient."

"I want a life, a family! With you and Tracy and Benji, The Kid and Maya, her girls, Barry! Even the Shlossbergs! The fuckin' Shlossbergs! Please Mary, I'm begging you, I'm—"

He's sobbing.

"Okay, okay, Eddie, I hear you, I hear you."

"Yes, Mary, yes?"

"I need a month — to do the paperwork... Eddie?"

"Yes?"

"Can you hang in there for another month?"

"Yes, yes."

"You don't sound good, Eddie."

"This is tough, Mary, so fuckin' lonely, tougher than I ever thought, so much tougher. I can't just move my life around anymore, Mary. I come with it. My life comes with me, I can't separate, can you understand?"

"You're sure about this?"

"Never been more sure in my life....I'm done, Mary, really done, please believe me."

"You know the risks."

"I know, Mary. I know the risks, but I already feel like dying. There's nothing anyone can do to me anymore."

He hangs up the phone and leafs through the New Testament, kissing King James.

Thank you God!

He takes a nap and wakes at seven in the evening. He turns on the local news with reports of fires, storms, accidents, powerlines down.

Holy shit! It's a storm out there.

He pulls a beer from the fridge, looks outside the window across the desolate two-lane highway, eighteen-wheelers pulled over on the side of the road waiting out the storm. He picks up the phone.

"Big-Below here."

"Oh, hi!"

"Bring the cookies, I'll put up the tea."

"Be right over, Tom, soon as Triple-A digs me out."

"You're the best, Midge."

"Room number?"

"I'll wave the lantern."

"You're so funny, Tom."

Eddie thinks of Ollie's story of when he first met Vickie, and how they didn't leave the motel, how dishes piled up, and dust became a friend. Eddie fucked his brains out, Midge cleaned his pipes, and the blizzard was over. Eddie returned to work, class, got his things in order, and felt better than he'd felt in years.

Three weeks to go!

He's making plans, thinking about taking trips with The Kid and little Benji.

Buy him that truck, go to Rockefeller Center, FAO Schwarz, Bronx Zoo, Central Park— do all the things I didn't do first time around. Take them on the Circle Line Ferry around Manhattan, Governors Island, Ellis Island, Statue of Liberty, put Benji up on my shoulders the way Sol did.

"DIS IS VAT I LIVED FOR!"

He picks up his manuscript. He hasn't touched it in weeks. Too jittery with anticipation, waiting to leave. But Luskin told him, "A writer writes every day." He sits down at the Olivetti and plunks out a chapter on sailing into the New York harbor. Phone rings.

"Hi Eddie, it's Mary..."

He got the call at ten, took a plane at twelve, hotel by two, out by eight the next morning for the one-hour ride from Toronto's airport to the chapel.

He missed Maya's wedding, the birth of her daughters, birthdays, anniversaries. He wasn't going to miss her funeral.

He should have known, because Maya called him every August twenty-third, the anniversary of their arrival to America on the S.S. Blatchford. This time August came and went, no call. September came and went, no call. October, Rosh Hashanah— the call.

All the sad thing in our family happen on the holidays .

He got to the funeral early and waited in the rain to see the twins Jessica and Jennifer, now ten. They came out of the hearse first, holding hands, crying, "Mommee."

Barry and his parents followed, broken and needing help getting out of the limo. Eddie walked back into the woods behind the parking lot, watching cars pull in. The receiving line extended from inside the chapel out to the parking lot, a sea of black umbrellas waiting patiently. Many broke down on line and the shock Eddie saw in mourners' faces mirrored his own. Maya was forty and died of a brain seizure in her sleep.

Where was I?

When everyone was seated in the chapel, Eddie stood behind closed doors, listening. He wedged the door open with his foot to hear. The Kid spoke beautifully as Mary and Tracy sat behind the Shlossbergs, and little five-year-old Benji sat quietly in the first row between cousins Jessica and Jennifer.

After the graveside service, Eddie walked from behind a tree, put a pebble on the headstone, said *Kaddish*, and left.

If it wasn't for funerals, I'd never see you, Eddie.

* * *

On the plane ride home, Eddie stops over in O'Hare and spends the one-hour layover in a bathroom stall bawling like a baby. The one hole left in his heart he saved for his sister. He ached for his son and grandson, but it's different— the loss of a sister who was with him all the way, who didn't give up on him, who loved him and cared about him, who forgave him more times than he cared to remember. It's hard for Eddie to think about her without feeling once removed.

First there were four, now there's one.

She was his last and final link to a world far away. A world of tyrants and gods, giants and midgets—Stalin, Hitler, Roosevelt, Churchill, controlling masses of humanity, moving them around, a world in ruins, a world in shock, and after-shock, the world of World War Two and its aftermath. The next war won't be this difficult. We'll all be pancakes.

He goes into a card shop, buys a calendar, circles August 23. He takes out his journal.

I used to be a son,
I used to be a brother,
I used to be a nephew,
I used to be a husband,
I used to be... a father.

* * *

"Dear Kid, I'm trying to put in words what's in my heart. I hurt you terribly and used you. I wrecked your career and destroyed your dream. I stole your childhood. I want you to know that every day of my life, I deeply regret what I did and I'm very, very sorry. If I could do it over, I would, but I can't. That time of my life I was sick and didn't know it, sick in my head, in my heart, and when you're sick like that, you do sick things. I know there's nothing I can say or do to make it go away, for you or for me, but, if I can, if you let me, I want to come back into your life and get to know you, and for you to know me. These are words I would have wanted to hear from my own father.

I went to see him several years ago in Israel to hear those words, but when I got there, he had already died. I missed him by a day or two, and now I'll miss him for the rest of my life. I don't want to die before you hear me say how much I love you, miss you, and want to get to know you in ways I couldn't before.

I hear you're a father and have a son. He shouldn't carry in him what I caused, and neither should you. I've changed and am no longer the person I used to be. The truth is, I still don't know who I am. But I'm trying to find out. It hasn't been easy, not when I've been caught up in a past I don't know, don't understand. But what I do know now is that I want to come home and be a part of family, *your* family.

I'm not sick, I'm not old, and I'm not dying. Although living in Iowa... I'm not writing this letter to get out. I'm leaving anyway. I need a place to go to, not run away from. I will certainly understand if you want nothing to do with me. And that's a choice. One I made with my father and regret very, very deeply. I'm reaching out to you so I can make peace with him, so you can make peace with your son, and for me to make peace with you.

That's all I have to say. If you're up for it, I'd like to break the old cycle and start anew. It's Rosh Hashanah. Think about it. But whatever happens, know I love you very much, you're my son and I'll keep trying to reach you.

I'm signing off this letter as the many I've written, but never sent. With love and regret, pain, joy, sorrow and hope, your father, Eddie.

Chapter Twenty-Four

Eddie moves to Brooklyn off Flatbush Avenue, several blocks from The Kid, Tracy, Mary, and Benji, who live on Fifth Avenue in Park Slope. He gets a job at Saperstein's Paint Store selling paint, and writes at night in a studio apartment above the store. He rarely goes out, and when he does, he walks cautiously with a gun in his pocket. On weekends, he's alone.

The Kid's recovered and functioning well, though he hasn't seen his father now in five years, and won't. Part of his recovery. The wounds are still too deep, too fresh. Eddie understands.

Took me twenty-five years.

Even though Mary and Tracy want him there, The Kid doesn't, so he bows out of any family occasions. He wants to be respectful and not complicate The Kid's life. But there are days when his heart aches so that he stalks them on Sunday mornings when The Kid takes Benji to Prospect Park. Eddie watches from behind a tree as The Kid sits on a bench, watching Benji bounce a beach ball.

Eddie moves from behind the tree and sits next to The Kid. He takes his hand and puts it in his. He raises The Kid's hand to his lips. They sit there crying. Eddie reaches in his pocket and hands him a Limoges figurine.

"He's Dutch, French, Limoges, made from thin shell, porcelain. There was another one with a striped hat. I'll get him that one next year for his birthday... start a collection...get him a new one every year."

They watch Benji bouncing a ball.

"That's some *boytschick* you got there."

"Yeah."

"Enjoying him?"

"Very much."

"Playin' any ball these days?"

"Just the Y, pick-up games."

Eddie reaches into a brown bag and throws the squirrels some peanuts. Pretty soon, he's got a group at his feet.

This irony of this moment doesn't escape them. The Kid laughs.

"I see you made friends, Pop"

"Yeah. They know me..."

Eddie offers. The Kid takes a few off Eddie's palm. They break shells and eat peanuts together.

"Heard you're doing better at AA."

"Tryin'."

"Bina used to call it *Aleph-Aleph*."

"Yeah... Bubbee... I miss her... and Aunt Maya."

"You spoke beautifully at her funeral..."

"You were there?"

"Yeah... I made that one. Listen Kid, next week is Yom Kippur and — there's a small Shul across the park"

"I'll go."

"And Benji?"

"Sure."

"It'll be nice, sitting together. It's the one day my Pop had to have me sitting next to him in Shul."

"Yes."

"Mostly old men in the Shul."

"I like old men."

"It smells a little, Shul smell."

"I don't mind."

"And the roof leaks."

"It's fine."

"It's a long day, I have to stay, but you —"

"It's okay, I want to be there."

"May be a little much for Benji."

"We'll let him run around."

Eddie walks over to Benji, bouncing the beach ball.

"I got lots of ground to cover, lot's of *al-chets* — you know *al-chets*?"

"Yes."

"Who told you?"

"Bubbee."

"My chest should be pretty sore by the time I'm done."

"Do it easy... take it easy on yourself."

"Yeah, I'll make it up in volume."

Eddie turns to the boy.

"Throw me the ball, Benji"

The little boy looks up and runs to his daddy.
"Who's this man, Daddy?"

* * *

We are the way we are not because it's how we want to be, but where we come from. Eddie comes from dislocation. A collection of broken bones set and re-set. They say a broken heart's the same, a bubble in a car wash pulled to its end, waiting for a swarm of down and outs to wipe the slate clean.

We fight so hard about things that have happened, long after it's happened. We shouldn't fight so hard, or else there's nothing left over for *this* life.

* * *

"*Zaydee*, look, look at me!"

Little Benji's on his father's shoulders and tosses the beach ball towards the basket. He misses. Eddie retrieves the ball.

"I gave it a shot, *Zaydee!*"

"You sure did, *boytschick*." He gives the ball to The Kid. "Here, try again." But this time, The Kid puts Benji on Eddie's shoulders.

DIS IZ VAT I LIVE FOR!

* * *

Eddie boards the Flatbush Avenue bus to go home. Sitting across from him is a wise guy. Eddie smiles and the wise guy gets off at the next stop. Eddie bends down to smell between his pants. He's okay. He gets off, walks up the street... some guys are in an alley throwing dice... he stands there a long time... too long... he starts shaking. A father and son walk by breaking his trance. He shadows them down the block. From the back they looked like he and Sol when he was a young boy.

Eddie veers off at Saperstein's and runs up the stairs, pours a shot of *schnapps*. He looks down at the family passport photo, the four of them in Bergen-Belsen. They're all in a frame now, sitting with him at his desk. His heart's racing. He goes to the window and looks down the block... Then looks back at the photo...

The Fix

He goes back to his desk, pours another shot, raises the glass, does a little dance.

"To Sol! Bina! Maya! Aryeh! Izzy! Harvey! Tom! Eddie! Zaydee! Whoever the fuck you are! *L'chayim!*"

He downs the shot, sits down and writes:

"It shoulda never happened. A bookie's life is relatively safe..."

End.

ACKNOWLEDGEMENTS

I've had many celebratory dinners over the past two years thinking *The Fix* was finished. I began writing it seven years ago, after my play *Magic Hands Freddy* was produced Off Broadway in 2004, another torturous experience in the theatre that cost me loads of money and *agasnayfush* (aggravation). But not as torturous as the Broadway production of *The Gathering* in 2001. The great writer Paddy Chayefsky (another Russian who loved to suffer), once said, "Every playwright should get to Broadway to see how meaningless it is."

I didn't know that at the time, and I don't think it's entirely true, but most of it, so that little venture of *meaninglessness* depleted my savings, pension and home, to the tune of $400,000, plus taking on ten years of debt at a time when our kids were starting College.

You see, I'm one of those writers who *really* believes in my work. I don't just write the goddamn thing, I go bankrupt. And my wife Esther is right there with me, body and soul through it all. So I surmised that a life in the *Thaytuh* is really a death wish. I didn't want to die or kill anyone, and yet I needed to write, but I was broke and had no more funds to give to *Thaytuh*. Don't get me wrong. I LOVE *Thaytuh,* there's nothing better, when it goes well, and I'm sure I'll come back to it, but at that time, seven years ago, it was the furthest thing from my mind. What to do?

Esther said, "Fuck plays. Write a novel."

Esther grew up on the Lower East Side and my first play, a comedy called *A Catered Affair* was based on her character. And character she is. I was forty-four having never written before, except some grocery lists, running a Jewish Community Center in Jersey, when I came to Esther one morning and said:

"I want to be a playwright."

"WHAT?!"

"I want to write a comedy about your catering business."

"You can't do that honey."

"Why not?"

"'Cause you can't write and you're not funny."

I had my central character. And so for these past 25 years, I wrote eight hours a day, seven days a week, loving it and living it. Writing saved my life. And taught me more about myself than I needed to know. But once it's out what are you gonna do?

"Fuck plays — write a novel."

"But I never wrote a novel."

"You never wrote a play and ended up on Broadway."

"What should I write about?"

"Tell 'em your story."

So I sat down and started writing *The Fix*. You write what you know, and I know sports. I played a lot of ball in my time and was always drawn to the CCNY basketball scandal of 1949-1950, when a rag tag group of city kids under coach Nat Holman stunned the basketball world, winning both the NIT (National Invitation Tournament) and the NCAA (National Collegiate Athletic Association), a feat never before accomplished in college sports.

The team made the city proud, for these were schoolyard kids, from working class neighborhoods and homes, with dreams and aspirations, worthy of the sacrifice of their parents, celebrating the opportunities given in this great country.

The team's remarkable victory gave so much to so many and the city was on a high, when it all came crashing down as players were arrested for "shaving points," for The Mob. The national scandal brought heartache and shame to the players, their families, and communities for decades to come. All for a few bucks, promising lives wrecked. These were good kids, innocent kids, who got mixed up with the wrong people. The money they received for fixing games was insignificant, pocket money. One had to wonder, what makes someone do that? *I* wondered. I wondered for over fifty years — one player said, "I didn't want to go to my father for money." So the genesis of *The Fix*.

In writing the novel, I knew the beginning and I knew the end. I also knew the story within the story, the theme of all my work. The struggle between fathers and sons, how little is written, how little is known. And the need for me to write about it was a way of understanding and healing my own relationship. So I started writing the novel seven years ago with the first line: "It shoulda never happened... " And that was certainly true in my life. The last thing in the world I ever thought I'd become was a writer. The last thing I ever thought I could do was survive. Born in Russia, immigrant family, Holocaust survivors, arriving in New York with my family at age eight, getting caught up with the wrong crowd... you get the story.

I wrote *The Fix* to 'tell my story'... and to keep my parents and sister alive. In the course of the writing, one by one they fell ill. I unconsciously slowed the writing, and it took me seven years when it should have only taken a few. I must have believed that if I kept the story going- they would. In the past three years, at the rate of one a year, I lost my mother, father, and sister. My sister was the hardest for me. She fought brain cancer for seven years, and when she passed last year, I finished shortly thereafter.

So I dedicate this book in memory of Gabriel, Bina, and Miriam, my family of origin. I think of them all the time, their love, and sacrifices, their hard life and their determination to make a better life for their children.

For the people in my life, my deepest gratitude goes to the love of my life, beautiful Esther, my best friend and partner for over 45 years whose strength, generosity, compassion, ballsiness, humor, and zest for life, lifted me in dark times and kept me afloat in lighter times. She made a home, stood by me, worked hard, and devoted herself to our children and family, showing me how good a person can be and how rich and joyous life is. Every man should be so lucky.

To Rachel and Michelle, my elegant daughters, bright, beautiful, brilliant, compassionate, and kind, proof that I did something right. I'm so grateful for their deep love encouragement, support, honest critiques, knowing their father, and making a mentsch out of me. So proud of them, the choices they made in their own journeys... and for me their presence and light reflect the strength and spirit of our people, and a comfort in remembering and honoring those who perished....

To my family, my wonder grandson Jai and dad, Bill, Nick, Steven, Josh, Joey, Joe, Nancy, Kriss. To Roger and Ellen, Sherry and Len, Don and Cathy, for opening your homes with great kitchen counters for me to write on in the wee hours.

To dear friends and a source of constant support, Marv and JoAnne, Ira and Paula, Norman and Anita, Lynn and Eddie, Augie and Susan, Sarah and Frank, Ginna and Charlie, Steve and Dorothy, Saskia, Ed... to the boys of Brooklyn, Henry, Herb, Barry, Danny, Allan, Don, Florio.

To my mentors Earl Graham and Rebecca Taylor, George W. George, and George DeCenzo who believed in me and settled for nothing less than the best. To David Friedman, and to Unity, a special place of spirit, and joyous friendship.

I'm especially grateful to Hilary Crist, my friend and editor, for her encouragement, and skillful shaping of the book. She "fixed" *The Fix* and made this book possible. Thank you, Hilary. And to Dr. Peter Crist and Dr. Paul Mestancik for their poignant lessons on the power of listening, loving and caring.

To Amy Ramsey, editor, and Melissa Gutman, two brilliant young women who allay my fear of reaching younger audiences. To my friend and dynamo publisher Usher Morgan, who can get anything done in record time. Thank you so much for believing in my work and publishing *The Fix*. I look forward to a long association.

GLOSSARY

Alte kaker — old man
Alte kakers — me and my friends
Antschuldik — excuse me
Aynickle – grandchild
Bobka – go to Moshes Bakery on Second Avenue and 7th Street
Ba-kaakd — pre-menstrual
Bahn-dit — little rascal
Balaboosta – women who scoot around the kitchen, ordering everybody around. Balaboostas walk into your home and take over.
Balagan — ruckus
Balagulas — not nice people, e.g., Madoffs
Baytzim — "I wish for you, my son"
Bobkes – got nothing
Boytschick — kid
Bris — no fun for the kid
Bubbe meise — old wives' tale
Bubbee — granma
Buzzhee — shoot the breeze
Chaseneh — wedding
Chazer — pig (trayph)
Chas-v' ha-li-la! — God forbid!
Chaverim — friends
Chazerrai — garbage
Chevra — friends
Chutzpah — the child who kills his parents and pleads to the judge he's an orphan
Cleantschick – yinglish for crazy clean
Dasvidanya — Russian for "see you later, gator"
Daven — pray
Der-cheretz — respect
Dybbik — bad guy
Ess, mein kind, ess — eat my child, eat (or I'll kill you!)
Farbissener — bitter person

Farblondget — in the desert for 40 years
Farbrengin — a gathering to celebrate
Farfoylte — spoiled or rotten
Far-haakd — chopped up
Farklempt - can't speak, overcome
Far-pitzt — shee-sheed to the nines
Farshtayst — understand?
Farshtopped — you'll know it when you feel it
Farshtunkene — like it sounds — bad odor
Flaysh — meat
Forshpeiz — appetizer
Fressers - on weight watchers
G'becks — baked goods
Gan-Eden — paradise
Gantze mishpoche — entire family
Gatkes — Calvin Klein would not wear
G'knipt 'n' g'bindled — tied up and packaged
Gelaymt - useless, person who can't do anything
Gelt — money
Gey nisht avek! — don't go!
Gey-a-vek — go away
Glet - loving glide of the hand
Goniff — don't let him into your house
Gornisht — zilch
Gott hot mir g'shtrofen - 'God punished me.'
Goy — gentile
Greps — belch
Gribenes - deep fried chicken fat mixed with fried onions. Cardiologists dream found at Sammy's on the Lower East Side
Grizzhes — Pepto
G'sheft — business
G'shry — scream
Gut Shabbes, gut Shabbes - 'Yo bro' on the sabbath
gute neshomeh — good soul
Ha-Shem — God
Hassaneh — wedding
Hev-a-b'ne-neh — have a banana

Hoyker — of Notre Dame
Ich vill shtarbin — I want to die
Kaddish — memorial prayer
Kaynahorah — Lawdy!Lawdy!Lawdy!
Kepee — small head
Kibbitz — pitter patter talk
Kiddish — blessing of the wine
Kishke — intestine
Kitzel — tickle
Knacker – big shot
Knaydle — matzah balls
Knish – made with potato or kasha
Knishes — go to Yonah Shimmel on Houston street
Krechtz – complaining moan
Kuzees — occupants in your nose
Kvell — beam with pride
Ligner — liar
Machataynim – in-laws
Machers — Trump, Gates, Buffett, Oprah
Malchome — war
Mazel tov – good luck
Mentsch — good person
Mentschlichkeit — humankind
Meshuge — crazy
Mezuzah — saves you from Pharaoh
Midbar — Hebrew for desert
Mishpoche — family
Mitzvah — good deed
Momzer — illegitimate child
Motze — blessing of the bread
Narishkeit — nonsense
Nebbish — don't date one
Nisht g'ferlach — not so terrible
Noodge — gentle bother
Nudnick – pain in the neck
Nuggee — knuckle on the head
Och 'n' Vay – Oy!

Oyfn pripitschock — by a fireplace
P'deshve – ball of your foot
Partizaners — guerrilla fighters
Paskudnyak – something the Bolsheviks may have called the czar
Pipick — belly button
Pisher – John Boehner
Pishka — can
Pitzeleh — tiny baby
Platz – bust
Playtzeh — "I got your back" or you can say, "I got your playtzeh!"
Pooritz — Prince
Putz – less than a shmuck
Rachmones — a pity
Rozhinkes mit mandlen — a lullabye about raisins and almonds
Rugelach — Moshe's bakery. Chocolate seven layer cake is phenomenal too. Say hi to Moysh, be generous, he has ten children.
Schmaltz — fat
Shaank — closet
Shabbes — sabbath
Shalom — peace
Shande — shame
Shema — wouldn't hurt to say before you go to bed
Shikse — hot
Shit a heen, shit a herr — not what you think; it means sprinkle here, sprinkle there
Shiva — mourn
Shlemiel – the one who spills the coffee
Shlemazel – the one who's spilled on
Shleps — heavy load
Shloch — unkempt, messy
Shluffee — nap
Shlump – pathetic
Shmatta — dish rag you should have thrown out long ago. If you want to take a minute and check, it fell behind the pipe under your sink.

Shmear – cream cheese on bialy or bagel
Shmeckel – little pecker
Shmuck — usually a male
Shmushkee — yinglish for kissing a newborn under the neck. Granma'a are the biggest shmushkiers.
Shmutz — dirt
Shnor — solicit or borrow without any intention of paying back
Shpatzeer — take a walk
Shpilkes — means needles, but used as impatience, can't sit still; "I have shpilkes," try it.
Shpritz — spray or P.E.
Shtarker — macho man
Shtetle — Anatevka, Lake Oy-be-gun, wherever Garrison Kheeler hangs out.
Shtick – literally "piece," but it's doing your act.
Shtimmer — Clint Eastwood
Shul — Synagogue
Shvitz — sweat
Siddur — Hebrew prayer book
Simcha — happy occasion
Sonim — enemies
Sveenia — pig in Russian
T'fillin — phylacteries, not prophylactics; prayer ritual
The Greene K'zeenah — greenhorn, right off the boat
Toches – booty
Toyve — favor
Trafe – can't eat
Tscha-tsch-kees — Crate 'n' Barrel
Tscholent — Jewish paella or chili
Tsheppa — pick, annoy
Tumling – make noise
Tzekrochen – coming undone
Tze-tootsed — prissy pissed
Tzitzkes — breasts
Tz-kaakd — cranky
Tzures — you shouldn't have
Valggering — slumming around

The Fix

Vantzes — cobwebs
Vie zogt men — how do you say
Yahrtzeit — anniversary day
Yeckes — German Jews
Yentas — Barbara Walters
Yidden — Jews
Yiddishe Momme — not Sarah Palin
Yoynee — kind of a nebbish
Yutz — cognate of *putz*
Zaftig — Latifa, Mo'nique
Zaftig shluffee — nap with Mo'nique
Zaydee — granpa
Zhlob — uncouth
Zifts — a sigh
Zolst zein g'zunt — You should be healthy
My wish for you

VISIT OUR WEBSITE

Join Our Mailing List

A fantastic new way to keep up-to-date with Arje Shaw!

Our Newsletter is a regular email with all the latest news and views from the author, plus information on her forthcoming titles and the chance to win exclusive prizes.

Visit www.TheFixNovel.com or www.ArjeShaw.com

LIBRARY TALES PUBLISHING

If you enjoyed this book, there are several ways you can read more by the same author and make sure you get the inside track on all Library Tales Publishing books.

Visit www.librarytalespublishing.com and find out first about forthcoming titles, read exclusive material and author interviews, and enter exciting competitions.

Visit www.LibraryTalesPublishing.com

Made in the USA
Charleston, SC
24 October 2011